DADDY'S GONE A-HUNTING

Other Books by Robert Skinner

Fiction

Skin Deep, Blood Red (1997)

Cat-Eyed Trouble (1998)

Blood to Drink (2000)

Non-Fiction

The Hard-Boiled Explicator: A Guide to the Study of Dashiell Hammett, Raymond Chandler, and Ross Macdonald (1985)

The Hard-Boiled Dicks: A Personal Checklist (1987)

Two Guns From Harlem: The Detective Fiction of Chester Himes (1989)

The New Hard-Boiled Dicks: Heroes for a New Urban Mythology (1995)

Edited Works

with Michel Fabre

(Chester Himes) *Plan B* (1993)

Conversations with Chester Himes (1995)

with Michel Fabre and Lester Sullivan

Chester Himes: An Annotated Primary and Secondary Bibliography (1992)

with Thomas Bonner, Jr.

Above Ground: Stories about Life and Death by New Southern Writers (1993)

Immortelles: Poems of Life and Death by New Southern Writers (1995)

DADDY'S GONE A-HUNTING

A Wesley Farrell Novel

by

Robert Skinner

Poisoned Pen Press 2000

First Trade Paperback Edition 2000

10 9 8 7 6 5 4 3 2 1

Library of Congress Catalog Card Number: 99-60513

ISBN: 1-890208-44-2

Front Cover Painting by David Bowers

Book Design by Susan Malling-Foster

Poisoned Pen Press
6962 E. First Ave. Ste 103
Scottsdale, AZ 85251
www.poisonedpenpress.com
info@poisonedpenpress.com

Printed in the United States of America

For Mom, who told many wonderful stories

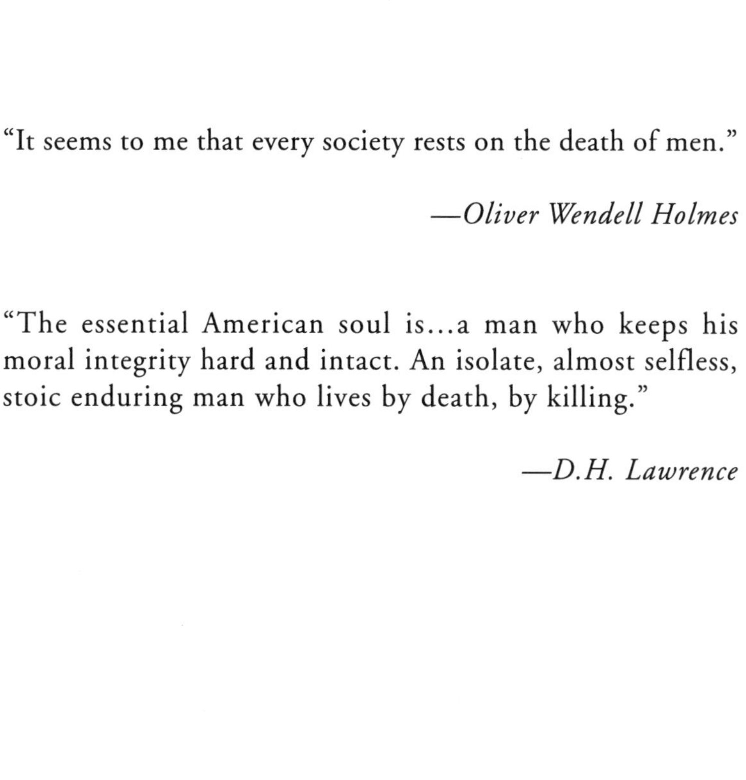

"It seems to me that every society rests on the death of men."

—*Oliver Wendell Holmes*

"The essential American soul is...a man who keeps his moral integrity hard and intact. An isolate, almost selfless, stoic enduring man who lives by death, by killing."

—*D.H. Lawrence*

"It was sometime in the summer'a nineteen and thoity-eight, and I was hangin' 'round wit' some'a my pals down near the Christ's Majesty Funeral Home. I weren't but a chile, y'understand, but they was already things I knowed 'bout the underworld life. Anyhow this Ford car pulled up in front of the funeral parlor and some people got out. What I mean to say is, some colored people got out along wit' a white man. Now that was kind'a funny right there, 'cause in them days, whites and coloreds didn't mix much.

"Anyhow, I seen this white man lookin' 'round real careful, like he was inspectin' and measurin' everything. He was dressed in one'a them white dinner coats, which would'a made him stand out anyhow, but then I got a look at his eyes—they was glowin' like coals of Hellfire in the shadow of his hat brim. I didn't reco'nize who it was, but I drew back, 'cause they was somethin' bad comin' off'n that man. For a second, I couldn't breathe nor nothin', and then I hoid one'a my pals say 'Great God Almighty, that there's Wesley Farrell.' Well, I packed up my shoeshine box and got me down to my own neighborhood, 'cause I knowed they was gonna be some dead men nearby soon."

—Moses A. Girod
shoeshine stall owner, age 83.
From an oral history tape in the
Historic New Orleans Collection.

Prologue

April 16, 1938

MALCOLM REDDING peered into the darkness around him as he eased his big Hudson sedan to a stop at the picnic grounds at Lake Pontchartrain. He looked at his watch and saw that it was nearly ten. He frowned. He was supposed to be at home helping his wife pack for their trip to Jamaica the next day.

It was dark and chilly out here, and the picnic ground was, as he anticipated, deserted. It was supposed to be spring, but the endlessly perverse weather in this part of the country had blown in a cold front that threatened to spoil the Easter weekend. He was glad he and his wife were taking a break. He was ready to feel the warm rays of the sun on his face. He got his tobacco pouch and the short briar pipe out of his pockets, and began to methodically pack the pipe. As he worked, he saw another car draw abreast of him, and heard the sound of the car door open and shut. Seconds later, his door on the passenger side opened.

"Well, it's about time you got here," he said irritably. "I've got other things to do tonight, so let's not draw this unpleasantness out any longer than we have to." He tamped the tobacco down in the bowl with the ball of his thumb, so engrossed in his task that he didn't see the cheap nickel-plated revolver appear in his visitor's hand, come to the level of his head, then emit a short, bitter roar.

The single shot knocked Redding sideways, his pipe and tobacco falling from his hands. Death was instantaneous. The killer's breath rasped harshly. With quick movements, the pipe and tobacco were picked up in gloved hands and placed in the glove compartment. Next, the killer wiped the cheap Harrington & Richardson .38 with a handkerchief, then pressed the gun into Redding's dead right hand.

The shrouded figure backed out of the car, stumbling as nausea roiled. The killer barely had time to bend over before the vomit rushed out onto the ground. The retching lasted for several seconds before it abated, then the killer used the handkerchief to wipe lips and chin. The stench of the burned gunpowder on the handkerchief nearly brought on another spate of retching, but breathing deeply and evenly caused the nausea to subside.

Within seconds, the killer was back inside the other car, threw it in gear, and headed back out onto Lakeshore Drive. The entire act of murder had taken less than three minutes to accomplish, but the killer knew with a twinge of fear and remorse that the memory would linger for a lot longer.

June 5, 1938

LATE IN THE afternoon, Ernie LeDoux rode the Algiers Point Ferry from the West Bank to New Orleans. It had been ten years since LeDoux had been in the city. A decade was a long time, particularly when you were a Negro in prison.

Ernie's memory replayed the images from that last time when he'd gotten ambitious and decided to knock over a Brinks armored truck carrying a payroll of seventy-five thousand dollars. He and his partners, Jack Solomon and Polly Flader, had stolen a Browning Automatic Rifle from a National Guard Armory which they'd used to blow off the truck's tires, then make mincemeat of the bulletproof glass. The guards gave up without a struggle, and were left bound and gagged in the ruins of the armored truck.

The trio of Negro hoods rode away from the wreckage, laughing and joking about what they'd do with their shares of the loot. They'd agreed that LeDoux should take it to a safe place, then they'd split up and lay low until things cooled off.

Things began to go bad for them almost immediately. Cops braced Solomon outside his rooming house on Perdido Street the next day and gunned him down when he went for his roscoe. That same evening, Flader was caught with his pants off and a whore's legs locked around his neck when the cops raided the whorehouse at Josephine and Constance Streets. They took him alive, but he refused to give anything up. He remained silent until the day a shank made from a teaspoon found its way into his back while he was showering at the prison farm to which he'd been assigned.

The news about his partners reached LeDoux quickly through the Negro underworld, and he knew something was wrong. How could the cops have tumbled to them so quickly? They'd planned it by themselves, and had remained together until the moment of the heist—there'd been no opportunity for one of them to get sauced and then spill something into the wrong ears. But somehow, somebody had learned about them, and was systematically exposing their whereabouts.

Knowing that the cops couldn't be far behind him, LeDoux cached the loot with an old friend, sharing the secret with no one else. After that, he kept constantly on the dodge, periodically phoning his sweetheart, Ruby Richoux, to let her know he was still free and alive. He managed to keep about one step ahead of the cops, but just barely.

The week after they killed Solomon, LeDoux crossed the parish line into Jefferson, hoping to throw the cops off his track for a while. He knew they'd be watching all the roads out of the area, and all the railroad depots and bus terminals, so he went to the only place left—a honkytonk called Avery's. He and Avery had grown up together, and the tavern owner was as true a friend as LeDoux had.

He was haggard from lack of sleep and jittery with nerves when the trio of plainclothes Negro cops came out of nowhere and surrounded the table. He could tell they were cops before they were halfway across the room, but they moved up on him fast, careless of their safety.

As the cops crowded in, LeDoux saw it was too late for gunwork. He came up with a German steel straight razor and cut two of them before the third put a .44 slug through his right leg. The three fell on him then, trussing him with cuffs and ankle chains within seconds. They rifled his pockets and discovered a few bills that they'd later found on a list of serial numbers from the stolen loot. It wasn't much, but it was sufficient to indict him.

LeDoux resisted various tortures, several offers of leniency, and the promise of a soft job in the prison library if he'd cough up the rest of the money. Ernie insisted on his innocence and played dumb. Only he and the man he'd left it with knew where the money was, and Ernie was damned if he'd give it up. He knew they couldn't keep him in prison forever.

That first year they tried to break him, placing him in solitary confinement. Months in the dark with bad food was almost enough to destroy him. He came out quiet and withdrawn, and from then on he did exactly what they told him. He knew he could not endure another stay in solitary.

Somehow he managed to survive through nine grueling years of killing toil under the hellish Louisiana sun and the shotguns of murderous prison guards. He had a goal, and he kept it fixed in front of him like a grail he could achieve if he were worthy. Eventually he was released for good behavior.

Now he was out and nearly home. He looked much the same as when he'd left. If anything, the years at hard labor had trimmed him down. His shoulders were the width of an ax handle and his massive square head sat atop a neck that was easily twenty inches around. His kinky black hair was still thick and full, with only a few errant strands of gray at the temples to give testimony to the hard years behind him. A part was freshly razored on the left side of his scalp, and but for a single scar on the left side of his jaw, his chocolate-brown face was remarkably smooth and unlined.

A trusted friend had arranged for Ernie's like-new 1926 Pontiac sedan, a suitcase of tailored clothes, and a .45 automatic to be waiting for him with a friendly farmer outside of Tunica. He made his way on foot to the farm, collected his belongings, and headed back to the city like a man of means rather than a broken-down ex-con. The clothes still fit him perfectly, and the engine of the old car purred like a sated tiger. LeDoux made his way to a small stash of run-out money, five thousand dollars, that he'd kept in a special place for an emergency. It was enough to tide him over until he could safely collect the stolen loot.

Ruby had written him sporadically over the years, but the occasional letters had assured him that she still carried a torch for him. He wondered how it would be with her after all these years. She'd only been a kid when they were together before. Now they were both older.

Unlike many of his fellow prisoners, he'd felt no desire to pleasure himself with another man—he'd put that part of himself into a box and locked it away. Now, when he tried to imagine himself with Ruby, he couldn't quite do it. It had been too long. He wondered if something inside him was broken, and the thought troubled him.

As he drove into the city limits, night was beginning to fall. He'd felt something electric in the air as he'd driven through Algiers to the ferry landing. Only a few other cars shared the brief voyage across the Mississippi with him. Now he stood on the steel deck with his jacket off and his tie undone, and watched the deceptively slow progress of the ferry coming from the eastern bank as his own trudged like a tired fat man in the opposite direction.

Finally the ferry's powerful diesel engines gave a huge shudder as the pilot signaled for reverse, so Ernie got back into his car and started the engines. Ahead of him he could see the lights of Canal Street, and he almost fancied he could hear the wail of trumpets, the low moan of a sax, and the deep hum of a bass beneath the noises of the dock. Then the cars were moving and he was off the ferry, heading Downtown to the Negro district.

He followed Canal Street as far as Rampart, then cut left across traffic. Rampart was as wide open as ever, and the smells, sounds, and sights were so powerful they were like a punch in the gut.

The neon sign advertising the Metro Hotel hove into view, and he pulled the Pontiac to a stop right outside the entrance. As he got out of the car, a young brown-skinned bellhop appeared to take his bags and car keys. He followed the skinny kid into the lobby and registered at the desk.

As the clerk read his signature, he said, "Everything's all taken care of, Mr. LeDoux."

"Huh?" Ernie said.

The clerk smiled broadly. "There's somebody waiting upstairs in Room 317. Go ahead, and I'll send your bags up with the 'hop."

Taking the key to his room, LeDoux went upstairs, with the bellhop directly behind. As he reached the door, he turned and handed the youngster a quarter, and fitted the key into the lock. The bellhop retreated down the hall, and Ernie picked up his bags and walked through the door.

It was a good-sized room for the Metro, furnished with a double bed, writing table, two armchairs, and a night stand. A framed photograph of a New Orleans marching band by Arthur P. Bedou hung on the wall over the bed. Sitting on the bed was a pretty girl—a woman, really. She'd grown up a lot in ten years, startlingly so. She got up while smoothing the brightly-colored dress she wore, her face smiling tentatively. Her shining black hair was chemically straightened now, and hung to her shoulders. Her skin reminded him of coffee with milk, and deep black eyes sparkled in her fine-featured face. "I wondered if you'd got lost," she said.

Ernie dropped his suitcases and closed the door behind him. His body felt like it was quivering all over, although when he looked at his hands, they were remarkably steady. He took off his derby and dropped it on the table, then he came to her slowly. When they were about twelve inches apart, she threw herself into his arms. The kissing seemed to go on forever, and when they broke, both of them were breathing heavily.

"Welcome home, baby," she said. "I feel like I been waitin' my whole life for this minute."

He smiled at her, blinking to keep the shine in his eyes from spilling over. "It has been a long time, honey," he said. "But the waiting's all over now." He put his mouth on hers hungrily, and they fell over gently onto the bed.

Outside his window, LeDoux could faintly hear music for real now—sweet, slow jazz from one direction, raucous Dixieland from another, mingling sweetly in the night like some kind of airy gumbo. He was home now, and he was never going to leave again.

Chapter One

A PAUNCHY, well-dressed Negro businessman named Ulysses Bautain came to consciousness gasping, shaking his head violently to escape the cold water that had been thrown into his face. He found himself lying on the filthy deck of a fishing boat that rocked violently in a choppy sea. The back of his head, over the right ear, ached abominably. He had a faint recollection of leaving the Sassafrass Lounge on his way to a lover's tryst with his lovely secretary, then everything going black.

"Where...am I?" he asked dully.

"You takin' a li'l cruise, bru-tha," a voice said from somewhere behind him. Then came the harsh sound of leather heels on the wooden deck until he saw a form looming over him. A match flared in the man's hand, and for an instant Bautain could see a long, humorous Negro face illuminated starkly as the man lit a cigarette. The match went out as he shook his hand, plunging everything back into darkness.

"What you want with me?" Bautain asked indignantly. He tried to sit up and found that his arms and legs were tied tightly, and his legs were weighted down by a length of heavy chain. "What's the idea?"

The other man blew out a lung full of smoke that was briefly visible in the night sky before a breeze snatched it away. “The big idea is, you should’a took the deal you was offered on that property.”

“Property?” Bautain asked stupidly.

“That’s right, cousin,” the man said. “That commercial property over Gentilly way.”

“But—but that offer was way too low,” Bautain said querulously. “It’ll be worth a hundred times more than that if—”

As he said the words, he understood immediately why he was tied hand and foot on a boat in the middle of Lake Pontchartrain. The old man in the wheelchair had contacted him through Bautain’s banker, had called him by telephone, and had finally come to his offices, offering to buy some relatively worthless property that Bautain owned in the marshy east side of the city. Except Bautain had insider information that it might soon be worth more—a lot more—and he’d dismissed every offer, the last one rather imperiously. He remembered now the flat, impassive face of the huge Negro who’d attended the old man, and the dangerous glint in the coal-black eyes of the old man himself. Bautain now knew he’d made a terrible mistake.

“No, wait,” Bautain said quickly. “call Lincoln up. I—I’ll deal with him. Tell him I changed my mind—that I’ll accept his original offer of two thousand dollars. I didn’t know he wanted the property this bad, I swear I didn’t.”

The other man laughed delightedly, a wholly inappropriate delight under the circumstances. A ray of moonlight fell across the upper half of his face, and Bautain could see the mad glitter in his eyes. “Nigger, you sure is doin’ some crawfishin’ now, ain’t you? Trouble is, it’s too late. Lincoln made you an offer, you turned it down. There ain’t no counter offers with Mr. Lincoln. After I get rid of you, Lincoln’ll make the same offer to your widow—or maybe he’ll offer less. Mr. Lincoln’s kind of a slick businessman.” The man laughed again, a jittery, nasty sound that reminded Bautain of rats skittering behind the wainscoting.

"You crazy, man," Bautain spluttered. "I'll give you five thousand dollars, cash money, tonight, if you'll lemme go. I won't even stop to pack or call my wife. Please, please don't kill me, please." Bautain was crying now, sobbing like a lost little boy. "Please, dear God, don't throw me in there tied up like this, please don't."

The other man bent down and dragged him upright, seemingly without effort. He held him like that, so he could look Bautain in the eye. "You fucked up, bru-tha. You thought you was tellin' some old handkerchief-head to go to hell. That was wrong. You was fuckin' with somethin' a whole lot bigger'n you. Now you gonna be fish food. Tell Saint Peter that Archie Badeaux said hello."

"No, No, NOOO—" Bautain's scream rose to an hysterical pitch as Badeaux dragged him to the gunnels and pushed him over. He was still screaming when the water closed over his gaping mouth. A big bubble burst on the choppy surface as the killer stood there, savoring each lung full of smoke until he was down to a butt of about a half inch. After one last shallow drag, he examined the glowing tip, then flicked it spinning into the troubled water. He patted his pockets until he found a antique snuff horn and a clasp knife with a long, thin blade. He opened the snuff horn, flicked open the knife, and plunged it into the white powder in the horn. Turning his back to the wind, he brought the knife point to his nose and snorted the powder into his left nostril. He repeated the procedure with his right nostril, then he stood there as the cocaine rushed through his system, making him feel like a giant.

As the rush subsided, Badeaux walked to the small cabin, cranked the engine, and as it caught, swung the wheel hard to port and headed toward the nearest navigation light that would point his way back to the New Orleans shore. He had one more stop this evening, one more murderous errand to fulfill for Mr. Lincoln before bedding down for the night.

Mr. Lincoln's quite an old heller, Badeaux thought to

himself. Wish I'd of known him in the old days, when he still had his legs. The two of us could've walked over this fuckin' town with hob-nail boots, took what we wanted, and then burned the rest. Those would've been great days, but these ain't such bad days neither. Got me a nice house, got me a new Dodge automobile, got me a pile of money in the bank, and a few stray broads to warm the bed at night. All I gotta do is kill anybody who gets in Mr. Lincoln's way. Yes, sir, not a bad life for a nigger from Philadelphia, Mississippi.

He laughed softly to himself as he entered the navigation channel that would lead him back to the docks at the village of Bucktown. And on top of that, there's that li'l piece of side action I got cookin'. That'll be one hell of a pile of kale. Maybe I'll retire. Maybe I'll just kill people for fun once in a while. He laughed again, more loudly, the sound floating eerily across the dark water.

A CLOCK SOMEWHERE in the apartment above Moise Cupperman's hardware store chimed four A.M. The large table was mostly in shadow, the big round dining table alone bathed in the harsh circle of light cast by a conical fixture suspended from the ceiling by a long, gilt chain. Five men sat around the table, their mouths set and their hooded, bloodshot eyes focused on their cards. Occasionally one of the men would venture a brief, furtive appraisal of the other faces around the table, but otherwise the five men might be statues, unmoving and solemn.

A big, black-haired Irishman named O'Connell grinned confidently as he folded his cards into a slender deck in the palm of his hand. His black eyes roved the table as he looked over the tops of his hands.

Moise Cupperman, a burly Jew with a shock of unruly gray hair and small round glasses that had slipped to the middle of his fleshy nose, frowned at his hand. It was a lousy two pair—all low cards. He'd taken a beating tonight, and couldn't understand how his luck could be so bad. He knew he was no riverboat gambler, but he was a better poker player than this. He wondered if he was getting old and his mind slowing down. A corner of his mouth quirked distastefully at the thought.

To Cupperman's left sat Art Frizzell, a crime reporter for the *New Orleans States-Item*. His nearly shapeless porkpie fedora rested on the back of his head, his chin cupped in his left hand as he surveyed the cards in his right. Cupperman had seen that look on Frizzell's face before, usually when he was about to fold. He couldn't bluff worth beans, the Jew thought, but he also knew Frizzell wouldn't go down without some kind of gesture. He had the kind of pride that a lousy poker player couldn't afford, and was always limping from one paycheck to another to make up for it.

Frizzell confirmed the Jew's thoughts, picking up a ten-dollar bill and tossing it into the center of the table. "I'm in for ten," the reporter said in a dry, nasal voice.

Sitting next to O'Connell was a small, neat man in his early twenties named Soto. His face was round and soft, like a young boy's, and he wore a thin, neatly-trimmed mustache that did nothing to detract from the boyishness. His eyes were a sparkling blue, and his lips full, sensual, and a bit red. His dark brown hair made his pale skin look like a baby's. He held his cards in a fleshy, pink hand near the surface of the table, angled slightly toward him. His other hand lay flat on the table between the hand of cards and his body. He wore a highly polished silver ring on the third finger of that hand, and he shifted it restlessly with his thumb as he studied his cards. Finally Soto said, "I'll see your ten." His voice was pitched a bit high, like that of a boy not yet through puberty. He threw two fives into the pot.

Cupperman wordlessly threw in a ten, then looked over at the other man at the table. The fifth man was tall and wide through the shoulders, and unlike the others, he still wore the jacket to his shantung silk suit of fish-scale gray with little herringbones running through it. A wide-brimmed Borsalino with a brown grosgrain band shaded all but his mouth from view. As he looked up from his cards, two pale gray eyes blazed for a moment from within the shadow. "See your ten, and raise you another twenty," he said. His voice was a smooth baritone with the clarity of a hammer striking stone, and with just that much emotion in it.

O'Connell smirked at the pale-eyed man. "See your twenty and raise you another twenty, Farrell," he said with a swagger in his voice.

Wesley Farrell's face was still lost in shadow, but his eyes seemed to smile in a particularly cold way. He picked up two more twenties and a ten-dollar note from the pile in front of him and dropped them on top of the confused mess of bills and chips in the center of the table.

O'Connell's grin grew into an obscene leer. "That's gonna cost you, hotshot. Show your cards and then stand back while I rake in that pot."

"Not yet," Farrell said in that same clear voice. "Before you move an inch, let me tell you what you and your pal there have in *your* hands."

O'Connell's grin hardened, and his coal black brows met in a hostile V over the bridge of his nose. "Is that some kind of crack?" he said in a voice that reminded the other men of gravel grinding under the tires of a heavy car.

"You boys need to work on your act," Farrell said, ignoring the menace in O'Connell's voice. "It sticks out like a wart on a debutante's nose."

"What you talkin' about?" Soto asked, his eyes big and his mouth open. His small chest worked as his breathing quickened. "We come here separate. I never seen this guy before in my life."

Farrell laughed mirthlessly and he shook his head from side to side. "If you can't lie any better than that, you better find another line of work, kid. You should see your face."

"Keep talkin'," O'Connell rasped, "and I'll kick your ass up into your hat, pen-wiper."

"Farrell, what the hell's goin' on?" Cupperman asked. His eyes had sharp points of lights in them, and his teeth were bared like a wild dog's.

"Just a little fun and games, Moe," Farrell said, his hands flat on the table. "These two boys have been in bed all night. Maybe before that, too."

Soto winced at the insinuation, and pushed himself away from the table as if to distance himself from the conflict growing around him.

"Talk clearer," Frizzell said, leaning over the table. "I'm a little slow tonight."

"It's not all that much," Farrell replied. "The nance is wearing a silver ring on his left hand. But it hasn't got a stone in it—the surface of the ring is a polished mirror disk. He uses it to show O'Connell what cards he's got, and then the two of them do some finger exercises on the table so O'Connell can tell Soto what cards he needs to build a winning hand. I think O'Connell's built a royal flush, with the ace of hearts the nance just gave to him."

"The ace of hearts?" Frizzell said.

"I've got the other three aces in the deck," Farrell said. "I've been watching you and Moe, and I'm pretty sure you didn't have it. O'Connell got very bold after the last time he picked up a discard. I think the nance broke up a straight in order to give him that ace he needed. Am I right, O'Connell?"

O'Connell's face had frozen into a hateful grimace, and the muscles in his shoulders bunched as he pushed himself violently upright. His right hand swept back to his hip and flew upward with a gun in it. Farrell, moving faster than the mind could register, rose, caught O'Connell's gun hand in his left as he shoved his old .38 Colt automatic into the black-haired gambler's face. As he thumbed back the rounded nub of a hammer on his gun, Farrell twisted O'Connell's gun wrist, and the gambler's hand opened convulsively. His Remington .380 automatic hit the table in the center of the pot as Frizzell, Cupperman, and Soto all jumped back from the table.

Farrell's face, no longer in shadow, was contorted with fury. The muscles along his jawline had grown lumpy, and his pale gray eyes flashed with an unearthly light. He still held O'Connell's right wrist at a painfully obtuse angle, and the truculence had drained out of the big man's dark eyes.

Cupperman's senses came back to him, and he reached over and grabbed the fallen automatic pistol, then he checked O'Connell's and Soto's forgotten poker hands. He turned each one over and opened them into fans. "God *Damn,* Farrell," he said in a hushed voice. "You had both hands dead on the button. A royal flush and a straight, minus the ace of hearts."

"What do you want to do with these guys?" Frizzell asked as he rolled up his shirt sleeves. "I think they deserve a beating at the very least."

Farrell released O'Connell's hand and shoved him backwards. He fell into his chair and nearly upset it. Soto had backed to the wall, his right hand slipping jerkily toward his hip pocket. His pale cheeks had reddened, and his baby blue eyes held a look of stark terror. Farrell shifted his gun muzzle until he centered on the boy's dark red necktie. "Go ahead," Farrell invited. "Pull that piece right on out. Show us how good you are."

Frizzell approached Soto from the side, jerked a nickel-plated Harrington & Richardson .32 revolver from the boy's pocket, and backhanded him across the face. Soto fell to his knees, blubbering, begging for his life.

Farrell turned his attention back to O'Connell who looked up at him with a sullen expression and scared eyes. "I'm going to give the two of you time to get to the railroad station this morning and get the first train going out of here—it doesn't matter which direction—just get out of town. If I see you again, I'll kill you on sight, you understand?"

O'Connell nodded jerkily. He'd heard stories about the tall man with pale gold skin before this night, but he hadn't believed them until now. He reached out a shaking hand toward the pile of money in front of him, his fingers curled to pick it up.

"Forget it, punk," Farrell rapped out. "You can keep what's in your pockets, and not a dime more. You're getting off lucky at that. Now get out of here and be quick about it."

O'Connell and Soto grabbed their hats and coats and disappeared from the apartment like a dream fades when you open your eyes. Cupperman looked down at the automatic in his hand, and saw his hand was shaking. He'd known Wesley Farrell a long time, but he'd never seen him in action before, and it scared him. He knew Farrell's reputation, and wondered how the man turned the violence inside him on and off like that. When he looked at Farrell, he was sliding his old Colt back into his waistband, and reaching for the money in the center of the table.

"And here I thought I was just going to have a quiet evening of poker," Frizzell said in his nasal voice. "Instead I lose my shirt and look like a dope in the process. Guess I'll go home and chalk it up to experience."

"Not so fast," Farrell said, holding out a sheaf of bills to the reporter. "Those guys cheated all of us, so we'll just split the pot and call it square."

"That's white of you, Farrell," Cupperman said. "But I don't think we deserve it."

"Don't take it so big," Farrell said as he handed the Jew a packet of bills. "They weren't too bad at their con. They just thought they were in the room with a bunch of rubes."

"You mean they weren't?" Cupperman said, with no attempt at irony.

Farrell grinned. "Think I'll call it a night, gents. I'll see you again in a couple of weeks, okay?"

The other men bade him farewell, and he found his way back down to the street. The darkness was giving way to a graying in the east as he got into his Packard Marlin and cranked the engine. Now that he was alone, he felt himself shivering and saw that his hands were shaking. He'd come within an ace of killing a man, and knew that he'd let the cheating go on far too long. He could have exposed O'Connell and Soto after the first couple of hands, but he'd let it build to a confrontation that some part of him had desired.

As he drove downtown on St. Claude Avenue, he knew he'd been out of control, and recognized how often and how easily that was happening. He was a stick of dynamite with a short fuse, and had been ever since Savanna Bealieu had left town, ten months before. He replayed their final conversation in his mind for the hundredth time, trying to find the right combination of words he might have used to keep her from leaving. "You don't understand," she'd said. "Well, make me, goddamnit," he'd shouted back at her. "I love you. What more can I say to you?" Saying the word "love" wasn't easy for Farrell, and he didn't understand why Savanna didn't recognize the power it had for him.

He hadn't seen Savanna cry many times, but she'd cried then. What was it she wanted him to understand? Sleepy Moyer had raped her just before Mardi Gras last year, but he was dead. She'd seen him die. "I still feel the same way about you," Farrell had said. "But I don't feel the same way about myself," she'd yelled back. He'd left in a huff, frustrated beyond measure that he couldn't get to the bottom of it; could not reach that secret place she couldn't, or wouldn't share with him. When he'd gone back the next day to apologize and try once more to patch things up, he discovered that she'd laid off all her people, put the building up for lease, and left town.

Another man might've gone off on a drunk or picked up another woman to help him forget, but there was a reserve in Farrell, a length of emotional steel that enabled him to absorb the blow and keep walking. But it had come at a price. He was often short-tempered, and violence welled up in him with such startling rapidity that even his friends had come to regard him warily, and always approached him from the front so he'd see them before he heard them.

He realized now that she was gone, that he wanted to marry Savanna, in spite of the seeming impossibility of it. He was a mixed-blood Creole by birth, but he'd been living as a white man for over twenty-five years. Marrying a Negro woman would mean giving up all that he had and was, but over a year ago, he'd recognized in himself the stirrings of a weariness with the role he was playing, and with the isolation into which it had driven him.

With Savanna gone, all that he had left was work and cards to fill up the hole in him. Much of the time he was able to make do, but at other times, like tonight, the emptiness demanded more from him than mere diversion, something with a dangerous edge, a rush of adrenaline that would drive the ache of loneliness back into its cave. Now that it was past, he realized again how foolish it was to court violence and risk killing someone. Or was it that he wanted someone to kill him? His eyes widened and his mouth fell open at the thought because he didn't know the answer.

ERNIE LEDOUX woke up, and for a moment didn't remember where he was. He saw the sunlight streaming through the windows and felt a moment's panic, thinking the guards would be on him because he wasn't up, dressed, and standing at the cell door. Then he remembered the drive down from Tunica, seeing Ruby again, and he relaxed.

He rolled over and saw that the bed was empty beside him, and he sat up. "Ruby?" he called softly. He pushed the sheets back, got up, and walked to the bathroom. He knocked lightly on the door. "Baby, you in there?" he called a bit more loudly. The door opened at his touch, and he saw a message written on the mirror in red lipstick.

Had to get to work
See you tonight
Love, Ruby

He grinned at that. He felt like a regular joe for the first time in years. *Love, Ruby*. God, that made him feel good all over.

He went to the telephone, called the desk, and asked them to send up a platter of ham and eggs and a pot of coffee. That done, he jumped into the shower and soaped himself all over, then shaved with his safety razor. He had gotten out and toweled himself dry when he heard the knock on the door. He hurriedly pulled on his pants, opened the door, and took the tray from the bellhop. He put it down on the writing table, got a quarter from his pocket, and flipped it to the 'hop, who grinned, nodded his thanks, and left.

The 'hop had also brought up the latest edition of *The Louisiana Weekly*, the city's Negro weekly newspaper. Ernie propped it up behind the tray and scanned the front page while he shoveled eggs and biscuits into his mouth. At first, none of the news meant anything to him because he didn't recognize any of the names. As he paged through the paper idly, he recognized some of the business names and many of the musicians and bands he saw written up.

He cleaned the remaining egg yolk from his plate with a biscuit half, washed it down with the remainder of the coffee, then got up and looked out the window. He guessed it must be midmorning by now. No need to wait any longer. He went to the telephone book, picked it up, and began looking under the "A"s for a joint called Attaway's Four Aces, but he found no listing for it.

He frowned and scratched his head at that. He then looked for a residential listing for Attaway, and found no Attaways at all in the book.

He put the book down, picked up the telephone receiver,

and asked the hotel operator to connect him with information. Within seconds a businesslike female voice came on.

"What name, please?"

"Benjamin Attaway, spelled just like it sounds," LeDoux said. "He lives on South Solomon Street."

"One moment," the operator said, then: "Sorry, sir, no listing under that name."

LeDoux's face took on a stunned look. "You—you're sure? No Benjamin Attaway?" He spelled it for her, but to no avail.

"Sorry, sir, no Attaways listed in Orleans Parish. Let me try Jefferson and St. Bernard." There was a long silence, during which LeDoux picked at his cuticles until they were ragged. Finally, she came back on. "No luck, sir. We can't find any Attaways in the area. I'm sorry."

"Thanks for tryin'," LeDoux said in a hollow voice. He put the receiver down on the cradle and stared at the wall. Ben couldn't have double-crossed him. He'd been like a father to Ernie.

LeDoux got up and went to his suitcase. He removed his trousers, then dressed himself in fresh linen, socks, shirt, and put his trousers back on. He knotted a tie around his throat, picked up his jacket and derby, and walked to the door. Something was wrong, and he was going to turn New Orleans upside down until somebody told him something that made sense.

A BEAUTIFUL NEGRO woman of about thirty came through the doors of the Café Tristesse like she owned the joint. She was about five-and-a-half feet tall, with skin so pale brown it was no darker than a suntan, shoulder-length jet black hair, and eyes like obsidian. The only makeup on her fine-featured face was lip rouge the color of ripe plums. Dressed in a pale yellow dress, yellow sling-back pumps, and a yellow hat that was like gold ornamentation on a queen, she was enough to make a Baptist minister drink swamp water, crawl inside a hollow log, and bay at the moon.

She walked through the lobby, past two of the janitors who watched her with big eyes, to the bar where Harry Slade, Farrell's bar manager, listened to the Boswell Sisters sing "Apple Blossom Time" on his radio. He looked up from an inventory sheet and nearly dropped his pencil.

"I wonder if I could speak to Mr. Farrell?" she asked politely.

"Well, yeah, I guess so," Harry said, struggling not to trip over his own tongue. He picked up a house phone, dialed a single digit, then spoke into the mouthpiece, his eyes flickering over the woman as he spoke. Finally he put down the telephone, and pointed across the large room to a door.

"Go right through there and up the stairs," he said. "Mr. Farrell's office is at the top."

The woman thanked Harry and followed his directions, pausing at a closed door at the head of the stairs and knocking on it. She heard a voice tell her to come in, and she opened the door and stepped through it.

Farrell was sitting at his desk with a cigarette in the corner of his mouth and a bottle of Jamaican Red Stripe ale at his elbow. A ledger was open in front of him, and he had a pencil in his right hand, poised over it. When he saw the woman, he put down the pencil, took the cigarette from his mouth, and stood up. "Can I help you?" he asked.

"Hello, Mr. Farrell," she replied. "I hope I'm not disturbing you by dropping in unannounced this way."

"Not at all," he said, offering her a chair with his outstretched hand. "Have a seat."

She stepped forward, smiling, and offered him a slender hand encased in an immaculate white glove. "My name's Carol Donovan." She gave him the full benefit of her dark eyes.

He took the hand. "Pleased to meet you, Miss Donovan. Can I offer you something cool to drink?"

"Some ginger ale would be lovely," she said. Her voice was just the right kind for a word like "lovely"—a cool contralto that perfectly enunciated every word. She talked the way Farrell imagined a graduate of Princeton might, except she was a Negro, and not many went to a place like Princeton.

He walked into his kitchen, put some ice in a glass, and filled the glass from a large bottle of White Rock he took from the refrigerator. He took it to her, then got his beer from his desk, sat down across from her and waited for her to get to the point.

"I own The Original Southport Club over in Jefferson Parish," she said. "I bought it last year from the previous owner, a white gentleman, and managed to turn it into a profitable venture."

"I know," Farrell said. "There are people who said a Negro club wouldn't have a chance in Jeff Parish, but you proved them wrong. You deserve congratulations." He was taken by her elegant demeanor, and the fact that talking to what she believed was a white man in an intimate setting didn't seem to bother her. He found that charming—and a bit intriguing. It wasn't what one would expect under the circumstances.

She nodded briefly, and smiled her appreciation. "You're too kind. But I know you understand this business, and the difficulties of making any nightclub a success."

"I've been at it a while," he said with a grin. "It's got its ups and downs."

She lowered her gaze to the amber liquid sparkling and fizzing in her glass, took a sip, then raised her eyes back to his. "Yes, ups and downs. That's actually why I'm here."

Farrell caught the sudden downturn in her mood and felt a strange fluttering in his stomach that had nothing to do with her looks or charm. "Trouble of some kind?" He heard the faint sound of warning bells in the back of his head.

"Do you know of a man named Archie Badeaux?" she

asked.

Farrell nodded. "He hurts people for a living—if they don't give him what he wants."

"He wants my club," she responded. "He came to my office earlier this week and offered a price big enough to lose under your thumbnail. Take it or get ruined was his proposition."

Farrell nodded his understanding, keeping his face neutral and his eyes opaque. Her bold confession of her troubles brought the warning bells to the front of his mind. He felt trouble circling him like wild Indians around a wagon train. He didn't like the way this was going. To stall for time, he reached for the cigarette box on the coffee table, opened it, and offered one to Carol Donovan. She took it, placed it between her plum-colored lips, and bent over for his light. He lit a fresh one for himself, then leaned back and looked at her again through the haze of the smoke he expelled. She didn't seem like a pushover to him, yet he knew she was here to ask for his help. Before he could say anything, she spoke again.

"I've heard some of the stories about you," she said. "About how you fought and killed a gangster named Emile Ganns a couple of years ago."

Farrell sighed. "There was a fight, Ganns was on the other side, and he got killed, yes. I'm not sure whose bullet did the job." He inhaled smoke and let it out through his nose. "You shouldn't get the idea from that that I'm the kind of guy who goes around kicking over anthills for the fun of it. Ganns was out for my blood, so it came down to him or me. I didn't look for that trouble, or any of the other troubles you might've heard about."

She leaned toward him and crossed her legs. They were long and supple, and he noticed she wasn't wearing any stockings. "I need help, Mr. Farrell. I'm not afraid to take up for myself, but I'm no match for a man like Archie Badeaux." She took a short drag from her cigarette and then placed it in the ashtray in front of her. "You're a brave man, a strong man. Even if the stories about you are only half true, you're still a generous man. Not many white men will help a Negro. You're one of the few."

He got up from his chair and walked around the room. She was good—awfully good. She almost made him forget that she was asking him to stick his neck into the lion's mouth. He walked over to the taboret and poured three fingers of Mount Gay Barbados rum into a tumbler, then walked back to his chair and sipped it. It had a heavy, sweet taste like the molasses it was distilled from. The bite was sharp enough to loosen his tongue again. "Regardless of what you might've heard, I'm not a strong-arm man. Getting into a head-butting contest with Archie Badeaux wouldn't do me any good, and it might get me killed." He sipped the rum again, then put the glass on the floor beside his right foot.

"For many reasons, I try to keep my nose clean and mind my own business," he continued. "I'm just like you—a nightclub owner. There are plenty of men—Negro and white—who make a living doing what you're asking of me. If you like, I can give you some names."

She listened intently as he spoke, then opened her bag and took out an envelope. She lifted the flap of the envelope and removed from it five one thousand dollar bills, which she arranged in a fan and placed on the coffee table between them. "I think Badeaux's just the tip of the iceberg, Mr. Farrell. There's five thousand dollars just for coming out to the club and looking things over. No catches, no commitments. They tell me you've got sympathy for colored people, Mr. Farrell. This is as much for the twenty-five colored people who work for me as it is for myself. Think about it, please."

She got up from the chair then, smoothing her dress with her white-gloved hand as she moved. To Farrell, it was like watching a poem come to life in front of him. "Please don't take too long to make up your mind. I don't know how long I can fight these people off by myself." She turned and walked from the room, leaving him sitting there looking at the money.

Twice he almost got up and ran after her to give the money back. He didn't need it, didn't even want it. He was certain it would bring him nothing but trouble. But what else do you have to do? he asked himself.

IN A LARGE downstairs room in a house on Melpomene Street, in what is known as the Lower Garden District, a painfully thin old man with lustrous black hair and tight, dry skin the color of buff writing paper sat in a wheelchair with his hands folded in his lap. His head swayed this way and that as he listened to Wanda Landowska perform the Goldberg Variations on his Capehart radio-phonograph. Landowska was one of the most spectacularly ugly women in the world, but she played the harpsichord with angelic perfection. The old man had played this album of records many times, and never tired of it.

From the front of the house he heard the sound of the doorbell. People seldom rang that bell, and when they did it was invariably someone to see him. He wheeled his chair to the phonograph, tenderly lifted the tone arm from the record, and regretfully switched it off. He deftly turned the chair with his strong, nimble hands so that he was facing the doors to the hall as they opened.

A large, bald-headed Negro stood there. The Negro wore a snow-white shirt, black bow tie, and black vest. His name was Albert Minshew, but the old man always called him "Albair," as though he were French. It was almost comical when you realized that Menshew had been imprisoned twice for homicide and jailed at least six times for assault with various deadly weapons. Almost. Until you looked in Albert's eyes, and noticed the queer light that sometimes lingered there. The old man might well have been the only person in the world who didn't fear Albert.

"Mr. Rogers Clifton to see you, Mr. Lincoln," the big Negro rumbled.

"Fine," Lincoln said with a sere smile. "I've been expecting him."

Albert turned and held the door so Clifton could enter the room. Clifton was a slender, elegant brown man dressed in a summer-weight wool blue suit with pinstripes. He wore a vest, even in the heat, with a gold chain that dipped from the top button of the vest into the pocket where his watch rested. Hanging midway down the chain was a keypin for the Negro law fraternity. His face was smooth and unlined, and he wore a trimmed mustache. His hairline had eroded back to the middle of his skull, leaving behind an unnaturally high forehead, and the impression of a greater age than Clifton actually was. He didn't look particularly happy.

"You wanted to see me, Mr. Lincoln?" Clifton asked in a carefully-modulated voice.

"I've some news on that property near the eastern edge of the city," Lincoln said.

"Yes?" Clifton replied. He said it in such a way that one almost thought he knew what Lincoln would say next.

"The owner has departed the city," Lincoln said, a small smile hovering about his lips. "I think his wife might be willing to sell it now. I suspect she'll want the money more than the bother of dealing with the property."

"Shall I call her tomorrow and ask?" Clifton asked.

"No, not so quickly," Lincoln said. "Give her a day or so to allow her time to get used to the fact that her husband probably won't be returning. Ladies sometimes take these things rather hard."

"I don't think I follow you," Clifton said carefully. His unwinking eyes never left Lincoln's face, giving the impression of a mongoose hypnotized by the eyes of a cobra.

"It seems," Lincoln said, making a steeple of his fingers, "that Mr. Bautain left the city with his secretary. The folly of middle age. Tsk, tsk. You'd think a man of his age and experience wouldn't act such the fool, would you?"

Clifton said nothing.

"I'd go and see her the day after tomorrow, or perhaps the day after," Lincoln continued. "Suggest the original offer for the land—two thousand, I think it was. I doubt her husband spoke of his business affairs in front of her. She won't be aware that I previously offered twice that much."

"Suppose she does—or suppose she refuses you—" Clifton almost said, "the way Bautain did," but he restrained himself at the last second.

"She won't," Lincoln said confidently. "Her husband's run off and left her for a younger woman. She won't know the true state of his affairs for a while, particularly since you'll be able to manipulate the bank records to make it seem he emptied several of his accounts. Leave enough for her to exist on—I have no wish to punish her further. Her husband's betrayal is enough for her to have to bear, don't you think?"

Clifton tried to keep his emotions from his face, but his eyes betrayed him. He was frightened of Lincoln, more frightened of him than anyone he'd ever known, and it particularly terrified him for the old man to spin these fantasies to him, knowing that Clifton knew they were lies, and yet spinning them anyway.

"Whatever you say, Mr. Lincoln," Clifton said finally.

Lincoln stared at Clifton for a moment. "You're making a great deal of money through your association with me, aren't you, Clifton?"

Clifton's face froze, and his eyes became opaque. "I'm comfortable. Quite comfortable."

The old man laughed, a harsh, dry clatter that sounded more like a serpent's rattle than the merriment of a man. His deep black eyes regarded Clifton as though he were a particularly interesting species of rat. Then the laugh cut off as though a switch had been thrown. "Comfortable, indeed. When I met you, you were a modestly successful fellow who'd suddenly been made acting president of a small bank. You might have become 'comfortable,' as you put it, but not soon. With me, you've made quite a bit of money through the little real estate deals on which we've collaborated, and when we dispose of this land at the eastern edge of the city, I will have the means to become a power in this city—and you will be part of it. Perhaps, then, you might feel a bit more enthusiastic about what we've accomplished—at what we will accomplish as we go on."

"I never wanted that," Clifton said. "My ambitions aren't as grandiose as yours."

"You're a prig, Clifton," Lincoln said. "A rather insufferable prig. But I need you, and whether you like it or not, you need my good will for as long as it lasts. Pray it doesn't run out." He half-turned the wheelchair until he was no longer looking at the bank president. "That's all for now. I'll call you if I have something else for you."

"Very well," Clifton said. "Good night." He turned and walked from the room. After a brief space of seconds, Lincoln heard the front door of the house open and close.

"Yes," he said to himself, smiling benignly. "Pray my need for you doesn't run out." He turned the chair again and wheeled it toward the Capehart, switched it back on, and placed the tone arm back on the record. His knowledge of the music was so precise that the needle landed on the exact spot where he had picked it up twenty minutes before. In seconds, he had put Clifton's visit from his mind.

Chapter 2

IN A SHABBY garage near the St. Bernard Parish line, a stocky dark-brown man with a neatly-trimmed mustache named Alex Mouton worked some figures in a ledger while his younger brother, Dominique, labored over the engine of an old Pierce Arrow touring car. The younger man's neck and shoulder muscles stood out in bold relief as he exerted all his strength to break loose a rusty bolt. Alex could hear curses punctuated by violent exhalations of breath, and he smiled. Dom thought he was such a he-man, but the car was proving to be more than a match for him.

The telephone rang at his elbow, and he removed the receiver from the hook. "Mouton Brothers Garage," he said.

"Gimme Alex Mouton," a gruff, muffled voice said. Must be a bad connection, Mouton thought idly.

"This is him," Mouton replied. "Who's this?"

"The name Archie Badeaux mean anything to you?" the voice asked.

"Hell, yeah," Mouton said. "I know his rep—a bad man with a gun, a real hard-boiled egg, is what I hear. What about him?"

"This is Badeaux talkin'," the voice replied. "How'd you like to do some work for me, a special job?"

"I ain't got nothin' against it, if the money's right," Mouton replied warily. He knew just enough about

Badeaux to want to be cautious.

"I want you to take a li'l trip to The Original Southport Club," Badeaux said.

"I dunno," Mouton said dubiously. "That's pretty rich for my blood. No place for a garage mechanic."

"You ain't goin' to have fun, fool," Badeaux said irritably. "How many boys you got?"

"Countin' me and Dom, eight," Mouton replied. "Why'd you wanna send a bunch of grease monkeys to a swell joint like that?"

"'Cause I want you to bust it up," Badeaux said forcefully. "I want you to smash it flat. I want it to look like a hurricane run through it, an' I want the customers scared so bad they're pissin' blood. Can you handle it?"

Mouton frowned. "I reckon. That all you want?"

"That's all," Badeaux affirmed. "I'll send eight hundred dollars over to you by special messenger—that's a century a piece. You do a good job, and I'll give you another eight hundred dollars as a bonus."

Mouton raised an eyebrow. This was good money, particularly for so simple a job. "Okay with me," he replied. "When you want the job done?"

"Tomorrow night," Badeaux replied.

"I hear you, boss," Mouton said. "You send the money over, and tomorrow we'll do the job."

"Good," Badeaux said tersely, then he hung up.

Mouton hung up his telephone and turned to where his brother was still straining against the engine. "Dom. Dom, let that alone for a minute."

"What?"

"Let that goddamn thing alone," Alex said. "We got a job."

"Huh?"

"Nigger, get the wax outta your fuckin' ears and listen."

IT WAS STILL early afternoon in Los Angeles, and a hot, dry wind known locally as a Santa Ana was blowing down

Central Avenue. Dressed only in a red silk slip, Savanna Beaulieu stood near an open window watching the hot wind expend its fury against the palm trees lining the street. Her brown skin had beads of perspiration on it, and her thick mane of black hair was pulled up off her neck into a twist. She plucked idly at the slip where it stuck to her skin.

She heard a rustling behind her, and turned to see a big, good-looking brown man yawning and stretching on the bed. He was naked, and had a thick mat of curly black hair on his chest. He ran his fingers through his long, marcelled scalp as he yawned hugely. "Hey, baby, he said lazily. "I'm lonesome. Come see me for a while."

"I seen you already, Harmon," Savanna said. "Cover it up and get lost, will you?"

Harmon looked at her with an insolent grin on his face. "You ain't tired of me already, are you? We just gettin' started."

"We *got* started at four this mornin'," Savanna said. "We got to know each other between seven and eight. Now it's two this afternoon, and time for you to get on outta here. I got work to do."

Harmon uncoiled his lanky body from the bed, then walked heavy-footed over to where Savanna stood with her back to him. He wrapped his long arms around her and began gently kissing her neck and shoulders as he kneaded her breasts with his large hands. She could feel his manhood begin to grow thick and heavy as he pressed against her buttocks. She reached around, found one of his thighs, and dug her nails into it.

"Hey," he cried, jumping back. "I was just bein' friendly. You don't have to act thataway. I'm leavin', okay?"

"Okay," Savanna said, "and don't let the door hit you in the ass on the way out." She was tired of Harmon and didn't care if he knew it. He was so good-looking and arrogant, though, she doubted he fully appreciated her disdain for him. She heard the rustle of cloth as he dressed, then a mumbled farewell as he left her rooms.

She was manager of a Negro nightclub called the Cotton Club West, and part of her contract provided her with a furnished apartment on the second floor of the club. The owner paid her well, and her experience running a club in New Orleans made the job almost like a paid vacation for her. Normally she didn't play with the customers, but something about Harmon had briefly attracted her. He was big, confident, and had a lazy smile, and she realized belatedly that he had reminded her of someone else—someone she'd come out here to forget.

She cut off that line of thought and went to the bathroom where she got into the shower and scrubbed herself vigorously with a big sponge. She also shampooed her hair, then got out of the tub, wrapped her wet hair into a turban, and padded naked about the apartment, letting her body dry in the warm air. When she looked up, it was nearly three o'clock, time for her weekly call.

She went to a small escritoire and lifted the receiver of a telephone. She got the long distance operator and gave a number in New Orleans as she sat down on a small upholstered desk chair. After a couple of minutes she heard a line ringing. Someone picked up on the fourth ring and a woman's voice said, "Hello?"

"It's Rosalee, 'Tee Ruth," she said. Savannna's real name was Rosalee Ortique, but she'd changed it to Savanna Beaulieu for business reasons years ago. Only her closest friends knew her real name anymore, and 'Tee Ruth Sonnier was one of the few.

'Tee Ruth was almost like a mother to her, and she'd gotten into the habit of calling her every week after moving to Los Angeles nine months before. She always got homesick afterwards, but Savanna could not shake the compelling need to keep in touch with home.

"Hello, Rosalee," 'Tee Ruth said. "How you makin' out, girl?"

"Makin' a lot of money and gettin' old," Savanna said

wryly. "It's hotter than blazes out here. I wish it would cool off."

"It ain't too bad here," the old woman said. "'Bout like usual for this time of year. You gonna come home and visit us soon?"

"I—I don't know," Savanna said haltingly. "Probably not."

"Lord, girl," 'Tee Ruth said. "You been gone for almost a year, and ain't been back once. You got to come home sometime. You could reopen your club and be back in full swing within a month, and you know it."

"I do know it," Savanna said, feeling herself being drawn into territory she didn't want to visit. "But I don't feel like coming back yet. Maybe I never will."

'Tee Ruth was silent for a while, and Savanna could hear nothing but crackles of static and the ghostly sound of two faint voices somewhere else on the line. Then the old woman said, "He'd forgive you if you came back. You know he would."

"Why should he forgive me?" Savanna flared. "I haven't done a thing but live my life the way I want. I got the right."

"Sure you do," Ruth said, "but you never even told him goodbye. I know why you left, and I understand the reason, but you didn't make him understand. You just left without even sayin' nothin'. He deserved better than that."

Savanna felt her face growing hot with shame. She and Ruth had had this talk before, but it never got any easier. "I tried to make him understand, but he couldn't. All he could talk about was love. He didn't understand that what I lost I had to get back without him. Without him having to come through a door and beat it out of somebody. He never understood that, and I couldn't make him."

"He ain't perfect, child," 'Tee Ruth said. "But who is? He just wanted to protect you."

"Goddamnit, I don't need protecting," Savanna said sharply. "I don't need somebody always lookin' over my shoulder, holding their breath in case I fall down. I never needed that, not even when Sleepy Moyer had me."

"So, because he cared enough to worry about you, you left him without a by-your-leave and ain't said nothin' to him for almost nine months," 'Tee Ruth said in a musing voice. "You can do what you want, I reckon, but if you don't make things right with him, you'll never know a peaceful day again. You can't leave business like that unfinished, not if you want to be able to look at your face in the mirror again."

"'Tee Ruth, please don't keep after me about this stuff. I called because I wanted to talk to you and hear how everybody is, not get some lecture about how bad I treated Wesley Farrell. For God's sake, he and I couldn't ever get married, have any children, or have any kind of normal life. What was the point of stayin' there with him?"

"You feel like God just naturally punished you, don't you girl?" 'Tee Ruth said. "But God don't work that way. And he don't send people to love you as a punishment. Love is what it is, and you got to take it or leave it. But if you leave it, don't go actin' like nobody's punishin' you. You doin' it to your own self."

"Goodbye, 'Tee Ruth," Savanna said. "I'll call you again sometime." She hung up the telephone before the old woman could reply. Tears were falling from her eyes onto her naked breasts, and she couldn't stop them. She went back to the bathroom, unwrapped her hair, turned on the cold water full blast, and stepped into it. She stayed until all the crying and shaking were out of her.

MARCEL ARISTIDE walked along Rampart Street as the evening was getting into full swing. He was a compact, good-looking octoroon of about twenty years, with light brown hair and large brown eyes that surveyed and filed everything he saw. He wore a light-gray summer-weight wool worsted and a pearl-gray Stetson cocked at a jaunty angle over his right ear.

He was on the street trying to lift his spirits, and he paused at each tavern, juke joint, and 'tonk, hoping that the smells and sounds of jazz that drifted out of each door would blunt the edge of the depression that bore down on him.

Two years ago he'd been a punk, a two-bit stickup artist on a fast track to the joint or an early gave, but his self-destructive path crossed that of his cousin, Wesley Farrell, and changed his life. Taking the younger man under his wing, Farrell had, in a sense, rehabilitated Marcel. He'd given him work, and eventually responsibilities to give him a sense of purpose. Marcel was grateful and tried hard, but his youth and inexperience sometimes tripped him up.

Some weeks before, Farrell had sent him to collect a debt of a thousand dollars from a gambler whose marker he held. It had seemed like a simple job—perhaps too simple. The man had let Marcel into his second-floor apartment, and had appeared genuinely glad to see him and to complete his business with Farrell. A woman had been with him, a very good-looking yellow chick with a body that could knock a man's eyeballs right out of his head at a hundred yards. She began playing eye games with Marcel as soon as he walked into the room.

The man excused himself to get the money, leaving Marcel alone with the young woman. She'd been a fast worker, moving to the sofa where Marcel sat, engaging him in light, bantering conversation, touching him in subtle ways to indicate her interest in him. Marcel was just fool enough to fall for it. By the time his brains checked back in, the man had back-doored him, leaving him with a handful of nothing. The woman lammed while he was in the bedroom looking through the open window at the empty fire escape.

Chagrined beyond words, Marcel trudged back to Farrell's office, expecting a tongue-lashing at the very least. Farrell listened to his shame-faced admissions, looking him in the eye and smoking silently throughout the story.

When Marcel finished, Farrell stubbed out the cigarette in an ashtray and said "Okay." He'd returned his attention to his ledger and paid Marcel no further mind.

Marcel wanted to say how sorry he was, how it would never happen again, but his voice was caught in his throat, and eventually he rose quietly to his feet and slunk from the office. Although his cousin treated him as though nothing had happened, Marcel could not get over it, and felt uncomfortable in Farrell's presence. He concentrated fiercely on the work he was given, and spent his nights prowling the streets of the Quarter, trying to distract himself from the burn of shame that seemed to have taken up permanent residence in his gut.

He was paused in front of Jake Itzkovich's Pawn Shop, inspecting the horns, guitars, and other instruments hocked by temporarily distressed musicians when he heard a woman hail him.

"Hey, good-lookin'. How's it hangin'?" she asked.

Without looking up from the window, he replied, "Straight and narrow, Mary Jack."

As the woman hooted, he turned and found an incongruously pretty black woman there, built like an Amazon warrior princess. They called her Mary Jack the Bear, and she was reputed to be the toughest woman in town. She sold sex most of the time, but occasionally took on bodyguard jobs if the money was right. She carried a Luger automatic in her purse and a razor in the top of her left stocking—at least so Marcel had been told. He'd never wanted to make an inspection just for curiosity's sake.

"What's a nice gal like you doin' on Rampart Street this time of night?" Marcel asked facetiously.

"Tryin' to make a livin', what else?" she asked with a grin. She had a lovely smile—if you liked sharks. "But I come to give you a message."

"Who from?" he asked.

She jerked her head across the street. "See that brutha over yonder?" she asked. "He knows you work for Farrell and he wants to ask you somethin'. Says it's important."

Marcel snorted. "Hell, that's what they all say. What's his grift?"

"He ain't got no grift," she said incredulously. "Look at the man for Christ's sake. He's so square the corners sticks out. I wouldn't carry no message for somebody I thought'd bring you grief, li'l Marcel. You're mine, all mine." She laughed deep down in her magnificent chest.

"He got a name?" Marcel asked, glancing over at the man. Marcel could see he was nervous or upset; he kept shifting his weight from one foot to the other, and he didn't seem to know what to do with his hands.

"Chet Daniels," she said. "He got him a dry cleanin' bidness on Washington Avenue, on the Lake side of Claiborne."

"All right," Marcel said. "I'll go talk to the guy."

"You an angel, li'l Marcel," she said. "I'll check you later now, hear?"

"I hear," Marcel said. He tugged his Stetson lower down on his forehead, and dodged a little traffic to cross the street. It took him only a few seconds to reach the man. "Your name Chet Daniels?" he asked as he drew near.

"Yessir, Mr. Aristide," the man said nervously. He looked to be somewhere in his early thirties, but they'd been a hard thirty from the look of him. His brown skin had deep lines etched in the corners of his mouth and his eyes. He was dressed in a cheap brown suit that nonetheless had knife-edge creases, and a well-starched white shirt. His necktie had little starbursts soaring across a blue background. On his egg-shaped head he wore a straw boater of the type that had been popular during the 1920s.

"What's on your mind?" Marcel asked.

"I got me some trouble," Daniels said. "I need to ask Mr. Farrell for a favor."

"We all got trouble," Marcel said. "What makes you think Mr. Farrell can help you?"

Daniels' face twisted with chagrin, and his hands shook

as they sought a place to rest. Marcel instantly regretted the harshness of his words. "Look, why don't we go in this café and have a little coffee. Then you can tell me what this is all about."

Daniels' face brightened. "That'd be real fine, sir."

Marcel felt vaguely foolish about this man mistering and sirring him. He couldn't be less than ten years Marcel's senior. Marcel gestured for the man to precede him into the café.

The place wasn't too busy yet, so Marcel pointed to a table against the far wall where they'd be able to talk in relative peace. When they were seated, a red-skinned girl in her late teens with a cute snub nose showed up to take their order. Marcel ordered coffee for both of them while he tried to ignore the come-on in her eyes.

"It's like this, Mr. Aristide," Daniels began. "I got me a brother. He ain't a bad fella, but he can't pass a punch-board without puttin' down a nickel. He gambles away just about every cent he makes."

"And loses every time, right?" Marcel asked, pausing as the waitress brought the coffee and another little come-hither glance.

"Yessir, that's a fact," Daniels said. "And he's into Nate Hopkins for near a thousand dollars."

Marcel whistled with surprise. "A thousand? How'd he get that much to gamble in the first place?"

"Ain't no tellin'," Daniels said, shaking his head. "All's I know is Hopkins sent a man 'round to see me, sayin' that if Ralph couldn't come up with the bread by tomorrow, he was gonna have to hurt Ralph. Also said if hurtin' Ralph didn't do the trick, he'd be 'round to collect the deed to my store. I ain't no fighter, Mr. Aristide. I worked for ten years to get my business together, and I got two li'l boys to raise."

"You got anything like a thousand to give Hopkins?" Marcel asked.

"I got some money, but a lot of it's tied up at the bank

for collat'ral on a business loan," Daniels said. "I got maybe seven hundred in a savings account that I was savin' for my boys' education, but that las' three hundred's a problem."

"So you're looking for a loan?" Marcel asked.

"Not exactly," Daniels said. "I heard Tommy Spence say that his cousin once got Mr. Wesley Farrell to stand behind him long enough to keep a loan shark from breakin' his legs. Ralphie and me can prob'ly get the three hundred if we got some time, but we can't do it with no broke legs, if you take my meanin'."

Marcel looked down at his coffee cup and idly turned it around in his fingers. The distress in the dry cleaner's eyes was genuine, of that Marcel was certain. He could go to Wes with it, and his cousin might agree to help the man. He might not, too. With Wes it was sometimes hard to tell what he would do. Marcel knew he was often sympathetic to poor Negroes in trouble, perhaps because he'd been one before he adopted the identity he now used. Marcel was one of the few who knew of Farrell's Negro blood, and it was a confidence he guarded zealously.

On the other hand, Nate Hopkins was a ruthless old bastard and would probably take the business if Daniels couldn't come up with the money. Marcel did a quick tally of his own assets, and made a split-second decision. He pushed his qualms to the side and sat up straight in the chair.

"Tell you what," Marcel said. "Mr. Farrell's probably tied up this late in the evening. I'll go over and see Hopkins myself, and I'll tell him that he'll get the seven hundred dollars tomorrow morning, and that I'll guarantee him the other three hundred dollars until you can come up with it."

Daniels' face was twisted into something that was nearly a smile but was dangerously close to tears at the same time. He grabbed Marcel's hand in both of his own and squeezed it mightily. "God bless you, Mr. Aristide. You and your boss are fine people. I'll see if I can't start lookin' for the rest of the money tonight."

"Okay," Marcel said, pulling back his hand. "Here's a number where you can reach me during the day." He passed over a plain white card with his name and telephone number on it, and got up from the table. "I'll see you later," he said, and then he turned and walked from the café.

Nate Hopkins owned an old three-story brick building on Frenchman Street about a block in from where it dovetailed into Esplanade Avenue. It took him a little more than a half hour to walk over there, but the air was cool since the sun went down and the evening was young yet. The building had once housed a business of some kind, but since Nate bought it, nothing went on in there that wasn't connected to gambling. Horses, dog races, numbers, prize fights—any game that would turn a buck, Nate Hopkins had his finger in it.

Marcel knew from another of Farrell's employees that most of the action went on in the upper floor of the building, so instead of bothering with the front door, he entered the right-side alley and climbed a tall steel staircase that ran up one side of the building. At the top, he knocked on a steel-reinforced door three times. It opened and a burly Negro about his own age and height stood there. He was dressed in a snow-white dress shirt a bit tight at the collar, a yellow tie with a red sailboat painted on it, and an underarm holster with a big .38 police Colt.

"We ain't buyin', so get lost," the man said. His round head had a ridiculous tuft of kinky black hair on top, but his eyes were suspicious and hostile.

"I ain't sellin' anything, brutha," Marcel said. "I just want to talk to Mr. Hopkins for a minute."

The Negro's mouth opened and a short bark of a laugh came out. "What makes you think Mr. Hopkins is interested in talkin' to a worthless pissant like you?"

Marcel had not uttered a harsh word, nor even raised a

fist at anyone since he went to work for his cousin, but this insult was too much. Without thinking, Marcel kicked out with his right foot and caught the other man in the shin. As the man yowled a curse and involuntarily bent forward, Marcel jerked the big Colt from the holster and shoved the muzzle into the other man's belly.

"I hate arguin' and fightin' and cursin'," Marcel said, his voice sounding calmer than he felt, "but I asked nice to speak to your boss. Do I get to do it easy, or do I shove you in ahead of your gun so your boss can see what kind of a monkey he's got guardin' his door? It's all one to me, brutha."

The other man looked chagrined, tried to look mad, then laughed out loud in a delighted way. "Okay, man," he said. "Look, I come on too strong. I'm like that some times. But you caught me fair and square. Toss me the rattle and I'll ask the boss to talk to you." He squinted at Marcel for a minute, grinning. "You got some good moves, man, you know that?"

Marcel grinned in spite of himself, twirled the revolver on his finger like Gene Autry, then offered it back to the man butt first. He caught the gun and shoved it back into his holster.

"Who do I say is askin'?" he asked.

"He won't know my name, prob'ly. Tell him I'm from Wesley Farrell."

The other man's eyes got big and recognition flared in them. "Why didn't you say you was from Farrell?" He let Marcel come into the hall, then left. He was gone about a minute and gestured for Marcel to follow him.

Marcel let the other man lead him through a dimly-lit hallway into a large room where about six men sat around a large table playing pinochle. An older man, perhaps fifty years old with skin the color of parchment and a scowl that looked perpetual, glanced over at them, laid down his cards, then got up and walked over to Marcel.

"What's Farrell want with me, boy?" he asked in a gruff voice.

"A favor," Marcel replied.

"I'm listenin'," Hopkins said, tugging at the brim of the dark hat that was already low on his forehead.

"You're holding paper on a jamoke named Ralph Daniels for about a grand," Marcel began. "His brother says he can come up with seven hundred dollars by tomorrow noon. I'm here to say I'll stand good the extra three Cees. You leave his brother Chet's dry cleaning business alone, okay?"

Hopkins looked Marcel up and down for a moment. "What does Farrell care about a wastrel like Ralph Daniels for?"

"His older brother did Mr. Farrell a favor once," Marcel lied smoothly. "He's just doin' one back."

"Shit," Hopkins said. "I don't want to take the brutha's dry cleanin' business no how. Do I look like a dry cleaner to you, boy?"

Marcel laughed. "No sir, you don't. Does Chet get the time to pay you off?"

"Hell, I reckon so," Hopkins said. "I'll do you a favor, too. I won't make you responsible for the rest. But you watch that Ralphie. He's a no-good punk, and he'll be into somebody else within a week. He won't be breathin' air this time next year, you wait and see."

Marcel nodded. "You're a gentleman, Mr. Hopkins. Mr. Farrell and I won't forget you."

Hopkins took Marcel's outstretched hand, shook it twice, then dropped it and went back to his pinochle game. The husky young Negro with the gun jerked his chin at Marcel and led him back out to the stair landing. They paused at the door.

"You're awright, li'l brutha," he said, offering his hand. "The name's Fred Gonzalvo. Let me know if you ever need a favor, hear?"

"I hear you," Marcel said, taking the hand.

Gonzalvo went back inside and closed the door. Marcel walked lightly down the stairs, breathing a sigh of relief. He hadn't run a bluff like that before, and felt a certain childish elation that he'd pulled it off. He almost wished he could tell his cousin.

NOT FAR AWAY, Ralph Daniels lay on a cast-iron bed, his hands behind his head, and an old single-action Colt six-shooter chambered for .38-40 Winchester lay on the bed beside him, his only company. He took a cheap Ingraham watch from his pocket and looked at it. It was nearing midnight—the deadline for paying off Nate Hopkins.

Ralph had exactly seventeen dollars and change in his pockets. About enough to get as far as Jackson, Mississippi, but not much left to live on when he got there. He'd considered selling the gun, but even that wouldn't get him that much farther away, or make much of a dent in what he owed Hopkins.

He cursed his luck as he lay there. Why in the hell didn't he quit while he was ahead? Why'd he ask Hopkins' man to take his marker as he bet on them damn worthless ponies? On an irresistible impulse, Ralph balled up his fist and hit himself in the face. His eyes teared from the pain, but it didn't make him feel any better.

Worse yet, he'd had to crawl to his brother Chet for help. He hated going to the sanctimonious sonofabitch, but it was that or nothing. How Chet had railed about his childishness, his inability to hold on to a decent job, his frivolous character. He'd wanted to smack the bastard, but he couldn't. He was too scared of Hopkins and what his men would do to him. As much as he hated to admit it, Chet was his only hope.

He got up and walked to the basin, ran cold water, and splashed it on his face. He looked up into the mirror and saw a hard, handsome face with high cheekbones, a bold nose, and slick black hair combed straight back from a high forehead. He looked a great deal like an American Indian and occasionally fantasized about going to Oklahoma or New Mexico and passing himself off as a Cherokee or Choctaw.

The trouble with that idea was that he'd still be a nobody. Indians were niggers in places where there weren't any real niggers to kick around. Ralph had always believed that with the right break, he could be somebody—somebody important. But the right break had never come.

Chet had it all. He had a pretty little yellow wife, two boys, money in the bank, and a successful business. Looking like a nigger had never hurt Chet. Ralph looked back on his childhood, and his tall, confident father, who'd been a mixture of Negro and Tangipahoa Indian. He'd married Chet's mother, who'd died in childbirth, then had convinced Ralph's mother, an ignorant Italian immigrant girl, that he was, in fact, a full-blooded Indian, and that Chet's mother had been a deceitful woman who'd passed herself off to him as white. Ralph shook his head. I come by it honest, he thought. The old man could spin a lie like a cowpoke with a lariat.

None of that mattered now. In a little while Nate Hopkins' men would be here to beat him, and he'd have to decide whether to take it, or kill them and run. The choices were so stark that chills ran up and down his spine and he shivered uncontrollably for a moment.

He was still staring at himself in the mirror when a knock at the door sent him diving for the bed. "W-who is it?" he quavered. He had the old revolver in his hand now, and he cocked it.

"It's me, Chet. Let me in."

"Y-y-you a-alone?" Ralph asked, still frightened and wary.

"Yes, you damn fool," Chet said in an impatient voice.

Still uncertain, Ralph crept to the door, stood well to one side, and flung the door open. As he looked over the barrel of his gun, all he could see was Chet standing there in that outdated straw boater. His long face was haggard.

"Put that gun down before you hurt yourself," Chet said as he walked in. "You won't need it. I got you off the hook."

Ralph was stunned. "But how? You said you didn't have all the money."

"I went and talked to a Mr. Aristide who works for Wesley Farrell," Chet explained. "He went to see Hopkins and got him to accept the seven hundred dollars I had in the bank. I'm gonna get it out tomorrow mornin', and then you're gonna take it over to Hopkins and get clear of him."

Now that it was over, Ralph began to shake. He'd been so keyed up that now he could hardly stand up straight. He put the revolver carefully on the bureau, then sank down on the bed. A muffled sob escaped his throat, and he put his head in his hands until he could get control of himself again.

"When you get through with Hopkins," Chet continued, "you're gonna clear out of this boarding house and move your stuff over to my house. We got an extry room there, and you can eat with us. I'll start you at the laundry at fifty cents a day, and you can keep twenty-five cents of it. The rest'll go toward payin' back the boys' college fund."

"What?" Ralph said, shocked out of his funk. "I don't know nothin' 'bout workin' in no laundry."

"You can learn," Chet said, his eyes hard and his mouth stretched tight. "You been skatin' by all your life, and it's time you started acting like a man and showing some responsibility. You work hard, and one day you can be my partner in the business, but for now you gotta pay off what you owe and get some decent work habits, you understand?"

Ralph looked at his brother with a stunned look on his face. He'd escaped the wrath of Nate Hopkins only to discover his brother owned him like some field hand. He wanted to rage and curse and swear that he wouldn't do it, but Chet had him by the short hairs. He had to get Hopkins paid off before he said or did anything else.

"Sure, sure, Chet," he said dully. "I understand."

"Good. I'll tell your landlady you're movin' out tomorrow. You come straight by my place at seven, we'll have breakfast, then go down to the bank. You can pay off

Hopkins while I get the store opened up, and then you can come down and join me. I'll show you the ropes, get you started." Chet straightened his shoulder muscles, to lessen the tension in them, and rubbed the back of his neck while he watched his brother. He'd felt sorry for him all his life, but right now he detested him. "I'll see you in the morning, Ralphie."

Ralph said nothing as his brother left, and remained there on the bed staring off into space. He should be feeling better now that Hopkins was off his back, but instead he felt dejected and forlorn. He'd been in the back of Chet's laundry and dry cleaning shop on a number of occasions, and the smell of steam and starch had sickened him. He didn't know how anybody could stand to live inside that smell every day, six days a week.

He got up, went to the closet, and pulled an old cardboard suitcase down from a shelf and began to pack his few belongings into it. He had three shirts, two pairs of slacks, and a black alpaca suit coat. He'd torn the matching slacks years ago in a bar fight, and had thrown them away. The coat was an unwelcome reminder of a time when he'd had freedom and some money to spend on good times. As he carefully folded the jacket and placed it in the bottom of the suitcase, he began working in his mind how long it would take him to pay back seven hundred dollars at twenty-five cents a day. It came to something more than eleven years. Meanwhile, he'd earn a grand total of twenty-five dollars a month.

He sank back on the bed again, overwhelmed by his situation. He looked across the room at the old Colt on the bureau, and wondered if it didn't make more sense just to end it all right here and now. A giant hand seemed to squeeze his heart in a vice, and he felt nausea roil his gut. No, there had to be another way. There just had to be.

Chapter 3

"WHEN WAS THE last time you saw your husband, Mrs. Bautain?" Sergeant Israel Daggett asked.

Lillian Bautain, a plump, dark woman in an expensive silk dress was slumped in her armchair, holding a crumpled white handkerchief up to her mouth. Her face was screwed into a tearful grimace as her bosom heaved with sobs.

"Late yesterday morning," the woman said, almost choking on the words. "He said he was going straight to the office. He called me late that afternoon and said he was going to meet his banker, Rogers Clifton, at the Sassafrass Lounge that evening, have dinner with him, and then come home. I woke up this morning and the bed in his room hadn't been slept in." She lost control of herself then, and sobbed hysterically for several minutes while Daggett silently turned over what little he already knew.

He'd been called into the case late that afternoon by one of the junior Negro Squad detectives, and after reviewing the known facts, had driven over to the Bautain home on Pelopidas Drive. It was a nice section of town where some of the more affluent of the New Orleans Negro community lived. The Bautain home was a large, rambling frame structure with Tudor features, and had a two-car garage in the spacious back yard. Mrs. Bautain's Chevrolet sedan was parked there now. Bautain's Lincoln had been found abandoned near the north boundary of City Park by a patrol car earlier that day.

Bautain was the third prominent Negro to fall victim to foul play in the past several months. There had been no developments on the other two cases, and Daggett was getting heat for it. So far, he hadn't been able to find a common denominator in the three cases. He'd already ruled out Ku Klux Klan activity—the Klan couldn't operate with the same impunity in the city as they could out in the countryside. Daggett suspected that the motive lay in some kind of business the men were conducting, but what that was, he did not yet know.

The woman took a deep, ragged breath, then let it out again. Daggett turned to her and saw that she was exhausted. Her skin had an unhealthy, gray pallor, and he immediately felt terrible for having to question her. But that's what I'm paid to do, he thought. Her man is probably dead, and I got to find him, and whoever did it.

"Listen, ma'am," Daggett said in a soft voice. "I hate to bother you at a time like this, but it might help us find him if we knew some things. Has Mr. Bautain spoken of any trouble with anyone recently?"

"Oh, I don't know," she said. "He didn't talk much about his business. He thought women were too stupid to understand serious things. As if I didn't go to the same college he did." Her voice held a trace of reproach, which she seemed to hear, because she caught herself and softened her tone. The question seemed to provoke something in her, though, because her face took on a thoughtful look."

"I did hear him grumbling about somebody who wanted to buy a piece of property he owned over Gentilly way," she said.

"Yes?" Daggett said.

"Yes, some undeveloped property near Eastern and Dwyer," she replied.

"Why was he grumbling?" Daggett asked her.

"Oh, he said they wanted him to give it away, and he

was annoyed that Mr. Clifton had bothered him with it." She paused and dabbed at the corner of her right eye with her handkerchief. "My husband was terribly close with a dollar, Sergeant. He didn't believe in doing business without making a profit."

"Mr. Clifton, you said?" Daggett said. "Would that be Rogers Clifton, the president of the Merchants and Farmers Homestead Bank?"

"Yes," Mrs. Bautain replied. "Ulysses said Mr. Clifton had referred the prospective buyers to him, and that Mr. Clifton had suggested a price that he thought they'd accept. Mr. Clifton doesn't know Ulysses very well, I'm afraid. Ulysses apparently knew the property might be worth more in the near future, because he wouldn't sell it."

"You have any idea who these prospective buyers might be?" Daggett asked, jotting notes in his pocket notebook.

"No," she said, shaking he head. "Like I say, he seldom discussed business with me." She paused, then said, "His secretary will know. She scheduled all his appointments."

"That'd be Shirley Macomb," Daggett said.

"Yes," she said. Daggett noted a small quirk in the corner of Mrs. Bautain's mouth, and remembered her saying earlier that the bed in her husband's room hadn't been slept in. That was a red flag right there.

"Do you suppose she might be at home this evening?" Daggett asked.

"Hummmmph," Mrs. Bautain snorted. "I'm sure I wouldn't know."

Daggett nodded slightly, raising one of his eyebrows. "Well, we'll check on that ourselves. Thank you, ma'am. We'll do everything we can to find your husband. And please let me know if you think of anything that might be of use to me." He took out a white card from his pocket and handed it to the woman, who looked at it once, then placed it on the table at her elbow.

Daggett went out of the room and past the maid, who held the door as he exited the house. His police cruiser sat just outside in the drive. Detective Andrews, a burly, mustachioed brown man with a cynical look in his eyes, waited at the wheel.

"You got a line on Shirley Macomb?" Daggett asked when he got into the car.

Andrews's heavy black mustache raised over a leering mouth. "I'd *like* to have a line on her," the detective said. "That gal's strictly high-octane."

"You already talked to her?"

"Nope, but I talked to some of the other tenants in Bautain's building, and the description they gave was of a woman who set the carpet on fire every time she walked into a room."

"Uh-oh," Daggett said. "The wife thinks something's goin' on between her and the boss-man. You find her at home?"

Andrews laughed nastily. "She didn't answer her phone, and the people at the building said she didn't come into the office today. You thinkin' what I'm thinkin'?"

Daggett shook his head. "Not yet. We'll drive over to her place and see if we can get inside the apartment. I don't want to make any assumptions until we've checked every angle. Let's go over there now and see what we can find out."

Andrews grunted. "Five'll get you eight she's wherever her boss is."

Daggett said nothing, but his face wore a thoughtful frown as they headed out Pelopidas Street. It took them about twenty minutes to make it to Shirley Macomb's apartment building on Abundance Street, off Elysian Fields. As they drove up to the building, Andrews let out a long whistle.

"Pretty damn nice for a secretary," he commented.

Daggett nodded. It was a three-story brick apartment building with a lot of rounded corners and concrete embellishments around the doors and windows. Each of the six French windows facing the street had a little wrought-iron balcony large enough to two people to sit on and take afternoon tea. Daggett bet himself these apartments cost more than a cop's monthly salary.

The two Negro detectives got out and walked to the entrance, where they scanned the mailboxes. There was a small brass marker stating that the building superintendent's office could be found at the rear of the building.

The pair followed a brick walk around the side, down a narrow but meticulously-kept alley until they found a door set flush with the building wall. There was a doorbell button, which Andrews pressed. After a few minutes, an elderly Negro wearing a white shirt and blue trousers came to the door. His hairline had receded all the way to the back of his skull, leaving behind a shiny brown dome surrounded by a cottony fringe of hair.

"Can I help you gentlemen?" the old man asked.

"You the building super?" Daggett asked.

"Thomas Morehouse," the old man said, nodding.

"I'm Detective Sergeant Daggett and this is Detective Andrews," Daggett said, holding out his badge. "Are you acquainted with Miss Shirley Macomb?"

"Certainly," the old man said gravely. "I've been here eight years, and she's lived here for the past two. Is something wrong?"

"We're hoping you can tell us," Daggett said. "Her boss has disappeared, and she didn't come in to work today. We've tried to reach her by phone, but no luck. I wondered if you'd come upstairs and open the door long enough for us to see if she's there and can't open the door for some reason."

Morehouse frowned and his eyes blinked a few times, then came out, closed his door behind him, and said, "Come with me."

They followed him to the front where he bypassed the electric lock with a key, and allowed them to go in ahead of him. He led them up all three flights of stairs until they reached the top level. Shirley Macomb's place was the one on the left. Using his key, Morehouse unlocked the door, opened it a crack, then said very distinctly, "Miss Macomb? It's Thomas Morehouse, the super. Are you there, Miss Macomb? Miss Macomb?" He raised his voice on the last try, but no answering voice could be heard.

Giving him a look, Daggett drew his .41 Colt off his hip and pushed the door wide. He went through it, Andrews in his wake with his own gun out. They called Shirley Macomb's name, but the apartment was silent.

Daggett walked into the bedroom and stopped there, surveying everything in front of him. The room was lavishly furnished with a tester bed and canopy and a matching dresser, dressing table, and night stand made of cherry. The bed had been slept in, but not made up. A silk bed gown lay carelessly across the foot of the bed. Everything else in the room was exactly as it should've been.

"Looks like she took off," Andrews said. "Maybe with the boss."

Daggett shook his head. "Nuh-uh, brutha. Not without her purse—not without some clothes. Look at the closet—nothing out of place, no empty hangars." He strode to it, picking up a purse from the dressing table and checking inside. He turned and looked up on the shelves in the closet. "Her suitcases are still here, her wallet, money, keys—everything here. Ain't never been a woman in the world who'd be in such a hurry that she'd leave all this behind."

"So she didn't leave by herself, and not by her own choice," Andrews said, stowing his gun back on his hip. He turned to the building manager, who stood there looking frightened and confused. "You see anybody here last night—anybody who didn't belong around here?"

"Well, no, I don't think so," the old man said, scratching his white fringe with his left hand.

"Think," Daggett said. "It wasn't necessarily someone coming to the building. Maybe somebody walking down the street, or passing in a car that seemed out of place."

The old man gnawed his lower lip, his eyes blinking as he tried to take in the enormity of the situation, then, suddenly, his eyes began to brighten and he snapped his fingers. "There was a man who passed by while I was gettin' the garbage cans put away yesterday evening."

Daggett turned on him. "What did he say?"

"Not much, really," the old man said. "He was just walking down the street, and he stopped to admire the building.

"He ask you about any of the tenants?" Andrews asked.

"Now I think about it, he asked me if somebody named Maxfield Parrish lived here," Morehouse said.

"And what did you tell him?" Daggett asked. His eyes held an intense gleam. He already knew the name was a phony—Maxfield Parrish was a painter who'd made it big back in the 1920s doing ads for Edison light bulbs and Jell-O desserts.

"Well, I told him no, of course," Morehouse said. "Told him that there was a couple of old ladies on the ground floor, a professional man and his wife and a dentist on the second floor, and a secretary on the top floor, and that none of them was named Parrish."

"Shirley Macomb was alone on the this floor?" Daggett asked.

"The other apartment's been vacant for a while," the superintendent replied. "He asked about the place, so I described it to him, asked if he'd like to see it, but he said it didn't sound big enough for him."

"What did he look like?" Daggett asked.

"Well, he was a young fella—not more than thirty or thirty two, well-built, but not as heavy as this man," he said, pointing at Andrews. "Tall, like you," he said, nodding at Daggett. "Dressed real nice. A pleasant-looking man—seemed to smile easy."

"So we got a guy about six feet, maybe one-sixty, 'pleasant looking,'" Andrews said, jotting it down in his notebook. "That oughta narrow it down a bit." He cut his eyes at Daggett, but Daggett ignored him.

"Was he afoot, or did he drive?" Daggett asked.

"Well, he was afoot the first time I saw him, but later I could've sworn I saw him drive by in a brand-new Dodge sedan—black four-door, it was."

"I guess you didn't catch the license number?" Andrews said.

"Well, only that it was a Louisiana plate—had the pelican on it," Morehouse replied.

"Did you see Miss Macomb at any time yesterday?" Andrews asked.

"Spoke to her when she came in about six thirty," the old man answered. "Just to say hello—nothing more."

"Thanks, Mr. Morehouse," Daggett said, handing him a card. "If you think of anything else, call me at that number, will you?"

"Sure will," the old man said. "You don't think anything's happened to the girl, do you?"

"We hope not," Daggett said, then he jerked his chin at Andrews and they walked away.

"What do you think, boss?" Andrews said when they were back inside the car.

"I think somebody wants us to think a middle-aged man ran away with his young secretary, but they were sloppy about it. No woman's gonna run off and leave a closet of expensive clothes nor a purse with her entire life in it. Get the lab boys to get in there as soon as they can to see what they can find. There's probably nothing there, but we might get lucky and find some prints."

"I hear you," Andrews said as he started the car.

WESLEY FARRELL strolled into the teeming midst of Rampart Street. The sidewalks were full of people seeking oblivion of one kind or another as they immersed themselves in the music, liquor, and drugs that were as much as a part of the night life as the miles of neon tubing that lit the famous street in garish tones of red, yellow, and green.

Located in the middle of the district was a particular tavern which had no name. The only clue to its whereabouts was a gaudy neon sign that depicted a red crawfish in a green top hat standing alongside a martini glass with two green olives in it. The regulars liked to call the place the "Happy Crawdad." Farrell stood under the sign long enough to drop his cigarette butt on the sidewalk and crush it with a quick twist of his toe.

Inside he found the place to be a bit more than half full. The dance floor was busy with Negro couples dancing to the sound of Hamp pounding out "Vibraphone Stomp" with Goodman and Teddy Wilson backing him. There were a few curious glances at the tall, well-dressed man with pale gold skin, but people of every stripe came to the Happy Crawdad, so most ignored him as they went about the business of their own pleasure.

Farrell spotted a Negro in the corner, playing a game of chess with himself. He was a big man, larger than average. His head was handsome and well-shaped, but it seemed a bit too small for the body that wore it. For that reason he was known far and wide as "Little-Head" Lucas.

"You beat it yet, Little-Head?" Farrell asked as he drew near.

Lucas didn't look up, fingering his chin with one hand and the head of a rook with the other. "It ain't about beatin' or losin'," Lucas explained patiently. "It's just a way of keepin' your mind sharp." He looked up finally and said, "What brings you down to this part of town, Mr. Farrell? No music at your place tonight?"

"There's always music there," Farrell said. "But I'm looking for other things tonight."

Little-Head Lucas considered Farrell's words, and let his fingers stray to the black knight, which he twiddled back and forth. "Something in particular?"

Farrell sat down and took out his Camels. He offered one to the big Negro, then took one himself. Lucas placed his between his lips, then leaned forward to accept Farrell's light. After he'd breathed in a lung full of smoke,

Farrell began to talk.

"What do you know about Archie Badeaux?" Farrell asked.

Little-Head Lucas put the black knight back on its square. "A mean mutha-fucka," he opined. "Come to town back in '29 or '30, worked for Straight-Flush Henry Alford for a while."

"Until Alford's guts got hung up on that whore's knife, you mean," Farrell said.

"Uh-huh," Little-Head replied. "He went free-lance after that, hurtin' people, sometimes killin' 'em, if somebody wanted it done bad enough and wanted to pay enough. He's bein' kinda exclusive lately, I hear."

Farrell's eyes glittered for a second. "Working for one man?"

"Uh-huh," Little-Head answered. "New player on the scene. Man from up Jackson way."

"How new?" Farrell asked.

"A year maybe—maybe a li'l more."

"Why haven't I heard about him?" Farrell asked.

"Playin' it cool," the big man said. "He got backshot up in Jackson, they say. Double-cross of some kind. They thought he was dead, 'til he turned up here, in a wheelchair. Not long after, he hired Badeaux to do his dirty work. Remember Four-Ace Johnny Clampett?"

"Gambler—got a little too big for his britches, I heard," Farrell said.

"He had control of some territory this Jackson man wanted," Little-Head said. "He wouldn't move, so Badeaux moved him—with a .45."

"How do you know this?" Farrell asked. "The cops don't seem to know who did it."

Little-Head Lucas's mouth smiled slightly. "A woman—Gladiola Haygood is her name. She's Badeaux's woman—and my second cousin. She's scared blind of him, but can't seem to get away. I told her I'd help her, but she's too scared to move."

"She see the killing?" Farrell asked.

Little-Head shook his head negatively. "Badeaux talks in his sleep. Woke her up ravin' one night, laid the whole thing out."

"The cops'd like to know that," Farrell said.

"They'll never get it from her," the big man said.

"This Jackson man—he got a name?"

"Lincoln. Jonathan Lincoln. Had a big rep back in the teens and twenties," Little-Head said. "Fast man with a gun, fast with cards, women, too. Went by the handle 'Greenback' when he was young. Built an organization in Jackson, stayed on top for a long time—till somebody shoved him off."

"Competition?"

"They said a woman did it—one of his own people," Little-Head replied. "She dropped off the face of the earth after it happened. She might be dead now, since she didn't finish the job on Lincoln."

Farrell nodded, tugging thoughtfully on his earlobe. "What else have Lincoln and Badeaux taken over here?"

Little-Head shrugged. "This and that—whores, numbers, some narcotics—the usual stuff."

"I heard something about Badeaux earlier today," Farrell said. "He's trying to push the owner of The Original Southport Club out of business—wants to take it over himself."

Little-Head cocked an eyebrow. "You're jivin'."

Farrell shook his head. "That's what I heard. You know anything about Carol Donovan, the club owner?"

"A very slick chick," the big Negro replied. "Pulled the Southport Club out from under that ofay who owned it like a magician snatchin' a tablecloth from under a pitcher of milk."

"He was a drunk and a lousy businessman," Farrell said. "He'd have lost it to the bank before long anyway."

"Uh-huh," Little-Head said. "But she's still good. I don't reckon a woman who'd do something as slick as that'd be no marshmallow. 'Course, Badeaux could make a marshmallow out of a slab of granite if he wanted to. I just can't figure what he or Lincoln'd want with a nightclub. Those boys are after real money—nightclubs don't make that kinda jack."

Farrell nodded, his eyes inspecting the pieces on Little-Head's board.

"Heard somethin' tonight," Little-Head said.

"What?" Farrell asked.

"Heard a big-shot colored man vanished off the face of the earth last night," the big man said.

"Who?"

"Know Ulysses Bautain?"

"Businessman of some kind," Farrell said.

"Real estate, mostly commercial property," Little-Head said. "He's the third prominent Negro to fall outta the picture since April."

"Who were the others?" Farrell said.

"Malcolm Redding, the president of the Merchants and Farmers Homestead, in April. Ezra Johnson, the owner of the Johnson Brothers Department Store, in May. Now Bautain in June," Little-Head said. "Mighty peculiar. They must'a all had something somebody else wanted real bad."

Farrell looked at the Negro sharply, and crushed out his cigarette in the metal ashtray on the side of the chess table. "Ever think of becoming a detective, Little-Head? You seem to have an instinct for it."

"Never," Little-Head replied. "Too much standin' around waitin' for stuff to happen, then too much runnin', screamin', and sometimes shootin'. I need time for my chess, and I wouldn't get it thataway, Mr. Farrell. Tell you what, though."

"What?"

"If Badeaux and Lincoln want that lady's nightclub, she oughta just give it to 'em and leave town. Ain't no woman can stand up to them, and mighty few men. Three of us has already disappeared, and for damn sure they had something somebody wanted. If it'd been the Klan, they'd been found hangin' from a tree somewhere, burnt. I'm bettin' they was killed by one of their own."

"You think Lincoln and Badeaux are behind it?" Farrell asked.

"I don't know, Mr. Farrell. There's bad colored men just like there's bad white. It could've been anybody."

Farrell stood up, and settled his hat down over his forehead. "Thanks for the talk. You keep it low, you hear?"

"Always, Mr. Farrell, always," the Negro said.

Farrell turned and left the juke joint. Rampart Street was as crowded and noisy as ever as Farrell hit the street. Horns were honking and friends were yelling across the street at each other. A tack-sharp mulatto girl in a low-cut violet dress and a wide-brimmed hat with a peacock feather in the band walked by him and smiled. He smiled back and touched the brim of his Borsalino as he continued past her.

His talk with Little-Head Lucas had been informative, but he wasn't certain what the information meant. If a Negro gangster was making a move within the Negro community itself, what was he trying to pull together? A banker, a real estate magnate, a department store owner, and a lady nightclub owner didn't seem to have anything in common with each other except for their color and the fact that they had more money than most of their race. There was nothing to say that Carol Donovan's troubles had anything to do with what had happened to the others, although Little-Head had drawn the connection between her, Badeaux, and the disappearance of the three men without Farrell's prompting. There wasn't much that got past Little-Head Lucas, and if he saw something in all that, maybe there was a connection.

What he had to deal with in his own mind was that none of this was any of his business. He'd done his best for years to avoid entanglements with others, not only because it was healthy to keep out of harm's way, but also because he was a man of mixed race. In Louisiana, any amount of Negro blood made you, by law, a Negro. That meant there were places you couldn't go, things you couldn't do, and some business you couldn't easily conduct. It was a bad position for a man who ran a nightclub catering to white people to be in.

For some reason he thought of his young cousin, Marcel Aristide. He'd never been a parent, but he'd taken the younger man under his care to get him away from the influence of a spiteful old aunt. Even though Marcel had been with bad people, he wasn't a bad kid himself. He was naïve in many ways, which made things a little tough. Farrell's life was the kind that demanded savvy and street sense, and Marcel wasn't showing much of that so far. He'd fouled up a few errands Farrell had sent him on, allowed himself to be tripped up by things that a more insightful man would've seen coming a mile away. Farrell shook his head. Maybe he should send the boy to college and find him some kind of honest profession. Living on the street by the rules of the street wasn't for everybody.

He looked up and down Rampart Street, feeling a strange electricity flowing through him. He'd spent a lot of his life on these streets, making up his own rules and taking the knocks when they came. Running the nightclub, living a manufactured life had softened him, he realized. In some respects, he wasn't doing much better than his twenty-year-old cousin. There'd been a time when he could walk into a room and people would freeze, waiting to see what Wesley Farrell would do, to find out why he was there. He realized as he stood in the spiritual heart of New Orleans that he missed the edge of those times.

He thought of another person who might tell him things tonight. He turned and headed in that direction.

Chapter 4

IT WAS PAST noon before LeDoux made it down to the neighborhood where Ben Attaway's speakeasy had been. When he got there, the building he remembered was boarded up and deserted. From the dilapidated condition, it was apparent no one had used it for a number of years. He walked across the street to a corner grocery that he remembered from the old days and went inside. He found a Negro of about his own age in a blood-stained white coat carving pork chops from a rack of ribs.

"Hey, man," LeDoux said by way of greeting. "Tell me somethin', will ya?"

"If I know it," the butcher said.

"Old Ben Attaway—that was his speak 'crost the street, weren't it?"

The butcher nodded. "Used to pass some time, and spend some money there, back in the old days. Went there after Prohibition, too. The whiskey was heaps better by then." He grinned. "Closed up now, though, for a few years."

"How many?" LeDoux asked.

The butcher put down his knife and scratched his head for a moment. "Reckon it must be about three at least. Was after Prohibition was lifted. Don't know why it closed. Maybe old Ben got too old to run it anymore. Ain't seen him since." He shook his head and smiled fondly. "Sure did have some pretty gals in there. There was this one who had a li'l mole right on—"

"Look, you don't know where old Ben might be now, do you?" Ernie interrupted.

The butcher shook his head. "Nope. Never knew the old guy that well. Don't reckon I can help you on that one, podnuh." He picked up his knife and resumed cutting pork chops.

LeDoux walked out into the waning sunshine, frowning. He went down the street for several blocks, button-holing everyone he saw. But no one had any information about Ben Attaway. Many didn't even remember him.

With a little effort he managed to recall where Attaway and his wife had lived, and hailed a Harker Brothers cab, one of two Negro-owned cab companies in the city. The cabbie took him over to Urquart Street in the Bywater section of the city, and after a little looking, he recognized the house. He knocked on the door and a girl of about sixteen answered.

LeDoux took off his derby and held it down in front of his stomach. "'Scuse me, miss. I hate to trouble you, but I'm lookin' for Ben or Marcella Attaway. They used to live here."

"Not no time lately," the girl said, her eyes busy on LeDoux's face and his out-dated clothing. "My mama and daddy bought this house through the Merchants and Farmers Homestead."

"How long ago?" LeDoux asked.

"Three years ago," the girl said. She was prevented from saying more by the appearance of a tall, stout woman in a faded print dress and a formidable look in her eye.

"Who're you, and what you doin' with my li'l girl?" she demanded.

"Nothin', ma'am," LeDoux replied. "I'm lookin' for the Attaways, who used to live here, but I reckon they don't no more."

"I should say they don't," the woman said. "We bought this house through the Homestead, all legal an' everything."

"You don't happen to know what happened to the Attaways, do you?" he asked in his politest voice. He could tell the woman was about to tell him to go to hell.

"Didn't know 'em," she said shortly. "Now you go on and quit takin' up all my time. Go on, now."

"Yes'm," LeDoux said, backing off. All he needed was for her to call the cops and he'd be on his way back to Angola.

He saw an old man and woman sitting on a porch directly across the street from the Attaway house. The old man was reading the newspaper and the woman was shelling peas. He walked off the porch and across the street to them.

"Good evenin'," he said politely.

"Evenin'," the old man said. "What can we do for you, young fella?"

"My name's LeDoux," he began. "I used to be friends of Mr. and Mrs. Attaway. I been away for a while, and can't find them."

"Well, you'll have to visit the cemetery for old Ben," the man said. "Died in the night about January or February of 1935. Heard old Marcella screamin' over there and run over with my shotgun. Thought somebody was killin' her, didn't I, ma?"

"Gospel," the old woman said. "Poor old Ben just died sittin' at the dinner table."

"I'm awful sorry to hear that," LeDoux said. "Me and old Ben was close."

"Sorry, young fella," the old man said. "Hate to give anybody bad news about a loved one."

"You wouldn't happen to know where Marcella is, would you?" LeDoux asked.

"Can't help you there," the old woman said, still concentrating on her peas. "Wasn't too long after that she put the house up for sale and left outta here. Ain't seen or heard from her since. If she's in the city, she's keepin' real still. Looked for her in the telephone directory for a few years, but never found no listin'."

Ernie sank down on the edge of the porch, rubbing his forehead. His feet felt unsteady, and his vision clouded for a few seconds.

"You all right?" the old woman asked. "Let me get you a glass of cold water. Maybe it'll make you feel better."

"No, ma'am," LeDoux said. "I was kinda shocked is all. I 'preciate y'all bein' so kind. Reckon I'll just be on my way."

"Good luck," the old man said. "Hope things begin to look up for you."

LeDoux walked back toward his waiting cab, his mind racing. He was running out of ideas. Midway across the street, it came to him where he might go. He leaned into the cab and spoke to the driver.

"You know Avery's honky tonk, over in Jefferson?"

The driver grunted. "Like my old lady's kisser."

"I wanna go over there," LeDoux said.

"Man, you're talkin' half the night to go over there," the driver said. "That's twenty bucks for goin' and comin'."

"Deal," LeDoux said. He got into the cab and the driver headed out of Bywater.

FARRELL HADN'T taken a gun with him, but he never went anywhere without the spring-blade stiletto and the Solingen steel straight razor in his clothes. He'd learned to use them early in his career, and they were like a part of his wardrobe.

As he walked farther down Rampart Street, the night grew darker, and the dives became less reputable, and even the neon signs grew fewer and farther between. His ears began to listen for the sounds of threat ahead and behind him, and his pale gray eyes inspected the shadows for stealthy movement. He felt strangely at home in this borderland between the respectable and the criminal.

The place he wanted couldn't rightly be called a juke

joint, nor an illegal gambling den or a bordello, but a man could find whatever he wanted there most nights. It had no name, no sign—only an open door. He paused at the opening, listening and waiting, then slipped inside.

His eyes, accustomed to the near darkness of the street, adjusted almost immediately to the dim light of the building's interior. Eyes from every table and each space at the bar took him in, measuring him, deciding whether he was an easy mark or someone to let alone. A mulatto woman of indeterminate years appeared at his elbow, slipping her arm through his so the side of her breast would rub against his arm.

"Hey, baby," she said in a husky voice. "You wanna fall in love for a half-hour or so?"

He looked down at her, and the flickering lights of the bar made a ripple across his pale eyes, and she drew away from him like he was a leper. He walked to the bar, his hands swinging easily at his sides. He dropped a silver dollar on the bar and it rang loudly as it spun down to a flat standstill. The bartender, a burly Negro of fifty or so, moved slowly to him, watching him closely.

"Whiskey or beer?" the bartender asked. "It's all we got, take it or leave it."

"Give me Molly Tatum instead," he said.

"Never heard of her," the bartender said, turning quickly to go.

Farrell's hand shot across the bar and caught him by the wrist. His fingers encircled the thickly-muscled wrist like a steel band, and the man let loose an involuntary gasp. "Tell her Wesley Farrell wants a few minutes with her. Don't make me ask you again."

He released the wrist and the barkeep staggered back, clutching the sore spot with his other hand. He looked at Farrell with a mixture of awe and surprise, and moved from behind the bar and into a back room. He returned in seconds and jerked his head toward the place from which he'd emerged. He said nothing, letting his eyes do all his talking for him.

Farrell moved away from the bar and threaded his way between tables where men and women watched him silently. A few drew away as he passed. Some knew him by sight; others saw the way he moved and the way his eyes roved over them, like the sights on a gun, and looked away quickly.

He reached the open door without incident, paused at the opening, then passed through. The back room was sparsely furnished, but a love seat sat against one wall, and on it a voluptuous blonde negress lounged with a tiny glass of sherry in her hand. Her hands were broad and large-knuckled, and her features were bold and handsome.

"Wesley Farrell," the woman said in a husky voice. "I haven't seen you in many a day. What brings you to see little me?"

Farrell saw a wooden chair in front of a desk and he caught the bottom rungs with his foot, jerked it toward him, and then straddled it, looking at Molly Tatum from over the back. "As much money as you've got, I don't understand why you stay in this pest hole. You could have a place as fine as the Sassafrass Lounge if you wanted."

"And then maybe one day you'd come in the door and beat me half to death like you did Sassafrass and run me out of town," Molly Tatum said. "No, I like it here. You'd have a tougher time messin' me over in here."

"Sass messed with *my* friends," Farrell said. "That was personal—not business."

"Oh, piffle," Molly said, sipping from her glass. "He's gone and I'm still here. I like things my own way, thank you. Now, why don't you tell me what you want so I can tell you to go to hell and leave me alone?" She smiled at him sweetly.

He returned her smile, tipping his Borsalino back on his head. "Don't try to get too tough with me, Molly. You got all the suckers fooled with that getup, but you and I both know there's nothing female under that wig and the dress.

And even if there were, if you got in my way, I'd leave foot tracks on you, woman or not."

Molly's smile faded, and her eyes burned hot for a brief second. "I don't like you," the transvestite said distinctly.

"Tell me about Archie Badeaux," Farrell said, changing the subject.

"What about him?" she snapped.

"For starts, where does he hang out?" Farrell said. "For seconds, where's his boss?"

A look of calculation oozed into Molly's eyes, and she plucked at her lower lip with long, carmined nails. "Why do you want him? Are you after him and Lincoln for some reason?"

"What do you think?" Farrell said. "And don't answer my question with another question."

She looked at him for a moment, her eyes flickering as the wheels in her mind spun round and round. Finally she said, "I don't know where Lincoln is. He keeps to himself and deals strictly through go-betweens."

"Such as who?" Farrell asked.

"All's I know is gossip," she said airily.

"Your gossip is better than some of the stuff they print in the *Times-Picayune*," he said with a small smile. "I'll listen to it."

She saw his smile and let her own lips curve seductively. Her eyes shone with what could've been lust or simply calculation. "What I hear is, he and Rogers Clifton have somethin' goin' between them."

"Clifton?" Farrell said. "He's the president of the Merchants and Farmers Homestead. What's he got to do with a gangster like Lincoln?"

She waved a dismissive hand. "Don't ask me. Like I said, it's gossip. But I know something else."

"Such as?"

"Clifton ain't been runnin' the Homestead all that long. He was head teller, and he and Malcolm Redding didn't get along all that well. Redding ended up dead."

"The cops said that was a suicide," Farrell said.

"When's the last time you took the word of a cop for anything, Farrell?" she said with a curl to her lips.

Farrell smiled. "Okay. Now about Badeaux..."

"He's bad," she said. "He's got him a house on Jackson Avenue, Lake side of Claiborne. Nice place, I hear. Rose bushes, trellises—you'd think he was a white man the way he lives now."

"I didn't ask you where he lived," Farrell said. "I asked you where he hung out."

She smiled again, enigmatically this time. "You should be careful of what you ask for, cher. You might not like it when you get it. He's a bad mutha-fucka, and no lie."

Farrell's eyes got flat and hard, and he leaned forward, resting his hands on his knees. "Molly, I could shut you down with a couple of phone calls. Men who owe me favors could be over here in about thirty minutes, reduce this place to kindling, and kick your candy-ass right out into the street."

The transvestite drew herself up, wrapping her long arms around her knees as though she were using them as a bulwark against him, and her face took on a look of petulance and hurt. "You're a brute, you know that? He might be at the Honey Pot. It's a dive down near the Desire Street Wharf. He owns it and everybody in there owes him or is scared enough of him that they'd curse Jesus if he told them to. If I had to guess, though, I'd go lookin' for a sweet shop on Clouet Street, 'bout two blocks off St. Claude, 'cept it ain't a sweet shop—it's a gamblin' parlor and he's got a room in the back where he entertains his lady friends. Go on down there, you mean sonofabitch. I hope he cuts you from your chin to your socks."

Farrell's lips drew back from his teeth, and he parted them in a smile that reminded Molly of an alligator she once saw in the Audubon Park Zoo. She was as big as Farrell, and if pushed she would fight like a demon, but she knew too many stories about Farrell, and the corpses he'd left behind him, to want to take such a risk.

He got up and pulled his hat down low on his forehead, his eyes never leaving her face. "Thanks, Molly. Maybe you'll get your wish. But if I get there and get blindsided because you warned him, you better hope I cash in my chips then and there, 'cause I'll be back to see you if I live, you hear me?"

She shuddered, hugged her knees tighter into her chest, and then blinked a big, fat tear out of each eye. They made muddy-looking rivulets in the rose face powder she had on her cheeks. When she said nothing, Farrell turned on his heel and left the room.

IT WAS NEARING closing at the Cotton Club West when the two tall, dark-brown men walked in. Savanna knew the minute she saw them that they were cops. She'd heard a few customers talk about them, and knew they were trouble.

"You Savanna?" the heavy-set one asked. His partner, of a more slender build, said nothing but looked at Savanna through eyes without a shred of emotion in them.

"That's right," Savanna said with her best smile. "Can I offer you gentlemen something from the bar?"

"Sure, girley," the second cop said. "Old Forester—bonded. None of that eighty-proof crap." He had the tails of his jacket swept back with his hands in his pockets, and Savanna could see the toe of his shoulder holster exposed at his left side.

Savanna snapped her fingers at the bartender and told him to bring double shots of the one-hundred proof bourbon. She could tell from the look in his eyes that the bartender was deathly afraid of the two cops. He had the drinks in front of them in seconds, then went back to the other end of the bar. Jimmy Lunceford's orchestra was just finishing up a set, and the sound of the music was quickly replaced by the buzz of people having fun.

The two cops picked up their glasses, and motioned for

Savanna to follow them to a corner table. She went along behind them, working to keep a look of strength and confidence on her face. She waited until the two men were seated, then sat across the table from them.

"We're here to make you a proposition," the heavy-set one said after he'd downed half his drink.

"You guys are cops, right?" Savanna said.

"Don't get cute," the slender one said. "You know we're cops. I'm Sergeant Manion and this is Lieutenant Stark. We're The Man for the Central Avenue District."

"Okay," Savanna said. "I always try to get along with The Man. I run a clean place and don't allow any dope in here. Anybody cuts up, we show them the door. And there's no back room for gambling here. You can see for yourself if you want."

Stark nodded his head approvingly, and looked at Savanna with dark, hooded eyes. She saw a predatory gleam in them that she didn't like.

"You're sharp as a tack, baby sister," Stark said. "We been hearin' things about you, 'bout what a clean joint you run. But this is a tough town. A place needs all the protection it can get."

"Protection? Against what?" Savanna asked in a bland voice. She'd been shaken down before and already knew where this was leading.

"You know—protection," Manion said nastily. "Against broken furniture, stolen stock, gange and morphine turning up on the premises—stuff like that. Your boss knows—we talked to him about it at the last place he owned. Maybe he thought by openin' up a new place and puttin' somebody from out of town to run it that he'd fool us. He didn't."

"Now, now, Manion," Stark said in an oily voice. "Don't be leanin' on the lady so hard. You can see that she's smart—a team player. She'll see the light."

"What's the pitch?" Savanna asked. She felt cold all over, and fought to keep her hands still in front of her.

"The pitch is two hundred dollars a week, baby sister," Stark said. "For now, anyway. Maybe later, you and me can get better acquainted, and the price won't go up. Get my drift?" His lips parted in an obscene smile.

"I'll get the money for you right now, if you want it," Savanna said, ignoring the innuendo.

Stark waved a diffident hand. "No need, no need. We'll come back tomorrow afternoon and get it. We know you're busy, and we don't wanna get in your hair durin' business hours, do we, Manion?"

"Not much," Manion said. His narrow face had a sly look, and the sharp edges of his teeth were just visible beneath his neatly-trimmed mustache.

The pair got up together. Stark straightened his suit and shot his cuffs. He squared his hat and looked down at Savanna, who hadn't moved.

"You're a real smart cookie, southern gal," Stark said. "You and me are gonna get along fine. We'll see you later now, hear?" He turned and walked across the club with Manion just a half-step behind.

Savanna felt sick at her stomach, and fought to keep from trembling. She'd come to California to escape her troubles, and now discovered herself neck-deep in an entirely new set. And in that terrible moment of discovery, another sickening realization: here, she was all alone.

AS THE DAY drew to a close, Marcel Aristide sat in the back room office of a quiet, productive little bordello that Farrell owned on Soraparu Street, about a block down from the Tchopitoulas Street Wharf. Farrell's original partner in the house, Marie Turnage, had been killed by Emile Ganns' men two years before. After teaching Marcel the ropes, Farrell had put him in charge to see what he could do with it. Marcel seemed to have a good business head because the place was making money.

He was listening to Louis Armstrong's Hot Five on the little radio that sat on his desk as he wrote checks to New

Orleans Public Service and the Sewerage and Water Board. Marcel loved music more than life, and even as he signed the checks and put them in envelopes, his feet were tapping in time to the hot Dixieland that gushed out of the small speaker.

He'd just re-capped his fountain pen when there was a knock at the door. "Yeah," he called.

The door opened and a young mulatto girl named Minette stuck her head around the door. "Mist' Marcel, they's a man out here askin' for you."

"Who is it, Minette?" Marcel asked.

"Said his name was Chester Daniels," she said. "He's awful upset."

Marcel got up, his face falling into a frown as he turned off the radio and pulled the door open. Chet Daniels stood there wringing his hands together, his face frozen with terror. Marcel took him by the arm and drew him into the room. Small grunts of anguish emanated from Daniels' throat as Marcel pushed him down into a chair, poured three fingers of Old Overholt into a water tumbler, then held it to Daniels' quivering lips. The man swallowed the rye whiskey like he was dying of thirst in the desert.

"What's the matter?" Marcel asked in what he hoped was a calm, soothing voice. Daniels' upset was so stark that it nearly had Marcel trembling in sympathy.

"Ralphie," Daniels said.

"What about him?"

"Nate Hopkins' men come to my store. They said Ralphie didn't show up with the money."

"What?" Marcel cried. His calm disintegrated with the disclosure of Ralph Daniels' perfidy.

Chet nodded his head jerkily up and down. "I picked him up this mornin', and we drove straight to the homestead to get the money out. I dropped him off near Hopkins' place and drove over to open my store up. I been waitin' on him to show up at the shop to begin work, but he didn't come and he didn't come. 'Bout noontime, two of Hopkins' men come to the store, wantin' to know where the money was. I—I didn't know what to say for a minute." He pulled out a crumpled handkerchief and used it to mop the perspiration flowing down his hairline.

"You been to his boarding house?" Marcel asked, feeling his blood start to boil.

"Yeah, I drove over there right after Hopkins' men left. The landlady said he come back not long after I took him to the Homestead, got all his stuff, and said he was takin' it to my house. But he never. I shoulda known last night he'd run off."

"What do you mean?" Marcel asked.

"Well, I said he'd have to pay me back for the money, and that he was gonna have to come to work for me at the laundry and live with me and my family. I could see in his eyes he didn't wanna do it, but it never crossed my mind he'd steal my money and run off. As God is my witness, I never thought that."

A string of curses came readily to Marcel's lips, but somehow he found the strength to shut them off. Swearing at Chet Daniels wouldn't help anyone, and it wouldn't help get the money back. He paced up and down the office for a minute, trying to think. Ralph Daniels was a weasel and a sneak, and his first thought would be to get out of the city. "So when did you drop Ralph off?" he asked quickly.

Daniels wiped his forehead again, then took a big, nickel-plated watch from his pocket and consulted it. "Well, we was at the Homestead when it opened at ten this mornin', and I reckon we was done there by ten thirty. It would'a been nigh on to eleven when I dropped him off near Nate Hopkins' place. The landlady said it was gettin' on to noon when he left there with his stuff."

Marcel looked at his strap watch. It was nearing three P.M. "What does Ralph look like?" he asked quickly.

"Well, he's about my height—five-eleven or thereabouts, but he's got a real slender build. He don't weigh more'n hunerd an' fifty pounds. He ain't as dark as I am. Fact is, he looks more like an Indian, with them sharp cheekbones and hawk nose. And there's that slick black hair he combs back over his skull."

"How old is he?" Marcel asked.

"Let's see, I'm thirty two, and he's about five years younger—that'd make him twenty seven."

Marcel picked up the phone and dialed an Uptown exchange. Someone picked up on the second ring. "Yeah," a deep voice said.

"Mickey, this is Marcel."

"Yeah, li'l brutha. What it is?" Mickey said.

"Look, we got a guy owes money tryin' to make a run-out, and I want him stopped. How many men you got there?"

"Oh, I reckon four boys 'round here somewheres," Mickey said. "What you want us to do?"

"I want you to send them to the bus and railroad terminals," Marcel said. "They're looking for a man named Ralph Daniels. He's a bit under six feet with a slender build. His skin's on the light side, and he's got a hawk nose and black hair he slicks back over his skull. His brother says he looks more like an Indian than a Negro, with sharp cheekbones. He's about twenty-seven years old."

"Awright," Mickey said. "What'll we do if we spot him?"

"Grab the sonofabitch and bring him to me," Marcel said harshly. "I put Mr. Farrell's reputation on the line with Nate Hopkins for this guy. If he gives you any trouble, you got my permission to break his neck."

"Hah!" Mickey roared. "What you gonna do?"

"I'm gonna go to the Union Passenger Terminal on Howard Avenue. The trains to Chicago and Los Angeles don't leave until early evening. He might be hanging around there. He ain't too bright."

"Hah!" Mickey laughed again. "You know somethin', li'l brutha?"

"What?"

"You soundin' more like Mistuh Wes every day."

"Get moving," Marcel said. "If this guy gets outta town—"

"Say no more," Mickey said. "We gone."

Marcel hung up the telephone and turned back to Chet Daniels. The other man looked a little calmer now—the rye whiskey had done him some good.

"I forgot to tell you somethin', Mr. Aristide," the laundry owner said.

"What's that?"

"When I saw Ralphie las' night, he had him a gun."

Marcel's mouth tightened into a thin, brittle line. He turned and opened the bottom drawer of his desk. He removed a bundle wrapped in an oily rag. He patiently unfolded it, and eventually uncovered an old .38 Owl's Head five-shooter and a cardboard box of Western brand .38 S&W cartridges. He broke the old gun, opened the box, then placed a cartridge into each of the five chambers. He closed the gun and placed it on his hip, then took five more cartridges, wrapped them in a piece of white envelope, then folded the envelope and tucked it into his left vest pocket.

As he stood there, he felt himself trembling inside because the gun reminded him of days and things he'd rather not remember. But common sense told him that if somebody as unpredictable as Ralph Daniels had a gun, he'd better have one, too.

Chapter 5

ERNIE LEDOUX'S cab swung into traffic and headed across town to Claiborne Avenue. The street had more houses on it than it had back in the '20s, and as the street left Downtown and skirted along the edge of the University section, it was plain that the homes he saw there were those of white people. No shotgun or Cajun cottages here—these were all fine two-story homes, many of them brick. The driveways were full of late-model sedans and coupes. Ernie shook his head in wonderment. It was almost like there wasn't any Depression in this part of town.

As Claiborne crossed the Jefferson Parish line, it became U. S. Route 90. Most of this part of Jefferson Parish was still rural, with some businesses and a few houses sprinkled along the sides of the road. After a few miles of fields and oak trees dripping Spanish moss, the taxi turned down a road surfaced with marl. Ernie could hear the shells crunching and popping under the taxi's wheels.

By now it was twilight, and long shadows had fallen across the landscape. He told the cabbie to pull up beside a group of parked cars and to wait for him. As he got out of the cab, he could hear guitar strumming and the wailing of a blues singer floating toward him in the dense summer air. Dim light could be seen ahead, escaping the doors and windows of a long, low ramshackle building. "This shouldn't take long," he told the driver, and handed him ten dollars to hold until he returned.

As he neared the honky-tonk, he could make out the firefly glow of cigarette ends in the hands and mouths of men and women lining the gallery. The music was louder now, and he recognized the voice of Bobby Jeeter, a bluesman he knew from times gone by. He passed a sedan with the doors flung open on both sides, and smelled the heavy redolence of sex in the air. He turned his head and caught a glimpse of a nude man and woman locked in a titanic struggle of love as they lay across the back seat, then continued on his way.

As he reached the gallery, he could make out the faces of men and women taking the air, sipping whiskey from Mason jars, or talking one kind of trash or another. A few couples were shamelessly necking in shadowy corners. LeDoux walked past all of them and into the building.

It was a long, low-ceilinged room with four-by-four posts holding up the roof. A layer of sawdust blanketed the floor. Near the center, Bobby Jeeter, dressed in a cheap blue suit and shoes and wearing a shapeless black fedora on the back of his head, sang "Pork Chop Blues" as he strummed an old Gibson five-string with most of the varnish worn off the sound box. His blind right eye blazed from his dark face like a window into Hell. He was surrounded by Negro couples who stood or sat around him, rolling their hips or snapping their fingers and nodding in time to the music.

LeDoux walked toward the bar, a long slab of rough-hewn cypress that had been smoothed black by two generations of work-roughened Negro hands. A short, stout man in a dirty white apron, white shirt, and red bow tie stood behind the bar, his eyes taking in everything in the room. Near to his hand on the long shelf behind him lay a shotgun with the barrels sawn off even with the fore-end, a cut-down baseball bat, and an ancient .38 Forehand

& Wadsworth five-shooter, nose down in an empty beer glass.

"Business is good, Avery," LeDoux said, tipping his derby on the back of his head.

Avery leveled his eyes at LeDoux, stared for a moment, then came forward, holding out a hand. "I'm a sonofagun—Ernie LeDoux," the stout bartender said, his dark-brown face split in a wide grin. "When did they let you out?"

"Two days ago," LeDoux replied.

Avery's face lost some of its glow. He shook his head. "I still feel bad about them catchin' you here. If I'd of knowed they had the place staked out, I coulda—"

"Forget it, man," Ernie said, waving a hand. "Somebody ratted me out, sure as you're born, but it wasn't none of your doin'. One day I'll find out who did, and pay 'em back proper." He took off the derby, removed a handkerchief from his back pocket, and wiped the sweatband of the hat. He let his eyes roam the bar casually. "I been tryin' to find Ben Attaway, but they tell me he's dead."

"It's gospel, brutha. I went to the wake and the funeral. Tough break."

Ernie leaned forward until his face was only inches from Avery's. "I ax'ed Ben to hold the money I stole before they got me. I figgered I could trust him—but I never counted on him gettin' dead."

"Shit," Avery said fervently. Then he snapped his fingers. "Wait—old Marcella's still alive. Still mean as hell, though. Stays drunk half the time."

"Where?" LeDoux asked, feeling excitement building inside him. "I looked all over—nobody knows where she is, and there ain't no telephone listed."

"Ben musta left her pretty well fixed," Avery said. "'Cause she bought a big old house on Leonidas Street, two blocks in from Claiborne on the Uptown side. It's a big green house with white trim. Reason I know is that she calls here after corn liquor all the time—knows I got a source down in Terrebone Parish. Maybe she's got one of them unlisted telephone numbers."

"That's what I was hopin' you could tell me," Ernie said. "Reckon I better go over there now." He pulled a gold Elgin watch from his vest and checked the time. It was a little past ten.

"Better take this with you," Avery said, passing over a flat, brown pint bottle. "Corn liquor. She won't drink nothin' else. Might make her a li'l more sociable—she's an ornery old bitch."

LeDoux grinned, taking the bottle. "Thanks, pal. I'll come back out again before long, bring Ruby with me."

"Ruby?" Avery said. "She around here? I heard she took off with somebody ages ago."

LeDoux looked startled. "Well, she was waitin' for me when I got to town, so that can't be true."

"Prob'ly just some damn rumor," Avery said with a diffident wave of his hand. "You come on back now when you can. Good seein' you back, brutha."

"Same here, man," Ernie said. He turned and threaded his way through the crowd, doffing his derby and waving it at Bobby Jeeter as he passed him. Bobby recognized him, and grinned hugely as the ex-holdup man walked by.

Avery walked back through the darkness toward his cab. Fireflies were winking in the air around him, reminding him of a carefree childhood long gone past. The sedan he'd passed was closed up now, and the lovers appeared to have dressed and gone back inside the 'tonk.

"Back to town, boss?" the cabbie asked as LeDoux came within earshot.

"Little side trip first, but it's on the way," LeDoux replied. He put the pint bottle into the inside pocket of his jacket, then leaned back in the seat, trying not to worry. Ben Attaway had been a good friend, and he'd trusted him implicitly, but Marcella was another story. If she didn't know where the money was, LeDoux knew he was in the shit.

Molly Tatum had directed Farrell to an illegal gambling parlor off St. Claude Avenue on Clouet Street. Molly claimed that Badeaux used it for a headquarters. Farrell was pretty sure that Molly was shooting straight with him. He'd made it crystal clear what he'd do to her if it was a lie.

St. Claude was dark, and he nearly missed the turn on Clouet. At the last minute he recognized a bakery on the corner and made the turn across traffic to the Lake side of the street. Two blocks down, he saw the building he was looking for—a crummy-looking dump with a sign reading "Luther's Sweet Shop." In local parlance, a "sweet shop" was a confectionery where one could buy candies, cakes, soft drinks, and cigarettes. Farrell got out and stood at the fly-specked window for a moment. He could see a dim light in the back. He tried the door, and it swung open at his touch. He unbuttoned his jacket and loosened the Luger in his waistband. Farrell had taken it from Sleepy Moyer the year before, and knew it shot straight—Moyer had nearly taken his head off with it. Sleepy didn't need it anymore—he was as dead as Abraham Lincoln's promise.

As he slipped through the door, he saw a sloppy-looking brown man with shaggy light-brown hair spilling over his forehead. He looked up from the pulp magazine he was reading, and Farrell saw narrow Gallic features set in a tan-colored face. "Help you, brutha?" the man asked. His hands were both below the level of the counter.

Farrell approached the counter, careful to keep both of his hands in sight. Odds were, the other man held a gun on him, and he had to get closer before making a play. "Lookin' for a guy," he said.

"Got a lotta things here, mister," the other man said. "Candy, cigarettes, RC Cola. Got some real good ice cream bars, and some li'l Hubig's pies, if you like lemon and apple. Don't carry much else."

Farrell smiled benignly. "Wouldn't have a floating crap game in the back, would you? I came all the way across town to rattle some bones. You ain't gonna send me back disappointed, are you?" Farrell let his eyelids down and assumed a sleepy, half-intoxicated look. The other man's eyes roved Farrell's face, checked his hands several times, as if expecting a .45 to grow there all of a sudden. He was about to let him pass when he realized Farrell was right up on him, and that something had happened to his eyes—they weren't sleepy anymore. He tried to back up quickly and bring the sawed-off shotgun from under the counter, but Farrell was on him, his right hand around the other man's throat, the other pulling him half over the counter, trapping the gun between his body and the countertop.

"Listen to me," Farrell said in a sibilant whisper. "I don't have to kill you. I want to see Archie Badeaux. I was told this flea trap belongs to him. That right?"

The other man's voice could emit only a strangled grunt, but he rolled his eyes and nodded as hard as Farrell's hand would let him.

"That's good," Farrell said. "Now, open your hand and let the artillery fall on the floor. I want to hear it hit. We'll just have to hope you didn't cock it."

The other man's mouth drooled as he again nodded. Something hard and metallic clattered to the floor. The man's eyes blinked as though the sound was a surprise to him.

Farrell relaxed his hold on the man's throat, but kept the fingers around it. "Tell me where Badeaux is. Yell, and I'll rip your throat out." His eyes had lost whatever human quality they'd had when he'd strolled into the sweet shop and now were like chips of broken glass.

"Far back," the man managed to say. "Office. Five guys in there runnin' some tables, between you and the office. You can't do nothin' in there without they fuck you up."

Farrell smiled then, and released the man's throat. The man heaved a sigh of relief just as Farrell's right hand traveled in a short, vicious arc to his chin. As the fist connected his eyes rolled up inside his head and he went limp. Farrell let him fall, then leaned over the counter, found the sawed-off shotgun, and picked it up. It was an old Remington twelve-gauge with outside hammers. He broke it, saw the brass bases of two shells, then closed it and walked to the passage between the sweet shop and the gambling den. He cocked both of the hammers, then held the scattergun down beside his right leg.

As he walked through the door, he found himself in a room twice as large as the front of the store. As the counterman had said, there were five tables, and between four and six men at each one. A light hung from the ceiling over each table, and the men were all thoroughly engrossed in their cards. He heard bets being made, called, and raised. Not a single man looked up at his entry.

He continued into the room, threading his way between the tables. He was nearly past them when one of the house men, a well-dressed Negro with a heavy-mustache and a thick head of hair marcelled in layers over his scalp happened to look up. He saw Farrell, saw the shotgun, and sucked his breath in sharply. The other men looked up then, and Farrell swung the shotgun up, letting the muzzles rove about the room.

"Stay in your seats," he said quietly. "Just keep on playing cards, and mind your own business if you want to stay healthy." He backed toward the closed office door, holding the shotgun easily in one hand. When he reached the door, he palmed the knob without looking, shoved the door open, and slid inside. As he closed the door behind him, the group of men rose as one and walked hurriedly from the room. In fifteen seconds not a single man remained.

Inside the room, Farrell heard the voices of a man and woman, gasping and panting. In a corner there was an army cot and on it a naked man labored over a woman. Her legs were locked tightly about his thighs, and he held himself up on his muscular arms as he plunged deeply into her. They were oblivious to Farrell's presence. Farrell pointed the shotgun at the wall over their heads and discharged one of the barrels.

The roar penetrated every recess of the room, cooling their erotic activities like a bucket of cold water. The woman screamed and the man rolled off her onto the floor. As he did so, Farrell put a foot down on his outstretched hand and bore down with all his weight. The man yelled, the fingers splayed out from around the perimeter of Farrell's shoe sole. Farrell kept his foot there, unmoved by the man's screams.

The woman's cries faded to a whimper, and she drew back against the wall, hugging a pillow against her breasts. She stared at Farrell as though he were a demon from the fiery furnace.

"You're Gladiola Haygood," Farrell said, just loud enough to be heard over Archie Badeaux's cries and curses.

She nodded, shocked that this violent apparition should call her by name.

"Get dressed and go home," Farrell said. "Your family's worried about you. If you stay with this piece of trash, one day somebody's gonna kill you just because you're with him. Get!"

She leaped from the cot, grabbing her slip, dress, and shoes as she ran. She was gone so fast that if Farrell had blinked, he'd have missed her.

With Gladiola gone, he turned his eyes down on Archie Badeaux. Badeaux had run out of screams, and all that came from his open mouth were grunts and loud exhalations of breath. Farrell pointed the shotgun at his head.

"Leave the Southport Club alone," he said.

Badeaux looked at him. "Man, what the fuck you talkin' about?"

"You heard me," Farrell said. "If I hear from Carol Donovan that you've been out there again, I'll find you and kill you. Just like that. No 'Hey, Archie, glad to see you'—just the sound of the gun going off, you understand?"

Badeaux, caught between rage and surprise, could only

gape. "Who the fuck are you, white man?" he asked.

"The name's Farrell," he replied.

Badeaux's eyes got a little wide, and he nodded slowly like a man just getting the answer to a question that had vexed him. "I heard of you," he said with no tone at all.

"Then you know I mean what I said," Farrell said. "Don't you?"

"Yeah, man, I heard you," he said after a brief silence. "I think you broke my hand."

Farrell smiled. "Good. Find another line of work while you still got the other one."

Badeaux said nothing. No one had ever taken him so completely by surprise, and his anger was overshadowed by his sense of awe. As he watched, Farrell broke the shotgun, removed the cartridges from the gun, and threw them on the cot. He pried the fore-end free from the bottom of the barrels, and let the suddenly disassembled stock, barrels and fore-end fall to the floor. He took his foot from Badeaux's hand, turned and left the room.

Badeaux waited for about a full minute, then he reached behind him, found his .44 Smith & Wesson under the cot, then scrambled to his feet and padded quickly to the front of the sweet shop. He heard groaning behind the counter, and went quickly to look over the top. He saw the unconscious body of his hireling lying there. He then walked naked out onto the sidewalk and looked up and down Clouet Street. It was empty and quiet, but for the sound of a barking dog somewhere down the block. After a moment, he went inside, locked the door, and went to throw water on his front man.

MUCH EARLIER that day, at about eleven in the morning, Ralph Daniels got out of his brother's car on Esplanade Avenue and watched while Chet drove back in the direction of the river. In the pocket of his coat he felt the lump of seven hundred dollars in twenties and fifties. In spite of the fact that he'd gambled away a thousand in credit, it was the first time in his life he'd actually held that much real money in his hand. His gambling debts were normally markers—credit for money he didn't have—and usually he scrambled for nickels, dimes, singles, and two-dollar bills to pay the debts off.

He'd been on an unprecedented roll the day he'd lost the big money. He'd won almost five hundred dollars, and a voice inside him kept urging him to quit while he was ahead and put the money in the bank, but that voice was small and weak compared to the other voice that kept urging him on to greater and greater risk, reminding him of all the things he could buy—clothes, fancy women, a big car—if he'd just have the guts to hang on a little longer.

He'd lost that five hundred almost immediately, but the loud inner voice fed his belief that it was only a temporary setback that had driven him to ask for credit, and to ask again. Only when the loss column showed him down four figures did the Voice of Caution gain the upper hand.

As he'd watched Chet's car fade into the distance, he thought about the afternoons he'd be spending in the hideous heat of the laundry, the back-breaking hours standing at the pressing machines. That was Chet's idea of a life, not his. Ralph Daniels had imagination and ideas. He was too good to sell himself down the river like that.

Ralphie turned and took a tentative step in the direction of Nate Hopkins' building. There was foot traffic all around him on the avenue, but he was alone with the voices in his head. They argued and struggled over his soul, first the Voice of Caution winning an inch, then the Voice of Reckless Abandon gaining. With seven hundred dollars, Ralph could go in almost any direction and have a sizable stake at the other end. He thought briefly of Oklahoma where he could perfect the image of a young Choctaw brave, and sample the pleasures of Indian maidens.

But Los Angeles—there was a real destination. It was

warm and sunny there almost every day, with sudden violent showers in the afternoon to wash the dust and heat away. He'd seen newsreels of Los Angeles, of the palm trees, the oceanfront, and tall, willowy women in bright print dresses. Could be the Indian act might get him some female action he couldn't expect in New Orleans—maybe get him some work in the movies. The thought put a smile on his face, and his tongue made a languid circuit of his lips.

Abruptly he turned and walked back in the direction of his boarding house. The landlady was expecting him to move out today, so she wouldn't think anything of his appearance that time of the morning. What he had didn't amount to that much, but he knew he might need the gun, and he was damned if he'd leave such a prized possession behind.

It took him about a half hour of pounding the pavement to make it back to his former address. The morning heat had him sweaty and a bit nauseous by the time the house finally came into view. It was mostly deserted that time of day, and the quiet was vaguely oppressive. He walked quietly up the stairs, past the landlady's apartment, and got into his room without being seen.

Most of his things were already packed in his cardboard suitcase. He looked at it, suddenly aware of its shabbiness, and vowed he'd get a decent case when he got to the West coast. He might go on a real vacation out there, and you didn't go on a vacation in that part of the world with a cheap, beat-up cardboard suitcase, no indeed.

He nestled his straight razor and shaving mug and brush beside his folded pants and shirts, and as he did so the black-and-white bone grips of the Colt peeked out. He grasped it in his hand, and a power seemed to flow from the blue steel up into his arm and chest. With the gun in his hand and the money in his pocket, Ralph had a momentary awareness of how the big-shots felt every day—strong, confident, rich. On an impulse, he tucked the pistol in his waistband, over his right hipbone, like he'd seen a guy in the movies do it. He let his coat fall back into place, then he closed the suitcase and set the latches.

He was at the door when a knock sounded. It was so unexpected that he nearly wet himself. "Wh-who's t-t-there?" he stammered.

"It's Mrs. Brown," a woman's voice said. Ralphie let out a deep sigh of relief, and went to open the door. His landlady stood there, wearing an ivory-colored sun dress that showed a lot of cleavage and fresh rose powder and lip rouge on her face. Mrs. Brown was a bit past forty, still trying for thirty five, and had been on the make for Ralph ever since he moved in. Ralph didn't understand women enough to be able to make sense of her attentions, and always felt ill-at-ease around her.

"Your brother told me you're leavin' today, Ralph," she said. "I—I'm sorry to see you go. It was so...pleasant havin' you here. Reckon you'll ever stop by again?"

Ralphie felt a flutter of excitement at this woman's display of her figure. Once upon a time he might've sampled some of that, but not now. Not with Los Angeles and all it represented hovering at the edge of his imagination.

"Well...I dunno, ma'am," he mumbled. "Reckon Chet'll have me pretty busy at the laundry and all." When words began to fail him, he reached impulsively into his trouser pocket and came out with a five-dollar note, which he shoved at Mrs. Brown.

She batted her eyelashes uncertainly at the money, then up at his face.

"It's the rent I owe you," he explained.

"Oh," she said, holding a hand up to her breast. "No, no, you keep it. It ain't that much to me, and you might need it. You been a good tenant, and you always paid your rent on time, and you was quiet. A woman couldn't ask for more'n that—at least not much." She batted her eyelashes again in a last-ditch attempt to convey what else she might've asked, if only she'd dared.

Ralph felt a flush crawl up his neck, and shoved the bill back into his pocket as he sought to avoid her eyes.

"I—I'll miss you, Ralph," she said. He looked quickly up at her face, and saw that now she was looking away, blinking rapidly to dispel the shine growing in her eyes.

"I—I gotta go now, so—so, g'bye, now," he said, and walked quickly past her and down the hall. He was afraid she was going to cry, and he almost ran down the stairs to get away. He didn't breathe again until he was out in the street, legging it downtown toward the railroad station.

It disturbed him to realize that a woman her age could feel like that about him. No one had ever loved him to his knowledge, not even his mother. She'd been an irritable woman, quick with a slap or a scold.

He had sought women out for sex many times, but never had he recognized any romantic feeling in any of them, nor had he experienced such feelings in himself. He shook his head to clear it, more disturbed by this than even the possibility of punishment at the hands of Nate Hopkins. But he continued to look behind himself occasionally, still trying to make sense of his landlady's behavior.

ROGERS CLIFTON sat in his office at the Merchants and Farmers Homestead Bank staring at the letter on his desk. It bore the letterhead of the Department of the Navy, Naval Aeronautics Board. He should have felt a sense of triumph at seeing the letter, but instead he felt sick inside. All he'd done—his banking degree from Fisk, law school at Howard, the logical steps on the path of gaining control of a bank to better the lives of Negroes in New Orleans—all for nothing. Instead of a community leader, he'd become the shill, frontman, and chief money launderer for the most vicious gangster he could ever imagine.

Ulysses Bautain had been a customer of the bank, and even though he was a little pompous and even a bit vainglorious at times, he hadn't been a bad fellow. Clifton had lunched with him several times, and had dined with him on the night he'd disappeared. He'd arranged the dinner meeting at Lincoln's behest. It had been one last-ditch attempt to get him to sell the property on the eastern edge of town, but it had failed. As Bautain exited the club, he'd nodded to Archie Badeaux across the room and Badeaux had gone out to commit murder. Clifton still felt queasy thinking about it.

Clifton had already gotten Lincoln title to the land surrounding it, meaning that once Lillian Bautain had signed over her husband's property, the control over the entire section would be exercised by Jonathan Lincoln. And Clifton would be the agent of change in one of the biggest land deals in recent New Orleans history—if he felt like admitting it.

Clifton got up from the desk and walked over to the window. It was getting dark outside, time to close up his office and leave the bank for dinner. He only wished he felt hungry. He heard the door open behind him and he turned to find his secretary there.

"Do you need anything else this evening, Mr. Clifton?" she asked. Her name was Barbara, and her pale red-brown skin and dark yellow hair made her particularly striking. He could only imagine what her racial mixture was. She had the hair cut short and it fit around her head like a feathery yellow cap. Her full lips were smiling gently at him. He'd been in love with her since before he became bank president, and he wanted more than anything to ask her to dinner.

"No, Barbara. Nothing that can't wait until tomorrow." He paused, and scuffed the rust-colored carpet with his toe. "I was wondering..."

"Yes?" she said. Was that a note of hope in her voice?

"Yes, well," he said, wringing his hands awkwardly. "I haven't had dinner tonight, and I thought..."

"Oh, how sweet of you," she said. "I'd love to, but I promised Mama I'd come over there tonight. Perhaps later in the week…?"

Clifton's face burned with embarrassment, but her response was so genuine that for a moment he was overcome with happiness. "Yes, perhaps Thursday night, if you're not too tired."

"I don't know why I should be," she said, favoring him with another smile. "I'll look forward to it very much."

"Oh," Clifton said, trying not to grin idiotically. "Good. Very good. I'll see you tomorrow, then. Have a good evening."

"Yes," she said. "You, too." She gave him one last smile, then left the room.

He stood there smiling, rocking back and forth on his heels for some moments after her departure. Then he remembered something—that Jonathan Lincoln owned him lock, stock, and barrel. So long as that was true, there was little hope that he'd ever know the kind of happiness that a woman like Barbara could give him.

He went to the desk and picked up the telephone, then dialed Lincoln's number. It rang only twice before Albert picked up. Clifton identified himself and asked for Lincoln. The old man must've been hovering at Albert's elbow, for he came on immediately.

"Well, Clifton, I hope you've got good news for me," the old man said.

"Of course," Clifton said. "The letter arrived from the Navy Department today. Their offer is in line with what you hoped for."

"Excellent," the old man said, rolling the word around on his tongue like French cognac. "As soon as that deal's signed, we can begin looking for other worlds to conquer." He paused for a moment, then said, "I know you hate me, Clifton, but that doesn't bother me a bit. In fact, I think your hate might just make you a better businessman than you were when I found you. You were far too fearful when I found you to ever be much of a success. You spent too much time worrying about what you had to lose. Now you don't worry about that anymore, do you?"

Clifton's mouth grew hard and his fingers tightened around the receiver. He wanted to hurl curses and invective at the old man, but he knew that Lincoln would think it childish. When he had mastered his hate, he said, "No, Mr. Lincoln. I think of nothing now but your death. All I want is to see it happen, then they can do with me what they want."

Lincoln chuckled for a moment. "You're becoming a real meat-eater, aren't you. I shall have to watch you more closely." He broke the connection, leaving Clifton sitting at the desk staring at the dead receiver for several long moments before he replaced it in the cradle.

Chapter 6

SAVANNA PULLED her car to the curb in front of the three-story office building two blocks off Central Avenue. The hot, dry winds continued to sweep through the city like avenging angels, scorching everything in their paths and leaving everyone feeling itchy and edgy. She'd passed two fist fights on Central as she'd driven, each surrounded by an excited crowd yelling encouragement to one fighter or the other.

The office building she sought was relatively new, attesting to the success of some of the Negro businessmen in that part of the city. It had a smooth, gray concrete skin with blocks of glass brick here and there to let natural light inside. She walked into a cool, empty vestibule. A glance at the directory told her the office she wanted was on the fifth floor. She pushed an errant lock of hair up inside the band of her wide-brimmed straw hat, shifted her handbag over her left shoulder, then asked the old man in the elevator to take her to the top floor.

There were four offices on this level; the one she wanted was at the end. A pebbled glass door had black letters painted on it that spelled out MARTY MADIGAN—INSURANCE—BAIL BONDS—REAL ESTATE. She tried the doorknob and found that it turned easily in her hand. The reception desk was empty—Madigan's girl must have been at lunch. Savanna saw that his office door was open a crack, and walked toward it. She heard talking on the other side and pushed the door open far enough to see the speaker.

Marty Madigan was sitting at the desk in his shirt sleeves, talking on the telephone. A small fan near the window whirred quietly, and Savanna could see the breeze ruffling the dark, shiny curls falling over Madigan's deep-brown forehead. He looked up as the door moved, saw it was Savanna, and quickly ended his call.

"Savanna, come in, come in," he said, getting up and gesturing toward a chair. "You're looking swell today, just swell." He smiled broadly at her. He wanted to make a play for her, but she'd managed to keep him at bay with a few looks, and by ignoring his effusive compliments.

Savanna strolled in casually and took the chair. "We got to talk," she said without preamble.

"Talk?" Madigan said. "Sure, I'm not too busy to talk to you. What's goin' on?"

"I'll tell you what's goin' on," Savanna said. "Last night a pair of colored cops came in to see me. They told me that I owed them two hundred a week for protection."

Madigan's smile melted from his face. "That's a lot of bread," he said.

"Why didn't you tell me about those guys?" she demanded. "Why didn't you tell me you'd had trouble with them before? They know you're the owner."

Madigan's face became flaccid and his eyes got a wild look in them. His hands, which had been clasped together on top of the desk jumped apart and began to shake. "Oh, God," he said in a low voice.

"What've they got on you?" Savanna asked.

Madigan tried to evade her glance, and got up from the desk. He walked jerkily to a window, wringing his hands. "What they ain't got on me is a better question," he said in a hoarse whisper. "They traced a drug dealer back to me a year ago. Threatened to kill me 'resistin' arrest' unless I cut them in on the action."

Savanna's mouth hardened. "Drugs. You been sellin' drugs—to kids, probably. They *ought* to've killed you."

Madigan swung around to face her, his eyes pleading with her. "But they ain't on the square neither. They use their badges to cut into every grift in this part of town. Did you see how good they was dressed, or that big Packard automobile Starke drives when the two of 'em are makin' the rounds to shake people down? They worse than me—a hundred times worse."

Savanna stood up. "Then pay them or disappear; either way I'm through. I didn't come out here to take on anybody else's troubles. I'll be out of my apartment by tomorrow night, and I'll take what you owe me out of the week's receipts."

"I need you," he said in a rush, reaching out a hand in supplication. "I need to keep that club goin', and I can't do it myself."

She looked at his hand, then back up at his face. "You need to stand up on your hind legs and quit crawlin' like some dog. If you don't want them squeezin' you, find some way to squeeze back. They're bad and they're tough, but they're still men. You can hurt them if you try hard enough. It's been done before."

"Please, I—I—" Madigan was stumbling over his words, and tears were spilling from his eyes. "I can't. They'll kill me."

Savanna turned and looked at him. She had never felt so much contempt for a man before. He had lied to her and put her at risk, and now was crying, begging for a woman to help him. "Not if you don't let them," she said flatly. Then she turned and left the office.

LEDOUX'S TAXI wound its way back out the marl road to Highway 90 and headed back to New Orleans. About forty minutes later, the driver slowed at Leonidas Street and made a right turn onto the street.

"You don't know the address, huh?" the driver asked.

"My friend said it was a big place, painted green with white trim," LeDoux replied.

The driver crept down the street, using his spotlight on the houses until they found one that matched Avery's description. "Reckon that's it," the driver said. He pulled to the curb and cut the engine. "Think you'll be long?"

"Hard to say, but I'll pay you extra to hang around." He pulled out his money clip and peeled off two more tens. "If that ain't enough, let me know when I come out and I'll square it with you."

"You the boss, boss," the driver said. He took out a package of cigarettes, put one in his mouth, and leaned back to wait for Ernie.

LeDoux walked through the yard and up on the porch. He could hear music playing on the other side of the door, so he pushed the doorbell button and stood back from the door. A light came on, bathing the porch in a pale, iridescent light. The door came open a crack, and a tiny old woman in a bathrobe stood there peering out.

"Miss Marcella, it's Ernie LeDoux. You remember me, don't you?"

"Ernie LeDoux's in prison," she said in a quavery voice.

"No, ma'am," he said, taking off his derby. "Take a good look—it's me, Ernie LeDoux. They let me out couple of days ago."

"My land," the old woman said. "I reckon it is you. What you want this time of the night?"

LeDoux shuffled his feet for a second. "It—it's kinda personal, ma'am. Could I come in and talk to you about it?"

"Well, I don't know—it's kinda late for callin' on folks."

LeDoux shifted his shoulders and felt the weight of the pint of whiskey in his coat. "Say, I got me a bottle of corn liquor in my coat here. Feel like sharin' a drink with me?"

"Corn liquor," she said, throwing open the door. "Why didn't you say so. Come on in here, boy." He could already smell alcohol on her breath.

LeDoux opened the screen door and walked into

Marcella Attaway's living room. It was a curious mixture of splendor and squalor. A Victorian sofa and chair covered in maroon horsehair dominated the room, but there were costly table lamps on the end tables. Near the fireplace, LeDoux noticed the pilot lights of a expensive Crosley radio phonograph glowing, and the sound of Fred Astair singing "I Found A Million Dollar Baby at the Five and Ten Cent Store" came from the speaker.

The rug was a thick Persian that nearly reached from wall to wall, but cigarette ends, bread crusts, and torn newspaper littered the surface. On the wall was a framed print by Romaire Bearden and a photographic portrait of Josephine Baker dressed in only a banana-leaf skirt. LeDoux was just close enough to read an inscription to Ben from the famous dancer, and he wondered where the old man could've met Josephine Baker.

He turned to find Marcella hovering at his elbow. "You said you had some corn," she reminded him.

He took out the pint and handed it over to her. She disappeared into the kitchen, and he heard the sound of glass clinking until she emerged with a pair of tumblers, neither of which looked too clean. She poured a healthy dose into each glass, grabbed one, and said, "Damn the French," before putting the glass to her lips and nearly draining it. "Ahhhhh," she said. "Why was it you said you was here?" she asked as she poured herself another slug.

"Well, ma'am," LeDoux said. "Before I got sent up the river, I asked Ben to hold somethin' for me—a canvas satchel with some stuff of mine in it. I was hopin' to get it back when I got outta the slam. You wouldn't know where it was, would you?"

She drank more liquor, and tapped her finger on her right temple while she rolled her eyes at the ceiling. "A canvas satchel, you said. Hmmmmmm—can't say as I recollect it. What color was it?"

"Just plain gray canvas, with a heavy clasp and leather handles. It was somethin' my daddy used and I had kind of a sentimental attachment to it. It had some stuff of mine in it, besides."

She looked at him sharply, fingering her chin. She took another sip of the corn, then shook her head. "My memory ain't what it was, but I reckon I'd remember. Ben woulda said somethin' to me about it, prob'ly."

Ernie felt like spiders were running around on his skin. "Well, maybe not. It was kind of a secret that Ben was keepin' for me. He said he wouldn't tell anybody about it. It must be with his things, or maybe in a place he kept valuables. It's real important that I get it back."

"You callin' me a liar?" the old woman flared. "I reckon I'd know what my own husband left behind when he went to the hereafter. If you don't know no better way to talk to a helpless old woman, you just get the hell on outta here. Go on, get." She got up and began shooing him away with both hands. LeDoux barely had time to grab his derby before the old woman had pushed him out the door onto the porch.

He stood there for a moment, breathing heavily, his fists opening and closing. He had the distinct impression that the old woman wasn't being on the up-and-up with him. She knew something, of that he was certain. He went to the window, and saw that Marcella had dialed someone on the telephone and was really laying into whoever was at the other end. He watched her for several minutes, then turned and trudged down the steps.

The driver saw him approach the cab, and pitched his cigarette end out onto the street. "All through for the night, cousin?" he asked.

LeDoux raised his eyes to the man, and smoothed the frown from his face. "Reckon so, for the time bein'. Take me on back to the Metro, will you?"

"You're the boss, boss," the driver said. He cranked the motor, waited for LeDoux to get back inside, then pulled away from the curb. LeDoux cast one last backward glance at the house and thought he saw the old woman standing at the window staring after him.

As Farrell drove back Downtown on St. Claude Avenue, he mulled over his confrontation with Archie Badeaux. It had almost been too easy, and Farrell wasn't the kind of man who believed in that kind of luck. It crossed his mind, too, that he'd just humiliated a man who made his living through the force of his reputation. It could be that he should've killed Badeaux. His own reputation kept some kinds of threat away, but a reputation also drew people who wanted to test it. He might come to regret this evening's entertainment, but there was no sense in worrying about it now.

He decided to head out to the Southport Club to see Carol Donovan. He'd said he would come out tomorrow night, but as long as he'd broken so many of his personal set of rules already, why not break one more?

The Southport Club was along the River, so he cut across town and found Magazine Street, then took it all the way down until it turned into Leake Avenue. Leake took him into Jefferson Parish; and about ten miles down he turned into a driveway that led him to a large parking lot. If the number of parked cars was any indication, Carol Donovan was doing a land-office business. He had to park about twenty yards from the front door. As he walked through the gravel parking lot, he saw on the marquee that Louis Bras and his Rhythm Sextet were out here. Farrell had used Louis before, and knew the little bald-headed trumpet player could really ball the jack.

He took off his hat as he entered the foyer, found the entrance to the main floor, and strode in past a tan-colored cigarette girl who wore the equivalent of two band-aids and a piece of cheesecloth as a costume. Louis and his boys were pounding out "The Joint is Jumpin'," and Farrell had to smile as he heard Louis sing the line that goes "check your weapons at the door."

He was at the bar only a moment when a white-coated

bartender appeared. If he was surprised to see a white man at his bar, he gave no indication of it. "Your pleasure, sir?" he said.

"A vodka martini with two olives," Farrell said. "And a word with Miss Donovan, if she's around."

"Can I give her a name, sir?" the bartender asked.

"Wesley Farrell." Farrell saw the recognition in the bartender's eyes, but the man said nothing. Forty-five seconds later he had a martini in front of him, and the bartender left again.

He was half-finished with the cocktail when her perfume reached his nostrils. "Evening in Paris," he said. "It's one of my favorites."

"Mine, too," she said. "What brings you here?" She eased up on a barstool beside him, her movements as elegant as a Russian ballerina's.

He turned on his stool to face her, and saw she was dressed in a mauve silk evening gown with a high-boned bodice and a half-cape that went over one shoulder and hung down her smooth brown back. She looked at what he was drinking, snapped her fingers at the bartender, and held up two fingers. "I didn't expect to see you so soon," she said. "Somehow I had the feeling you'd be the kind of man to think about things a little."

"I thought about them," he said. "When I thought about them enough, I went out and hunted up Archie Badeaux." His new martini arrived along with Carol's. He picked it up and raised it to her in a silent toast.

She smiled over the rim of her glass, answered his gesture with her own, then sipped the martini. "And you found him," she said.

"Yes," Farrell replied, getting out his cigarettes. He offered one to Carol, took one for himself, then lit them both with a nickel-silver lighter. "He was occupied when I found him, but I got his attention. I told him to leave you alone."

Her eyes got a little wide, then she lowered them as she

let smoke curl out of the corners of her mouth. "What did he say?"

"He was having a little trouble talking just then," Farrell said. "He was looking at a shotgun at the time." Farrell knew he was talking too much, but it must've been a reaction from the confrontation with Badeaux. He felt a need to get it out of his system.

"Was—was anybody hurt?" she asked, still not able to meet his eyes.

"Not in any way that shows," Farrell replied. "Everybody went home, so far as I know."

Carol turned to him, her black eyes now flat and impenetrable. "Why don't we go up to my office and talk more privately. I've got some single malt scotch up there that just came in." She stubbed her cigarette out in an ashtray on the bar.

Farrell felt something electric coming from her, but didn't know what it was about. "Sure," he said. "Single malt's pretty rare in these parts—like some women." He crushed out his cigarette, got up and let her put her arm through his, and then he let her lead him to the end of the bar and through a door that opened onto a lighted stairway. The soundproofing in the building was good. Louis and his sextet were almost inaudible once the door closed behind them.

Carol led him up to the second floor, and then through a door to a luxuriously furnished room. There was a desk in there, but the rest of the room was like a spread from *House Beautiful*. There was a black leather sofa and two chairs, a curly maple coffee and end tables, and torchères made of brass and black enamel with globes of green glass.

There was a taboret near the desk with about a half-dozen bottles and decanters and a row of heavy crystal tumblers. She opened a bottle of Laphroig and poured about two fingers each into two of the tumblers, humming a little song as she worked. When she was finished, she corked the bottle, picked up the tumblers, and brought them over to the couch. She sat down beside him, handed him a glass, and lifted it to him.

"Happy days," she said.

"Are here again," Farrell countered. He touched his glass to hers, then sipped the rare old scotch. "Mmmmm. Not bad."

"At twenty-five dollars a bottle, it ought to be better than that," she said, one corner of her mouth curving up. Her eyes sparkled now, and seemed less opaque than earlier.

He leaned back and looked at her. He noticed for the second time that she didn't seem the least uncomfortable about being in an intimate setting with him. He found that interesting. It suggested things about her background and experience that didn't come across in other ways.

"That little song you were humming," he said after a second sip. "I've heard it before, but don't remember the name."

"It's a nursery rhyme," she replied, turning her body enough so she could face him. "'Little Baby Bunting, Daddy's gone a-hunting, to get a little rabbit skin to put my Baby Bunting in.' My mother used to sing it to me a long time ago."

"Is your mother still alive?" he asked.

"No," Carol replied. "She had a hard life and died young."

"Your father?" he said.

"He went away one day and never came back," she said. "No rabbit skin for baby, I'm afraid."

"That's tough," Farrell said solicitously. His own mother had died young and he hadn't known his own father until a bit more than two years ago, and he felt an immediate sympathy for her that he didn't know how to express.

She got a cigarette from an enameled box on the coffee table, put it into her mouth, then held it for him to light. When she'd taken in a lung full of smoke, she let it out her nose and looked at him frankly. "Why did you come here tonight?"

He smiled and drank more of his scotch. "Not for the reason you're thinking. I did something pretty rash tonight—something that might cause you more trouble than you originally had. I gave Badeaux a hotfoot—I don't know for sure that he won't decide to come out here and try to push you again. That means I either let you handle it from here, or I make it a point to be around in case there's more trouble."

She regarded him intently, searching his face with her eyes. "I shouldn't have asked you to do what you've already done. Badeaux's trouble—I'd never forgive myself if—if anything happened to you because of me."

He smiled easily. "It's too late for that now. We'll just have to play it out. Chances are he won't bother you again. If he does—"

"Then what?"

"We'll cross that bridge when we get to it." He finished his scotch and stood up. She stood up with him.

"Thank you for all you've done. I've been alone most of my life. It...it's good not to feel that way now."

She was standing very close to Farrell, and the smell of her perfume made him feel loose and reckless. He caught her around the waist and pulled her closer to him. Her eyes widened, but she didn't resist. Her mouth came up to meet his, but then she hesitated, and her hands came up and flattened against his chest. "Don't," she said. "Not yet. Not like this."

He looked into her eyes, saw things there he didn't understand, but he nodded, let her go, and stepped back from her. "Thanks for the hospitality. I'll see you tomorrow night."

"Yes," she said. He turned and left the office. She looked after him until he was gone, then she put both of her hands on her face and held them like that for some time, giving into the tremors that she'd held back while Farrell was still there.

Marcella Attaway was asleep on the horsehair sofa with a needlepoint pillow under her head. Her gray curls were messy and her mouth gaped as a noise like a buzz saw escaped from it. Her slack fingers cradled the empty pint bottle that had held Ernie LeDoux's corn whiskey. She didn't hear the front door open and close, nor the muffled footsteps of the intruder crossing the Persian carpet.

The intruder stopped at the fireplace and picked up a poker from the rack of fireplace tools. It had never been used, and the brass sparkled in the light of the chandelier that burned overhead. The intruder walked toward the sleeping old woman, the poker half-raised to strike. Eyes focused on the old woman, the intruder didn't see the teacup and saucer near the end of the sofa until a careless foot sent it clattering.

The old woman snorted as her slumber was disturbed. She brushed at her nose with her hand, then rubbed her eyes as she came awake. "Wuzzat?" she mumbled. "...the hell's that racket?" She opened her eyes and saw the figure looming over her.

"What in the world are you doin' here this time of night?" she asked, surprised. "You always call first." She struggled to a sitting position and saw the poker. "What's that for? We don't need no fire this time of the year. No, wait—no, no, NOOO—" Her cries were cut off as the poker struck her over the right ear. She put up her hands to fend off the poker, but blows fell relentlessly, battering away her puny defense. She crumpled, then rolled off onto the floor. Her small body made barely any noise as it hit the carpet.

The killer dropped the poker from a gloved hand, then bent, removed the glove, and shoved fingers into the old woman's neck. When no pulse could be felt, the killer's hand withdrew, shaking now. A feeling of nausea struck with terrible fury, and suddenly the killer turned away from the body, vomiting on the rug. It took a moment to regain control, but with remarkable speed the killer left the house and walked down to a gray Chrysler coupe. In seconds the car was in gear and rolling Uptown on Leonidas. The car passed a bus and an old man walking his dog, but there was nothing about the Chrysler to attract any attention as it made the turn onto Oak Street, heading for Carrollton and Downtown. The killer was all the way home before the realization stuck that the right hand glove had been left beside the old woman's body.

WHEN MARCEL ARISTIDE arrived at the Union Terminal on Howard Avenue earlier that evening, it was past seven. There was still some time left to find Ralph before the departure of the Panama Limited to Chicago and the Sunset Limited to Los Angeles. He only wished he had a photograph of the guy to show at the ticket windows. Hopefully a description would be enough—Ralph Daniels appeared to be a distinctive-looking man that people would remember.

He walked through the doors to the main waiting room and paused to scan the crowd. There were a lot of people sitting and milling about, but the terminal was nowhere near filled to capacity. He began a slow walk around the perimeter, studying each individual row of chairs in the place, paying particular attention to anyone with a newspaper in front of him or a cap over his face. By the time he'd made one full circuit, Marcel was pretty well convinced that Ralph at least wasn't in the waiting room.

Marcel approached the ticket window for the Chicago train, his mind working furiously. He was a Negro about to ask a favor of the white man behind the counter. He knew he was probably going to have to appear obsequious and not particularly intelligent. It made his gut roil at the thought, but there was really no alternative. It was imperative that he catch Ralph before he boarded one of the two departing trains, otherwise he could kiss the money goodbye. Marcel would be honor-bound to pay Nate Hopkins out of his own pocket. The thought of being rooked by a penny-ante hustler like Ralph Daniels was just the spur he needed. He got furiously angry for a moment, and that flash of rage was sufficient to propel him into the potentially humiliating encounter.

"Uh, 'scuse me, suh," Marcel said in a cracker voice. He held his hat in front of his abdomen and played with the brim like a bashful cowpuncher in a Republic western film.

"Yeah, what is it?" the ticket agent said brusquely, not looking up from the papers he was sorting.

"Well, ya see, suh, I was s'posed to meet my cousin, Ralph, down heah to give him somethin' impo'tant to take to our mammy in Chicago, but I done fo'got the time the train leaves so's I could catch him. I was wonderin' if he'd done come heah and bought his ticket awready."

"Your cousin, huh?" the white man said, still shuffling papers. "What's he look like?"

"Well, suh, he's 'bout my height but kinda on the skinny side, an' he looks kinda like a Injun—you know, sha'p cheekbones and nose, and straight black haih he slicks back like Ru-dolph Val-un-tino?" Marcel mimed slicking back his hair, wearing an idiotically hopeful grin on his face.

"Nah," the ticket agent said impatiently. "I been here since noon and ain't nobody like that come through here." He still didn't look up at Marcel. "You sure it's today he's leavin'?"

"Well, suh," Marcel said stupidly. "I thought it was today, but mebbe I got the days confused. Thank you, suh, thank you ver' much." Marcel backed away, still grinning, and turned back into the terminal.

It appeared that Ralph hadn't gotten a ticket for the Chicago train. It might be that he went to one of the bus terminals or one of the other two railroad stations in town, but Marcel had a hunch that wasn't true. For the first time in his life, Ralphie had a sizable chunk of cash in his pocket. He might go east, or he might take a bus, but

Marcel had Ralphie sized up as a loser with dreams of grandeur. If he didn't go to the large Negro community of Chicago, Los Angeles was the best bet. It was warm and sunny there most of the year, very much like New Orleans. Plus, Los Angeles was a dream that beckoned to many a southern Negro. It was like a new paradise where things impossible at home became real in the golden sunshine of a city on the make.

Marcel turned next to the window for the Sunset Limited and saw an elderly man behind it, his arms folded on the counter in front of him, his green eye shade at a cocky angle on his white head. Something told Marcel that he wouldn't need the shuck and jive with this old fellow.

"Excuse me," Marcel said. "I'm trying to catch my cousin before he leaves on the Sunset Limited this evening. Is it possible he might've gotten his ticket already?"

"Sure, it's possible," the old man said. "I sold quite a few tickets already, but not many for the colored car. What's this cousin of yours look like?" His baby blue eyes twinkled intelligently behind thick glasses in gold-filled rims.

"He's about my height, but thinner," Marcel began. "He's got some Indian blood, and looks like an Indian brave—high cheekbones and a hawk's nose. Combs his hair straight back over his skull. He's around twenty-seven years old."

The old man's eyes roved the ceiling for a moment while he drummed his fingers on the marble counter. "Sounds familiar. Yeah, I think I sold him the ticket a while ago. You look around for him in here?"

"Yes, sir," Marcel said. "But I didn't see him."

"Well, there's a colored lunch counter over yonder." He pointed over Marcel's shoulder. "And there's some colored cafés and joints a few blocks away—you probably know all that. There's still a little while to wait until the train boards. He's gotta be at one of 'em. If he comes back, should I say you're lookin' for him?"

Marcel waived a hand, smiling gratefully. "No, sir, I'll

probably be able to locate him now that I know he's got his ticket. If all else fails, I'll just catch him at the track doors. You've been real kind."

"Hell," the old man said, shrugging, "it weren't nothin'. Good luck finding him."

Marcel touched two fingers to the brim of his hat and walked over to the tiny sandwich counter that served Negroes. It was small, with only a couple of tables. Several Negro men and women were standing up eating sandwiches and sipping sodas or cups of coffee. There was a large, handsome black woman of about forty behind the counter making up a sandwich when Marcel walked up. She saw him and turned to take his order.

"What'll it be, sugah?" she asked, wiping her hands on her apron.

"I'm looking for my cousin who's leaving on the Sunset Limited this evening," he replied. "I wondered if he'd been in here. He's about my height, slender build, features like a movie-show Indian, and slick black hair."

"Noooo, baby," she replied with a lazy smile. "Men as good lookin' as you and your cousin don't come in here ever' day. I remember them kinda men. Try some of the joints in the neighborhood. Maybe he in one of them makin' time with some waitress."

Marcel grinned and tipped his hat, then turned to leave the terminal. As he got to the street, he paused to look at his watch. It was six thirty—about two hours before the Limited pulled out for Los Angeles. He looked around, wishing he had Mickey or a couple of the other men with him. They could split up and cover this entire end of town. He knew of several colored cafés in the vicinity of the railroad terminal, not one of which was much different or better than any of the others. He knew he was just going to have to choose a direction and hope to get lucky.

Chapter 7

ARCHIE BADEAUX got dressed and managed to slap some sense back into his man, Luther Devereau. Luther explained how he'd been sucker punched, doing his level best to make himself out to be the aggrieved party in order to keep Badeaux from punishing him further.

"He was real sneaky, Archie," Luther said, rubbing his sore jaw. "He acted like he knew the place was a gamblin' hell and all's he wanted was to lay some bread down; you know what I'm sayin'?"

Archie's lip curled. "I know what you're sayin' all right. You let an unarmed man come in, take your gun, and slap you into the middle of next week. Then he runs off all the boys with your gun, comes in and scares me and Gladiola so bad we're pissin' blood, and then warns me off of something I don't know nothin' about. Hell, I could see he was Wesley Farrell the minute I laid eyes on him. Everybody in this fuckin' burg knows that mutha-fucka, 'cept you, I reckon." Badeaux took the snuff horn from the pocket of his vest and the bone-handled clasp knife from his coat. He snapped open the blade of the knife, pushed it into the white powder in the horn, then brought it to his left nostril and snorted it up noisily. He repeated the process, snorting that load up the right side of his nose. He coughed a few times, snorting again to clear his nose as he put the horn back into his pocket. He tested the edge of the knife blade with a broad, spatulate thumb as he turned his gaze back to Luther.

Luther knew he had to get Archie's mind off the unwarranted attack and his own unwilling complicity, or Archie might do something bad. He'd hurt Luther once before when he was feeling mean and had taken on a load of coke. "This Carol Donovan—you don't know her, do you, Archie? I seen her picture in *The Sepia Socialite,* though—man, what a dish."

"I don't give a shit if she's the fuckin' Queen of France. I ain't done nothin' to her nor her place. I wanna know what call she's got to sic Farrell on me," Badeaux said in a thick, mean voice.

Luther, the wheels in his mind spinning madly, came up with something that might get him back in his boss's good graces. "Why don't I go out there and lay the fear of God on her, Archie? Let her know what messin' with Archie Badeaux's likely to get her. Huh? What you say?"

Badeaux looked at Luther, half-way interested in his employee's brainstorm. Luther wasn't good for much, but he was good enough to go out and have a talk with a woman, no matter who she was. He'd sent Luther to discipline unruly whores a few times, and they'd always toed the mark afterward. "Maybe you're right, Luther." He looked at his watch. "It ain't but eleven thirty. That place'll be open for another couple hours yet. Go out there and tell that bitch that if she uses my name to anybody else, I'll come out there and make her wish she'd never been born. You get me?"

"Yeah, right, Archie," Luther said quickly. He knew he was out of the doghouse, at least for the time being. He'd slap ten Carol Donovans around if it kept Archie off his neck. He buttoned the collar of his shirt and went to get his jacket and tie. On the way, he stopped in the bathroom to wash his face and run his wet fingers through his hair a few times. With the tie around his neck and the

Windsor knot snug at his neck, he didn't think he looked too bad. Farrell's fist had discolored the skin alongside his chin, but luckily the skin wasn't broken.

He went back to the front of the store and got a set of brass knuckles and a .380 Remington automatic pistol, which he shoved into his pants' pockets. He grabbed his hat and was on the point of leaving when Badeaux stopped him.

"Luther, don't you mess this up, you hear me? If I have to go out there and clean up a mess you made, you better get on the first bus outta town, else I'll rip the skin right off your bones." Badeaux's eyes were still full of fury and his teeth looked white and sharp against the backdrop of his dark brown face.

"Sure, Archie," Luther said, trying to grin at his boss. "It'll be a snap. Don't worry 'bout nothin'."

"It ain't me that's got to worry," Badeaux said ominously. Luther didn't hang around to prolong the conversation. If it went on much longer, he might just disappear off the face of the earth.

Luther locked the door to the sweet shop behind him and walked across the street to the old Willys-Knight coupe parked near the corner. He got in, cranked the engine, and left the neighborhood. He was ten blocks down St. Claude before he noticed that sweat was dripping down his face from the hairline. He found a crumpled handkerchief in his coat pocket and used it to blot himself dry.

He'd worked for Archie Badeaux in a number of capacities, mostly running errands and disciplining whores, but he considered himself an integral part of Badeaux's operation. He'd gotten to know Badeaux right after he came to town from Philadelphia, Mississippi, where he'd been chief driver for a bootlegger up there until the 'legger crossed the wrong man and ended up dead.

Badeaux, figuring his fortunes in Philadelphia were on the wane, came south to New Orleans and became a bodyguard for Straight Flush Henry Alford, a Negro racketeer who specialized in narcotics and women. Badeaux had chosen Luther from the gang of hard-faced young men on Alford's payroll and after that he became Badeaux's man exclusively. When Alford was murdered in his sleep one night because his snoring had bothered the coked-up whore in his bed, Badeaux split away from the rest of the gang, taking Luther with him.

For a while, most of what they'd done together was hire out for protection, kidnap people, and kill those who'd become inconvenient to other mobsters in the city. Luther rarely used his gun—Badeaux never needed any help in killing. He did it the way some men ate breakfast in the morning—without much thought and with dispatch, particularly when he'd had a sniff of nose candy.

It was Luther's idea to open up some illegal gambling dens, and Luther had found the sweet shop and set it up. He'd made a success of it, prompting Badeaux to invest in several others. Luther wasn't much good with cards or dice, but he had good organizational skills and covered the front. Farrell was the only person, so far, to breach the operation, and Luther felt pretty bad about it. He hated to let Archie down because Archie had given him an opportunity to shine in the world. What Farrell had done to Archie was an affront to Luther as well. He knew he wasn't as good as Farrell with a gun or knife, but maybe he'd find some other way to get even with him. Archie would be pleased with that.

It took him about an hour and a quarter to make it from Downtown to the location of The Original Southport Club in Jefferson. Although it was nearing closing time, there were still cars in the lot, and Luther recognized the sound of Louis Bras' trumpet leaking out as someone opened the club front door.

Luther figured that going in the front door might not be the best way to handle this. The fewer people saw him, the better it would be. If he had to get tough with the

Donovan jane, it wouldn't do for anyone to've seen him go in to talk to her.

He circled around the perimeter of the building until he found a service entrance that was unlocked. He palmed the knob, peeked inside, then slid through the opening. As he looked around, he figured that if the Donovan woman wasn't on the floor, she'd be in an office. Likely enough, the club offices were upstairs. He walked farther inside until he found a hall. The hall led to stairs and he crept up them, listening between footfalls for the sound of another person.

The upstairs was dark for the most part, but he caught a glow of light puddling at the foot of a door. He walked closer until he saw the door was open just a crack. He peeked inside, and saw a woman that made his mouth run water. Her back was to him, and all he could see was flawless brown skin with a kind of cape of purple silk hanging over one shoulder. Lustrous dark hair fell to the woman's shoulders, and the curves of her body made Luther's fingers itch just from looking at her. He pushed the door open and walked softly inside.

When he closed the door, the sound it made was enough for the woman to whirl around at him. Her movement was such a surprise that Luther jumped back a step. Her face was the answer to the promise her body made.

"Who are you?" she demanded. Her face was set like stone and her black eyes blazed at him imperiously.

"Devereau's the name," Luther said. "I work for Archie Badeaux."

"Get out," she said, holding her fists down at her side. "Get out before I call downstairs for help."

Luther moved like a snake, rushing up on her before she could move. She raised her fists to hammer at him, but he caught both of them in one hand, then clapped his other hand over her mouth. "Yellin' like that wouldn't be polite," he said. "Not before I give you a message. Archie Badeaux said for you not to use his name no more to Wes

Farrell. Mr. Badeaux don't like punks like Farrell comin' around, botherin' him and all."

She struggled against his hand, her face darkening with blood as she struggled to break free and cry out for help. Luther grunted as her fury tested his strength. He knew that she'd get free of him soon, so he did the only thing he knew—he took his hand from her mouth and slapped her as hard as he could. The blow rang out like a pistol shot, and she went limp in his arms.

It took him aback for a second. He hadn't thought he'd hit her that hard, and he realized her ruse just in time to keep from catching her knee in his groin. "You li'l bitch," he said through his teeth. He slapped her again, catching her over the ear this time. She went limp again, for real this time, and he dragged her to the leather sofa, pushing her down on it. He was breathing heavily now, her flesh under his hands having inflamed his passions in more ways than one.

"You—asked—for it," he said, panting. "That was just a sample. You fuck with Archie Badeaux again, and he'll come here personal and settle your hash." He put his hands on his hips, talking down to her like she was a defeated enemy, captive in his hands.

"You bastard," she said. "I'll fix you for that." She wiped her mouth roughly with the back of her hand as though trying to remove the taste of something vile from her lips.

"Hah!" Luther said. He took out his brass knuckles and slid them over the fingers on his right hand. He slapped the armored fist into his left palm, full of bravado. "If you think that, you got another think comin', babycakes. You say that again, I'll leave some marks on you that won't come off." He raised his hand threateningly, and was gratified to see her draw back. "You better be scared. If I come back, it'll be for the finish, get me?"

She looked at him speculatively, seeming to measure him with her eyes. He could detect no fear in her in spite of his threats or the pain he'd inflicted. Confused, he took the knuckles off his hands, and turned to go.

"How much is Badeaux paying you?" she asked in a clear, distinctive voice.

He whirled around, surprised by the strength and resolve he heard there. "What you say?"

"I said how much is Badeaux paying you?" she repeated. "Because I could probably pay you more."

"Hah!" Luther said, sneering, but he was intrigued. He'd never beaten a woman and had her talk to him this way. "You ain't got enough money for that. Me and Badeaux are pals. I been with him for years. You don't know what you're talkin' about."

She raised up from the leather sofa, her body unwinding like a cobra from a fakir's basket. She reached under her left arm and pulled down a zipper. The mauve silk came apart like the skin from a banana and Luther saw her flawless breasts come free of the dress. His mouth fell open and he backed up a step, surprised, frightened, and confused. He'd thought he had the upper hand, but she'd turned the tables on him with this move.

"What the fuck you think you're doin', woman?" he asked in a hollow voice. The breasts were round and perfect and pale tan with nipples the color of Belgian chocolate. In his entire life he'd never seen anything like them.

"I know what you're doin', and it ain't gonna work," he said weakly. His mouth and throat felt like a sand storm of epic proportions had whirled through him, drying up every drop of life-giving moisture in his body. "I ain't some kid never had a piece of tail before," he continued. "I done had dozens of women every bit as good as you—better, even."

She continued to walk toward him, ever so slowly. As she moved, the dress seemed to melt from her body, the cape catching first on her shoulder, then hanging on her right breast for a brief second before falling in a puddle at her feet. Her legs had the perfection of a Greek statue and the triangle of night black hair where her legs came together seemed to glisten in the light. She stepped free of the dress and he saw her lips had curled into a smile that had no humor in it, and that her left eyebrow had arched rakishly over her left eye. She put her arms around his neck and drew him toward her. His mouth was open and his tongue was trying to make words, but his mind had gone numb. All he knew at that moment was her arms and breasts and red lips and tongue and that strange glint in her eye. After a while he forgot his name and most everything else he knew, but by then he didn't care.

ISRAEL DAGGETT was asleep in his house on Dauphine Street, dreaming about his wedding day. He was standing before the priest in his best blue suit, and Margurite was there in a gown of the purest white. The priest was saying the wedding mass, but the bells were ringing too soon and drowning out the priest's words. "What did you say?" he kept asking, but the bells rang louder and the priest continued to say the mass without being heard. He turned to Margurite, and she was shaking his arm.

"Baby, wake up," she said. "It's Sam Andrews. Wake up, Iz."

He came awake all of a sudden, his heart pounding and his eyes wild. He looked around, saw he was at home in bed, and saw Margurite bending over him in her nightgown. "It's Detective Andrews. He said he needed you right away," she said.

He got up and took the phone from the night stand. "Yeah," he said.

"We found Shirley Macomb," Andrews said without greeting.

"Where?" Daggett asked, knowing the news would be bad. He looked at his watch and saw that it was five.

"The Zachary Taylor Bridge in City Park," Andrews said.

"I'll be there in twenty minutes," Daggett said.

He hung up the telephone and went to the wardrobe. He stripped off his pajama bottoms and threw them in the floor of the wardrobe. He quickly dressed in underwear, socks, white shirt, and the trousers of his brown suit. He stuffed the tail of the shirt into the waistband of the trousers, then threw a tie around his neck without knotting it.

"Is it bad?" Margurite asked from the bed.

"It's bad," he replied.

She said nothing. Daggett would sometimes share with her the things he experienced, but the murders he never spoke of, and she'd learned not to ask. He shoved his feet into a pair of shoes, then got his long-barreled .41 Colt Army Special and shoved it into the leather holster sticking out of his right hip pocket. He grabbed the jacket to the suit and his yellow Stetson, then went to her and kissed her on the cheek.

"You want me to make you some coffee before you go?" she asked.

"No time," he said. "I'll call you later, baby."

She nodded and he left the room.

As he walked out the front door and locked it behind him, it hit him that less than two years ago he'd been walking out of Angola State Penitentiary a convicted felon and a ruined man. He'd returned to the city to find a murdered sweetheart and his life shattered. Through some quirk of fate, he'd been thrown together with Wesley Farrell and the two of them had cut a swath through New Orleans that had turned the city inside out—but in the end he had been cleared of the false charge of murder that had stripped him of his police career and robbed him of five years of his life. Captain Frank Casey had gotten him his old job back with the police force, at his old rank, and money to help make up for all he had lost, and he had ended up marrying Margurite Sonnier and starting life over.

He had stepped back into his old career like he'd never left it—the rhythms of a cop's life were like something ingrained in him that he could never lose—like the flinty taste in his mouth when faced with yet another murder.

It took him twenty-five minutes to reach the bridge in

City Park, and as he got out of the car he saw Andrews and Martinez, another Negro Squad Detective, standing guard over a sheet-covered form. Standing at a distance were a few uniformed men and the intern and ambulance attendants in their white jackets. Daggett felt his heart accelerate, and the familiar flinty taste grew on the back of his tongue.

Andrews looked at him, and for once the man didn't have a leer on his face or a smart crack in his mouth. "Is it her?" Daggett asked.

Andrews bent down and lifted the sheet. She'd been in the water for a while, but not long enough to have bloated too badly. The face was still recognizable. She was dressed in a nightgown that was plastered obscenely to her body. Her jaw muscles were clenched and her eyes were wide open. Daggett couldn't look in them.

"A couple kids down here tryin' for some catfish before the sun come up found her," Andrews explained. "Looks like she was thrown in the water with a weight tied to her feet. They hooked her and dragged her to the surface."

"The doc's looked her over and couldn't find any bruises or cuts suggesting she might've been knocked unconscious," Martinez said. "Chloroformed, maybe." His eyes looked sick. "We found a gold identification bracelet on her arm," he added. "It says 'To Shirley from Ulysses.' It's got some little hearts engraved around the names."

"How long's the doc say she was in the water?" Daggett asked.

"About thirty-six hours," Andrews said, "which would be just about right if she disappeared when we think she did." He was quiet for a moment, then he said, "I want the man who did this. I want him to resist arrest."

"Okay," Daggett said. "I don't know if it'll do any good, but we gotta look for anybody who might've seen something. It will have happened during the night she disappeared. Check cab companies to see if any of their cabs came through here then, milk delivery trucks, mail carriers with special delivery mail—the works. Check the headquarters for this police district and see if they got any reports of suspicious activity. There's a bus that runs down this street—call New Orleans Public Service and find out who drove the bus that night. Move, before this trail gets any colder than it is now."

Daggett's outrage and energy seemed to flow from his words sending each officer off in a different direction, eyes hard and mouths set. Daggett nodded to the ambulance men and they put the body on a stretcher and loaded it into the wagon. In less than two minutes, Daggett stood alone at the murder scene.

Shirley Macomb was dead because Ulysses Bautain was dead, he reasoned. There had been some attempt to make it look like they'd run away together, but the killer's luck was bad. Finally, after months of dead ends, he had something to hang his theory on. A shame somebody else had to die to get you this far, he thought ruefully. If Bautain was dead, then it followed that the other Negro businessman who'd suddenly disappeared the month before was dead, too. Daggett didn't know what the connection between them was, but the disappearance of two such men was too much to call a coincidence.

Daggett had another theory, too. He believed that somehow the death of Malcolm Redding was connected to these other three deaths, but he didn't know how it fit yet. Everyone but the killer believed that Redding was a suicide, and Daggett had allowed them to keep on thinking that. He knew for a fact that it was a murder, but he didn't want the murderer to know he knew it yet. He was saving that little edge for later.

There was something else about that killing that was different from these others. Whoever had killed Redding hadn't been used to killing. He or she had puked their guts up outside the victim's car. Whoever had thrown Shirley Macomb, probably still alive, into the City Park lagoon hadn't been that squeamish. That could mean that the killer had gotten hardened to it as he'd gone along—or it could support the theory that there was more than one suspect involved in all four murders.

Daggett had a line of inquiry he wanted to follow today. He didn't know if it would pan out, but it was a place to start. He walked back to his car and started the engine. Before he could put the car in gear, the dispatcher radioed his call sign.

"Inspector thirty-seven, over," he said into the microphone.

"Signal Thirteen at 1757 Leonidas Street. Detective Gautier requests you meet him there, over," the dispatcher said.

"Roger," Daggett said. "I'm rolling." A Signal Thirteen was a murder. It was going to be a long and unpleasant day. He might not be able to call Margurite after all.

EARLY THE PREVIOUS evening, Ralphie Daniels had breathed a sigh of relief as he walked inside the air conditioned railroad terminal on Howard Avenue. Although he had few friends of his own, many of his brother's friends and business acquaintances knew him by sight and he dreaded the possibility of being seen by one or being stopped for idle conversation. He doubted his ability to get through even a few minutes of meaningless talk without somehow conveying his guilt. He knew beyond doubt that in order to stay out of trouble, he had to remain under cover until the train began to board.

He walked to the ticket window and found there an old white man wearing a green eye shade. The old man was peering at a schedule through thick glasses, making notes with a pencil. Ralphie cleared his throat.

The old man looked up. "May I help you?" he asked.

"Yes, sir," Ralphie said in a hoarse voice. He cleared it noisily and repeated himself. "Yes, sir, I'd like a ticket on the Los Angeles train." Ralphie felt that his entire body was quivering inside, and he wondered why it didn't show on the outside. He fidgeted and reached into the pocket where his money was hidden.

The old man wordlessly got out a ticket and began writing on it. It took him a few minutes to do everything he needed to do, and all the while Ralphie stood there trying not to shake while sweat ran down his face and back.

"That'll be tenty-seven seventy-five," the old man said finally. His words were so sudden that Ralphie nearly jumped a foot. He took out the roll of cash that his brother had given him and peeled off two twenty-dollar bills, which he handed to the old man. The ticket agent quickly made change, and counted it out exactly into Ralphie's waiting hand.

"The train leaves at eight, and I reckon they'll board a half-hour before, like usual, so you've got a couple of hours to kill, young fella," the old man said. "You can check your suitcase over there." He pointed over Ralphie's left shoulder, and Ralphie nodded. He turned to go, only to be halted by the old man's voice.

"Hey, wait a minute," the agent cried. "You near walked off and left your ticket." He held the ticket out at arm's length.

Ralphie gave him a sickly smile, took the ticket, and walked hurriedly to baggage check-in. He left his cardboard suitcase with the baggage man, received a chit for it, then walked slowly away as he consulted his pocket watch. He briefly considered taking a seat and just waiting there. But what if someone Chet knew came through and saw him? Chet had to know by now that Ralphie had double-crossed him and was running somewhere. Any friend of Chet's would be sure to tell his brother immediately. That might mean cops, and if the cops caught him, Ralphie knew Chet would have him sent to jail, sure as shooting.

Ralphie turned away from the waiting area and left the terminal by a side entrance. There were a few Negro cafés and joints not far away. One or two were disreputable enough that the likelihood of being seen there by any of Chet's upstanding, church-going friends was relatively small.

He hiked several blocks past Lee Circle to Erato Street, then cut down Erato for three blocks before he came to Mason's, a hangout favored by dock workers and less savory sorts. A tan barmaid three sizes larger at the bottom than she was at the top switched over to him with her tray held flat to her side. "What'll it be?" she asked around a wad of gum.

"Gimme a shot of Schenley's and a glass of Dixie to wash it down," he replied in a husky whisper. He had his collar turned up and his porkpie hat jammed down over his eyes, a gambit that caused more people to look at him than might've if he'd just walked in without a care in the world. Several peered at him over their shoulders, and briefly confided in whispers their opinions of what crime he might be guilty of. The barmaid brought him his drinks, took his dollar, and left him alone.

He bolted the shot, nearly strangling on it, then sipped the beer until he got his breath back. The knot in his stomach gradually loosened up, and he began to relax in the dim quiet of the tavern. Day after tomorrow, I'll be on Central Avenue in Los Angeles with a gal on each arm, he told himself. And Chet'll be in that hot dry cleaning shop with sweat down to his ankles. The image made him smile a little, and gradually he began to feel good about his life and forget the risks he was taking.

DAGGETT ARRIVED at the Leonidas Street address about forty minutes after receiving the call at City Park. Already on the scene were several uniformed cops questioning neighbors and bystanders, a couple of Negro detectives, and the ubiquitous ambulance with its crew of white-coated personnel. It reminded Daggett uncomfortably of what he'd left in the park. He got out of his car and began to hastily knot his tie as he walked toward the house where he saw Gautier on the porch. Daggett rubbed his face and realized that he hadn't shaved yet. It don't matter to the dead, he thought grimly.

"What we got here?" Daggett asked as he mounted the steps.

"Old lady with her skull caved in," Gautier said. "Neighbor saw her door wide open when he went out to get the morning paper. Come over, looked in the door, and found her on the floor with brains all over her face."

Daggett walked past Gautier, who fell into step behind him as he went inside. He saw a couple of print men at work, dusting everything in sight. There was a bloody poker lying beside the old woman's body. "What's her name?" he asked.

"Marcella Attaway," Gautier replied. Her and her late husband used to run a speak called Attaway's Four Aces. The old man died not long after Prohibition was lifted and the old lady eventually sold out."

"Jesus," Daggett said. "This place is a dump. I've seen pigs in cleaner places."

"Neighbor said she stayed drunk half the time. Never saw anybody, never came outside that he knew of. She'd have groceries and liquor delivered to her from the stores. Once in a while, he said, a delivery van would come through and deliver something. That radio-phonograph," he said, pointing to where the set remained with its dials glowing, "was something he remembered the Radio Center deliverin' a couple years back. It's a beauty—reckon it must cost about five hundred dollars."

Daggett let his eyes wander around the room, taking in the expensive furnishings amid the squalor. Expensive bottles of scotch and bourbon lay about—all empty. He tried to imagine why the old woman could afford such luxuries, yet lived in such unmitigated filth, and couldn't come up with any reasonable suggestion.

"The old man must've left her pretty well fixed," Daggett said.

"Not according to her bank balance," Gautier said. "I

found it in a desk drawer—got about a hundred bucks and change in it. It's been dormant for several years. Either she's got money hidden somewhere, or somebody else was buying the stuff for her."

Daggett went closer to the body and knelt down beside it. Her arms were flung out from her body. He picked up one of the chilly hands and inspected it. There was a diamond and emerald ring on her ring finger, and a delicate bracelet of gold mesh encircled the wrist. "Whoever killed her didn't do it for the money—she's got a fortune on this hand," he said in a musing voice.

"That ain't all," Gautier said. "After she was killed, whoever did it upchucked all over the rug here."

Daggett came erect with startling speed. "What?"

Gautier looked at his boss with a curious expression. "Over here, boss," he said, pointing to his right. "Left his dinner all over the carpet. Real mess."

Daggett walked over to where Gautier pointed, and saw the drying puddle of vomit on the rug. It wasn't the most unusual thing in the world, but it had been his experience that people driven to murder were usually pretty keyed up until some time after the killing was done. They might get sick later, they might be overcome with remorse and drink themselves into a coma, but he'd seen very few killers who stopped to vomit right after the killing. They wanted to get away as quickly as possible.

"Anybody see anything?" he asked Gautier.

"So far, the only thing we know is that somebody in a Harker Brothers cab stopped here late last night, and the driver parked out front of the house until the passenger came out again. We're checking with them to see what the driver can tell us. Found one other thing, too."

"What's that?" Daggett asked.

"Killer left a glove behind—a right hand glove made of gray suede. Probably wore it in here, took it off to check the old woman's pulse, then forgot to pick it up again. The sonofabitch was some rattled, I guess."

"Any maker's name in the glove?" Daggett asked.

"Yeah, but not a local company," Gautier said. "It's for a small hand, which means a woman could've done the killin'. It fits with the vomiting."

"Maybe," Daggett said, but he doubted it. There were some bad women in the world—he and Wesley Farrell had jailed one of the worst he'd ever known the previous year—but this kind of savagery was unusual in the female criminals he'd known. "We gotta get something together fast. We got another woman killed over in City Park—we need a break on both of them. I'm gonna put the whole squad on these two killings. You run this half, I'll put Martinez on the other."

"What're you gonna do, boss?" Gautier asked.

"I got some people to see," Daggett said, then he walked away, got into his car, and drove away, leaving Gautier staring after him with a puzzled expression.

Chapter 8

WESLEY FARRELL slept only a few hours, awaking sometime after seven. He lay in the bed for a long time after waking, studying the ceiling in the gray light of dawn, thinking back over the previous night. He'd spent much of his adult life minding his own business, thinking over a situation before he'd commit himself to it. Last night was a change from that. He'd deliberately sought out a man who was no threat to him personally, threatened him, humiliated him in front of his woman. Then Farrell had gone to see a woman, he realized now, with nothing more on his mind but going to bed with her. He'd pretended to himself, and to Carol, that he hadn't come there for that, but at the last minute his desire for her was so strong that it nearly overpowered both of them.

He turned over on his side and looked at the empty pillow beside him. His longing for Savanna had become more intense, if that were possible. His loneliness was making him reckless, and that, he knew, was not a good thing.

He sat up and threw his legs over the side of the bed, then got up and went to the shower. He spent a long time in there, shaving in a small mirror he'd had installed, then got out, toweled himself dry, dressed in a fresh singlet and shorts, then went to the kitchen and made a pan of ham and eggs, a pile of whole wheat toast, and a pot of coffee. He sat down and devoured it, not really tasting it, and feeling surprised when he looked down at the plate and found it empty.

He put the dirty dishes in the sink, brushed his teeth, then dressed himself. He spent some time at his desk taking care of invoices, business correspondence, and his ledger. When he was finished, he saw from the clock on his desk that it was nearly noon. He found himself restless, got up and walked around the apartment, then went downstairs and talked to Harry Slade at the bar, inspected the kitchen, then went back upstairs.

He looked at the telephone and thought about calling Carol. He had no idea what he'd say to her, and felt vaguely foolish. He turned to look out the window and thought back again over what he'd learned from Molly Tatum. The transvestite seemed to know a great deal about the doings of Badeaux and his boss, Jonathan Lincoln. Farrell didn't like the idea that a new player could come into town and burrow his way into the fabric of the community without him even knowing it. It bespoke a calculation and shrewdness beyond the average—it reminded him uncomfortably of the late Emile Ganns. He thought, too, of some rumors that had been circulating about some Negro businessmen—rumors that linked them with the mysterious newcomer. The possible involvement of Rogers Clifton, president of the largest Negro-owned bank in the city, heightened Farrell's sense of disquiet. He knew nothing bad about Clifton, but even the suggestion of an involvement between Lincoln and a man trusted with the savings of hundreds of Negro families left a bad taste in Farrell's mouth.

He opened the top right-hand drawer of his desk and took out the stiletto, razor, and a Luger automatic, and stowed them about his person, then he got up, retrieved his pearl gray Stetson, and left the office.

Ten minutes later he was parking down the block from

the offices of *The Louisiana Weekly*, the most important Negro newspaper in Louisiana, and one of the most influential in the region. At the reception desk he found a young woman with dark brown skin and large brown eyes. She wore a pair of glasses with heavy black bakelite frames, and her black hair was gathered at the back of her neck with a black velvet ribbon. She was just finishing up taking notes over the telephone when Farrell walked up.

"Yes, sir," she said as she hung up the phone. "How may I help you?"

"Is Sam Whately in?" Farrell asked.

"I think so," she replied, picking up the receiver of a house phone. "Who can I say is asking?"

"Wesley Farrell."

The girl dialed a two-digit number, spoke quietly into the mouthpiece, then hung up. "He'll be right out," she said.

Almost as she finished talking, a short, thick-bodied Negro in his early fifties strolled in from the back. He was dressed in a rumpled pair of brown trousers and matching vest. His white shirt was open at the neck, his tie pulled askew. The vest was unbuttoned and held together by his heavy watch chain, with both shirt sleeves rolled to the elbow. "Afternoon, Mr. Farrell," Whately said around the butt of a well-chewed cigar. "What's up?"

Farrell went to him and shook hands. "Can I talk to you for a minute?"

"Sure," Whately said. "C'mon back." He turned and led Farrell back through a maze of desks and copy tables to a large rolltop in a rear corner. He took the oak swivel chair, and pulled up a battered side chair for Farrell.

"You worked the Redding case, didn't you?" Farrell asked.

"Yeah," Whately said, "but I ain't happy about it. I never seen a bigger mess than that, and I was never completely satisfied we got the whole truth. Redding was a good man—not one of them guys who goes to church on Sunday so everybody can see him slip a twenty into the collection plate—a man who did a lot of good in the community."

"That tallies with what I've heard, too," Farrell said. "He didn't sound like the kind of guy to pull a dutch act, either. He was supposed to've had guts."

"He didn't commit suicide," Whately asserted, "no matter what anybody says. Israel Daggett really disappointed me on that one."

"Iz is a good cop," Farrell said. "He must've had a reason for issuing that kind of a report."

"What he did was give rise to a lot of rumors about the man," Whately said angrily. "Such as the one that had Redding carryin' on with some tramp, that he embezzled money from his own bank and was about to be exposed—trash like that. I tell you, it makes me wild sometimes."

"Yeah," Farrell said sympathetically. "It's tough, all right."

"Whately's eyes narrowed as he looked at Farrell. "If you don't mind my askin', what makes you so interested in Redding, especially now, so long after the fact?" He took the cigar butt from his mouth, threw it into the trash, and leaned back, his fingers busy on the Phi Beta Kappa key that dangled from his watch chain. Farrell knew Whately had attended the prestigious journalism school at Indiana University.

"I was just thinking about some things," Farrell said. "None of it amounts to much." He paused and rubbed his chin in a thoughtful sort of way. "You know of any bad blood between Redding and Rogers Clifton?"

Whately stared at him for a second, his eyes shifting as they inspected Farrell's face. "What do you mean by 'bad blood,' exactly?" the old newshawk asked slowly.

"Clifton gained the most by Redding's death," Farrell said. "A man desperate enough might decide to remove his competition and then be ready to step into his shoes. It's happened before. And you said yourself that Redding's death was no suicide."

Whately's eyes became hooded, and he took a fresh cigar from his shirt pocket, bit off the end, then struck a kitchen match on his thumbnail. He took his time lighting the cigar, running the match flame up and down the length of it, toasting the outside as he puffed it into life. Finally, he said, "You sound like you know something the rest of us don't."

Farrell shrugged. "Just thinking out loud. What I really came to ask you is if you know anything about a man named Jonathan Lincoln."

Whately's eyes got a gleam in them, and he leaned forward in his chair and lowered his voice. "He worries me, Mr. Farrell. I don't know much about him, but I keep hearing rumors about him."

"What kind of rumors?"

"Well," Whately said, scratching his head. "Confusing things. Quiet little power plays, takeovers of land and businesses. Nothing blatant, mind you. You have a run-in with him?"

Farrell's face took on that unreadable quality that all gamblers cultivate, and his eyes got a little chilly. "Not really, but I heard some things about him—enough to make me want to know more. I figured if anybody in the city would know about him, it'd be you."

Whately smiled at Farrell's subtle flattery, and leaned back in his chair again. "He's been kinda quiet since he came here," Whately said. "It's known that Archie Badeaux and a few other local punks are on his payroll. Badeaux's been seen all over the place, but he ain't done anything to get himself arrested. I think Lincoln's playin' some deep game, something that'll make him a power in the colored underworld here."

"What do you know about him, personally, that is?" Farrell asked.

"He started out as just a cardsharp," Whately said. "Nobody knows where he come from, but he's got a lot of white blood in him, which might mean he's some planter's bastard. He made a rep in the Mississippi Delta back in the '90s and early 1900s, both as a card player and as a gunman. He couldn't possibly have killed all the people laid to his name, but he never minded killing.

"He went to Jackson about the time of the Great War," Whately continued, "and built an empire of sorts up there—gambling, women, booze, even narcotics after Prohibition set in. Not that Prohibition bothered him much. He had a fleet of transport trucks and stills, too. Half of Western Mississippi got liquored up on Jonathan Lincoln's hooch every Saturday night during the '20s."

"So why's he down here?" Farrell asked.

"Factions in his empire got to fightin', and even he had trouble keeping them at bay. There was a woman he was close to—ran a house full of women—prime stuff, no street trash—named Manda Hayes. Kinda funny, that name, too. Lincoln sometimes called himself 'Greenback' Hayes when he was young. Anyhow, there was a brawl at this place, he got shot in the back and left for dead. The Hayes woman disappeared, and it was rumored that she'd been the one who killed him—except he wasn't dead."

"That's why he's in the wheelchair," Farrell said.

"Bingo," Whately said. "The shot cut his spine in half, but it didn't kill him. He had a couple boys who were loyal to him to the end. Supposedly they got him to a doctor, saved his life. Without his legs, he probably felt like a sittin' duck up there in Jackson. He dropped out of sight, turned up here a bit more than a year ago."

Farrell nodded. "Tell me, Sam. What do you know about Carol Donovan—the woman who owns The Original Southport Club?"

"Not much," he confessed. "Went out there once and spoke to her. Pleasant enough—a real looker, too. I heard she was from up Memphis way, had run something similar there. Why do you ask?"

"I heard a rumor," Farrell replied. "That Archie Badeaux was trying to force her to sell out."

Whately gazed at Farrell speculatively. "If that's true, it's mighty funny," the reporter said. "A nightclub's a bit out of Lincoln's line, unless he wants to use it as a front for something else. I know one thing, though."

"What's that?"

"If Badeaux told her to get out, she better get. Ain't been a woman born who could stand up to that murderous bastard. He'd gut her, use her for fishbait, and eat ice cream while he was doin' it."

Farrell nodded, his face expressionless. "Thanks, Sam. I appreciate the time. Call me if you need anything, hear?" He got up and stuck out a hand.

Whately rose from his chair and shook Farrell's hand. "Sure, thanks, Mr. Farrell."

Farrell turned and left the newsroom. Whately watched him thread his way through the crowded room, his mind working like a calculating machine. He sat back down, consulted an address book, and then began dialing the telephone.

ISRAEL DAGGETT stopped in at the barber shop on the ground floor of the Astoria Hotel and got himself a shave, then he made a trip over to the Merchants and Farmers Homestead Bank. It was mid-morning by the time he got there, and most of the tellers' windows were occupied with lines of Negro men and women there to do their banking. The Homestead was a three-story structure of heroic Georgian architecture. The inside had impressive marble columns. Paintings of the two Negro businessmen who'd started the bank near the end of the nineteenth century were enshrined over the elevator door. Daggett got in and asked the operator to take him to the top.

The elevator opened onto a reception area lushly carpeted in red shag. A beautiful woman with red-brown skin and dark blonde hair sat at a mahogany desk typing on a big Underwood. She looked up as the elevator door opened, and turned to greet him.

"Good morning," she said in a cultured voice. "May we help you?"

Daggett took out his badge case and opened it so she could see his gold star-and-crescent shield. "Sergeant Daggett, ma'am. I'd like to speak to Mr. Clifton."

"He's rather busy," she said, folding her hands on the desk. "Perhaps I can help you."

"I don't think so," he replied. "This is in regard to a murder case we're working on."

"Oh," she said, a little shocked. "Surely you don't think..."

"I don't think anything—yet," he said. "I'm still investigating, gathering facts. I hope Mr. Clifton can enlighten me on some things."

He could tell from her eyes that she was disturbed, but she kept her composure, picked up the intercom phone, and buzzed Clifton. "Yes, sir. There's a Detective Daggett with the New Orleans Police out here. He wants to ask you some questions. About a murder, he said. Yes. Yes. Of course." She put the phone back in its cradle and got up from the desk. "He'll see you right away," she said. She opened the door to Clifton's office, stood aside so he could enter, then closed the door behind him.

Daggett found himself in a beautifully-decorated office with oak panels on the walls, leather sofa and chairs, and an oak desk large enough to land an army bombing plane on. Clifton stood behind the desk in his shirt sleeves, his expression neutral.

"Sergeant Daggett, isn't it?" he said as he gestured at a chair across the desk from him. "I read about you in the papers some time ago. Something about you being cleared of an old murder charge, I believe."

"You've got a good memory," Daggett said, placing his hat on the edge of the massive desk and sitting down in a red leather side chair. "I didn't think that news mattered to anybody but me and the men who framed me."

"What happened to you was disgraceful," Clifton said with a trace of mild outrage. "So typical of how our people are treated."

Daggett said nothing to that. This wasn't where he wanted the conversation to go. "I'm here about Ulysses Bautain," he said.

"Yes?" Clifton said, his eyebrows raised interrogatively.

"According to the *maître d'* at the Sassafrass Lounge, you had dinner with him there two nights ago," Daggett said.

"Yes," Clifton said, nodding. "We had some business to discuss."

"What was the nature of the business?"

A curtain came down behind Clifton's eyes, and he laced his fingers together on top of his desk. "I'm not at liberty to discuss the business of bank patrons, Sergeant."

"Let me put it another way," Daggett said. "After you had dinner with him, Bautain disappeared."

Clifton's face lost some of its haughtiness. "Ridiculous," he said. "He's one of the most successful businessmen in the city—he wouldn't just up and leave the city."

"No," Daggett said. "It seems unlikely to me, too. But then his secretary disappeared, too."

"His secretary?" Clifton's face was shocked, and his professional demeanor seemed to slip a little.

"That's right," Daggett said. "Shirley Macomb's body was fished out of City Park lagoon early this morning. We don't know for certain, but she might've been thrown in there while she was still alive."

"Dear God," Clifton said in a hushed voice.

"Whoever killed the Macomb woman killed Bautain, too," Daggett said. "We don't have a body, but the Macomb woman's death makes it almost certain. She and Bautain were having an affair, and the killers made a sloppy attempt to make it look like they'd run away together. What I want to know is why Bautain was killed."

Clifton's professional face came back. "Why come to me?

"Because you're probably the last person to see him alive before the killer got to him," Daggett said. "I can't help but wonder what you talked about—and where you went after the two of you parted company."

Clifton got up from his desk, his face a mask of fury. "This is the most outrageous treatment I've ever had in my life," he stormed. "You can't come in here and accuse me—"

Daggett held up a hand. "You're jumpin' the gun, Mr. Clifton. I didn't accuse you of anything. I said you were probably the last person to see him alive. What was it you talked about?"

"We talked about a dozen things," Clifton said impatiently, striding back and forth behind the desk. "Merchants and Farmers is the most important Negro lending institution in the state. He was a man of many different enterprises—naturally he'd come to me and talk about investment opportunities."

"Did you talk about a piece of land on the eastern side of the city?" Daggett said quickly.

Clifton's mouth was still open, but he stopped, closed his mouth, and looked down at Daggett, who hadn't moved. "I—well, we may have, I don't remember," the banker said.

"His widow says you were talking to him about selling it, and that he was a little steamed up about it," Daggett said. "She said he believed the land would be worth a pretty penny, and that you were trying to get it cheap."

"Well, if I was," Clifton said huffily, "I was only practicing normal business. For the love of God, Sergeant Daggett, any businessman tries to get something for the least possible price. So would you, if the circumstances were reversed."

Daggett nodded, "Maybe so, maybe so." He got up and picked up his Stetson from the desk. "Thanks a lot for your time, Mr. Clifton. I may call you again if I've got more questions. Have a good day now, hear?"

"Yes, good day," Clifton said. He sat down at his desk and made a show of rustling papers. When Daggett was gone, he picked up his private telephone and dialed Lincoln's number. Albert picked it up on the second ring.

"Put Lincoln on," he said. "This is Clifton."

It was only a matter of a moment before the old man came on the line. "Yes, Mr. Clifton, what may I do for you this afternoon?" The old man was positively insouciant.

"What may you do?" Clifton said in a hoarse whisper. "The police were just here. They said you've killed Ulysses Bautain's secretary. They found her in the City Park lagoon this morning. What are you thinking?"

"Perhaps something went wrong," Lincoln said calmly. "I suspect the men handling that didn't deal with the situation in the best way they could."

"For God's sake, Lincoln, when I agreed to help you, I didn't sign on to be your accomplice in wholesale murder. Killing an innocent woman—how low can you get?"

"That's an interesting question for you to be asking," the old man said calmly. "You're in this up to your neck, Clifton. The better part of wisdom on your part would be to do what you're told and not do anything that would bring undue comment on our operations."

"But you've killed three people," Clifton said in a pleading voice. "Bautain and Johnson I could understand—they were an obstacle to your plans—but the woman—"

"Tut, tut, tut," Lincoln said. "What's done is done. Do what I said, and you'll have nothing to worry about. Get out of hand, and there's no telling what may happen. Do you understand me, Clifton?" The old man's voice had become brittle and cold, and even the show of *politesse* with which he normally conducted his conversations fell away like dust.

"Yes. I understand," Clifton said in a hushed voice.

Lincoln hung up the telephone, and after a moment, Clifton placed his in the cradle. He put his forearms on the desk and put his face down in the cradle they made. He remembered the time he'd broken a stained glass window in the parish church with a rock, and felt the same hopelessness he'd felt that day, as though he were forever damned, with no hope of redemption in this life or the next.

Ernie LeDoux woke to the sun streaming in from the street window. The curtains billowed gently in with a cool breeze. He sat up and rubbed his face. He'd slept badly the night before after his inconclusive meeting with Marcella Attaway. As he sat there thinking, he became more and more certain that the old woman was holding out on him—that she'd found the stolen payroll and was living it up. She'd no doubt bought the house, the expensive phonograph, the glittering jewelry she had on her unwashed limbs. He got angry thinking about it, remembering the times he'd chopped cane in hundred degree weather. Three times he'd been bitten by rattlesnakes out there in the cane fields. Once he'd nearly died from the bite. It came to him that he'd have to go back there and make her tell him where the money was. He couldn't let this lie after all he'd been through.

He heard Ruby come to beside him, yawning and stretching. He turned and saw her tawny body come loose from the sheets, and he momentarily forgot Marcella Attaway as she reached for him. They were busy with each other for the next fifteen minutes or so, and the material world fell away from him.

Afterward, he lay in the bed listening to her sing in the shower, and he had time to remember what he was thinking about before. He frowned as he lay there.

Ruby came out of the bathroom wrapping a towel around herself and she went to the window to look out on the street. She stiffened as she stood there, and her right hand reached involuntarily behind her, as though she were trying to touch him. "Ernie," she said. "Ernie, get up, sugar."

"What?" he asked.

"Baby, they's two cars fulla cops just pulled up out front," she said. "What could they want here?"

LeDoux jumped from the bed and ran to the window, being careful to keep out of sight. He saw two Negro detectives and four uniformed officers getting out of their cars.

"Ernie, you better get outta here," she said, an edge of hysteria in her voice.

"Why?" he asked. "I ain't done nothin'."

"Baby, you're an ex-con. It don't make no difference if you did or you didn't. They liable to shoot you on sight. C'mon, we gettin' outta here."

With a speed that was truly remarkable, Ruby wriggled into her dress and shoved her feet into shoes. LeDoux, confused but caught up in her alarm, hurriedly pulled on pants and shirt, grabbing his jacket, tie, wallet, and the .45 automatic from his bag. They ran into the hall, leaving the room door ajar, and raced to the fire stairs at the opposite end. LeDoux figured they might cover the front and the service door, but they might not think of the fire escape until later.

Their shoes rang on the metal steps as they hurled themselves down at a breakneck pace. They made the alley, and Ruby pulled him in the direction of Canal Street. Somehow they got by the cops because they heard no whistles or shouts behind them. An old hand at eluding notice, Ernie jerked Ruby to a more sedate walk and used the time to straighten his clothes and knot his tie around his neck. Ruby took a hair brush from her purse and gave her hair a few licks as she walked beside them. Within a block they looked reasonably respectable again.

"If it turns out they was lookin' for somebody else, we're gonna look mighty stupid," LeDoux said. "I hardly been out of the room since I got to town. Fact is, only places I been was to Avery's 'tonk out in Jeff Parish, then to see old Marcella Attaway."

"Why'd you wanna go see that miserable old bitch?" Ruby said as they crossed Canal and entered the Quarter.

Something that Ernie couldn't explain made him decide not to answer that question with the whole truth. "Oh, well, you know, I was mighty fond of Ben, and when I heard he was dead I just wanted to go say I was sorry and ask her what I could do for her. She didn't need anything, though. Looked like Ben left her pretty well fixed."

"Humph," she snorted. "They didn't act like they had a pot to pee in nor a window to throw it out of after you got sent up, 'specially after Prohibition got repealed."

"Yeah?" LeDoux said casually. Inside he was castigating himself for not being completely straightforward with Ruby—after all, this was the woman he wanted to spend the rest of his life with. But he recalled that she'd been evasive about her goings and comings lately, and he'd begun to feel a little uneasy about the way she'd just disappear or drop in without any warning or notice. Besides, there might be some danger for her in knowing too much about his troubles.

"We gotta go somewhere and lay low until we find out what's what, Ernie," Ruby said.

"I ain't got a place in this world to go," he said.

"I know a place," she said. "It ain't much—fact is, it's a parlor house."

LeDoux looked at her sharply.

"Don't go lookin' at me like that," she said with heat in her voice. "I wasn't but a kid when you got sent up. What was I supposed to do, anyhow? Scrub floors?"

"Well, I don't know," he said for lack of a better thing. He'd been wondering where she been keeping herself, and now he knew, and was strangely crestfallen. "Don't worry about it, baby," he said in a dull voice. "Ain't many of us has done all the right things all the time."

A Harker Brothers cab rolled down toward them, and Ruby stepped into the street and flagged it down. She and LeDoux piled into the back seat.

"Where you folks wanna go?" the driver said over his shoulder.

"Take us to the Desire Street Wharf," Ruby said. "I'll show you where to go from there."

"You called it," the driver said, and he headed out toward Canal Street.

LeDoux looked at Ruby without saying anything. Ruby ignored him, and used her compact mirror to make up her face.

THE SUN WAS getting low in the sky as Marcel began his search of the juke joints, taverns, and cafés within easy walking distance of the railroad station. Along the way he resisted the blandishments of two banana-skinned prostitutes who wanted to take him around the world, talked to a numbers runner who wanted a job, and bought two cups of coffee he really didn't want. It was getting closer and closer to train time, and so far not even a glance at anyone who remotely resembled Ralphie Daniels. If he somehow eluded Marcel and made the California train—Marcel didn't want to even contemplate the possibility. He didn't know how he'd be able to face Wes with such a failure.

It was about seven fifteen when his luck turned. He had wandered over to Erato Street, thinking to try his luck at Mason's Tavern, when he saw a man emerge from the joint. Although Marcel was a full block away, the man fit the general description he had of Ralphie Daniels. Moreover, the man was nervous—it was evident in his posture and in the way he continually moved his head from side to side, up and back, surveying and measuring everything in his path. Marcel was careful to continue on at a lazy walk, not seeming to pay attention to the man.

The man crossed Erato and headed back in the direction of the terminal. Marcel, on the opposite side of the street, pretended to be deep in thought until they were abreast of each other. He turned quickly into the street and headed toward Ralphie.

"Ralph Daniels," Marcel called in a loud, clear voice.

Daniels froze for a second, then turned quickly, his hand streaking to his waistband. Marcel saw the revolver sweep up just in time to throw himself face down in the street. The gun exploded and Marcel heard the bullet whine past him. He looked up in time to see Daniels legging it for all he was worth away from there.

Marcel was up in a flash, running flat out behind the other man. "Daniels," he yelled. "Stop now."

Daniels didn't even look back, but Marcel knew he couldn't start shooting back at him. Hitting a moving target was chancy at best, and the likelihood of hitting a bystander too great. Marcel wasn't thinking much about shooting, though. He wanted to get his hands on Ralphie Daniels' neck and pound his head into the pavement. Marcel had discovered in that split second that he didn't like being shot at a damned bit.

Daniels could run like a rabbit, and he darted down an alley. Marcel followed at full speed, knowing that he couldn't lose sight of him or the man might successfully make the train. He careened into the alley in time to see Daniels reach over his shoulder and fire again. This time the shot was high and Marcel didn't even feel the need to duck. If the fool kept shooting, though, somebody would call a cop, and if a white cop got his hands on Ralphie, Marcel knew he and Chet could kiss the money goodbye.

He saw Ralphie cut down Thalia Street and head toward the River. Although his breath was becoming labored, Marcel knew that Ralphie had to be tired, too. The riverfront was a dead end, and he figured he'd be able to cut the other man off pretty soon.

They were nearing Tchopitoulas Street when Marcel saw a car two blocks down turn on to Thalia and head toward them. Then Ralph did something completely unexpected. He ran into the street toward the car, shoving his gun out in front of him. The car skidded to a stop. Ralph tore open the door, dragged the driver out by his collar, then jumped behind the wheel. Marcel had his Iver Johnson .38 out at arm's length. The car roared toward him, the still-open door flapping as the car picked up speed. Marcel was forced to throw himself to one side to escape being hit, and by the time he'd found his feet again, the car was turning the corner two blocks away.

"Goddamnedsonofabitchingbastard," Marcel swore. He'd never felt so frustrated in his life. He turned and found an old man trying very painfully to get to his feet, so he walked over and helped the old man up.

"Wh-what happened?" the old man ask in a dazed voice. His skin was the color of red clay, and he had enough wrinkles for three men. His straw hat had fallen from his shiny bald head, so Marcel bent over and picked it up for him.

"I was chasing that guy," Marcel said bitterly. "And he stole your car to get away."

"Y-you a po-leece man?" the old timer asked.

"No, just a sucker," Marcel replied. "What's your name?"

"Willard Tomkins," the man replied. "What am I gonna do?" His voice nearly broke, and Marcel knew without being told that the car was important to him.

"Do you live far from here?" he asked.

"Down off'n St. Roch Avenue," Tomkins said. "I don't think I can walk it, not with this leg feelin' this way."

"C'mon," Marcel said, getting an arm around him. "Lean on me, and we'll get you a taxi. I'll pay for it, and leave you enough money to get around on for a few days. He'll probably abandon the car, so call the police as soon as you get home so they can get a message out to their patrols. With any luck, you'll have the car back in a day or so."

"Oh, you think so?" Tompkins said hopefully. "You're mighty kind, mister. What's your name?"

"Aristide. Marcel Aristide," he replied. He felt pretty useless at that moment, and wondered how he'd ever explain all this to Wes when he saw him. He didn't even know what he'd tell Chet Daniels, and dreaded having to let him know that his brother was still loose with his seven hundred dollars. Marcel knew that if he couldn't get Daniels' money back, he couldn't stand by and let Nate Hopkins take the laundry away from him.

As he walked down the street supporting the wounded old man, he found himself wondering if this was how Wes got the reputation he had for helping people out. All you had to do was have a soft spot and be in the wrong place at the wrong time, he thought dolefully. Now there would be two of them with a reputation that neither wanted.

As soon as he got the old man situated, he'd return to the railroad depot, but he had a hunch that Ralphie, in his panic, would not return there, fearing that it might now be watched. With Marcel's men at the other terminals, Ralphie couldn't get out of town through any of them. As scared as he was, he'd probably go to ground somewhere in the city. Marcel thought that he'd really relish breaking both of Ralphie's legs himself if he ever found him.

Chapter 9

BADEAUX WAS in the kitchen at the back of the sweet shop on Clouet Street when Luther came back in. Luther was still wearing the clothing he'd worn the night before, and looked a little hung over.

"Where the hell you been?" Badeaux demanded. "I sent you out to knock a bitch around, not go on no vacation. Did you tell her?"

"Huh?" Luther asked. He walked to the stove where coffee was on, got himself a clean cup from the dish drainer and poured himself a cup. He could tell from Archie's voice that he'd just taken a hit of the white power. At times like this, a man had to walk soft if he wanted to go on walking.

"Don't 'huh' me, nigger," Badeaux shouted. "I said did you tell her?"

"Oh, yeah," Luther said. "I told her. I smacked her around plenty, Archie." He sipped his coffee, and didn't look at Badeaux.

"Then where the hell you been all night?"

Luther turned and looked at Archie for a moment, then smiled and looked away. "Aw, after I'd slapped her around a while, I got me a head of steam up and hadda find a stray broad to work it off on."

Badeaux's face got hot. His woman had been chased off,

and here was this fuckin' errand boy of his gettin' his itches scratched. It made Badeaux feel meaner than forty hells. "I'd still like to know what the fuck's goin' on," Badeaux grumbled. "I never once crossed Farrell's path, and never even heard of that bitch, and I get stepped on—hard, I mean. He might'a slugged you, Luther, but he shoved a scattergun in my fuckin' face."

As Luther listened, he realized that probably for the first time in his life, something had scared Archie Badeaux. Luther was a shrewd judge of human nature, and he knew that sooner or later, Archie would want to do something about that—would want to get back up on the horse that had bucked him off. Luther knew Archie'd want him along to help him, and that was a job Luther wanted nothing to do with. He'd seen how fast Farrell had moved, and how little he regarded the shotgun in Luther's hand when he struck like a rattler. He nodded vaguely, kept his mouth shut, and sipped some more coffee.

"Well, what'd she say?" Badeaux demanded. "What'd she say when you slapped her around and told her what was what?"

"She cried and screamed a li'l—you know how women is, man. She said she'd lay off you, is what she said." Luther went to the electric icebox and rummaged around in there until he found a couple of fried chicken breasts and a left-over piece of French bread. He took the food to the table, sat down, and began to eat. He studiously avoided looking at Badeaux, because he feared that if Badeaux looked in his eyes, he'd know he was lying—would know that he'd been disloyal, and would be disloyal again. Archie would kill him on the spot. He needed to change the subject.

"Y'know, Archie, I was thinkin' maybe we oughta start havin' a man—somebody pretty tough, I mean—to hang around outside the places where we got action goin' on. He'd be like a—what do you call it?"

"How the hell do I know what you call it?" Badeaux said

irritably. "I don't even know what the fuck you're talkin' about."

"A—a first line of defense, that's it," Luther said, suddenly remembering the line from an article he'd read in *Time* magazine. "That way, if somebody like Farrell shows up, tryin' to get tough, this guy could maybe take him out. And if the tough guy gets by this outside guy, the guy inside the joint—me—would have that much more warning that trouble was comin' through the door."

Badeaux looked at Luther, bent over his plate munching chicken like it was the best thing God ever made. Luther acted stupid sometimes, but there was a brain under there and every once in a while he'd use it and surprise the shit out of you. "Maybe you got somethin' there, Luther. We'll get some guys in and try it out." Badeaux sounded calmer now, and Luther felt the muscles in his neck and shoulders loosen as the tension in the room diminished.

"Right, Archie. You're the man," Luther said around a bite of chicken.

Badeaux looked at Luther some more. Something wasn't right, or at least it wasn't the same, and he couldn't quite put his finger on it. It made him itchy, and he didn't like it.

The telephone rang, and Badeaux went to it. "Badeaux," he said into the mouthpiece.

"It's Ruby," a woman's voice said. "Some shit is hittin' the fan."

"Where you at?" Badeaux asked.

"I'm at the house near the Desire Street Wharf," she replied. "He's here with me. Some cops decided to raid the Metro. I figured they hadda be there after him, and I didn't figure we could afford to let them grab him before we found out where the money was."

"Shit," Badeaux said. "Reckon it was the right thing, baby. He tumble to anything yet?"

"I had to tell him I'd been turnin' tricks while he was in the slam. He ain't takin' it too well, but other than that everything's jake," she said. "You better find out why the cops were after him. If they grab him before he leads us to the money, we're up the creek."

"You ain't got to tell me that," Badeaux said testily. "Keep him occupied for a while, and don't let him go out without you. I'll call my man at the police station, see what he can tell me. This week ain't been nothin' but trouble since it began."

"What're you talkin' about?" she asked.

"Wes Farrell come in here last night, cold-cocked Luther, shot the place up, and told me to stay away from somebody I never even heard of," he replied. "Other than that, life's a *fuckin'* bowl of cherries."

"Watch out for him, baby," she said. "He's poison."

"Fuck it. Just stay glued to LeDoux. Hit him on the fuckin' head if you got to."

"I hear you," she said, then she hung up the phone.

Badeaux hung up his receiver, his face a darkening thundercloud. He turned to where Luther was sitting, but the man was gone. He looked in the office, the gaming room, and out in the sweet shop, but Luther had vanished.

AFTER FARRELL left the newspaper office, he began to see a picture forming, but he also knew there was more going on than this brief glimpse had furnished him. There was more—a lot more, and he felt a genuine hunger to get to the bottom of it all. He drove back Downtown and found himself on Rampart Street. He slowed for traffic, and recognized Savanna's old joint, the Club Moulin Rouge, to his left. He pulled to the curb on an impulse, cut the engine, and got out of the car. He walked to the front door of the club and stood there quietly, as though listening for some hot jazz licks to escape from behind the locked door, or for Savanna to walk out in her red sheath to invite him inside.

You got to get a grip on yourself, he said in his mind. You lost her, plain and simple, because you were too goddamned stubborn and full of pride to get on an airplane and find her. You blew it, and that's what you've got to live with now—not the fact that she's gone, but that you wouldn't get up and go after her. Now you're running all over like a chicken with his head cut off just trying to fill up the empty hole that you dug in your own heart.

The truth of his self-imposed lecture was so devastating that he felt his knees tremble for a second. He turned around on the sidewalk, oblivious to the foot traffic that flowed around him as though he were a huge rock in a rushing river. He didn't know what to do with himself, or with the new revelation. He got back into the car and turned it around and then headed for Police Headquarters. Ten minutes later he was parking his Packard convertible a half-block down.

He found Mrs. Longley, his father's secretary, at the desk typing correspondence when he came through the reception room door.

"Mr. Farrell," she said brightly. "Here to see the Captain?"

"Yes, ma'am," Farrell said. "If he's not too busy."

"I think he'll see you," she said with a smile. She was somewhere in her middle forties, auburn-haired and blue-eyed, and there seemed to be an inexhaustible well of youthful good cheer in her. He wondered if his father had ever noticed that. She punched the intercom button, spoke briefly with Casey, then got up and opened the door to his father's office for him. He smiled, walked inside, and took off his Stetson.

"Well, the prodigal returns," Casey said, getting up from his desk. His shirt sleeves were rolled up over thick forearms that had a sprinkle of red hair on them. A lock of red hair, shot with a bit of gray, fell over his right eye, giving him a boyish look. He looked into Farrell's eyes, saw trouble in them, but remained smiling until Farrell took his seat.

"You're looking a little like somebody who's bicycle was stolen," he said in a softer voice. "Come to the old man to fill out a theft report?"

Farrell, realizing his father was trying to cheer him up, gave him a little smile which never quite reached his eyes. "How did you stand it, Frank? How did you stand it when you lost mother and realized you'd never get her back?"

Casey leaned back in his chair and rubbed his chin. The smile left his face and his blue eyes became serious. "That's a question, kid," he said. "The truth is, I wasn't much good to myself or anybody else for a few years after that. I tried drinking to forget, but only felt hung-over all the time. I had friends who covered for me when I'd screw up. I tried to dig a hole and bury myself in it, but nobody would let me." He opened the drawer to his desk, pulled out a pint of Old Forester and two jelly jars. He put about three fingers in each jar and pushed one across the desk to Farrell.

"The trouble was, nobody'd let me crawl off and die, in spite of how hard I tried to do it. Finally, I got tired of fighting off their kindness and started living again. It was less work, in the long run." He lifted his glass to Farrell and took a sip. "I think you're a better man than me, son. I think you're stronger inside than I was. You've gotten up every day since Savanna left, you've taken care of business, and you've helped your friends when they asked for it. You feel like a piece of chewed gum, but nobody'd blame you for that. I know how you feel about her. I know all you did to help her through things after what Sleepy Moyer did."

"I tried, but I couldn't," Farrell said glumly. He took a drink and felt it burn its way down his throat to his stomach. "I've helped people I never cared anything about, but the one time I wanted to help somebody I did care about—I might just as well have been somewhere else."

Casey leaned across the desk and pointed a finger at his son. "Listen to me, Wes. It wasn't for you to do. You didn't fail her. She was going through something no man can even understand, and the sad truth is, there wasn't really anything you could do for her. She's got to do it herself, and she probably couldn't do it here with all her loved ones around her."

"But why?" Farrell asked. "What good are friends if you can't ask them for something?"

"You and Savanna were as close as a man and woman could get, but it's kind of funny that you don't understand the most elemental thing about her—she's genuinely independent, and got everything she's ever had on her own—with nobody to help her. I don't think she really knows how to accept help, and maybe that's the best way to be. After all, we all come into the world alone, and we go out the same way. Nobody can spoon-feed life to you, or put a Band-Aid on it when things get a little tough."

Farrell looked down into the amber glass of whiskey in his hand and swirled it around until he'd created a little whirlpool, then he looked back up at his father. "I guess I should've known that. My life's been the same way. I don't know why I forgot it." He drank the rest of the whiskey, then put the glass down on the edge of Casey's desk.

"Sometimes it helps to have somebody remind you of what you already knew," Casey said. "It may be the main thing a friend's good for."

Farrell nodded. "I'm kind of forgetful now and then. Thanks for jarring my memory, Frank."

"Forget it," Casey said. He drank off his whiskey, then put both glasses and the pint back into the bottom drawer of his desk. "What're you up to these days?"

Farrell knew he couldn't tell his father anything about Carol Donovan without getting his bowels in an uproar, so he said, "Just the club and a little business. I'm a little bored, to tell you the truth."

Casey laughed. "Then take a cruise to Trinidad, get some sun—or go to Arizona and ride a horse or something. You've never taken a vacation in your life, have you?"

Farrell grinned. "No, but I'm not sure riding a horse and looking at cactuses is my idea of a vacation, either."

"Hell, just get away," Casey said. "It'll do you good. Just don't send me any of those postcards of cute fillies in cowgirl outfits saying 'wish you were here,' all right?" He laughed.

Farrell smiled and got up from his chair. "You got a deal. Thanks, Frank—for everything."

"Get out of here," Casey growled good naturedly. "I've got city work to attend to."

"Let's go to Galatoire's this weekend," Farrell suggested. "You in the mood for Chicken Clemenceau?"

"Always," Casey said.

Farrell smiled at Mrs. Longely and left the office, feeling unexpectedly buoyed from his visit. He left headquarters, got into his car, and headed back to the Café Tristesse.

SAVANNA WAS downstairs at the Cotton Club West working with her bar manager on the liquor inventory when Sergeant Manion strolled into the room. He had his jacket thrown over his shoulder and the big revolver he carried under his left arm was ostentatiously exposed. He had a smile on his face, as though he were making a visit to an old friend, but even from a distance she could see that the smile had things wrong with it. His eyes were glassy, and his swagger was just a bit too insouciant.

"Well, well, well," he said. "The li'l southern gal hard at work. Good seein' you again, sugar." As he drew close, Savanna saw that his pupils were no bigger than pinpoints. On top of everything else, this dangerous asshole was a snowbird. That really puts the cherry on the cake, she thought.

"You've come for the money," Savanna said. She looked at her bar manager and jerked her chin at him. Careful not to look at Manion, he put down his inventory sheets and left quickly.

"I didn't come especially for the money," Manion said in a low, seductive voice, "but if you got it handy, I'll sure take it, honey-lamb."

Savanna reached under the bar and came up with an envelope, which she placed on the bar and shoved over to Manion. With the speed of a striking snake, his right hand shot out and captured her hand and the envelope and pulled them toward him with painstaking slowness. Savanna met his eyes, not flinching. She knew she could not match his superior strength, so she let him drag the hand until she was leaning across the bar toward him. She could smell the Old Spice he was wearing, and the faint trace of oil on his gun. She tried not to register the disgust and contempt she felt, and let a small smile curve her lips.

"You're kinda cute, honey-lamb," he said, showing his teeth. "Maybe you and me could be friends, huh?"

"Starke already made it plain that he's got me staked out as his personal territory, Manion," she said in a soft voice. "He don't look like the kind of man who'd appreciate anybody poachin' on his preserve. If he found out, he might kill both of us." She let herself smile, in a sorrowful way this time, like the princess whose father won't let her out of the prison turret.

The mention of Starke's name seemed to have an effect on the police sergeant. The grin melted off his face, leaving behind a slit in his mouth lined with narrow yellow teeth. His eyes flattened, and he took his hand off Savanna's. Savanna lifted her hand off the envelope, and Manion picked it up and shoved it inside his hip pocket.

"Starke don't know everything I do, and he don't have to know, understand?" Manion said. "I want somethin', I go out and get it, and don't worry 'bout tomorrow, see."

"Sure," Savanna said in a calm, reasonable voice. "But Starke, he prob'ly don't miss much. I wouldn't want to come between y'all. It don't look like a healthy thing to do."

"You let me worry about that," Manion said. "He's senior to me and he gets a whole lot more of the gravy. Maybe I'm gettin' tired of that crap."

"Sure," Savanna said. "Any real man'd get sick of bein'

another man's hound dog. I can see you're a real man, prob'ly a whole lot more of a man than Starke. But for my own sake, I gotta let y'all figure out the peckin' order in this deal. I'm just a woman, see, and a woman can't get between two men, if she knows what's good for her."

Manion nodded wisely. "You're sharp, baby sister. Got any liquor around here?"

Savanna smiled far back in her jaws, and let her eyes sparkle at Manion's show of wit. "Sure, baby. It's a bar, ain't it?" She reached under the bar and brought out a bottle of the bonded Old Granddad. She filled a tumbler about half full, pushed it over to him, and watched as he picked up the glass and drained it in a single draught.

Manion's body quivered and the muscles in his face rippled as the hundred-proof bourbon whipped at his nerves. "Damn," he said. "That stuff's got a hell of a kick." He lifted his lip up from over his top teeth and leered at her. "I'll see you some more, toots."

"Sure, baby," Savanna said. "I'll be around." But not for much longer, she thought. Something's gonna blow up, and I ain't gonna be here when it does. She watched Manion stroll cockily out the front door, then went upstairs to begin packing her things.

After Carol Donovan sent Luther Devereau away at six, she got up and went to the private bathroom in her office suite, stepped into the shower, then began to scrub herself with a long-handled bath brush. Luther had proven to be an energetic lover, although he didn't have much finesse. He'd done exactly what Carol had told him to do, moving her body around on the bed, mounting it this way or that.

Carol had been a prostitute a time or two and had learned to make a man work for his pleasure so he thought he was getting something extraordinary. Luther took longer than Carol had expected. When it was over, though, she'd extracted promises from him, which he had faithfully agreed to. She'd promised to meet him again the following afternoon, and he'd promised to do what she asked of him.

He was pathetic, really, she thought, after his bluster and his proclamations of friendship and loyalty to Archie Badeaux. It seemed to her that any man alive would give up his soul just to get his hands under a woman's dress for a few minutes.

She knew she couldn't depend on Luther for much, but he might be able to get her into Lincoln's lair. If she handled it right, she could arrange for Farrell to track her there and take care of Lincoln for her. He was taking just a little too much time to track Lincoln on his own, and Carol didn't want the old man to smell a rat and bolt from the city before her work was done.

She scrubbed herself with the brush until her skin tingled, then douched herself twice with the little rubber bottle and hose that hung in the shower, perhaps overdoing it a bit to get Luther's stink off her body. She kept the feelings of disgust at bay by thinking back over her early life. Her mother had been a prostitute and Carol, called Mattie Roker in those days, had been the offspring of the man who'd tempted her mother away from her family and then turned her out. The man had wanted Lucinda Roker to abort the baby, but she'd refused, and run away to have it. She was already a whore, so she supported herself with her body until she became too big with Carol to attract anyone.

After that, her mother had traveled from one house to another, sticking to the fancier bordellos because the men who came there were at least clean and had some manners.

When Carol was nine, social workers for the county found out about her and took her away, placing her in a series of foster homes, from which she became a chronic runaway. She was then assigned to an orphanage run by the African Methodist Episcopal Church. There she got liberal doses of religion, castor oil, and beatings when necessary. Carol kept herself strong by thinking of her mother and the reunion they would one day have.

The orphanage educated her, taught her manners and how to speak proper English without an accent, and housekeeping skills that might attract a husband. By then a seasoned dissembler, Carol gave the outward appearance of docility and squirreled away every nickel and dime she could lay hands on for her eventual escape.

At the age of seventeen, with a stake of forty dollars and a belly full of religious and domestic training, she escaped one night during a storm, made her way to the railroad station, and bought passage for Memphis, the place from which she'd been sent eight years before.

Eight years is a long time in a prostitute's life. Carol eventually found the house where her mother had worked, but it no longer housed prostitutes. She visited bordellos until she found someone who remembered the name of the madam of her mother's place of employment. Eventually she found the old woman living in a church-sponsored old folks home, an irony sufficiently delicious that it didn't escape the young woman's notice. She'd already learned the meaning of irony while being beaten by church people.

The old woman, now fat and feeble, remembered Carol's mother with a bit of prodding, but could recall little of what had happened to her. She gave Carol some names and some possible addresses, and sent the young girl on her way. The search consumed several years, and along the way Carol took odd jobs in houses cooking, cleaning, and sewing for the whores. She made enough money to get along and rebuild her stake periodically.

When she could no longer endure the domestic drudgery, she took a job as a prostitute, herself, thinking it must surely be better than what she'd been doing. She was only half right. She made a great deal more money, but found that the work wasn't so easy. She noticed, too, that women she worked with sometimes turned up with syphilis, and learned to take precautions against it.

Finally, after having worked her way across most of

Tennessee, she got word that her mother was dying in an insane asylum, a victim of syphilis, herself. Carol went to her, and barely recognized the pitiful wreck in the gray nightgown. By then she'd been looking for her mother for seven years. She took up residence there and began caring for her mother day by day, calling on the skills she'd learned as a reluctant home economics student, domestic, and familiar of whores and johns.

There were days when her mother was almost lucid and seemed to know her. During those times, Carol gradually found out about the man who'd sired her and destroyed her mother's life. As the sick woman descended more and more into madness and deteriorated physically to nothing, Carol thought about that man, thought about finding him, and thought of what she'd say when she did. When the woman died, old before her time, Carol buried her in the asylum cemetery, then returned to Memphis to start all over again.

She got out of the shower, her skin glowing from the workout with the brush. She toweled herself dry, went to her dressing table, and began to make herself up for the night. Wesley Farrell was coming that evening, and she wanted to be ready for him when he arrived.

ISRAEL DAGGETT left Rogers Clifton's office and drove to the Johnson Brothers Department Store on South Galvez Street and parked across the street from the entrance. The store was the most successful of its type in the region, and the doors were busy as new shoppers entered and others exited with their arms full of packages. Margurite liked to shop here, so many of their furnishings and draperies had come from Johnson Brothers.

A pretty brown girl dressed in a gray military tunic with frogs and gold braid smiled at him as he entered the elevator and asked to be taken to the administrative floor. He got out and went down the hall until he found a pebbled glass door with painted on it. He walked through it and took off his hat as he approached the secretary's desk.

She was about forty-five, and wore a gold *pince-nez* with a gold chain that was pinned to her blouse. As she looked up, he took out his badge folder and opened it for her. "Sergeant Daggett, ma'am. I wonder if I could speak to Mr. Johnson."

"Well," she said, "I don't know if he's free at the moment."

"You might tell him I've got some questions in regard to his late brother."

She surveyed his face again, made some sort of decision, then pushed a button on her intercom. A voice said something, then she pressed a key and said, "There's a detective from the city police, Mr. Johnson. He says it's about your brother." The speaker crackled again, then the woman got up and led Daggett to the door. She opened it, gave him a non-committal smile, and nodded for him to go in.

Elijah Johnson wasn't a big man, but he held himself stiffly erect like a soldier on parade. Even in his office he wore the jacket to his gray gabardine suit, and his tie was precisely knotted, with a diamond stickpin in the center of the knot. He held out his hand to Daggett.

"What can I tell you that you don't already know?" he asked by way of greeting.

Daggett shook the older man's hand and nodded. "Sergeant Daggett, Mr. Johnson. I came up with some ideas and wondered if I might bounce them off you for a couple minutes."

"I don't see why not, although my level of hopefulness about this sorry situation is not particularly high after all the months that have gone by. Have a seat, Sergeant."

Daggett took the chair in front of the desk while the store owner resumed his high-backed red-leather chair. "Your brother handled many of your investments and real estate, didn't he?" he asked.

"Ezra had a head for such things," Johnson affirmed. "It left me free to manage the store, although I often miss his wise counsel."

"Tell me, Mr. Johnson, did you and your brother have any dealings with Mr. Clifton at the Merchants and Farmers Homestead prior to Mr. Ezra's disappearance?"

Johnson's eyes narrowed to a squint as he considered the question, and he tapped his temple with his right index finger. "I didn't, personally," he said, "but Ezra may have. He and I talked whenever a decision on something had to be made, but often he didn't bother me if he didn't think a situation warranted it."

"Who would know?" Daggett asked.

"Well, Mrs. Tandy, my secretary would," he replied. "She served as Ezra's secretary, too." He leaned over to his intercom and pressed the buzzer.

"Yes, sir?" Mrs. Tandy's voice said.

"Can you come in for a moment, please?" Johnson asked. Within a few seconds, she walked through the door.

Daggett stood up as she approached the desk, and held a chair for her to sit in. Her eyes were full of questions, but she remained silent, waiting for one of the men to speak.

"Mrs. Tandy," Daggett began. "Mr. Johnson says that you served as Mr. Ezra's secretary while he was here."

"Yes, sir, that's correct," the woman replied.

"I want you to go back in your memory a few months," Daggett said. "Do you recall Mr. Ezra having any business meetings with Mr. Clifton, the president of the Merchants and Farmers Homestead?"

The woman sat there for a moment, and then nodded. "Yes, sir, I believe I do."

"Do you have any idea of what their meetings were about?" Daggett was leaning forward now, his eyes fiercely intent.

"It isn't too difficult," she replied. "There's a parcel of land over on the east side of the city. Not a very good parcel of land, either. Mostly bayou and prairie. It was something Mr. Ezra and Mr. Elijah inherited from a relative years ago. Mr. Clifton was representing a local Negro consortium, he said. Mr. Ezra wasn't too keen on it, I seem to remember, but he never said why he didn't want to sell. After his disappearance, the same people approached Mr. Elijah, and he went ahead with the sale."

"Yes," Elijah said, snapping his fingers. "A piece of fairly worthless land. Would cost a fortune to drain it. I ended up selling it to a local company."

"You don't have any idea why Mr. Ezra viewed the sale unfavorably?" Daggett asked.

"He didn't discuss it with me, and he probably wouldn't have gone to Mr. Elijah unless he thought something was important enough to require a joint decision."

"That's right," Elijah said. "We trusted each other implicitly. He knew real estate, and normally he didn't bother me with any of that."

"You recall the name of the company that was interested in the land?" Daggett asked.

"We've got the contract and bill of sale on file," Mrs. Tandy said. "Excuse me for just a moment." She got up and went into the outer office. Elijah Johnson got up and looked out the window, his hands clasped behind him. Daggett noticed that he rocked back and forth on his heels, and that his hands were clasped so tightly that the skin grew pale. It was probably the most emotion the old man ever showed.

Mrs. Tandy came back in with a manila file folder, which she laid on Elijah's desk. He opened it and drew out the bill of sale, which he handed to Daggett. The purchasing company called itself Anchor Properties, and listed as chief operating officer one J. Lincoln.

"What was Mr. Clifton's role in this transaction?" Daggett asked.

"Well," Elijah said, "he had no official role. He knew of the property and brought somebody from this Anchor Properties together with my brother. More than that I can't tell you. They paid us a few thousand dollars for the tract of land, and that's the last I knew of it, and the last time I had any face-to-face dealings with Clifton, although the Homestead is Johnson Brothers' bank."

Daggett made some notes in his notebook as the store president spoke, then closed the notebook and replaced it in his inside coat pocket. "I appreciate you letting me take up all your valuable time like this, Mr. Johnson."

Johnson leaned forward across the desk, his face suddenly bleak. "For months I've hoped that you'd come here and tell me that you'd found my brother. Does what we spoke of today have anything to do with his disappearance?"

Daggett stood up and looked at Johnson. "All I've got right now are theories and some suspicions, Mr. Johnson. And police business being what it is, I can't talk about any of them until I've got some hard evidence." He picked up his hat and set it upon his head. "But I can tell you this—your brother's case isn't closed. Before it's all over, I'm gonna find out what happened to him, and then I'll bring somebody to trial over it."

Johnson stood up. "Good luck, young man. Let me know if I can help you further."

Daggett nodded. "Count on it. G'day, ma'am," he said to Mrs. Tandy, then he turned and left the office.

Chapter 10

NIGHT FELL and Yvonne Fasnacht's Southland Rhythm Girls were downstairs in the Café Tristesse heating up the joint with "Stars Fell Over Alabama." Their leader, known as Miss Dixie, was jittering madly on her clarinet.

Upstairs, listening on his special speaker, Farrell changed into a pair of formal black trousers, a white shirt with diamond studs, and a pair of soft leather evening shoes with tassels on the front. Before slipping on the white dinner jacket, he got a tan leather shoulder holster from a drawer and strapped it on over his shirt. From the felt-lined drawer of his desk, he removed a long-barreled .38 Colt army automatic, loaded it with a fresh magazine, then stuck it into the holster clip.

As he was getting ready to go, he put on a black Borsalino with a slate gray grosgrain band, then went back to the desk, got his bone-handled straight razor and the five thousand dollars that Carol Donovan had offered him two days ago to come to her club. He'd give it back, since there was no longer any doubt in his mind that his motives toward her were purely personal. When he spent time with her, at least he wasn't thinking about Savanna.

In a sense, there seemed no other reason to go to the Southport Club tonight. He'd warned Archie Badeaux off, and somehow he doubted that Badeaux would pick up the dare. Whatever else people knew about Wesley Farrell, they knew he made good on his promises. He left the office and walked down the metal stairs at the rear of the building to where the cream and red Packard waited for him.

It was nearly eight as he drove out of the French Quarter and onto Claiborne Avenue. The long street wound from the clutter of Downtown through neighborhoods of prosperous homes, past an art-deco monstrosity that housed a high school, and the campus of St. Mary's Dominican girls school. The road took him past working-class neighborhoods into the semi-rural edge of Jefferson Parish.

The moon was high and nearly full, floating among feathery gray clouds. For a second he was reminded of a poem by Alfred Noyes about a dashing highwayman riding below a moon "like a ghostly galleon, tossed upon cloudy seas." As he crossed the parish line, he turned toward the river and followed the road until he reached The Original Southport Club.

He pulled into the large parking lot of the Southport Club just before nine o'clock, and saw immediately from the number of cars that the club was doing a good business tonight. He knew that middle-class and professional Negroes from as far away as Little Rock and Jackson came to sample the jazz played here. He was forced to leave his car some distance from the club entrance, so it took him a moment or two to reach it.

As he sauntered through the lot, he noticed a couple of cars, one an old Pierce Arrow touring car and the other a Nash sedan, pulled in near the entrance. Eight men got out and walked inside. The sight of that many men visiting a nightclub without women struck Farrell the wrong way, and he felt something uncomfortable grow inside him.

He followed them into the lobby, pausing to leave his hat at the cloak room. The colored hatcheck girl gave him a tentative smile, but her eyes examined every inch of his face as she tried to decide what had brought this tall white man to a Negro club. Farrell had seen that look before when he'd patronized other Negro establishments, and had learned, with difficulty, to ignore it. Favoring her with a smile, he drifted past her onto the main floor of the club.

The men who had come in ahead of him broke into twos and threes and went to different tables. He noticed that they carried their hats with them, and that their suits were rumpled and not particularly new. Some instinct told him to mark where each of them went as he continued on his way to the bar.

"Dry vodka martini," he told the bartender. "And a word with Miss Donovan, if she's not busy."

The bartender remembered him from his previous visit, and silently complied with both requests.

Louis Bras and his sextet were up on the bandstand having a little fun with "Deep River," giving it a lot more bounce than the composer originally intended. The people on the dance floor loved it—they were jitterbugging up a storm. He remembered Bras and his boys playing that same number at Savanna's club once, and he could not help but smile at the memory of that night.

"Having a good time?" Carol Donovan asked. "The smile says you are."

He turned his body on the stool so he could face her. "Who wouldn't have fun with Louis Bras on stage? He can make you smile no matter how you feel."

"You're right," she said. "Everything feels perfect tonight." She put her hand on top of his and smiled at him. He looked down at her hand, then back up at her face. He smiled back at her. She was wearing a strapless evening gown of pale green taffeta with a heavily boned bodice that seemed to serve her creamy bosom up like an offering to a starving man. She had jade buttons set into her earlobes, and her dark plum-colored lip rouge was the perfect accompaniment to her jet black eyes.

He put down his cocktail and got out his cigarette case. He opened it and offered one to Carol. She reached out a long, graceful hand with plum-colored nails and selected a cigarette. Farrell took one for himself, then lit both of them with a lighter. "Everything all right out here tonight?" he asked when the cigarettes were going.

She blew out a long stream of smoke from between her lips and smiled at him again. "It's been a wonderful night so far, and I think it'll get better."

"With any luck, your troubles in this town are over," he said. "You've got a good start here, and with a little luck, it'll grow into something big." He took in some smoke and then let it out again. "You look like a million bucks tonight, Carol."

She lowered her lashes as though embarrassed by his flattery, but her mouth smiled. When she looked back up at him, the black eyes had a sparkle in them. "You're good for a girl's ego, you know that?"

"Just telling the truth as I see it," he said. "Could be you're overdue to hear those kinds of things from a man." He was being even more reckless than he'd meant, but the impulse had momentum now, and he couldn't seem to stop it.

She nodded a bit seriously. "You might be right. It might be that I am. How come you're walking around loose? Men like you usually have a woman to keep them company."

He inhaled some more smoke and blew it out with a sound like a sigh. "There was somebody a while ago, but she left town. I guess you could say I was just letting nature take its course from there."

"Sounds wise," she replied, but she kept her hand on top of his.

The orchestra had moved into "Embraceable You" and Carol had opened her mouth to say something when a disturbance erupted on the floor. Men were punching some of the dancers, and others were flipping over tables and chairs. Women were screaming as the melee swept out from the center to envelope the entire floor.

Employees ran into the pit and began trying to break up the fight, but they, too, were quickly overwhelmed by the more fight-savvy perpetrators. Farrell could see that the men who'd preceded him into the club were, as he'd half-suspected, some kind of hired muscle, and two of them were laying about with blackjacks. Bodies were trampled to the floor as people fought to get away from the escalating violence.

Farrell's mind went over what he'd said to Archie Badeaux the previous night, and the way the man had behaved during the confrontation. This scene made no sense in light of those memories, but he weighed that against what he was seeing with his own eyes. These men had deliberately been sent here to wreck the place and hurt the business, and he felt a cold rage grow at the thought that Archie Badeaux had decided to test him.

He moved away from the bar, realizing he'd wanted somebody to hit every since Savanna left, and now he was getting what he wanted. A man with a blackjack was directly ahead, his back to Farrell. Farrell hit the man a terrific blow over the kidneys, and as he doubled over and half-turned, Farrell threw a crushing right to the hinge of his jaw. He felt bone crack under his fist and the man crumpled. He pulled the sap from the man's hand as he fell.

Two of his partners saw Farrell's intrusion and turned on him together. The one wearing brass knuckles Farrell took out with a foot to the groin. Using that man as a fulcrum, Farrell pushed his body sideways in time to sidestep the other man's charge. Farrell stuck out his right arm and caught the man in the throat. As he hit the floor, Farrell kicked him in the temple and silenced him.

Blood was surging through Farrell now, and he felt a curious pleasure in the pain he was inflicting. He found another of the gang struggling with a waiter and dropped him with a practiced flip of the blackjack to the base of the man's skull. With the troublemakers dwindling, the other employees were managing to bring the customers back under the control. The fight was losing momentum.

Farrell's bloodlust began to ebb and he felt vaguely sick

from what he'd done. Then a woman screamed his name, and he turned to see a man drawing a gun from his hip. Farrell's right hand streaked to his shoulder, the .38 automatic cleared his coat and fired, fired, and fired again. The gunman's hand opened and a revolver fell to the floor. He looked down at his riddled chest, then back up at Farrell with a look of disbelief as his life drained away.

Farrell swung the barrel of the gun left and right, looking for other threats, then he saw two men break off from the crowd and race for the exit. As one of them flung a desperate look behind, he recognized the man as Alex Mouton, a garage mechanic and part-time punk for hire. Alex Mouton would talk to him later that night, and through him he might find out why Archie Badeaux wanted this club bad enough to risk a war with Farrell.

The dance floor was hushed for a moment, then came a hubbub of muttering and whispering among the remaining guests. Fear and shock were on almost every face. Farrell felt a hand on his shoulder and turned to find Carol Donovan looking at him.

"You all right?" he asked.

She nodded jerkily. "I thought he was..."

"He tried, but you yelled in time," he replied. "Thanks."

She was still touching his arm, and didn't seem to want to let go. He put his hand over hers and gave it a gentle squeeze. "Better go call the parish sheriff's office and report this. I'll be here when you get back." He squeezed her hand again, and she left him.

He let the hammer down on the Colt and returned the automatic to his holster as he walked over to the body. The man lay sprawled in that bag-of-old-clothes fashion that the violently dead assume. His eyes were wide open, and still held a look of surprise. Farrell bent down and went over his clothes until he found a tattered leather wallet. It had a new hundred dollar bill in it, along with several singles and fives, and a driver's license made out to John James Johnstone, Jr. Farrell had heard of the man—a street punk with fists bigger than his brains—now a lifeless heap of meat and bone. Farrell hoped he had no family, but figured they were better off without him if he did.

He got up and walked back to where the dregs of his martini sat. He finished it, then had the bartender bring him another. By the time he'd worked his way through that one, he was beginning to lose the feeling of lassitude and vague nausea that the violence had engendered in him.

Carol came back and sat next to him on a barstool. "The sheriff's sending out an ambulance," she said as she settled her hips on the barstool. Her suntan complexion looked a bit pale, and a few errant strands of black hair had fallen over her left eyebrow. Farrell could not quite resist reaching out to brush them gently back into place. Carol let him do it, her dark eyes drinking him in, seeming to search his face for the answer to some unspoken question.

"Let me do the talking," Farrell said. "They don't have any Negro cops in this parish, and the white ones aren't always very sympathetic. I did the shooting, so if there's heat, I'll take it."

"I didn't—I didn't mean for this to happen," she stammered. "I didn't mean to get anybody else—I mean for anybody to get killed."

"Badeaux's responsible for this, not you," Farrell said. "I told him to lay off and he sent these punks out here to wreck the place. Maybe he thinks I'll let it lie. I'll have to go and see him again."

They heard a commotion near the front entrance, and turned to see several men come in dressed in the khaki uniforms and Sam Brown belts of the Jefferson Parish Sheriff's Department. They were led by a big man who wore his hat like an army aviator, without the grommet, so it looked "crushed." Farrell had dealt with him before, and while he couldn't exactly call him a friend, Farrell knew him at least to be fair. He stopped long enough to look at the body, then looked over and saw Farrell. He stalked over with a scowl on his face.

"This your doin'?" he asked without any greeting.

"Hello, Lieutenant McGhee," Farrell said. "You're looking well tonight. Yep, I shot him, but he drew first. This lady yelled in time and saved my life."

"That so?" McGhee asked, turning to Carol.

"Yes, Lieutenant," Carol replied. "That man was one of a group who came in and tried to smash up my club. Mr. Farrell tried to stop them, and that man drew a gun. Any number of these people will certainly testify that Mr. Farrell shot in self-defense."

Farrell noted that Carol had no trepidation about speaking up to a white cop. That wasn't a usual thing among southern Negroes, many of whom had been mistreated and abused by white cops and sheriff's deputies, or knew others who had. It was one more thing in her to admire, as if he needed any others.

McGhee made a disgusted face, displeased either that Farrell was in the right or that his badge seemed to inspire so little awe in this Negro woman. "Lemme see your piece," he said to Farrell.

Wordlessly, Farrell removed the automatic from his holster, ejected the magazine, then cleared the chamber with a quick jerk of the slide. He handed the gun and magazine to McGhee who appraised the gun for a moment, then looked at the magazine. "You put three in him. You wanted to make damn sure he didn't get up again, didn't you?" Without waiting for an answer, he bent to the carpet, picked up the cartridge Farrell had ejected, and pressed it back into the magazine. He replaced the magazine in the butt, let down the hammer, and handed it back to Farrell, butt first.

"You got a license for this?" McGhee asked.

Farrell removed a leather case from inside his dinner jacket and opened it so that his driver's license and New Orleans City firearms permit showed from behind celluloid windows.

"This is a New Orleans permit," McGhee said.

Farrell smiled. "And you know good and well that Jeff Parish doesn't require a permit to carry a concealed weapon. Most of your parish is rural, and your parish council won't make farmers and trappers apply for a piece of paper to carry a gun, Lieutenant."

McGhee made another face, closed the case, and handed it back to Farrell. "One of these days, hot-shot, I'm gonna have a question that you won't have an answer for." Before Farrell could reply, a junior deputy came up, pulled McGhee to the side, and they staged a whispered conversation for several minutes. Finally McGhee broke away and came back to Farrell and Carol.

"The guy you shot's called Jay-Jay Johnstone," McGhee said. "According to my man, he's got an arrest record as long as your arm. He was also carryin' an unlicensed .38. That seems to bear out your story, lady."

"I could've told you all of that, McGhee, and it's *Miss* Donovan," Farrell said pointedly. "She's the owner of this club."

McGhee didn't answer Farrell, but he gave him a withering look before touching the bill of his cap with his fingers. "Ma'am," he said by way of farewell. Then he looked at Farrell again and said, "I'd appreciate it if you'd take yourself and your gun back into Orleans Parish. I got enough trouble out here without you makin' me any more." When Farrell said nothing, McGhee glared at him, which Farrell returned, pound for pound, until McGhee gave up and stalked away.

"He doesn't like you," Carol remarked.

"He's not bad, for a cop," he replied. "He just hates mess, particularly when it's got Negroes connected to it. They make him uncomfortable." He looked down at Carol and said, "I've got someplace to go."

She looked up at him with a stricken expression. "No, you can't."

"You don't have anything else to worry about tonight," he said. "And I want to go and talk to the two men who got away. I know who they are, and I want to find out as much about this as I can before I go after Badeaux."

"Take me with you," she said. "I can drive."

He raised an eyebrow, and said, "Where I'm going a lady can't travel. It might be dangerous for you."

"What about you?" she said. "You might need somebody to watch your back. I must go with you."

"Not on this trip, sugar. It'll go easier if I'm alone, and besides, they won't be expecting me." He took her chin in his fingers, lifted her face, and kissed her lightly on the lips. "Stay out of trouble until I get back," he said. Before she could respond, he had turned and was walking toward the lobby.

ISRAEL DAGGETT was at the station late, going over the reports of the various investigators involved in the Shirley Macomb and Marcella Attaway murders. Hours of investigation into the Macomb murder had so far turned up nothing at all, and Daggett was frustrated over that. Seldom had a murder so enraged him, and he knew that was not good. You had to keep yourself on an even keel, and not get too personally involved, or you ended up missing something vital. So far, though, there'd been nothing vital to miss.

There was information on the Attaway murder, but it seemed to lead nowhere. A neighbor had reported seeing a Harker Brothers cab waiting outside the murdered woman's house during the night, and the driver had been found by mid-day. His name was Aaron Theobald, and he was a man who noticed things. It took him only about an hour of staring at mug books until he identified Ernie LeDoux as his passenger. Daggett had discovered from the warden at Angola that LeDoux had given the Metro Hotel on Rampart Street as his temporary forwarding address, and had sent officers to pick him up. They'd arrived to find his room vacant and the door standing open. Thus far there'd been no word on his whereabouts from any of the snitches the Negro Squad depended on.

On the face of it, it looked bad for LeDoux. They could place him at the scene at the approximate time of death and he'd just served a term for armed robbery. On the other side of the coin, LeDoux had no record of violence against anyone. All his life he'd used his brains to keep out of violent confrontations, and had no record of assault. Additionally, they had Bertillion records of LeDoux's hands, and they were too large to fit the suede glove found beside the body. Moreover, LeDoux was as tough as nails. Daggett could not believe that if he had to kill somebody, he'd vomit his guts out. Men didn't survive ten years at 'Gola with weak stomachs.

The puddle of vomit haunted Daggett, because of the similarity to the Redding murder. He needed a connection between those two cases, and so far he didn't have it. He rubbed his forehead, worked the stiff muscles of his neck, and got up to stretch. It was after nine and he hadn't found the time to call Margurite. He felt like a louse and walked over to pick up the telephone. He'd dialed most of his home number when the door to his office opened and Andrews walked in with a grin on his face. Daggett put down the phone. "Something?" he said.

"Something," Andrews said. "Not enough to shoot off any fireworks, but a solid lead, boss."

"Lay it on me," Daggett said, feeling his pulse rise.

"Found the driver of the bus that runs through City Park on that route," Andrews said. "Early that morning he saw a car pull out from the area on the other side of the bridge. Said the guy pulled out without even looking and he had to jam on the brakes. Scared him silly, he said."

"Yeah?"

"Yeah. Driver stuck his head out the window and cussed the guy out. Driver said it was a Negro driving the car, said the Negro stuck his hand out the window and gave him the finger. Driver's white, so you can guess how that went over."

"Uh, huh," Daggett said dryly. "What did the man see?"

"Car was a '38 Dodge four-door deluxe sedan, black," Andrews said. "He pulled right out into the bus driver's headlights so he got a good, clear look at it.

"Tell me he got a license number," Daggett said.

"No license, but maybe something just as good," Andrews said.

"What?"

"Driver saw that winged-wheel trade mark plate on the bumper that New Orleans Motors puts on their merchandise," Andrews said.

"That's the place on Broad, over near the Washington Avenue Pumping Station," Daggett said.

"Right. Boss, that's a pretty expensive car," Andrews observed. "Ain't many colored folks got that kind of bread these days."

"So if we go to the dealership and ask for a list of buyers of that model—"

"We can pick off the Negro buyers from the addresses," Andrews concluded.

Daggett's face split in a huge grin. "Sammy, I'd promote you if there was anything to promote you to."

"Hell, boss, just give me the money," Andrews said. "I can't spend no title."

"I'll ask Ray Snedegar to get in touch with them first thing in the morning. If they can give us a name, we might have the sucker in jail coveralls by dinner time," Daggett said. "Good job, Sammy. Better go on home and get some sleep. Tomorrow's gonna be a long one, prob'ly."

Andrews turned to go, and Daggett stopped him one more time. "Did Gautier come up with anything from the Secretary of State's office on that land yet?"

Andrews scratched his head. "Not yet. He said it's a lot of paper shufflin' goin' on over there. Maybe tomorrow, he said."

"Okay. Good night, Sam," Daggett said.

Andrews left and closed the door, leaving Daggett alone

again. He found himself praying that they'd find the killer of Shirley Macomb tomorrow. There were things he wanted cleared up, and he planned to get the answers if he had to handcuff the guy's feet and hang him upside down from the office door. He started to call Margurite, then just picked up his hat and coat and left the office. She was probably gonna be mad whether he called or not.

ERNIE LEDOUX stalked up and down in the room they'd given him upstairs at the Honey Pot like a caged tiger. It was bad enough that he was on the run from the cops for a crime he didn't commit, but he was also smarting from the realization that Ruby was a prostitute.

LeDoux hadn't led a sheltered life, and in his early days had shacked up with any number of working girls. But Ruby had seemed so pure when he'd first known her. She was still a kid and unspoiled, and being with her had been such a pleasant change from the hard-edged dames he'd known before. Now she was one of them, and she was more or less blaming him for the turn her life had taken.

The doorknob turned and LeDoux whirled about, his hand on the butt of his .45. He relaxed as he saw Ruby enter the room. She looked at him with a dull expression on her face.

"No need to go off the deep end," she said. "The cops don't know you're here."

"Do you know why they want me in the first place?" he asked.

"They think you killed Old Lady Attaway," she said. "They talked to the cab driver who took you there and traced you to the Metro."

"Great," LeDoux said bitterly.

"Why'd you really go to see the old woman?" Ruby said. "And don't give me no more of that bull about you bein' so fond of Ben." She paused and studied him through slitted eyes. "It's the money, ain't it? She knew something about the money. You could'a had the money by now—if you knew where it was. Did she tell you?"

"It ain't none of your concern," he said roughly, turning toward the shaded window.

"Bullshit," she said. "I was your woman when you stole it, and I waited all these years for you to come back. I deserve some of that money." Her voice became shrill and as he turned, he saw that her face was full of rage and that her fists were bunched at her sides.

"So, that's why you made such a point of bein' there at the Metro when I got back to town. It wasn't me you was waitin' for—it was the money." He laughed mirthlessly. "Man, time sure does things to some folks."

The door opened and Archie Badeaux stood there in his dark blue suit and gray homburg tipped low over his right eye. LeDoux went for his gun, but Badeaux's hand flicked up and the muzzle of his .44 Smith & Wesson settled on Ernie's midsection. "Loose the piece, brutha," Badeaux said. "Make like a tree leakin' sap, or my gun might have a sympathetic reaction."

Ernie pulled the .45 out with his thumb and forefinger and dropped it on the floor.

"Kick it over here," Badeaux said. "I wouldn't want you to trip over it or nothin'."

LeDoux did as he was told, then stood there with his fists clenched impotently at his sides. His face was twisted with anger, but his target was Ruby. "You two-timin' li'l tramp," he said.

Badeaux laughed. "Man, you is the biggest sucker I ever saw. She was mine even when she was with you before. We played footsies with you from the time you come up with the idea to knock over the Brinks truck. Trouble with the whole thing was we played it too cute. I should'a just put the arm on you the minute you had the loot and got it over with." He jerked his chin at Ruby and said, "But I let her talk me into this complicated scam and ended up with nothin'. Now it's ten years later, and I want the money ten times as bad. Start tellin' me where it is."

"Why don't you just take a bite outta your own ass, nigger," Ernie said. "If I had the money, I'd be gone by now. I left it with Ben Attaway to keep for me, only he died and I never knew it. The old woman had the money, but somebody else got to her before I could figure out a way to make her talk. Whoever croaked the old woman's got the money—but it wasn't me. What I got is what I'm standin' in."

Badeaux shook his head. "Tsk, tsk, tsk," he said. "It ain't much of a story, Ernie. I figure you beat it out of the old woman before you left. You didn't have time to go get the money before the cops landed on you, but I figure the old woman told you where it was before you finished her off. Old ladies tend to be kinda soft. A li'l whippin' is usually enough to get anything they got."

"You're a hell of a lot dumber than you look, man," LeDoux said. He looked at Ruby and smiled nastily. "You really hooked yourself up with a winner, didn't you, honeylamb. He's carryin' all his brains in that rod he's holdin'. I feel sorry for you. I mean *damn* sorry, you two-timin', stupid li'l twist."

"Nobody calls me a stupid twist, you bastard," Ruby yelled. She pulled a .25 Colt automatic pistol from the pocket of her dress and pointed it at LeDoux.

"No, you idiot bitch," Badeaux yelled, but it was too late. The little pistol cracked sharply and LeDoux fell senseless to the floor.

Chapter 11

SAVANNA WAS at the desk in her office going through papers: discarding some, filing others, placing a few in a folder to take with her. Her bags were packed and soon she'd be checking out of the Cotton Club West for good.

She'd nearly finished when she heard loud knocking on the door. She froze as the knocking became kicking, then the door flew open and banged into the wall. Starke stood there with a terrible look on his face, and his normally fastidious dress was disheveled. He walked into the room and slammed the door behind him. Savanna went on with her paperwork as though nothing untoward had happened.

"I went to see your li'l friend, Madigan," Starke said, staggering a little as he walked. "He said you'd quit him and was leavin' today."

"That's right," Savanna said in a toneless voice. "I'm out of this. Madigan's the one you want to talk to from now on."

"Nobody said you could go any fuckin' where," he said in a slurred voice. He leaned on the desk and she could smell the reek of bourbon coming from him, and she caught her breath to keep from gagging. "You and me ain't got acquainted yet, girley," he said with a snicker. He reached over to grab one of her wrists and she danced nimbly away, seeming not to see him.

"Sorry, Lieutenant," she said pleasantly. "I got business back in Louisiana. I've overstayed my welcome here. Time to go home." She hadn't thought of Louisiana as home in a long time, and realized as she said it that home was just what she meant. She wanted to shake the dust of Los Angeles from her feet and return to what she knew.

"Not yet, baby sister," Starke said thickly. "Not before we have a li'l session in that bedroom yonder." He dropped his hat on the desk and began to pull his tie loose from his neck. He lurched around the desk, bumping his hip on the sharp corner. He cursed, and his bloodshot eyes got the look of a rabid dog in them. A strange humming emanated from deep in his throat as he advanced toward her.

Savanna had handled many a drunk in her day, and some aggressive men who weren't drunk, but as she looked at Starke, the image of Sleepy Moyer came into her mind and she remembered how he'd hummed a song as he cut off her clothes and then raped her while she was tied to a bed in his deserted boarding house. She backed up, fear and anger warring inside her as her eyes roved the room looking for escape or some kind of edge.

Starke laughed way down deep in his barrel chest as he took off his coat and pulled the tie from around his neck. His shoulder holster was so large it looked like a wooden leg strapped to his body. He shrugged off the harness and let it fall to the floor with a thump.

Savanna found herself pressed inexorably toward the bedroom door. She had a gun in there, but she'd never get to it before Starke jumped her. He was going to rape her—it was in his eyes, in his ugly face, and in the way his thick-knuckled hands reached out for her. She remembered how she'd struggled against Sleepy Moyer, and the rage she'd felt at her helplessness. She felt again his filthy hands and mouth violating her body as she squirmed helplessly under him. She'd never feared Sleepy, only hated him—but he was dead. It was Starke in front of her now.

Without conscious thought, she stepped toward him and kicked the crooked detective in the groin with all of her 140 pounds behind it. A loud chuff of air escaped his lips and his eyes blared with pain and disbelief. As he crouched there in shock, Savanna threw a savage right cross to the hinge of his jaw. The blow made a solid, meaty pop as it landed, and he fell to the carpeted floor with a muffled thud. As he hit the floor, Savanna finished him off with a kick to the face. He bleated once and then lay still.

Savanna stood over him with her fists cocked and her teeth bared, breathing heavily. She walked around him to make certain he wasn't playing possum, but there was no need. He was canceled out. A sound like a ragged snore came from his broken nose.

Savanna knew she had to get out and quick, but she wanted to make certain she wouldn't be followed. She picked up the discarded holster and gun and threw them out into the alley behind the club. She removed his handcuffs from his belt, then had an inspiration. She rolled him over onto his back, unbuckled his belt, and then tugged his trousers off over his shoes. Then she tugged off his boxer shorts and threw all the clothing out into the alley after the gun.

He'd fallen not far from one of the radiators, so Savanna locked one of the cuffs around his left wrist, then dragged him close enough to the radiator to lock the other cuff around the steam pipe.

Moving quickly, she went into the bedroom and got her two suitcases and her handbag. She was about to leave the room when she heard the doorknob rattle. "Hey, man, lemme in there. Quit hoggin' that broad and lemme in there." It was Manion. "I'm gettin' sick and tired of gettin' your leavin's."

Savanna put her suitcases down and reached into the bag over her shoulder. From it she removed a .38 Colt Banker's Special with ivory grips. It was the gun Farrell had given her, and even though she'd left him, she hadn't been able to leave the gun. It was her single tie to him over the last year. She looked down on it with an affectionate smile, then she walked to the door, unlocked it, and jerked it open.

Manion's leer turned to shock as she shoved the muzzle into his face.

"Get in here, you stinkin' piece of rat meat," she hissed. "And don't go for your gun unless you wanna go through life minus your balls." She cocked the pistol and Manion's complexion turned gray. Then she backed up slowly, waggling the pistol at him to bring him further into the room.

As he got past the door, his hands raised in the air, she pushed the door shut and made him take out his gun and handcuffs. "Now take off your pants," she said.

"What?" he said, his voice pitched high with fear.

"You heard me," she grated. "Take 'em off, now, or I'll make a steer out of you." She pointed the cocked pistol at his groin, and he nearly fell down shucking his trousers. "Now walk over to the desk and sit down," she commanded.

"What're you gonna do?" he asked in a shaky voice.

"I ought to kill you, you sonofabitch," she said, "but I think I'll fix it so you can't hurt anybody else with your badges. Pick up that pencil and write down what I tell you."

Manion, his face caught between humiliation, fear, and impotent anger, did as he was told, keeping his hands in sight.

"What's your first name?" she demanded.

"Huh?" Manion said stupidly.

"Your first name," she repeated.

"It's—uh—Fred," he said.

"Here's what you're gonna write. 'I, Sergeant Fred Manion, hereby admit to extortion against Marty Madigan, owner of the Cotton Club West, and against other Negro business owners in the Central Avenue District. I and Lieutenant Starke were partners in this extortion, and have been guilty of this for several years.' Now sign it."

"W-what are you gonna do with that?" Manion asked as

he wrote.

"I'm gonna give it to a friend before I leave town," she replied. "I'm gonna leave it up to him what he does with it. If he's any kind of a man, though, he'll make copies of it and send them to the chief of police, the commander of the Central Avenue Precinct, and to the *Los Angeles Times* and all the Negro newspapers."

"You can't do that," Manion said. "We'll be sent to jail—we'll get killed in there. You know how many people we done sent to the pen?"

"What I wonder is how many you framed into the pen," she said. "But I'm doin' it anyway." She threw his handcuffs on the desk in front of him. "Now put them on and go cuff yourself to the radiator next to your partner."

"You can't just leave me like this, woman," he cried, his voice cracking with panic. "I won't stand a chance."

"I can, and I will, you dirty bastard," she said. "I wish I could kill you, but you're not worth the bullet. Besides, if you died too quick, you wouldn't suffer enough for all you've done. They'll teach you some things you didn't know at San Quentin, I imagine."

Once he was fettered, she turned and got her bags, then turned back to him once more. "They might not put you in jail—the law's a funny thing. But let me give you fair warnin'. If you get any fool thoughts about followin' me down to Louisiana, I got friends down there that'll cut off your balls, fry 'em in corn meal, and make you eat 'em, and then they'll feed the rest of you to the 'gators. And I'll be there to watch." Her voice had become thick and guttural, and Manion shuddered, then looked away.

Savanna left the room, locking the door after her. As she made the street and put her bags in the trunk of the car she'd been leasing, she felt free and in possession of herself again. For the first time in a year, she couldn't recall the smell of Sleepy Moyer's hot breath on her face, nor the feel of his hands on her body. Those memories were as dead as the man, himself. She could go home now.

She got into the car, turned it over, and left the alley. An hour later, with Manion's letter in the mail to Marty Madigan, she was in the Jim Crow car of the Southern Pacific's east-bound train. She watched the shadowy landscape of Los Angeles County slide past her window for a while, but soon had leaned back in her seat and closed her eyes. Shortly, the rocking motion of the train lulled her into a deep, dreamless slumber.

FARRELL FELT his muscles loosen once he was behind the wheel of the car. Badeaux had made a move and he'd successfully countered it. But now that the battle was joined, there were nagging doubts in his mind about it all. He still didn't understand why Badeaux wanted the club in the first place. Badeaux was a professional at hurting people. It was all he did and he did it well. If he was pushing Carol for Lincoln's sake, that didn't really make any sense, either. Lincoln was an empire builder, not a punk looking to gain a little respectability by running a legitimate operation. Did the Southport Club represent something to the shadowy gangster that was invisible to Farrell? If so, he couldn't imagine what it would be.

Farrell got out onto U. S. 90 and followed it back through New Orleans until it joined State Route 1. It was a long drive, and it was nearing two o'clock as Farrell drove over the Intracoastal Waterway bridge and on through the villages of Arabi and Chalmette. Leaving the intrusive lights of the city behind, the sky became velvety black, studded with brightly-winking stars.

The village of Mereaux wasn't more than a wide patch in the road, but Farrell knew it was where the Mouton brothers lived. He was acting on gut instinct, but he had a feeling the two of them would go somewhere to lick their wounds. There was only one place in Mereaux that they could go. A Negro bootlegger he'd dealt with during Prohibition had told him about the honky-tonk just off the highway on Parish Road Seven. He almost missed the sign, which leaned over drunkenly where weather had undermined the ground it stood in. In the high beams of his headlights, he saw it was pocked with several rusted .22 bullet holes, but the number 7 was clearly visible.

He heard it in the darkness ahead of him before he saw it. It wasn't much more than a shack, but light escaped from the windows facing the road. A raucous Negro voice was singing "Poor Man Two-Step" in Cajun French, and a banjo, guitar, and washboard accompaniment could be heard just beneath him.

He parked beside an ancient Reo and looked around him. Near the entrance was the old Pierce Arrow that had carried the Moutons to The Original Southport Club. Farrell pulled his hat low over his eyes and walked to the entrance, his eyes and ears probing the darkness around him.

He paused just outside the door and inspected the interior. The musicians, a quartet of rawboned black men in overalls and broad-brimmed straw hats, were standing in a cleared spot near the back wall. The scene was lit by kerosene lanterns hanging from pegs along the wall. Men and women were gathered around them, clapping and tapping their feet in time to the music, some dancing in a small cluster. The bar, a couple of rude pine planks lying between a pair of wooden kegs, was vacant except for two burly men in cheap, wrinkled suits of town clothes. They stood shoulder to shoulder, their backs bent and a certain hangdog quality to their posture.

Farrell moved quietly through the door, his hands swinging easy at his sides, his eyes focused on the Mouton brothers, but also conscious of everything around him. A Negro woman happened to turn her head and saw him, and her face froze. A tall white man in a snow-white dinner jacket was like a ghost to her in this environment. He fixed her with his pale eyes and drew his hand across his throat, and she hurriedly turned her attention back to the musicians.

Farrell's right hand made a movement and the Solingen

steel razor whisked open in his hand, gleaming in the harsh light of the kerosene lanterns. When he was within six inches of the two men, Alex Mouton happened to turn his head. He saw Farrell's face, and opened his mouth to yell. Farrell's left hand shot up and captured his throat, and his right hand held up the razor in front of Mouton's eyes, which bugged in unspoken terror. Farrell's mouth was close to his face. "If you want to live, follow me outside. Yell, and I'll slice you from gullet to gizzard."

Dom had turned at his brother's sudden movement, and in his eyes Farrell could see something stupid welling up.

"Your brother wants to fight. If his hands move at all, I'll slice your head right off your shoulders. Tell him." Farrell shook Mouton's neck for emphasis.

Alex turned his head slowly, and wagged it back and forth at his brother, knitting his brows in a comically authoritative manner. Dom's hands twitched several times, but then they relaxed. Farrell linked arms with Alex, then jerked his chin at Dom, indicating that he should precede them through the open door. They walked quickly and quietly, and no one seemed to notice their departure.

When they were about twenty yards outside the 'tonk, Farrell let Alex go and shoved him over toward his brother. The razor disappeared from his hands and he spoke in a hard, menacing voice.

"Why did Badeaux send you out to wreck the Southport Club tonight?" Farrell demanded.

"Huh?" Alex said. "How'd you know Badeaux sent us?"

"Answer the question."

"Well, he didn't say," Alex Mouton replied. "He called us two days ago and said we should go out there tonight and wreck it. He give us a hundred bucks apiece, and said there'd be an extra hundred for a bonus."

Farrell stared at him. "You say he called you two days ago and said you should do it tonight."

"That's right," Mouton replied.

Farrell was silent for a moment, letting his pale eyes rove

over the two brothers. "How'd he pay you off?"

"He sent the money to our garage by a messenger," Mouton said. "Railway Express Agency truck."

Again Farrell was silent. Then he said, "The Jeff Parish law's got all the rest of your guys on ice, except for Jay-Jay. They've probably turned you up already, so you better get out of town."

"Huh?" Alex said. "You're lettin' us go?"

"That's right," Farrell said. "You better stay gone for a while until things blow over."

"Why you doin' this?" Alex asked suspiciously.

"Because you're a couple of chumps, suckers," Farrell said contemptuously. "You shouldn't go to jail just because you're stupid."

Alex looked dazed and shook his head, but Dom became bellicose. "This is shit, man. We get our asses kicked, lose out on that extra money, and now this ofay is runnin' us outta town. Fuck that." He made a run at Farrell, who sidestepped him and hooked him in the gut with a hard left, then followed through with a hard overhand blow to the temple.

Farrell stood there massaging his knuckles, then looked up at Alex. "Get him out of town before he gets himself killed, and you along with him." Then he turned and disappeared into the night.

RALPHIE DANIELS flung a last look over his shoulder as he tried desperately to urge the ancient automobile to a higher rate of speed. He heard the clatter and wheeze of the engine as it struggled to maintain thirty-five miles an hour, and knew he couldn't go much farther.

He didn't know who the man was who'd chased him, but guessed it was someone working for Nate Hopkins. A cold sweat broke out on his forehead as he thought how close he'd come to a beating—or worse. It puzzled him as to why Hopkins had sent only one man after him—normally leg breakers worked in teams, yet he had never spotted more than the lone man who'd almost chased him down.

He cudgeled his brains as he tried to make sense of his situation. How'd the man find him? Then it came to him—he must've tracked him to the railroad station, somehow discovered he'd bought a ticket, then guessed he was hiding in some colored joint until train time. Jesus Christ on a bicycle, he thought. What rotten goddamned luck. If he'd been a moment earlier or later, he might've missed the guy on the street, made it back to the train, and now be on his way west. Shit! He pounded the seat with his fist, raising such a cloud of dust that soon it had him sneezing uncontrollably.

He looked quickly at his pocket watch and briefly considered driving to the Southern Pacific terminal or a bus station, but wait—Hopkins would have those covered, too. That old man was no fool. His eyes widened as he urged the battered car onward, realizing he was probably trapped in the city with nowhere to hide. For a moment he knew such stark terror that he nearly lost control of his bladder. His breathing was rapid and shallow, and he felt faint. If only he'd been able to steal a better car, but this piece of junk—. As the thought crossed his mind, the engine began to cough and miss, and he barely had enough power to ease the ancient buggy to the curb before it died entirely.

As he sat there with his head leaning against the steering wheel, tears sprang to his eyes. It seemed to him that God, Himself, was conspiring against him, blocking his one chance to get a leg up on life. He lifted his head and leaned back in the seat wearily. Where could he go? He briefly considered going to Hopkins and giving him the money, but about fifty dollars of it was gone, and in any case, Hopkins might have him beaten just for trying to run away.

Then it came to him. Mrs. Brown might hide him. The way she'd looked at him earlier in the day, she'd have taken him to her bed right then and there. He shivered at the prospect, but soon convinced himself that crawling into bed with a woman almost fifteen years his senior was a better alternative than sneaking from street to street until Hopkins's men found, and dealt with him. He got out of the car and began walking back in the direction of his old neighborhood.

It was now full dark, and he gained some feeling of comfort in knowing he was hidden in the shadows. He avoided walking directly under street lamps, even though it sometimes took him partly out of his way. He had the old Colt in his front pants pocket now to facilitate a more rapid draw, having already replaced the expended cartridge cases with fresh loads. It was killed or be killed now, he told himself, and he felt desperate enough to do whatever it took in order to escape punishment.

Finally, more than an hour after abandoning the old car, he saw his old boardinghouse ahead of him. He ducked into an alley and surveyed the street for a long time before he was sufficiently convinced that no one waited for him in the shadows. He crept the remaining steps to the house and pressed the doorbell button. In spite of the warmth of the evening, he felt himself shivering, and fought to keep it under control. Then the door opened.

"Why, Ralph," Mrs. Brown said. "What a surprise. Did you forget something?"

"Well, uh," Ralphie began haltingly, scuffing one foot on the step. "I, well, I was, uh, thinkin'—'bout what you said earlier today. 'Bout comin' back for a visit, that is."

Mrs. Brown's mouth smiled, but uncertainly, as though she couldn't quite believe this was happening. "Oh. I—I'm so glad to see you. Would you like to come in, maybe have a little something?"

"Uh, sure," Ralphie said.

She stood aside from the door and allowed him to come in. He brushed against her as he passed, and it was like an electric shock for both of them. Each jumped back a little, Mrs. Brown uttering a little sigh as she did so. Ralphie smiled at her nervously, trying to appear happy to be there.

She took him through the door to her parlor and closed the door behind her. "Have a seat there, Ralph. Make yourself comfortable. Wouldn't you like to take off your coat? It's awfully hot outside tonight, isn't it?"

"Yeah," he said. "Yes, it is." He knew he was sweating and didn't know how to stop. The knowledge that Nate Hopkins' men were combing the city for him, combined with his proximity to this lovelorn female made him feel faint and weak. He went to a love seat that rested under a large painting of a lighthouse, its yellow beam reaching far out into the ocean. A clipper ship under full sail seemed to be beating toward the light as dark clouds muddied the night sky. The picture seemed strangely significant to him.

Mrs. Brown, after slipping him a shy smile, went through a door. While she was gone, Ralphie tore off his jacket and shoved the Colt six-shooter down in one of the pockets. He laid it over the back of the chair with his hat just as Mrs. Brown returned to the room. In her hands was a tray bearing a bottle of Kessler's American, two glasses, and a small crystal ice bucket with a bail handle and a set of tongs. She put the tray on the coffee table and sat down beside Ralphie on the love seat.

"Well, how was your first day at the laundry?" she asked, putting ice cubes in each glass and then pouring some of the whiskey over them.

"Well, it was—you know—kinda hot," he stammered. "What with all that steam—well, a body gets all—"

"Yes, steamed up. Oh," she said, making a *moue.* "I made a joke." She tittered behind her hand, and even Ralphie gave a nervous little laugh.

She reached over, picked up the two glasses of whiskey, and handed one to him. "Let's make a toast," she said brightly. "To good times."

"Yeah," Ralphie said. "Good times." He clinked his glass on hers, then tipped it up and drank half of what was in it. The whiskey burned down his gullet and made his head grow warm and fuzzy inside. He cleared his throat twice to keep from coughing. As he watched, Mrs. Brown put her glass to her lips, closed her eyes, and drained it in one long swallow.

"Oooh, that was good," she said in a shivery voice. "Let's have another."

Before he could say anything, she refilled her glass and topped his off. He drank some of it, trying to keep up, and this time she drank only a small sip, but her eyes were glowing in her dark brown face.

"I'm so glad you came back," she confided softly. "I—I always wanted us to be—well, you know—friends."

"Oh, me, too," Ralphie said quickly.

"Really?" she said, her face glowing with pleasure, and a girlish prettiness was evoked by her smile. He noticed for the first time that she was still wearing the white sun dress, and that her ample bosom was straining the fabric as she leaned toward him. He almost could not take his eyes off her breasts, and fancied that they moved independently under the revealing bodice, enticing him toward them.

"Uh, yeah, really," he said. Then he drank the rest of his whiskey. This time it didn't burn quite so badly, and he felt strangely giddy and confident. He put down his empty glass, looked into her eyes, and pulled her toward him. The suddenness of the move made her eyes widen and her mouth fall open. Before she could say anything, he molded his mouth onto hers and held it there for what seemed like a full minute. When he took his mouth away, she looked at him, and a wicked grin formed on her mouth.

"You sly li'l thing," she said. "And all this time I thought you weren't interested in me." She pulled him tightly against her and kissed him until he thought his brains would melt and trickle out of his ears. Her hands were rubbing all over his back and down over his hips. His clothing suddenly felt very tight and constricting.

Before he knew it, she was pulling at the buttons on his shirt and the buckle of his belt. He was kissing her back just as frantically, slipping the straps of her sun dress down over her shoulders, grabbing whatever flesh he could expose. Suddenly, she didn't seem too old to him anymore. After a time, the love seat became too small for their needs and they dragged each other out of the parlor and into an adjoining room, trailing clothing as they went. There they fell across a convenient bed, where they remained for the rest of the evening.

ROGERS CLIFTON dreamed he was walking in sunshine on a cloudless day. A breeze came off the lake and plucked at the white tennis shirt and trousers he wore. He'd never contemplated beauty of this magnitude. He walked along the shore, taking great strides, moving toward a beautiful cottage on a hill. He could make out the figure of a woman waving to him, a woman with a feathery cap of dark blonde hair. He waved back, and stepped up his stride, hurrying toward the love she had to give him.

But for some reason he wasn't able to walk as quickly as before. She was still waving, urging him to hurry, and he waved back, but his breath was becoming labored. The day was still majestically beautiful, and his happiness seemed assured, but he was moving now with almost agonizing slowness. He was leaning forward, struggling with all his might. He looked down and saw that there were hands grasping at his legs and ankles, hands that were bones with shreds of flesh still adhering to them. And attached to the skeletal hands were corpses, skulls with skin stretched tightly over them, faces of dead people that he recognized. He screamed and screamed and kept on screaming.

He found himself sitting bolt upright in his bed in the bungalow he owned on Wallace Drive near Dillard, one of two Negro colleges in the city. He untangled the sheets from around his legs, staggered into the bathroom, and bathed his face and neck in cool water, careless of his silk pajamas. He looked up into the mirror, and the terror in his eyes almost unmanned him. He grabbed the edges of the wash basin to keep from falling, and forced himself to a standing position. Eventually he was able to walk out of the bathroom, and into his living room.

He went to a cabinet, opened it, and took out a decanter of cognac and a small balloon glass. He managed to open the decanter without dropping it and slopped some of the contents into the snifter. He raised it to his mouth and drank deeply, letting the fire of it burn away some of the fright. He filled the glass a second time, then put the decanter down and walked to a leather club chair beside a window.

He fell down into the chair and looked out at the clear moonlit night. The moon was so large and perfect that it was oppressive to him. He looked around his comfortable house and saw that he had everything, knowing at the same time that he also had nothing. He'd thought that he could shake hands with the devil, but keep his fingers crossed behind his back and somehow save himself. He knew now that the devil would not be tricked.

In the beginning, what he had done hadn't seemed so terrible. Fate had offered him an opportunity to take the fruits of a bad thing and make something good out of it. He'd be helping his people and advancing his own career at the same time. It hadn't turned out to be that simple, though. There'd been complications—big ones. He'd had to cover up one thing by doing another. It shouldn't have happened the way it did, but once it was done it couldn't be undone.

And then came the day when Lincoln entered the picture. He'd been charmed by the old man at the time, imagining from his light skin, cultured conversation, and genteel surroundings that he was a Creole gentleman, someone who'd be an asset to the Negro community, and to his own advancement. His smile was so genial, it wasn't until the day he explained some things that Clifton realized how much his smile was like that of a crocodile.

Clifton had thought he was the equal of any man he'd

meet before Lincoln. His Howard University law degree, his Phi Beta Kappa, his membership in some of New Orleans' most prominent social clubs—he realized now that with all those advantages, he was tainted by a few fatal flaws. He believed he could be clever and a bit unscrupulous at the same time, do good things for his people while occasionally sweeping a little inconvenient garbage under the carpet. Lincoln's capacity for immorality and moral degradation so far outstripped his own that he felt like a child in the old man's presence.

Lincoln had found out about all his sins—every one of them—and had held them up to Clifton for his own brand of amusement. "Cooperate with me," the old man had said, "and we'll make certain you continue to be the admired Negro banker, worshipped by those less fortunate than you, even idolized by well-meaning white people. Don't cooperate, and your life will experience unfortunate—reverses." Clifton recalled just how he'd steepled his fingers when he'd said that word, and how he'd drawn his mouth into a prim little line. His black eyes had been as flat and empty of feeling as a pair of old pennies.

Clifton got up and walked to his desk. He sat down, opened a drawer, and took out a handsome mahogany box. He unlocked the box with a key, and looked inside. Lying in the box was another key, one for a safe deposit box, and a .32 Browning automatic pistol he'd purchased on a trip to Belgium some years before. He'd never fired it, but he knew it held a full magazine. He picked it up and hefted it experimentally in his hand. He sighted down the barrel, and pantomimed squeezing the trigger. Then he turned it, looked at it, and placed the muzzle against his temple. Even though the gun wasn't cocked, he found he couldn't pretend to pull the trigger. His throat felt thick and hot, and tears gathered in the corners of his eyes. He put the gun back in the box, and then locked the box, placed it back inside the drawer, and closed it.

He stared across the expanse of the desk and looked at a

series of family photographs, most taken when he was much younger. His parents had both had family in New Orleans and had sent him here every summer to visit cousins, uncles, and aunts. Those times had been so happy that it had caused him to decide to locate here after law school. How he regretted that decision now. He continued to stare sorrowfully at the photographs until the sun came up several hours later.

Chapter 12

MARCEL ARISTIDE had returned to the parlor house on Soraparu Street tired in body and spirit. He'd gotten reports from most of his men, none of whom had gotten even a glimpse of the elusive Ralphie. Feeling lower than he ever had, he pulled the telephone toward him and dialed Chester Daniels's number.

"Hello?" the dry cleaner said in a timorous voice.

"This is Marcel Aristide. I thought I'd call you and let you know how things stand."

"Oh, Lord, Mr. Aristide," Daniels said. "I been hopin' and prayin' you'd call."

"I wish I could give you some good news," Marcel said, "but Ralphie's still out there. I traced him to the railroad depot and had him in sight, but he took several shots at me and ran off."

"Merciful God, Mr. Aristide," Chester said in a low, anxious voice. "I pray you ain't hurt, sir."

"No, but he hijacked an old man's car and got away from me near the River," Marcel said."

"Oh, Lord," Chester said, his voice even lower, and more hopeless than before.

"Listen," Marcel said, talking as much for his own spirits as Chet Daniels's. "We've got all the railroad and bus terminals covered. The car he stole was a wreck, and frankly I don't think he's gonna try to get out of town that way. The Louisiana State Police would shoot him as soon as look at him, and he's bound to know that."

"You think?" Chester asked.

"Definitely," Marcel said. "What I'm thinking is that he'll go to somebody in the city, ask them to hide him for a few days. Who are his friends?"

"Well, sir," Chester began. "Ralphie's always been too centered on himself to have much in the way of friends. I'm most all he's got, and I ain't feelin' too high on him myself, just now."

Chester Daniels's lugubrious description of his brotherly feelings almost made Marcel laugh out loud, but he kept his composure, then Chet said something that hit him like a jolt of electric current.

"I'm just thinkin', though," Chester began. "I'm a man who notices things, and earlier today I noticed something that might be some help to us just now."

Suddenly alert, Marcel felt a strange humming in his ears. "Lay it on me," he said.

ERNIE LEDOUX felt he was climbing up through the darkness, laboriously, hand over hand. Light was so far from him that he wondered if he'd ever see it again. He remembered Ruby screaming things at him, and then everything dissolving in a welter of red and yellow lights. He wondered if he was dead, and thought that if he was, this darkness must surely be Hell. He heard what he thought were the moans of people around him, suffering the torments of the damned. And then he heard a voice.

"Well, I reckon you ain't dead yet," the voice said. "But things could change, if the right answers don't start comin'."

With Herculean effort, LeDoux managed to open his eyes, and for a second the light blinded him and he moaned aloud. He realized then that the cries of the damned he'd been listening to had actually been his own.

For some reason, that didn't make him feel any better.

"Water," he said. "Water."

A tin cup was pressed against his mouth, and cool water washed over his teeth and tongue. He managed to swallow it without choking, then fell back against the blanket he was lying on. He reached up a hand to his aching head, and found cloth bound there, sticky with his blood. He suddenly remembered the sharp crack of the .25. "Damn, I been shot," he said.

A man started laughing then, and he opened his eyes and recognized the man who'd burst in on him and Ruby.

"Who're you?" he asked in a dry, cracked voice.

The man straddled a wooden chair with his arms folded across the top. He held a big Smith & Wesson .44 Special negligently in his right hand, as though he didn't really need it, but simply wanted LeDoux to understand the pecking order in this world. "They call me Archie Badeaux," he said, "but you can call me Mr. Badeaux." He grinned in an ingratiating way, but his eyes had strange lights dancing in them. He swiped at his nose with the back of his left hand, and LeDoux saw flecks of white powder there. He'd known coke-hounds in his life and knew a man lived longer if he steered clear of them. A fine time to remember that, he thought.

"You're the fool thinks I still got the hold-up money," LeDoux said after a moment. "You got a lot of sorrow and upset comin' to you, cousin."

Badeaux's smile remained in place, but it took on a fixed, humorless quality, and his eyes brightened to a single pinpoint of light. "May be, but if that's the way you want to play it, you'll die, as slow and painful as I can make it. Seventy-five gee is enough money for me to put out a little effort, and you'll wear out long before I do."

LeDoux struggled to a half-sitting position, and managed to prop himself up against the wall. He'd been through so much already that Badeaux didn't scare him. "Look man, I ain't ready to die yet, and you're right—the seventy-five gee is enough money to make a man do damn near anything to get it back. But this ain't the way."

"You got a better way, I reckon," Badeaux said, intrigued by LeDoux's show of moxie and the bold, commonsense tone he adopted.

"You're damn straight," the ex-convict said. "I was beginning to think about the thing when the cops nearly got me at the Metro. Since I been cooped up in this whore house, I had all the time I wanted to think about it."

Badeaux twirled his revolver on his finger, then on an impulse, shoved the gun back under his arm. "All right then, let's hear what you got to say."

"When I went to see the old lady, the more I pressed her about the bag I left with Ben, the more agitated she got. She got so wound up toward the end that she run me out of there, yellin' and cursin' at me. If I'd had time to think about it, I would'a just pushed her down in a chair and made her talk. She was already scared enough that I could'a made her spill what she knew."

"How you figure?" Badeaux asked, more intrigued than ever.

"After she threw me outta the house, I peeked into the window and saw her on the phone with somebody. I could hear her yellin' and screamin', wavin' her hands around her head like a crazy person. My figurin' is that she had a friend or a relative or somebody she was partnered up with. My showin' up so sudden like got her in a tizzy. She called the partner in a panic, and whoever it was came over and shut her up before I could come back and make her talk."

Badeaux was silent for a long moment, his eyes darting this way and that as he weighed LeDoux's explanation. "You know, you might just have somethin' there, brutha. Now the question is, who was the old lady partnered up with?"

"I been thinkin' on that, too," LeDoux said. "That house was a shithole. It looked like she couldn't take care of herself no more, and that somebody must be lookin' out for her. She had that big house, that expensive radio-phonograph, and she had a ring and bracelet with diamonds the size of your thumbnail in 'em, but she was dressed in filthy old rags and she smelled like a dead 'coon."

Badeaux's teeth showed as his lips peeled back in a grin. "Man, you ain't so stupid, you know that? I been out here for ten years lookin' for that dough, and it was under my fuckin' nose the whole time. You been here two days and already figured all that out." He laughed and slapped his thigh.

"Ain't nothin' to laugh at yet," LeDoux said. "Whoever it is has the stash knows I'm here lookin'. They'll be damn careful now, 'specially after killin' the old woman. We got a pile of diggin' to do in order to find it."

Badeaux's grin took on a chilly edge. "What do you mean, 'we?' Maybe you forgettin' your situation, cousin."

LeDoux sat up, his eyes full of his old forceful spirit. Bullet wound and all, he was still Ernie LeDoux, the man who knocked over a Brinks truck and got away with seventy-five gee. Badeaux remembered all of that, and made a move toward his gun.

"Listen, man," LeDoux said. "I don't know you, but I figured out Ruby used you to help double cross me in order to find the money ten years ago. I still got considerable investment in that money. I got shot in the leg, spent near a year in solitary, then nine years choppin' cane. Then no sooner than they let me out, I got the cops on my ass for somethin' I didn't do, and then got shot in the fuckin' head by a woman I thought was solid in my corner. The way I see it, you owe me the chance to see that money again, and even give me a split of it if I help you find it."

Badeaux's hand still fingered the butt of his revolver, but there was wisdom in LeDoux's argument. Besides, neither Ruby nor Luther had the strength, savvy, or sheer ruthlessness required to track down the killer and the money. Badeaux let his hand fall away from his gun. "Okay, cousin, you got yourself a reprieve. If we find the money, we split it down the middle. If we don't..."

"Nothin' from nothin' leaves nothin'," LeDoux said. "I

won't be no use to you and I'll just be on my way, no hard feelin's."

Badeaux found himself nodding. "Yeah. I think so. Yeah."

IT WAS NEARING dawn when Farrell rolled back into New Orleans from St. Bernard Parish. In spite of the rigors of the past day, his eyes were bright and alert. For the first time in a long while, he felt fully engaged in life, his mind clicking like a calculating machine.

The Mouton brothers would never know it, but they had given him a lot to think about with the superficial story they'd told him. Archie Badeaux was a man who persisted and survived through the force of his personality. Farrell, himself had seen it while looking in the man's face over the barrel of a sawed-off shotgun. Badeaux hadn't been afraid. Surprised and a bit angry, but not afraid.

And yet Alex Mouton claimed that Badeaux had hired him over the telephone to wreck the Southport Club, and had then sent their payment via a Railway Express Agency messenger. A man like Badeaux wouldn't be likely to involve an honest middleman in a criminal transaction—he'd take care of it himself, to make sure of the men he'd hired, and to let them know on the spot that they'd better not fail him. The Moutons were a couple of stumble-bums. They might do for back-alley mugging, but not for going into a high-class nightclub where a hundred witnesses could get a look at them. And Badeaux would know that.

He thought back over some of the things that Molly Tatum had told him. Badeaux was supposedly working solely for Jonathan Lincoln. Sam Whately had opined that Lincoln was playing some deep game that would make him a power in the New Orleans underworld. Could a man whose boss had those kinds of ambitions afford to spend the time it would take to run a nightclub owner out of business?

There was, too, the business of the three dead businessmen.

Making a murder look like a suicide, as Malcolm Redding's was made to look, was Badeaux's natural métier. So was making two other businessmen vanish off the face of the earth, as Bautain and Johnson had. If Badeaux had murdered three men in cold blood, would he stop at killing a problematic woman if his boss wanted her club? Farrell was forced to doubt it.

So why had Carol concocted this charade? She wanted Farrell involved in her life for some reason, but what was it? He looked at his strap watch and saw that it was nearly six. If she was anywhere, she was at home. He'd checked on her address earlier, and knew that she lived on Press Drive, in the Gentilly section. He turned the wheel of the Packard and headed across the Downtown section. The town was dead at that hour, and with little traffic to impede his progress, he reached her home in about thirty-five minutes.

He pulled up at the front and saw nothing unusual. The neighborhood was still slumbering, and no one, not even a family dog was about. He got out of the car, pushing the door shut, rather than slamming it, then moved silently up the walk on the soft soles of his evening pumps. As he reached the door, the fine hairs on the back of his neck and hands began to prickle, and without consciously planning it, the Colt automatic appeared in his hand. He looked down at the latch and saw that the door was ajar. He felt cold all over as he pushed the door open and slipped inside, quickly stepping to one side and dropping into a crouch.

"Carol?" he called. "Carol, it's Farrell," he said again, a bit louder. Again, nothing.

He rose and began moving deeper into the house, his eyes and gun muzzle inspecting every corner, every hiding place. He found her bedroom, and saw clothing strewn about and the bedclothes torn from the bed onto the floor. There was disarray everywhere he looked. He wasn't quite certain what had happened, although it seemed clear that there'd been some kind of violent activity here before Carol left.

He heard water running, and saw water coming from under the bathroom door. He went to the door, flung it open, and found the sink overflowing. On the bathroom mirror, in Carol's distinctive plum-colored lipstick, was the hasty scrawl of one word: *LINCOLN.*

SAM WHATLEY sat in the nearly deserted newsroom of *The Louisiana Weekly* with his eyes closed, fingers laced across his belly, his chest rising and falling regularly with sleep. He'd been sleeping in one place like this or another for most of his adult life, and often found it more restful than his few actual nights spent in a bed. His jowls were pouched where his chin was sunk on his breast, and his lips were pursed, making little poooohing sounds as he exhaled.

Before slipping off to dreamland, he'd called everyone he knew in Memphis, and had remained in the office in the hope that one of his sources would call with some information. He'd fallen asleep in his desk chair at two, and it was past six now.

The telephone on his desk began to jangle, and it rang several more times before he was jarred from his slumber. He started, snorted, then broke wind as he shifted in his chair. Wrinkling his nose at the smell, he reached over and grabbed the receiver off the hook. "Whately," he said.

"Sam, it's Drew," a voice said. "Sam, you there?"

Whately rubbed his face briskly with his free hand, and sat up a bit straighter in the chair. "Sorry, Drew. Dozed off. Gettin' too old for this night owl stuff."

"You and me both," the other man said with laughter bubbling in his voice. "Listen, I got some dope for you on that question you asked about. That photo of that woman you wired up here—where'd you get that?"

"No big secret," Whately said. "She owns the first Negro nightclub in Jefferson Parish. We did a story on it and one of the staff photographers went out there one night and snapped a few shots of the place and the owner. Swell dish, huh?"

"No lie," Drew said. "And real respectable-lookin'. It was a good enough photo that it helped me nail down a few things."

Whately grabbed a pen and pencil. "Go ahead. I'm listenin'."

"It's quite a story," Drew said. "Your nightclub owner wasn't exactly a member of the Ladies' Aid Society up here. Fact is, she never owned anything like a nightclub in these parts."

"What did she do?" Whately asked.

"Better ask what she didn't do," Drew replied. "She used three different names while she lived here. She was a high-class hooker by the name of Mattie Roker, ran an illegal gambling dive under the name Ann Lou Donovan, and managed a fancy house under the name Manda Hayes."

"Damn," Whately said. "Busy lady. Why all the shiftin' around?"

"Not completely sure," Drew replied. "Could be the name shifts and the job changes were just how she kept one step ahead of the law. It's a common thing among underworld types, as I'm sure you know."

"Yep," Whately said. "I've known yeggs who had as many as fifteen aliases, and a whore in Biloxi who used twenty-five—that gal was *somethin'*."

Drew laughed appreciatively. "Did come across one thing that was a little peculiar."

"Go on," Whately said.

"An ex-cop on the vice squad said he'd heard some peculiar things from this old drunk who used to be a press photographer for one of the New York Negro papers," Drew continued. "I found him, bought him a few drinks and he told me this story about workin' for a colored gangster name of Lincoln who'd been a big noise over in Jackson."

Whately perked up and leaned forward in his chair, as though straining to catch every word that Drew uttered.

"Jonathan Lincoln?"

"That's the one," Drew said. "Said this Lincoln had used him to trap influential types in compromisin' positions with this young whore. He took me to his flop and showed me copies of some of his pictures—they'd peel the paint right off the wall, I tell you."

"Jesus," Whately said, scribbling rapidly.

"He had pictures of a couple of Negro ministers, businessmen, bank officers, and a school principal with this gal. And that's just the start. There was white men they trapped like that, too. Drunk said there was a couple'a state senators, three judges, and the man who was the Jackson chief of police at the time."

"Damn," Whatley said. "How'd they manage all that?"

"The li'l gal would give them a come-on, get them a li'l bit likkered up, lure 'em to a room she had in a house somewhere, and this drunk would be on the other side of a two-way mirror with his Graflex. He told me that a couple times, when she couldn't get the marks to cooperate, that she'd drop chloral hydrate into their drinks to knock them out. Afterwards, some of Lincoln's men would take the unconscious man to the gal's rooms, strip him, and let the gal roll around in the bed with him while the drunk took pictures. He told me this, all of his own free will, too."

"How'd the drunk end up in Memphis?" Whately asked. "He must'a been makin' good dough with a racket like that."

"He got scared after they got to messin' with white folks," Drew answered. "A respectable colored person'll lay down for something like this—he's got too much to lose. But you start trying to hold up a powerful white man with friends, he'll get those friends together and they'll shoot your ass right off—if you're lucky."

"Yeah, and if you ain't lucky, they'll hang you up in a tree and set the tree on fire," Whately said. "It's a great story, Drew, but what's it got to do with the woman I asked you about?"

"Well, this drunk worked for her for a while," Drew replied. "When she ran the fancy house, she also did a small business in pornographic pictures for a while. The drunk was her photographer—while it lasted. Anyhow, they got on pretty good, he said. She appreciated his work and laughed at his jokes. Made him feel almost human at times, leastways that's how he put it. Over a period of time he told her quite a lot about his experiences, and he happened to tell her about workin' for this Lincoln."

"So that's the connection," Whately said under his breath. "What'd she do after he told her the story?"

"She left town," Drew replied. "Just packed up her stuff and left without a word. He found one of the girls in her house who'd seen her put her suitcases into her car early the next morning and then drive away. She never came back, and the man's still pretty upset about it. I think he was kind'a in love with her," Drew said with a wistful note in his voice.

Whately sat there for a moment, tapping the point of his pencil against the surface of the stenographer's notebook he'd been using. "That's damned interesting," he said after a moment's pause. "Good work, old friend. When you comin' down this way the next time?"

"Hard to say," Drew replied. "Gets harder and harder to get away every day."

"Too bad," Whately said. "After all this work, I figured I owed you a crawl through some of the dives down here, if you could get away, that is."

"Hell, why didn't you say so? I'll try to get down there the first week of July." Drew's voice was suddenly as enthusiastic as a teenage boy's.

Whatley laughed. "Good. Let me know if you change your plan."

"Okay, Sam. Talk to you soon."

"Right, 'bye now."

Whatley replaced the telephone on the cradle, then lifted

his feet as the night janitor made a pass with his push broom. He looked at his watch and saw it was nearly seven. He got out his personal phone directory and began looking up his Jackson, Mississippi, contacts.

DOM MOUTON came back to consciousness in the front seat of the Pierce Arrow, cool breeze rushing over him through the open sides of the car. He shifted himself, sitting straight up and rubbing his eyes.

"Where we at, Alex?" he mumbled.

"Through Slidell, goin' east," his brother replied. "I got a couple'a pals in Mobile could give us some mechanic work. Enough to keep us alive for a while, anyway. If things there don't pan out, we could try our luck over in Pensacola. Always wanted to see that beach over there, maybe get a look at them flyin' boats that the Navy's got. That must really be something, flyin' way up in the sky, and then landin' on the water—kinda like bein' a pelican."

Dom leaned forward, rubbing his forehead with his hands. Alex saw that his brother had a big discolored place over his temple where Farrell had slugged him. Damn, that man could move, he thought. Too light on his feet for a white man, Alex thought. "If you're feelin' a li'l bit rocky, there's a pint of Old Crow in the glove box."

Dom fumbled with the latch to the glove compartment until it came open, then rummaged around in there until he found the brown glass bottle. He uncorked it, tipped it to his lips, and drank a long swallow. "Ahhh," he said, wiping his lips on the back of his hand. Blinking his eyes, he seemed to be truly conscious of his surroundings for the first time.

"What the hell happened? My head feels like a split melon."

"You went up against Wesley Farrell and he 'bout knocked your damn block off is what happened. You lucky to still be breathin', boy."

Dom shifted in his seat again and muttered a curse under his breath. "I don't like this runnin' off without gettin' some payback. Badeaux set us up for some reason—I don't know what he's got against us, but he set us up."

Alex shrugged. "Maybe. I don't understand none of it—never did. All's I understood was the money."

"Shit," Dom said. "He give us a measly hundred skins to go up against a life-taker like Farrell. He owes us for Jay-Jay. That boy was kin to us, Alex."

"Jay-Jay was always one to jump before he looked," Alex said. "He shouldn't of never pulled that gun. He'd be in jail right now if he hadn't, but he'd be alive. I feel sorry for his mama."

"Goddamn it, Alex," Dom exploded. "You always makin' excuses when things don't go right. Archie Badeaux set us up to take a fall. We got us a cousin dead and five friends prob'ly gettin' the rubber hose treatment in the back of the sheriff's lock-up. I say we go back to town, look him up, and squeeze him 'til he pops." Dom's body was rigid with anger, and he leaned over toward his brother. Alex could smell the hot fumes of liquor on his breath.

"Archie Badeaux ain't nobody to fool with," Alex said nervously.

"Hell, we the Mouton brothers," Dom said. "We the same guys who went in that 'tonk in Terrebone Parish that time, took on that bunch'a goddamn Cajuns, and beat the dog shit out'a them. That was two against six, remember? We cut them down like they was wheat and we was the scythe."

"That was different," Alex said prudently. "They was just bayou peckerwoods. You're talkin' about goin' up against Archie Badeaux."

Dom reached into the glove compartment and came out with an old .44-40 Smith & Wesson revolver. "Archie Badeaux's a man. You punch a hole in him and he'll bleed. Besides," he said, glowering, "he owes us somethin' for sendin' us into that trap—more money, or his skin. Hell, we'll be lucky to be able to come home for a year."

Alex's mouth took on a sulky cast, and he half-shrugged his meaty shoulders as he tried to think of a reasonable excuse to keep going east. But he couldn't. Dom was a hothead, but he was right. Badeaux owed them. He didn't know why the man had set them up like that, but the inescapable conclusion was that he had. Alex had to admit that he was curious about what they'd done to merit the set-up.

As he thought about Jay-Jay and the other boys getting worked over by parish deputies, he felt an ember of hate down inside him suddenly burst into full flame. He applied the brakes to the old touring car, and worked the wheel to get it turned around in the highway. Within seconds, they were headed west again.

He flicked a glance over at his brother, and saw Dom smiling, his eyes hot and mad-looking. Dom reached back into the glove compartment and brought out a mate to the old Smith & Wesson in his hand. He broke it, made sure it was loaded, then closed the old gun and laid it in his brother's lap. After a moment, Alex picked up the old gun and shoved it down in the left side of his waistband.

LINCOLN WOKE before the sun came up, as he often did. Sleep was so close to waking for him now that it was more like he was in a daze, rather than experiencing actual slumber. He was getting old, as much as he hated to admit it. The bullet that had cut his spine in two had probably shaved ten years off his life, pushing him closer to the grave than he was ready to be. It wasn't that he was afraid of dying, exactly—it was more that there was too much that he still wanted to do. More than anything else, he wanted to resurrect the empire he'd lost in Jackson. He was wise enough to know he couldn't take an earthly empire with him—but he wanted to know if he was still good enough to do it one more time.

His mind began to float back over the years, another sign of advancing age, he thought wryly. He'd been a happy little boy once, back in the Mississippi Delta. He'd lived an idyllic life then, wrestling, and fishing, and playing hide and seek with the plantation owner's sons, taking lessons with the boys and their sister from the tutor the planter had imported at no small expense. If it had continued forever, he'd have been content.

But something had happened the year he turned twelve, though, something that had changed his life forever. Some cousins had arrived, and like usual, he was with the other boys. They gathered at the coach door and young Jonathan stood with them with a feeling of heightened expectation. They didn't get company with children all that often, and he wondered what wonders these strangers would bring from the outside world.

The family with their two boys aged nine and twelve got out of the coach and all the children began talking at once, but as he pressed closer, Jonathan noticed that a reserve come upon the visitors' children. They ignored him studiously, paying an exaggerated attention to their cousins. The planters' children noticed the change, too, but ignored it, and in the ignoring, put Jonathan outside their group. Dazed and confused, he remained rooted to the spot as the children went inside the big house to play games.

The rest of that day seemed impossibly lonely to him and he drifted from place to place about the estate. Toward the middle of the afternoon, he wandered into the kitchen where Aunt Sallie was up to her elbows in pie dough. Jonathan lived with Aunt Sallie in a cabin nearby, something he'd always known, yet never bothered to question. A few times he'd seen himself alongside the planter's sons and daughter, and noticed no difference in them. At times, he fancied he could even see a resemblance, although it meant nothing to him besides an interesting coincidence.

"What you mopin' around for, boy?" Aunt Sallie asked in a soft, mildly disinterested voice.

"Some folks come to visit at the big house," he said. "They brung some chirren with them."

"So why ain't you with 'em?" Aunt Sallie asked. "Every time I sees one of 'em, I sees you right behind. Y'all have a fuss?"

"No," Jonathan said. "The other chirren—the ones come to visit—they act like I ain't there. They wouldn't talk to me—they wouldn't even look at me. Why'd they wanna do that, Auntie?"

Sallie sighed deep within herself. She'd been wondering when this day would come, and had actually dreaded it. She hated to take a child's innocence away from him, but she'd known ever since she took the infant Jonathan from his dead mother's arms that the day would come. "Reckon their folks don't like 'em to play with coloreds," she said offhandedly.

"Colored?" the boy said. "Who's colored?"

"You is, son," she replied.

"No, Auntie. I'm as white as they is. I seen it in the mirror."

She put her pie to one side and sat down on a chair so she could be on his level, and put an arm about his shoulders. "You don't look colored, but you is, down where it can't be seen. You see, a body can be white on the outside, but it's the colored in the inside that they judges you by. You got a little of that colored in you, and to them other folks, you all colored. You'll never be anything else."

"No," he said in a dazed voice. "It ain't true."

"The white folks makes the rules, son, and this a rule that can't be broke," she said, blinking to keep a shine from growing in her eyes. "You'll get used to it, by and by. After a while, you won't even think about it no more."

The boy staggered off from her then, and she had to restrain herself from running after him. She'd dealt him a cruel blow, but he'd have to find a way to live with it without anyone's help.

He ended up in the cabin he shared with her, dazed and sick inside. He felt the world whirling around him, and he fell down on the old braided rug and ceased to know anything. Sallie found him there several hours later, with a raging fever and his clothes soaked with sweat. She stripped the sodden clothing from him and spent the rest of the night bathing his body in cold water to bring down the fever. It was still raging the next day, and the plantation owner was prevailed upon to send for a doctor.

Toward evening, the doctor arrived. He couldn't tell what had brought the fever on, but he knew that like any fever, it had to break. He applied himself to that principle, and two days later the fever did break, and the boy returned to a semblance of consciousness. His body looked wasted, and the hollows around his eyes seemed to have been burned there. By the end of the week, he had taken enough nourishment to be able to get up and around again. Soon he was like himself in all but one respect—he no longer played with the other children. He continued to take lessons with them, but afterward kept to himself.

At the age of fifteen, he asked the planter to let him go to work with the other young Negro men. "You don't have to do that," the man said. "Continue with your lessons, and then I'll send you to Tuskeegee. You can learn to be a school teacher or some other useful occupation. You don't need to grub in the dirt for a living."

"No, sir," Jonathan replied. "I wish to be with my own kind."

The planter's face reddened, from embarrassment or anger the boy could not tell. After a lengthy silence, the man replied, "As you wish. But don't come to me later with any complaints about the hard road you've taken. You made the choice yourself."

"Yes, sir," Jonathan replied. He met the man's gaze, and his jaw hardened stubbornly.

For the next three years, the boy worked as a laborer, and his body became toughened to the demands of physical work. He spent his spare time listening to the older men, learning much. From one, he learned the skills of card-playing and dice. Another showed him the tricks of wrestling, boxing, and infighting. Yet another taught him how to make a knife from an old file, then worked patiently with him in the art of knife-fighting and throwing.

Other parts of his education also received special attention. One of the older girls, noting what a fine, well-built youth he'd turned into, invited him into a barn one evening and initiated him into the ways of sex. He proved to be a particularly apt pupil, and subsequently used his new knowledge with a considerable number of the other young plantation girls.

On the day he was eighteen years old, he counted the money he'd made, and found that he had amassed, through his wages and gambling, a sum of one hundred dollars. He went to Aunt Sallie and informed her of his decision to leave and find his own way in the world. She didn't want him to go, and tried in every way she could think of to keep him by her, but he was adamant in his refusal. There was one thing he demanded of her, and he would not let her alone until she relented.

"I want to know who my sire is," he'd said.

"What difference does it make?" she asked. "It can't do you no good to know." But in the end, she told him what he'd half suspected for years—that the planter, himself, was his father. He nodded, a half-smile hovering at his lips, as though she'd told him some mild and harmless joke.

The next day, carrying a flour sack containing his few possessions and with the hand-made knife on his belt, he left the plantation and didn't stop until he'd reached Memphis. The years that followed were years of blood and thunder. He killed a man in a knife fight over a game of cards. The man had called him a cheat, which Jonathan was—he'd learned his lessons well years before. He already knew that if a man backed down from a direct challenge like that, he'd be despised from then on.

The fight had begun without any preamble, and was

savage in its intensity. The duration was short. With two quick slashes, Jonathan disabled the man's knife arm, and as he tried to switch hands, the youngster went in under the other man's guard, disemboweling him with a single stroke. The man looked down in shock as his insides poured out of him onto the sawdust floor. He was dead in minutes, and Jonathan found he had a new reputation, one that brought him admirers, and challengers, as well. His life became that of an itinerant gladiator, and he made more money hiring himself out to maim or kill those who'd become inconvenient to someone, or who were owed punishment or retribution of some kind by those powerful and rich enough to purchase it.

Over the years that followed, Jonathan found a solid place in the Beale Street underworld, dealing in women, illegal whiskey, extortion, and murder. His pale skin, educated manner, and the black broadcloth that he wore made him stand out in any company. Another man might've chosen to live as white, but Jonathan's desire was to live with those who'd accepted him rather than with those who'd arbitrarily rejected him for a thimbleful of blood.

When Memphis became too hot to hold him, he migrated to Jackson, and took on a new name—Lincoln. He found an amusing irony in using the name of the Great Emancipator, the man who'd freed Negroes—freed them to starve, to be murdered, to be in a state of constant fear. Lincoln feared no one, and in the years that followed, both white and Negro came to fear him.

As he lay there in semi-darkness, he thought again of the day he'd returned to the plantation where he grew up, riding the back of a prancing roan gelding. Dressed in the black coat, hat, and trousers, he made a sight that caused the Negroes in the fields to straighten up and stare after him.

When he reached the plantation, he rode to the kitchen door, dismounted, and walked inside. He found a younger Negro woman of perhaps twenty five there, busy with, of all things, pie dough. "Where's Aunt Sallie?" he asked.

"She been out there in the ground these seven years now," the young woman replied, wiping her forehead with the back of her hand. She left a streak of flour on her coal-black forehead, reminding him of Aunt Sallie for a moment. She'd often been streaked with flour. "It was the fever done her in," the woman said. "That and just not carin' no more. She pined for this li'l boy she used'ta have, but he been gone a long time by then."

He nodded, his eyes cast down at the floor. Nothing had hurt him in a long time, but he felt a curious sense of loss and remorse at the discovery of her death. He left the kitchen, remounted the gelding, and rode back to the Negro cemetery that had been there as long as the plantation, itself.

He found her grave after fifteen minutes or so of looking. He knelt down by the grass-covered mound and took off his hat. He didn't know how to pray, and didn't believe in God anyway. He removed from his vest a locket on a chain, and draped it over a corner of the wooden marker with her name burned into it.

He got up and mounted the horse again, then trotted out to the front of the big house. The master was there, now grown old, but still spare and straight in his black riding boots. Jonathan rode up to him, his left hand tangled in the reins and his right atop his thigh.

"It's normal courtesy for a man to call at the door to a house before he starts gallivanting all over another man's property. Who are you, sir?" the old man demanded.

"One who carries your blood," he replied melodramatically. Lincoln had learned to love a bit of theatrics for moments like these. When the man looked at him blankly, Jonathan said, "Little Jonny. Surely you remember. Your bastard son by a woman named Lucille. She died bearing me, but you never owned up to it."

"You've got a hell of a nerve..." the old man began. Jonathan held up a hand.

"You got off cheap, old man," he said. "I went away a

long time ago, and took away all of a hundred dollars of your money. By rights, twenty-five percent of all this ought to be mine—if you'd ever been man enough to acknowledge me as your son."

The old man's face flushed the color of blood, and he stepped down off the porch, raising a riding crop. "You dare to come onto my land and lecture me. I'll pull you down from there and—"

Before he could finish the threat, Jonathan Lincoln's right hand flashed to his right hip, and a long-barreled Colt appeared, exploded twice, and then with a single smooth gesture returned to the holster. The old man looked down at the blood welling up on his chest, and collapsed.

Jonathan Lincoln looked down on him, trying to find some emotion, but he could find nothing for the heap of flesh at his horse's hooves, not even hate. What he had done was just paying off an old score. Now that it was paid, there was nothing more to feel, and no reason to linger. He tugged on the reins, and as the horse turned around, he saw Negro men and women clustered in the yard, their mouths open with shock.

He held them with his eyes for a moment, waiting to see if any of them would be brave enough to attack him or attempt to hold him in any way. Most of them looked away, unable to meet his gaze.

"Man," one of the bolder men said in a hushed voice. "What you done?"

"I took away your reason to stay here. The white daddy's dead," he told them. "Go find your own way now, or just keep on being niggers forever. He can't help you anymore." He kicked the gelding lightly in the ribs and it broke into a trot, cutting a wake through the crowd of Negroes like a big red ship splitting the waves.

The old man known as Lincoln lay there in his bed, feeling in his mind the bucking of the .45 against his hand, the strength of the horse between his legs, wishing again to feel the exquisite pleasure of sliding into a woman, knowing that all the money in the world couldn't buy it back for him.

Chapter 13

FRED GONZALVO pulled in front of the boarding house at about six A.M. As he got out of his Chevrolet roadster, he saw Marcel Aristide get out of a brown Ford sedan and stride across the grass toward him.

"Hey, li'l brutha," Gonzalvo said in a low tone. "What's the word?"

"Remember Ralphie Daniels?" Marcel asked.

"Remember? The old man's havin' a fit 'cause the li'l weasel still ain't been in to pay off." Gonzalvo chuckled juicily.

"He's in there," Marcel said, hooking a thumb over his shoulder. "He's been keepin' the landlady warm all night, from what I can tell."

"What?" Gonzalvo almost shrieked. "My mama goes to the same church as that lady. She'd have a fit if she knew a man that young was haulin' her ashes."

"From the look of things, the landlady's been doin' the haulin'," Marcel said.

Gonzalvo grinned. "How you wanna handle this?"

"You go around the back in case he hears me and tries to pull a sneak. I'll go in the front and try to corner him in the bedroom."

"That li'l creep," Gonzalvo said. "I ain't busted me a head in about six months. I hope he tries a run-out, I purely hope he does."

"Just don't kill him," Marcel warned. "He ain't no good to anybody dead."

The pair split up and Marcel walked up to the front door, removing from his pocket a ring of skeleton keys. He tried about a half-dozen before he found one that would work. Quietly he opened the front door of the house and made his way to the landlady's ground-floor apartment. He found that the front door key fit the lock, here, too.

He passed through the parlor, noticing the open bottle of whiskey, the glasses, and the bucket of melted ice, and then followed the trail of discarded clothing to the bedroom. He leaned against the door post and shook his head. Gonzalvo joined him a minute later, and grinned, hunching Marcel in the ribs lightly with his elbow.

Ralphie lay on his back, one arm trailing down the edge of the bed to the floor. His face was slack, and he breathed heavily like a man who's just run a marathon and come in dead last.

The landlady, her nicely-rounded *derrière* only barely covered by the sheet, lay face down on the bed. In spite of being on her stomach, a noise escaped her mouth—it sounded very much like a file being rubbed across a wooden chair leg.

Marcel nodded to Gonzalvo, who went to the landlady's side of the bed and then pulled out his .38. He put a stern look on his face, and stared down at the occupants of the bed. Marcel took out his Owl's Head, then reached down and pinched Ralphie's nose shut. The runaway-gambler, his breathing cut off, came to violently, starting so that the bed shook.

The landlady, jolted out of her own slumber by Ralphie's sudden movement looked up, saw Marcel, and pulled the sheet over her. As she rolled over, she saw Fred's hard face and she shrilled out, "Don't kill us, for the love of God don't kill us."

"Good morning, Ralphie," Marcel said. "You're late for

your appointment."

"Ralph," Mrs. Brown said from behind her sheet, "what business do you have with these gangsters?"

"You see, ma'am," Marcel said, "Ralphie, here, is in hock to a gambler named Nate Hopkins for seven hundred dollars, which he was supposed to've paid back by yesterday noon. And here we find him, without his pants, long overdue to make good on the debt."

"Ralph, there must be some mistake," Mrs. Brown protested. "We can straighten this out without any violence, can't we?"

"Ma'am," Fred said heavily. "We don't aim to hurt no women, but this boy's done broke the rules. Reckon we gotta start by bustin' that dumb head of his, and then..."

"No, no," Mrs. Brown shrieked, throwing her body across Ralph's, and all but losing her sheet in the process. "Don't hurt him, for God's sake, please don't hurt him."

Fred, no longer able to contain himself, burst out laughing. "Boy," he said to Ralph, who was struggling to remain under the body of his middle-aged lover, "you ain't much of a gambler, but at least you can do somethin' right. You might just come outta this with a whole skin." He laughed again, uproariously. Marcel found that he, too, could no longer keep a straight face, either.

Marcel spun the old revolver on his finger and shoved it into his hip pocket. He was amused by the ridiculous scene, but he felt a strange satisfaction at that moment. He'd taken a risk, had the cards go against him, but had somehow turned things around. Nate Hopkins would get his money back, but for Marcel the big thing was that he had erased the doubts from his own mind that his earlier failures had put there.

He had an understanding now that in the kind of business that Farrell had him doing, whether you were vigilant or careless, things could come unglued, and a man had to move fast and make the right choices in order to come out on top. There would be other times like this as long as he worked for his cousin, but he knew now, beyond a doubt, that he could play the cards as they fell from now on. He felt calm and strangely at peace.

He turned and looked down on the two people tangled in the sheets, then back up at Fred.

"Why don't you go out in the parlor, Fred."

"Huh?" Fred said, wiping the tears of laughter from his eyes.

"Give us a little privacy for a second," Marcel said quietly.

Still chuckling, Fred walked around the bed. "Whatever you say, boss." He shoved his big revolver back under his jacket and walked out of the bedroom.

"Mrs. Brown," Marcel said. "Nobody's going to hurt Ralph, so you can let him up now. Ralph, you come on out from under there and put your pants on. This ain't no way for a man to act."

Marcel's calm, patient voice seemed to soothe both of the bed's occupants, because Mrs. Brown eased over, taking care to keep the sheet over her. Her eyes were still uncertain, but she was considerably calmer. Ralph, still blinking rapidly as though he expected a bullet or a fist to come his way, eased out of the bed, fumbled for his boxer shorts and trousers, and pulled them quickly on. He stood up slowly, his mouth working to relieve the dryness left there by his fright.

"What you gonna do with me, man?" Ralph finally asked.

"Nothing at all," Marcel said. "You still got the money?"

"Most of it," Ralph said, unable to meet Marcel's eyes.

"Well, we'll come up with what's missing somehow," Marcel said patiently. "They we're gonna take you down to see Nate Hopkins, you're gonna pay him what you owe him, and then you're gonna take whatever lumps he dishes out, you hear?"

Ralph's eyes were bright with fear, but after casting a quick glance down at Mrs. Brown, he faced Marcel again and nodded vigorously. "What then?" he asked.

"That'll be up to your brother, but I figure if you agree to go on and make an effort to work off your debt, he'll give you a break somewhere down the line," Marcel said. "He seems like a decent, hard-working guy."

"Reckon he is at that," Ralph said, lowering his head.

"Finish gettin' dressed then," Marcel said. "I've spent too much time on this as it is. I'm gonna let Fred take care of you until I check back with my boss, then we'll meet up later and go to see Nate Hopkins, all right?"

"Yes, sir," Ralph said meekly.

RUBY RICHOUX was still jittery from shooting Ernie LeDoux, and angry for the bitching out Badeaux had given her. Rather than stay there with the body on the floor or put up with him any further, she'd left and spent the rest of the night at Lincoln's house, using her key rather than waking Albert or Lincoln.

She got up from the bed feeling strung out, her nerves completely raw. She'd consumed a pint of Calvert's Reserve trying to calm herself down, but it had produced the opposite effect. Her eyes were shot with broken blood vessels and her skin had an unhealthy tinge. Her body, unclad but for her step-ins and a brassiere, was clammy from the sticky sweat that dotted it.

She got up, went into the bathroom, and stood in a hot shower until she could no longer stand it, then stood under the cold. It washed away the sweat and with it the stink of cheap whiskey, but nothing else. She still felt like a piece of chewed gum. She wrapped her wet hair in a turban, put on a light cotton robe, then went downstairs to the kitchen. Albert was already there, dressed, as always, in his white shirt, bow tie, and black vest. He was scraping scrambled eggs and bacon from a skillet as she came down.

"Want some of this?" he asked.

"No," she said. "I want coffee."

"It's on the stove," he said. "Help yourself."

"Why don't you pour it for me?" she said nastily.

"Mr. Lincoln hired me to look after him, not you," he replied. "You're old enough to look out for yourself—if you'd smarten up enough to do it. Messin' with that Archie Badeaux ain't gonna get you nothin' but trouble, baby sister."

"Drop dead," she said. "Go look after the old man. It's what you're good for." She had her head in her hands, looking down at the porcelain top of the kitchen table where she sat. She didn't see the look he gave her, nor the way his right fist gathered and trembled for a second. When she did look up, he was gone with Lincoln's breakfast tray.

She got up and walked over to the stove where Albert had left a drip pot of strong black coffee heating in a pan full of water. A saucepan of milk still warmed on another burner, giving off a thick, sweet smell. She poured some of each into a mug, sweetened it with four teaspoons of sugar, then took it back to the table and began sipping.

She'd thought when the old man brought them down to New Orleans that she'd get a chance to get out on her own, but it hadn't worked out the way she'd hoped. She'd schemed on and off for ten years with Badeaux to find LeDoux's missing treasure, and still they had nothing. And you're the damn fool who shot him, she reminded herself. It took all her will power not to throw the mug across the room and smash it.

Albert came back into the room and put a stock pot onto the stove. He filled it with water, added some diced salt pork and chopped onions he'd browned earlier, added a generous portion of red kidney beans, then turned the fire on beneath it. Without looking at her, he said, "Mr. Lincoln wants to see you."

"So?" she said out of the side of her mouth.

"So go up there. Or he said I should bring you." Albert's voice was still low and without expression, but she looked up at his face, and received the full intensity of his eyes. They were not the eyes of a humble domestic servant. She'd heard that he once threw a baby into a furnace because the mother had tried to break away from her pimp. For the first time in her acquaintance of Albert Minshew, she fully believed it.

"Awright, I'm goin', already," she said. Her voice was soft, but there was a teaspoon of acid lying at the bottom of it. She cut her eyes at Albert as she spoke, but he was back at the stove, ignoring her.

She trudged up the stairs like a toddler forced to go to bed before time. She didn't like these summonses, because it placed her in an inferior position. She'd dealt with enough men to know how to get the upper hand and keep it, but there was no getting the upper hand with Lincoln. His was always up, and encased in steel.

She knocked on his bedroom door, then stood there waiting.

"Come," he said in a firm, resonant voice.

She opened the door and walked into the bedroom. Albert had arranged pillows so that he was propped in a sitting position and banked on both sides to keep him from slipping sideways. He had a bed tray of lacquered white pine in front of him, and he was busily eating the scrambled eggs, bacon, and toast Albert had brought up. He had doused the eggs in ketchup, something that she found repulsive. Ketchup always reminded her of blood.

"I heard you come in last night," he said. "It was rather late."

"Yeah, I thought I'd come over here and get some sleep. It was too noisy at the house."

He glanced up at her, still working busily with his knife and fork. "From the look of your eyes, you didn't sleep much here, either. Whiskey won't put you to sleep. Hot milk would do it. You need to keep better care of yourself, girl. I'm not going to be around forever, and I want to leave you in such a way that you can manage things."

"Yes, daddy," she said.

"I know you aren't interested in this," he said as though she hadn't spoken. "But you can't count on people like Badeaux to take care of you. He'll get tired of you and walk away to the nearest floozie who crooks her finger at him."

The force of his words struck her painfully, and she caught her breath, feeling tears about to overflow her eyes. "He's a bastard. He treats me like dirt sometimes."

"Archie wasn't raised by a good family. He was jerked up, I suspect, by a drunken father or a whore for a mother. I saved you from all that. I knew your mother was no good."

"If she was no good, why did you lay with her?" she said, trying to control the emotions about to break loose in her.

"I was a man, she was there," he replied bluntly. "There was no love to it. She wasn't a very lovable person, your mother. But you—the moment I saw you, I felt something paternal. I'd sired children in the past and had not been fazed by it. But you—you were different. I saw things in you, the way you waved your little fists and screamed with such abandon." He paused and looked over her face, as if marking the resemblance to the infant who had so charmed him. "I'd mellowed a bit by then."

"I wouldn't know," she replied.

"Of course you wouldn't," Lincoln said. "By the way, where is Badeaux? I haven't spoken to him in over twenty-four hours."

"He's busy," she said evasively.

He looked at her sharply. "I supposed that much. But busy with what? My business, or his own business? I don't like it when my people get too independent. He needs to remember that he works for me, exclusively. No private errands, no side deals."

"That's all you know about Archie," she said derisively. "He's got a hell of a lot of things on the side."

Lincoln put down his knife and fork and looked over at his daughter, his black eyes boring into her like augers. "Enlighten me, then. Because I have this feeling that wherever he's been, you've been there, too."

She wouldn't look at him, but she could feel his eyes digging at her.

"You've been making the mistake of thinking that because I don't leave this house that I don't know what my people are doing. You should know better. I warned you back when you set up Ernie LeDoux and then gave him up to the police. I know all about that. I also know that Badeaux was playing house with you at the time and put that stupid little idea into your ear."

She was facing him now, her eyes wide and blank-looking. She tried to think of a plausible denial, but it was already too late. He'd cut right into her and opened her up like a butcher slitting open a carcass of beef.

"That's it, isn't it. LeDoux's sentence ended a few days ago—oh, yes, I kept track, even up in Jackson. You and Badeaux thought you could cozy up to him, thinking that ten years in the pen had turned his brains to oatmeal. Oh, you should see the look on your face, my little darling. You look like someone just told you there's no Santa Claus." He laughed at her, a brittle, humorless cackle that seemed to reverberate from the walls of the room.

"He's dead," she said.

Lincoln's laugh cut off clean, although he didn't look particularly disturbed by her confession. "Who's dead? LeDoux or Archie?"

"LeDoux. I—I shot him last night. In the head."

"Well, that was brilliant," Lincoln said. His voice was perfectly neutral, but his sarcasm was evident in his choice of words. She'd known him long enough to understand that much about him. "But I suppose if you left the body with Archie—he at least knows how to dispose of one. God knows, he's disposed of enough of them lately. Come over here," he said, patting the edge of his bed. "Come sit by me and eat a piece of this toast. It'll make you feel better."

It was always like this, she thought. He'd ridicule you until you wanted to cry, then he'll make like he loves you for a minute or two. Dumbly, she got up and trudged to him. She eased her hips onto the side of the bed, and laid her head on his thin shoulder. "There, there," he said. "You can't lose what you never had. There, there."

But, he thought silently. It's time to remind Badeaux

who he's working for. He's been getting too independent lately, and that's not good in a hired killer. It may just be time to retire him and find someone else. Ernie LeDoux, indeed. "Besides, the thing you thought you lost you could never really have. I've had control of it for some time now."

Israel Daggett had received a telephone call before he left home that morning that might promise some enlightenment on the Marcella Attaway murder. He hoped it would, anyway.

Instead of driving directly to the station, he headed for the Mid-City area, and twenty minutes later eased his car to a stop in front of the *Louziana Lou Foods* plant at Jeff Davis Parkway and Howard Avenue. As he strode up the walk to the building, he found himself wondering how this large, white, art-deco monstrosity with all its rounded corners and oval windows had ended up here on the edge of Gert Town, the worst ghetto in the city. Zoning in New Orleans had befuddled smarter men than he, and he soon put it from his mind.

At the main reception desk inside the building, he took off his hat and showed his gold star-and-crescent shield to the young white receptionist. "I wonder if I could have a word with one of your Negro employees," Daggett said. "His name's Percy Godine."

The receptionist looked mildly alarmed. "Percy's not in any trouble, is he, officer?"

"No, ma'am, not at all," Daggett said, wagging his head. "I just want to ask him a question about something that happened in his neighborhood the other night.

Mollified, the receptionist dialed a number on an internal phone line, spoke quietly into the handset, then put it back and looked up at Daggett. "He'll be right down. You can have a seat over there if you like," she said.

"Thank you, ma'am," Daggett said, and he walked over to a leather sofa and sat down. On the coffee table was a recent issue of a locally-published Negro magazine entitled

The Sepia Socialite. Daggett picked it up and began leafing through it idly. There was an article about The Original Southport Club, which Daggett read through. He'd been meaning to take Margurite over there, but hadn't had the time. There was never enough time, he thought a trifle bitterly. He hadn't noticed it when he'd been a single man, but now that he was married, he was constantly afraid that Margurite was getting shortchanged because of his devotion to his job. He was a little worried that she might think so, too.

He put those thoughts aside when he came to the posed portrait of Carol Donovan. Something about the image interested him, but he wasn't completely certain what it was. Before he could finish the thought, he heard the sound of leather heels on the gleaming marble floor and looked up to see a man coming toward him.

Percy Godine was about twenty-five, a serious-looking young man with an erect athletic carriage and a dignified bearing. He walked directly to Daggett without any outward appearance of upset or worry.

"Are you the police officer asking for me?" Godine asked.

Daggett got to his feet and showed his badge. "Detective Sergeant Daggett, Mr. Godine. Why don't you have a seat for a minute. This won't take long."

Godine came around the coffee table and sat down with the detective, then half-turned so he could look Daggett straight-on. If being interrogated by a cop bothered him, he was doing an excellent job of concealing it.

"You're a hard guy to catch up with," Daggett said. "We've been trying to catch you at home for two days now."

"Well," Godine said, "between my night job, college, and my part-time job here, I don't have a lot of free time."

"I see what you mean," Daggett said. "You don't get much sleep, do you?"

"No, sir," the young man said. "But once I get out of college and get myself into a better situation, I can sleep all I want."

Daggett smiled at the young man's self-assurance, then got down to business. "The reason I'm here is because an old woman who lived in your neighborhood got murdered a couple nights ago."

"You mean Mrs. Attaway," Godine said. "That was really a shame. She seemed harmless as a fly."

"Somebody didn't think so," Daggett said. "We're working on the assumption that she was dangerous to somebody and they killed her to shut her up."

"Gracious," the young man said, looking shocked.

"We don't have much to work with right now, and we're hoping that you might've seen or heard something that might help us out."

The young man folded his arms and leaned back on the sofa, his eyes focused on a spot above him on the ceiling. After tugging thoughtfully at his lower lip for a moment, he said, "The neighborhood was pretty quiet when I went to sleep, but I did hear a dog barking later on. It woke me, and I got up to look out the front window."

"Did you see anybody?"

"Not somebody, but I did see something a bit out of place."

"What was that?" Daggett asked.

"Well, there was a car I'd seen in the neighborhood a few times—not often. It's been several months since I saw it the last time. It was a Chrysler coupe—a deluxe 1935 model with a lot of chrome trim. I happened to see it one afternoon when it was still light. It was a light gray two-door. I'd never seen it there that late at night."

"So you'd seen the car before," Daggett said.

"Yes, not often, but a few times a year for the past three or four," he said. "I'd mentioned it to some of the other neighbors, thinking it belonged to some friend of theirs."

"But it didn't," Daggett said.

"No, but I wasn't surprised," Godine said. "Nobody in my neighborhood has two dimes to rub together, and they don't know anybody who has. They're all workin' folks, just scraping by."

"Okay," Daggett said. "Let's get back to that night. When did you see it?"

"It was about one at the time," the young man said. "I went to the kitchen to have some milk and a few ginger cookies my mother sent over—was in there maybe fifteen minutes. I came back to look out the window before going back to bed, and the car was gone."

"It might be useful if I could find the owner and talk to him or her," Daggett said. "Did you notice the license number or anything like that?"

Godine considered a minute, then said, "Not all of it, but the first two numbers were six and eight. That's my birthday, June eighth. I probably wouldn't have noticed at all but for that. I'm always playing games with numbers—I'm studying to be an accountant."

Daggett looked up from the notebook he was writing in with a grin on his face. "A man who notices all this in the dark just because he hears a dog barking might just think of becoming a cop. This might just be useful information." He stood up, and Godine, sensing the interview at an end, stood up with him.

"Thanks for your help," the detective said. "If you think of anything else, give me a call at this number." He fished a card out of his vest pocket and handed it to the young man. Godine took the card, looked at it, and nodded.

"What's a man got to do to become a cop, if you don't mind my asking?" Godine asked.

Daggett grinned again and scratched the back of his neck. "He needs to like long hours, not much money, and a flair for writing reports—that and not mind getting shot at occasionally."

Godine cocked an eyebrow at the detective. "Take away the report business, and that describes what a Negro does every day."

"You got a point," Daggett said. "Better continue on

with your accounting. Let me know how it turns out." He shook hands with the young man and walked back over to the reception desk. "Excuse me, miss," he said. "Would you happen to have a phone I could use for a minute? I need to call headquarters."

She pointed at a desk phone on a long, low table under a large window that looked out on the parkway, and he nodded and walked over to it. Within a minute or two, he had Andrews on the telephone. "Sam, I think I got something on the Attaway case. Get somebody to start lookin' at vehicle registrations for the surrounding parishes and see if you can find a 1935 Chrysler deluxe two-door coupe, light gray in color. The first two numbers of the license are six and eight."

"You talk to the Godine kid?" Andrews asked.

"Yeah, he turned out to be a gold mine. Says he saw the car there on and off for the past several years, and knows from talkin' to the neighbors that the driver isn't acquainted with anyone else in the neighborhood. He woke up because of a dog barking and saw it parked in front about the time we think the Attaway woman got killed."

"I like the sound of this," Andrew said. "I'll get that new kid, Patout, to work on it."

"Tell him to work fast," Daggett said. "I got a feeling about this. And Sam?"

"Yeah?"

"Get Gautier to go over to the Notorial Archives and look up the title to that house the Attaway woman lived in. I got a feelin' about that, too."

"What're you thinkin' about, boss?"

"It's hunch," Daggett said. "Nothing more than that."

Andrews had heard that tone of voice from his boss before, and didn't believe it a bit. "Okay, play it close to the vest. I don't have to know anything but what you tell me."

Daggett chuckled. "Don't worry, grandma. It's just a

crazy idea I got. I don't want to look like a clown if it doesn't pan out. Anything from New Orleans Motors?"

"I called Ray Snedegar, and he said he was going over there this morning first thing. Maybe we'll have something by early afternoon."

"I hope so," Daggett said.

LUTHER WOKE up about three A.M. feeling like he'd climbed the mountain and then was too worn out to even roll back down. Carol Donovan had really put him over the jumps. He couldn't admit it, but he knew beyond a doubt that he didn't know a thing about women at all. Carol's attentions to him were a surprise—one that puzzled and worried him a little bit.

He looked at her bare back as she sat at her dressing table, brushing her dark hair out with a brush. She caught a glimpse of him watching her in the mirror, and paused her brushing long enough to smile at him. Her smile wasn't like any woman's smile he'd ever seen. It reached down your throat, punched a hole in your heart, then continued on down until it exploded in your testicles. He felt himself getting stirred up just seeing her face.

"What're you looking at?" she asked.

"Why, you, honey," he said. "It's a pretty wonderful sight, I swear. There's somethin' I don't understand, though."

"What's that?" she asked, resuming her brushing.

"Why a classy lady like you wants to bother about a scuffle-town nigger like me. I ain't nobody—just a flunky for Archie Badeaux."

"You're more important to Badeaux than that," she said. "After all, he sent you to bully me, to shut me up. He wouldn't just send anybody to do that. He trusts you—you're important to him."

Luther couldn't help but be flattered by Carol's words. He thought about them for a second and allowed as how there was some truth to her description of him, although it was considerably prettied up from the way Badeaux usually described him.

"You're too good to waste yourself on Badeaux," she said. "You could throw in with me and we could do some business." She put down the brush, turned her buttocks around on the stool, and leaned toward him, her breasts swinging elastically from her chest. It was almost enough to make his heart stop for a second.

"Gee, whiz, honey," he protested. "I don't know about all that. Archie ain't some guy you just go foolin' around on. He's bad medicine when he gets riled up."

"If we handle things right, you can take over Badeaux's action after he's out of the way," she said, kneeling on the bed, hovering over him like a bird.

He'd been on the point of pinching one of her chocolate-brown nipples when she said that, and his hand jumped away from her like he'd been stung. "What'd you say?" he squeaked. "Honey, Archie ain't some punk you can just sweep out the front door. He's the baddest man I ever worked with. Why, I once seen him walk into a room full of men, and when the dust cleared, he was the only one still standin' up."

She smiled and put her hand on Luther's belly, rubbing it softly as it traveled down his front to the tangle of brown hair where his legs came together. His manhood stirred in response, in spite of the frightened look in his eyes. She lowered her mouth to the base of his neck and began to gently chew and lick the tender flesh there. He moaned, and his hands reached around and caught her buttocks and began to knead them.

"You just don't appreciate what you've got, honey," she murmured to him. "You're smart and you're strong. With a little help, we could make a place for ourselves with Badeaux's boss. He won't care who does his dirty work for him, so long as it gets done and gets done right."

Luther moaned again, and his hands began to move up and down her thighs. She knew he wouldn't hear anything else she said for a while, so she continued to use her mouth and hands on him until he was ready, then she lay down on top of him and loved him until he screamed.

She rested on her side, stroking his ear playfully with her index finger until he turned on his side and looked into her eyes. "Goin' up against Archie won't be easy," he said. "He's smart. He can smell trouble comin' a mile away. We got to have us an edge of some kind, or he'll kill both of us."

"We'll have to do some thinking, then," Carol said. "Before we act."

He looked at her for a little while, rubbing her hip with his hand. "You ain't told me why you wanna do this."

She pulled herself closer to him until she could feel his heart thudding against her ribs. "Because I want to form a partnership with his boss—the kind of partnership that'll make me somebody in this town. The nightclub is just a front. I wanted to attract Lincoln's attention, then do something to get next to him. If I can outsmart Badeaux, I'll be more valuable to him than Badeaux ever was. It's as simple as that."

He shook his head a little. It was hard to do on the pillow, but the trouble in his eyes made plain his worry. "I don't know Mr. Lincoln well enough to say how he'd act if somebody cut his A-Number-One out from under him. Could be he wouldn't take it kindly. He's got some other boys, includin' a big sonofabitch named Albert. I believe Albert could rip the head off'n a bull if Lincoln told him to, and I wouldn't wanna be standin' between Albert and the bull if Lincoln give the word."

She raised up on her elbow and let her long hair swing over Luther's face, sending waves of perfume down into his face. He shuddered, but didn't move. "I've got something that Lincoln wants," she said. "He doesn't know it yet, but he will once I get to talk to him. It might be that we won't have to get rid of Badeaux. If I play it right, he'll decide Badeaux's got to go, and get rid of him for us. Like you say, he's got Albert."

"There's that," Luther admitted. "I ain't exactly on first-name terms with Mr. Lincoln, but I reckon I could ask him if he'd see you. It might be an easier way to go."

"And if he won't, we can always hit Badeaux and use that as a way to get in to see the old man," she said.

Luther propped himself up on a pillow, some of the worry leaving his face. This woman was too good to let get away from him, and he'd even buck Archie to keep her, but he was just as happy not to have to go that route. "Why don't we call at the house and we'll see if he'll let us in," he suggested. "It'd be easier and cleaner in the long run to do it like that."

She smiled at him like he was the cleverest, slickest yegg to ever walk the underworld, her eyes shining with pride in him. At least that's the way it looked to Luther.

Behind the smile, Carol knew that she had entered a game that would require nerve and luck. She had everything in play now, even Wesley Farrell. Now, if only she could get all the players in the same place at the same time.

IT WAS PAST noon when the Sunset Limited arrived at the Union Passenger Terminal in Downtown New Orleans. Savanna Beaulieu's makeup had been freshened and she wore a smart-looking twill suit with a blouse of rose pink silk and her wide-brimmed straw hat with a pink ribbon band. The closer to New Orleans she'd gotten, the more excited she'd become. Putting on fresh clothing and makeup was her own special way of coping with the excitement.

As the train eased to a stop alongside the platform, she made her way down the aisle with her overnight bag, and out to the vestibule, where a courtly porter in a white jacket helped her descend from the car. Even though there was no one to greet her, she wore a smile just to be back in the city. She'd thought several times about wiring 'Tee Ruth Sonnier or her daughter, Margurite Daggett, or even

Farrell, but in the end, she'd decided to just return to town and rediscover everything on her own.

Another porter helped her get her bags and saw her out to the taxi stand, where a Harker Brothers cab driver helped her get her things into the trunk of his taxi. Once she was situated, he got in behind the wheel and said, "Where to, ma'am?"

She considered for a moment, then said, "Take me to the Café Tristesse on Basin Street."

"Okay," he said, and then started the car. It took less than ten minutes to make it there. He helped her get her bags into the club vestibule, after which she paid him and sent him on his way.

It struck her as ironic that she'd never entered the club from the front entrance. Farrell had been the most important person in her life for a few years, but as a Negro, she couldn't expect to be treated like any other club guest. She wondered if Farrell ever considered that particular irony, and eventually decided that he had. Farrell's inability to deal openly with his identity was painful for him sometimes, as she well knew from observing him.

She walked through the lobby into the main floor and continued past the cleaning crew to the bar, where Harry Slade, as always, stood working on inventory and other bar concerns. He heard her footsteps coming up behind him, and turned, smiling when he saw her face.

"Miss Savanna," he said, beaming. "When did you get in?"

"Just got off the train about a half-hour ago," she said.

"Seems like you been gone a long time," Harry said. "About a year, ain't it?"

"A little less, but sometimes it seemed a lot longer," she said.

"The boss is really gonna be glad to see you," Harry said, then caught himself. His boss's relationship with Savanna was something he'd figured out for himself long ago, but he pretended that he thought their friendship was strictly business. The world being what it was, he knew nobody could afford to talk openly about such a liaison.

"I'm lookin' forward to seeing him, too," she said. "Is he here?"

Harry raised a corner of his mouth and scratched his head quizzically. "Truth is, he ain't been in much this week. I don't know where he is, to be honest, since he ain't checked in recently. It might be that Marcel knows. He's upstairs now, if you wanna talk to him."

"That would be okay," she said. "I haven't seen him in a long time, either."

Harry called upstairs to Farrell's office, told Marcel about Savanna's appearance, and agreed to send her up.

"My suitcases are in the vestibule, Harry," she said. "Would you look after them for me?"

"Sure thing," he said. "You know the way up, right?" He instantly realized what he'd said, grimaced, and turned his face back to his inventory sheet. He didn't see Savanna's grateful smile before she walked toward the staircase leading to the second floor.

She found Marcel pacing up and down the floor of Farrell's office. He had filled out a little since she'd seen him last, and his face had lost some of the boyishness it had previously held. He reminded her jarringly of Farrell; the worried look he wore she'd seen on Farrell's face more than once. "Savanna," Marcel said, meeting her at the door. "Where did you drop from?" He smiled and walked over with his hands held out.

She took his hands and smiled back at him. "I got sick of Los Angeles and decided to come back home," she said.

"Where you belong," Marcel said with a nod of approval. "Wes isn't around just now," he added. She could tell by the look in his eyes that there was more to the story than that, but she let it lie for the moment.

"I heard," she said with a touch of rue on her lips. "I wasn't sure comin' here was exactly the best idea. I—I kind of wanted to come and tell him I was sorry—for walking away from him the way I did. I half expect him to tell me to go to hell."

Marcel nodded sympathetically. "I can't tell you what's on his mind, but I do know one thing—he's been a changed man since you left. I don't think I've seen him smile once in the past year." He paused to knead the muscles and tendons in the back of his neck with his hand for a moment. "I think your being so far away has been tough on him, but don't tell him I said so."

"No," she said, "of course not." She paused to look at Marcel, then said, "Something's wrong, isn't it?"

Marcel cut his eyes away from her for a moment, then brought them up to meet hers again. "I don't know," he said. "I've kind'a had my own troubles for the past few days and haven't been in touch with him. Once I'd tied up all the loose ends, I came here to check in with him, and found him gone."

"He gets wrapped up in things all the time, doesn't he?" she asked, trying to resist the feeling of panic that Marcel's worry was trying to set off.

"I know that," Marcel said, shrugging "But after I started checking with people who know him, I found out he was at The Original Southport Club last night, and that there was some shooting done. He came out on top, but that's the last time anybody in the grapevine's heard anything from or about him."

Savanna felt an involuntary shudder run through her body. To have come so far and find him missing—she couldn't lose him now—it would be too much. "The Southport Club? That's the place that drunk ofay was runnin' into the ground, wasn't it?"

"A woman named Donovan bought it out from under him," he replied. "It's a colored joint now. Harry said the woman had been to see him, but he didn't know what about."

"Could he be in some kind of trouble?" Savanna asked.

"Don't know," Marcel said. "but you know Wes as good as I do—he's got a way of stirrin' things up, and when he does—"

"Things—and people—start gettin' wrecked," Savanna finished for him. Her dark brown eyes were troubled. "We got to find him."

Marcel nodded. "I'm with you. Let's go out to the Southport Club and see what we can find out. We can check in with Harry from time to time to see if he's checked in."

"Let's go," she said.

As Marcel grabbed his hat and they turned to go, Savanna reflected on how each of them had drawn strength and emotional sustenance from Farrell, and had learned from him that curious drive to get into motion when a crisis loomed. She knew that neither of them was as good as Farrell, but she hoped that together they'd manage to be at the right place at the right moment, and be of help to him as he'd so often been to the pair of them.

Chapter 14

THE MESSAGE scrawled in lipstick on Carol Donovan's bathroom mirror hit Farrell like a punch in the gut. It was clear that Carol had left the message for him, but since he didn't know where Lincoln was, he was at a dead end. But Badeaux would know.

Farrell knew a man like Badeaux would have plenty of places to lay up and it was hard to say exactly where he'd be. He'd already gone to the sweet shop on Clouet Street after leaving the Mouton brothers, and had found it deserted. He'd known before going there that it wouldn't be that easy, but it was worth a try.

He recalled hearing that Badeaux had a house in a working class neighborhood on Jackson Avenue, and decided to go there next. If nothing else, he might find something that would help him find Lincoln's address.

He walked back into Carol Donovan's living room and sat down at the desk. He removed the telephone receiver and began calling people, people who seemed to always be awake, no matter what time of the day or night; people who had answers to questions and would part with them for money, or a the promise of a favor down the line. Eventually, after calling every Negro contact he had and coming up empty, he turned to a white man who always knew far more than was healthy for anyone, black, white, or Cherokee Indian.

"Let me talk to Nate Styles," he said to the man who answered. "Tell him it's Farrell calling."

He heard the sound of the phone being dropped on a hard surface, then a long silence. Finally Styles picked up.

"Well, well, it's Farrell again," Styles said archly. "You're gonna owe me favors into 1950, pal, the way you keep callin'. What is it this time?"

Farrell did a slow burn. He'd had to come to Styles more times than he'd wanted for information in the past few years, and it was just like the punk to make an issue of it. "Before I tell you that, let me remind you that a year ago, a guy had his foot on your neck. You'd be dead right now if I hadn't stepped in, Styles, so cut the crap and tell me where Archie Badeaux lives."

Styles was quiet for a moment. "Okay, pal," he said in a quieter voice. "No need to get riled up. I was pullin' your leg is all."

"Badeaux," Farrell repeated. "No more small talk."

"He lives at 4756 Jackson Avenue," Styles said in a rush. "How I know that is on account of he was messin' with a woman that was friendly with one of my boys. The guy followed his woman there, tried to put a snatch on her, and Badeaux beat him until he was nearly dead. Time was I thought of takin' care of that nigger punk."

"You wouldn't call him a nigger to his face, Styles," Farrell said in a cold voice. "Just like you wouldn't try to take care of him. He's better than you and any six boys you got. I'll tell him you sent your regards, when I find him."

"Hey, wait a minute," Styles began, but Farrell had already hung up the telephone. He got into his Packard, cranked the motor, then drove back out onto St. Claude Avenue, following it back into town, where it became Rampart. He followed Rampart until he could cut over to Claiborne Avenue, then followed that to Jackson Avenue. Badeaux's address was on the Lake side of the avenue, so Farrell made a right turn onto Jackson and followed it in a couple of blocks. He'd parked and gotten out of his car when he saw three men approach. It was Israel Daggett with two men. They had shotguns in the crooks of their arms. Farrell had seen a man shotgunned once. He never saw a shotgun that it didn't make a thrill race up his spine, and for the memory to flash in front of his eyes.

"What's with the scatterguns?" Farrell asked when he had closed the distance between them.

"We got a warrant for Archie Badeaux," Daggett said. "We got a witness that places him near the scene of a murder in City Park yesterday."

"Murder?" Farrell said. "Who?"

"A secretary named Shirley Macomb," Daggett said. "A bus driver gave us a description of the car and we got it from a dealer's list that he owned the same make and model," Daggett said. "The superintendent of her apartment building just identified a mug shot of Badeaux as the guy who was hanging around the building just prior to her disappearance."

"Jesus," Farrell said. "You hit the big number on this guy."

"And that ain't all," Daggett said. "We also suspect him of killing her boss, a real estate man named Bautain, and a department store owner named Johnson." Daggett paused, took in the rumpled evening clothes and the stubble of beard on Farrell's face, then he looked in the gambler's eyes and saw trouble in them. "Now's the time you get to tell me what you want with him."

"It's kind of a long story," Farrell said, "and I'll tell it to you once we've checked his house. If he's there, he might be able to answer some questions I've got."

Daggett smiled. "You want to invite yourself in on this, is that it?"

"I know it's against the rules," Farrell said, "but there's a woman who might be in trouble. She may not be, too, but if Badeaux's there, I'll know the answer pretty quick."

"Just don't get in the way if he starts shootin'," Daggett said. "I don't need any more teeth marks in my ass for gettin' you killed."

"Fair enough," Farrell said.

Daggett sent Andrews and Maxwell, another member of the Negro Squad, down the alleys on either side of the narrow shotgun house, then he and Farrell went through the gate, across the immaculate little yard to the front porch. They each took a piece of wall on either side of the front door, then Daggett pounded on it with the butt of his shotgun.

"Archie Badeaux," he called out. "This is the New Orleans Police. Come on out with your hands up where I can see 'em." When no answer came, he called out twice more, but was met with more silence. He looked over at Farrell, who nodded and reached over gingerly to the doorknob. To Farrell's surprise, the knob twisted easily in his hand, and then the door opened smoothly inward.

Daggett went in first with the shotgun held level at his hip. Farrell followed him in with his Colt drawn. Andrews and Maxwell met them at the middle of the house and exchanged looks that were partly relief and partly chagrin.

"Back door was unlocked, boss," Andrews said. "Dirty dishes in the sink and some kitchen trash that hasn't been taken out in a while—it's smellin' a little. Two days since he's been here, I'm guessin'."

"So much for this bright idea," Daggett said archly.

"Where else might Badeaux be?" Farrell asked. "I checked at a illegal gambling parlor over on Clouet Street, but no luck. Actually I wasn't expecting to find anybody there—I kind of knocked the joint over the other night, with Badeaux in it."

Andrews smirked. "I'd of give a week's pay to see *that.*"

"Sam, keep a watch on the front in case our prodigal son shows up," Daggett said. "Max, call the office and let them know we turned up an empty here. Ask if they got anything for us there."

"Right, boss," Andrews said, and the two detectives went separate ways while Daggett and Farrell made themselves comfortable.

Daggett threw a hip over a table and leaned his shotgun against his leg. "Maybe you'd like to tell me now, why you're here lookin' for Badeaux in that monkey suit with that roscoe in your fist."

Farrell holstered the gun, hooked a wooden chair with his right foot, and pulled it over to sit on. He took his black Borsalino off and dropped in on the table beside Daggett and ran this fingers through his hair several times.

"A couple days ago, a woman named Carol Donovan came to see me," he began.

"She's the hotcha mama who owns The Original Southport Club," Daggett said. "I was just readin' about her earlier today."

"Right," Farrell said. "She told me that Badeaux had been to see her, and was trying to force her to sell out to him, cheap. I went around asking questions, and the general consensus was that Badeaux didn't give a hoot in hell about a nightclub."

"Because he's up to something else," Daggett said.

"Working for a guy named Lincoln," Farrell said.

"Right," Daggett said. "And Lincoln's here tryin' to put together a power base. We think the reason Badeaux killed Bautain and Johnson is because they owned land that Lincoln wanted—property we discovered the Navy Department wants to build a naval air training station on—to the tune of a half-million bucks. Bautain wouldn't sell, and we think Johnson refused him, too."

Farrell nodded. "But that makes the Donovan story make less sense than ever. If Lincoln's playing a game with those kinds of stakes, a nightclub's the square root of nothing to him."

"So why's the Donovan dame layin' off all this crap on Badeaux?" Daggett asked.

"I wish I knew that," Farrell said. "It was already smelling a little funny when I went out there last night. But then a gang showed up and tried to wreck the place. I mixed into it, knocked a few guys around and shot another—"

"You're the guy made Swiss cheese outta Jay-Jay Johnstone?" Daggett interrupted.

"Yeah," Farrell said ruefully. "I'm not crazy about it, either. I spotted the Mouton brothers running off after the fireworks were over. I played a hunch that they'd be in a place I knew of, and I found them there. I got them to talk, and they told me that Badeaux had hired them over the telephone, then sent the payoff to them by a Railroad Express Agency messenger. They never saw him in person."

"So maybe it wasn't Badeaux who hired them," Daggett said.

"But somebody wants him to take the fall for it," Farrell said.

"There's something we can check out," Daggett said. "Max," he called.

"Yeah, boss."

"When you get through to headquarters, ask one of the guys to get in touch with the Railway Express Agency. Find out what they can tell us who arranged a parcel delivery to the Mouton Brothers Garage."

"Right," Max replied.

Daggett was silent for a moment, plucking at the pleat in his trouser leg. "There's another angle to this I can't quite figure out," he said. "There was a third Negro businessman who was killed the month before Ezra Johnson disappeared. It seems like it ought to dovetail with these others, yet it doesn't quite fit the pattern."

"You talking about Malcolm Redding?" Farrell asked.

Daggett nodded. "He was the first to be killed, and I think there's a connection—three Negro businessmen, each killed a month apart—but Redding's was made to look like a suicide, and the other two disappeared. They tried to make the Macomb woman look like a disappearance, too, but they were clumsy about it—we found her within twenty-four hours of the disappearance."

"So you don't think Redding's *was* a suicide," Farrell said.

"It definitely wasn't a suicide," Daggett said. "Redding

was found with a pawn-shop special in his right hand, one shot to the right temple. But Redding was a southpaw, raised in Arizona before he came to New Orleans. He was also an expert marksman and had two guns of his own—a .38 Colt Officer's Match target revolver and a silver-mounted .380 Beretta automatic he'd bought on a trip to Rome a couple years ago. He didn't need to go out and buy a piece of junk like that, and even if he did, he wouldn't have put the gun in his right hand to do it. And besides, at the time he was killed his wife was at home packing for their vacation to Jamaica the next day, a vacation that Redding himself had planned and bought the tickets for."

"Does she know where he was going that night?" Farrell asked.

"He told her he had some urgent business that wouldn't wait until they returned from the Caribbean," Daggett said. "She didn't know what it was, although she said he'd discovered something at work that had really disturbed him."

"Who'd benefit from his death?" Farrell asked.

"The main candidate is the guy who stepped into his shoes," Daggett said. "Rogers Clifton."

Farrell's head snapped up. "I crowded Molly Tatum for information about Badeaux two nights ago, and she told me there was bad blood between Redding and Clifton over something. She also said that Lincoln was involved in some business with Clifton. If she knew what, she wouldn't say, but it couldn't be anything legit—not with Lincoln in the picture."

Daggett scratched his nose reflectively, then said, "Elijah Johnson said that Clifton worked as some kind of go-between for his brother and Lincoln in the land deal. There's a connection, but I wonder if it's the only one."

"Redding's dead because of Lincoln, just like Bautain, Johnson, and the Macomb woman are dead because of Lincoln," Farrell said. "What else is there?"

"Because of the link with Lincoln, but not killed by Badeaux, as the others were," Daggett said. "Somebody else in that group did the killing, and I'll tell you something else, I think that person also killed an old woman named Attaway on Leonidas Street last night."

"Huh?"

"When we found Redding's body, whoever shot him had puked up his breakfast right outside the car," Daggett said. "The old woman was beaten to death, but whoever killed her vomited all over the rug afterward. Both those killings were done by an amateur—not a pro like Badeaux. They killed out of hate or out of fear—driven to it, but not hardened enough to do it without flinching."

"Man," Farrell said in an admiring tone. "Does this stuff ever make your brain swell up? I can see how you got to that conclusion, but the trail's kind of convoluted."

"Tell me about it," Daggett said ruefully. "We don't even know who we're lookin' for, much less why."

"Badeaux might talk if we could find him," Farrell said.

"I doubt it," Daggett said. "He's gonna go to the chair. Clarence Darrow couldn't save him if he's done three murders. He'll shoot it out, unless we can take him by surprise. But we got to find him first."

Maxwell came into the room and pointed a finger at Daggett. "Bossman, Gautier's on the line. He says he's got some dope he thinks you wanna hear." Maxwell's voice was pitched low, but there was a trace of excitement in it that Daggett heard. He turned and followed Maxwell into the next room.

BADEAUX FOUND LeDoux some alcohol and some sticking plaster, and the ex-convict was able to clean his wound and place a fresh, and considerably smaller, bandage on his head. The under-powered little jacketed bullet had made a neat, clean crease in the right side of his forehead, producing a spectacular amount of blood, but not much of a wound. LeDoux removed his shirt, on which there'd been a considerable amount of gore splashed, then put his suit coat on over his singlet.

"What's your idea?" Badeaux asked when they were inside his big Dodge.

"I knew some people of Ben's who might be able to help us," LeDoux replied. "If anybody can tell us who was helpin' old Marcella out, it'll be them. How's about givin' me my gun back?" he asked.

Badeaux favored him with a broad grin, but shook his head in the negative. "Nigger, do I look like I just got off a fuckin' banana boat or somethin'? I give you a loaded .45 and the next thing I know, you're makin' alterations in our partnership. Nope, reckon I'll keep the .45 for now—leastways until we find out where the money is."

"Suit yourself," LeDoux said. "But it's your ass hangin' out in the wind with nobody to look out for it."

"I been lookin' out for it just fine for quite a while without no help," Badeaux said. "Let's just get on to where we're goin'. Gimme a direction."

At LeDoux's instruction, they left the vicinity of the Honey Pot and traveled north on Piety Street about ten blocks until they reached Dorgenois, where they turned right and continued on until they were near the St. Bernard Parish line. "Drive slow," LeDoux advised. "I ain't been here since before I went to the slam. They might'a painted the house a different color or somethin' by now."

"Hell," Badeaux said. "People in this part of town have to eat fish-head soup half the time. Ain't none of them gonna waste no money on paint."

They drove through the neighborhood at a snail's pace, LeDoux looking first to the left, then to the right. Twice he had Badeaux come to a stop while he got out and stared at particular houses, but each time, he would crawl back inside and shake his head to the question on Badeaux's face. LeDoux hated to look at him, because he could see some fire building behind the killer's eyes. He knew that if he couldn't come through with something soon, Badeaux might just kill him and forget the money.

They were six blocks down on Dorgenois, nearing the parish line when Ernie held up a hand and said, "Stop. Pull over there." Badeaux did as he was told, and LeDoux got out of the car, put his derby on his head, and followed the walk up to the porch of a sagging shotgun cottage with relatively new lime green paint. "Somebody got some money," Ernie said. "And I think I know where."

The place hadn't had a fresh coat of paint the last time he'd seen it, but unlike many of the other houses in the neighborhood, this house had a front door with a large beveled-glass window in the upper third, which he particularly remembered. There was also some gingerbread trim holding up the overhang on the porch that he recalled.

Badeaux got out and walked briskly behind him until they reached the front door. LeDoux beat a rapid tattoo on the door with his knuckles.

An old woman came to the door wearing a formal black dress and carrying a black hat with a veil in her hand. She looked out the window at the bandage on LeDoux's head and at the white singlet showing under his suit coat. LeDoux quickly took off his hat and held it in front of him, and tried to erect a pleasant expression on his face. It seemed to work, because she opened the door a bit.

"What can I do for you?" she asked.

"Miss Lina, don't you remember me? It's Ernie LeDoux. I was a good friend of Ben and Marcella Attaway."

She looked him up and down for a moment. "I thought you was in prison," she said a bit warily.

"Yes'm, I was, but I served my stretch and they let me out for good behavior. I come home to see Ben and Marcella and found out they was both dead."

She nodded at him, some shine growing in her eyes. "Yeah, it's true. Ben's been gone 'bout four years now. Somebody done murdered poor Marcella night before last. Just beat the poor old thing until they knocked the life right out of her." She pulled a scrap of lace handkerchief from the pocket of her dress and dabbed the corners of her eyes with it. "I just come from a visitation, is why I'm dressed up like this. She sure looked pitiful in that big coffin, li'l as she was." She blew her nose daintily into the handkerchief. "I hope you'll pardon me," she said. "My manners has slipped some. I should'a ax'ed you two gentlemen to come in." She held the door open wider and stood aside to let them both enter. After she closed the door, she gestured at the sofa and then sat down in a matching armchair upholstered in dark blue material with small white pinstripes.

"I was sure sorry about it when I heard, Miss Lina," LeDoux said after they were seated. "Ben and Marcella treated me like a son."

"Yeah," Badeaux said ingratiatingly. "They was the finest kind of people." He smiled that pleasant smile of his, and nodded.

Miss Lina stared at him for a moment, as if trying to place him. "I don't recollect you, young, fella," she said. "Have we met before?"

"No, ma'am," Archie said. "But I was acquainted with the Attaways all the same. They was fine, generous souls."

"Lord, ain't that the truth," Miss Lina said. "After Ben died, she come over one day and give me five hundred dollars to get the house painted and to buy some new livin' room furniture. Anybody else would'a been bound up with their own concerns, but not Marcella. She dipped right into what Ben left her and give me that five hundred dollars like it weren't no more than pocket change. It touched me so much I just busted out cryin', I swear I did." She burst out crying at the memory, sobbing throatily into her tiny handkerchief.

Badeaux and LeDoux exchanged a glance. Badeaux's eyes were hot and excited.

"You reckon Ben left her that much money?" LeDoux asked in what he hoped was a solicitous voice. "The poor old guy didn't seem to have all that much when I knew him. They was livin' in a real small house before—I visited it couple days ago, lookin' for Ben."

Miss Lina blew her nose again, more loudly this time, and shook her head. "I don't know nothin' but what poor Marcella told me. She said Ben had an insurance policy that 'set her up for life'—them's almost her exact words. She give some to others in the family, too."

"So was anybody takin' care of things for the old—the poor old soul?" Badeaux asked. LeDoux looked over and saw that he was considerably on edge. A nerve at his right temple had begun to pulse and his eyes were flickering rapidly.

Miss Lina wiped her nose with her handkerchief, and shook her head. "Well, I ain't seen her in a li'l while. Y'know," she said, pitching her voice in a low, confidential tone, "after she got to drinkin' so heavy, I sorta lost touch with her. I'm a church-goin' woman and I don't hold with no drinkin'. I s'pose losin' Ben broke somethin' in her up and she turned to drinkin' to ease the pain. I hope the Good Lord won't judge her too harsh." She put the damp handkerchief on the arm of her chair, and narrowed her eyes as something seemed to come back to her. "Now I think on it, though, I did hear her say once that she was pretty much alone in this town, 'cept for the child of one of her second cousins."

LeDoux's heart gave a little jump. "She happen to mention a name?"

"No, sorry," Miss Lina said, shaking her head. "Like I said, I ain't seen her in a while. This would'a been a year or two ago. She was in the big house by then, but seemed like she was havin' all she could do to keep up with it. It was kinda messy, and wasn't smellin' too good. She said this cousin of hers was givin' her advice on what to do. The way she talked, he was pretty slick—a real go-getter who knew how to handle things."

"Boy," Ernie said. "I'd sure like to talk to him—to

express my sympathy, that is."

"Well, shucks," Miss Lina said. "I reckon he must be takin' care of the funeral. I didn't see nobody at the visitation I didn't know, but I reckon if you go on down to Christ's Majesty Funeral Home, they can tell you who he is."

LeDoux looked over at Badeaux to see the killer's face had undergone a transformation. His eyes were bright and hard like ball-bearings and his teeth were bared in a smile that was terrible to see.

ALEX AND DOM MOUTON rolled into New Orleans about seven o'clock as the gray skies of early morning were giving into the more brilliant blue of summer. They stopped off at a diner on Gentilly Road and ordered up platters of ham, eggs, grits, and biscuits. Dom ate with his normal gusto, and Alex, preferring not to think about confronting Archie Badeaux, ate as hard as he could, too.

As he rubbed a biscuit half around in the egg yolk on his plate, Dom looked up at his brother with a questioning look in his eye. "Alex?"

"Huh?" the elder brother asked, sipping black coffee.

"Where we gonna find Badeaux? Ain't neither one of us even seen him, much less knows where he lives."

Alex put down his cup and put his chin in his hand. "I been thinkin' about that," he replied slowly. "It come to me a li'l while ago that we know somebody who used to know Badeaux pretty good."

"Who's that?" Dom asked.

"Annabelle Melancon," Alex replied. "She used to lay up with Badeaux before he got too tired of her. He dumped her for some floozie, so I reckon if she knows where he is, she won't mind tellin' us."

Dom smiled as he crammed the biscuit half into his mouth.

Alex got up and left his brother at the table while he walked to the pay telephone at the other end of the diner. He got into the booth, fished around in his pocket until he found a nickel, then dropped it into the slot and dialed a number. It rang six or seven times before someone picked up.

"Man, you sure callin' early in the mornin'," a woman whined. "This better be good."

"Annabelle, this is Alex," he said, grinning.

"Alex who?" she asked suspiciously.

"Alex Mouton. Don't act like you don't know me, honey. We had too good of a time last time I saw you."

"Hah!" Annabelle snorted. "You men think rollin' around in the bed for a half hour is like a cruise on the White Star Line. If you'd of took me to a nice place, I'd remember that better."

Alex laughed softly. "I will next time."

"Next time, hell," she said. "What makes you think there's gonna be a next time?"

"On account of I want to pop Archie Badeaux, and I figure you'd be willin' to help me on that."

Annabelle was silent for a moment, then she spoke up again. "You're gonna try to kill Archie Badeaux and you want me to help you? Damn, Alex. How do you know he won't kill you and then come after me for helpin' you?"

"'Cause I'm gonna have my brother with me and he'll be outgunned. He crossed us up, Annabelle, and we're gonna pay him back for it. He crossed you up once, too, 'less'n I misremember. I figured you'd like to make a li'l contribution to the project."

Again she was silent for a moment, then, "I misjudged you, Alex. You got some big ideas. You kill Archie Badeaux and you'll be a big man in this town. That'll make up for you not callin' me for the past four months."

"Aw, honey, I been busy. You know how it is."

"Hell, yeah, I know how it is," she came back. "Okay, but I mean it—you can't tell him where you got this, no matter what."

"I ain't gonna do no talkin', woman," he said impatiently.

"He got him a house on Jackson Avenue, 4756 Jackson,"

she said. "He use to take me there, before him and that bimbo got together."

"What bimbo?"

"I don't know her, just of her," Annabelle said. "He was two-timin' me with her before I found out about it. Come to the house lookin' for that mutha-fucka, and here he is in the bed with that slut. I tried to kill both of them with a whiskey bottle, but Archie knocked me down and damn near killed me. He threw me out on the porch and said if I come back there again, he'd throw me in the Lake."

Alex listened to this narrative carefully. He knew little about Badeaux, and anything he could learn about the man might be useful later. "So what did you find out about her, baby?" he asked in a solicitous voice.

"She's some slut he hooked up with back at the tail-end of the '20s," she said. "She been outta town for a while, then come back in last year. That's when he started two-timin' me with her."

"You know her name, baby?" Alex asked.

"I seen her in the Brown Fedora one night six months ago. She was alone at the time, and I was gonna go over and cut her, but some of my friends held me down and got me outta there before I could do it. Heard one of them later say her name was Ruby Richoux."

"You know where she lives?" Alex asked.

"I spent some time lookin' around for it, thinkin' for a while I might shoot her," she replied. "She livin' in a big house on the River end of Melpomene. It's gray with blue trim. A real swell place, too. Reckon she's got money or somethin'."

"Or somethin'," Alex agreed. "We'll try Badeaux's house first, and if he ain't there, we'll take a plant on this Melpomene joint. Thanks, baby. I'll pay you back for this."

"You can pay me back by stompin' his two-timin' black ass into the sidewalk," she said bitterly.

Alex laughed good-naturedly and hung up the phone.

He left the booth and came back to where Dom was working over his teeth with a toothpick.

"C'mon," he said. "We got a place to go."

Traffic in the Downtown section made it slow going for a while, but about three-quarters of an hour after he talked to Annabelle, Alex Mouton turned the Pierce Arrow off Claiborne Avenue into Jackson. Alex was surprised to find a hired killer like Badeaux living in such a swell neighborhood. The yards were all well-cared for and the houses painted and in good condition. The air was thick and sweet with the smell of flowers. It was so pretty that for a minute Alex was a little jealous.

He pulled the old car to a stop across the street from Badeaux's place, which was surrounded by a white picket fence with little boxwoods planted around the border. They took out their guns and checked them, then stared at the house like they thought it would give them some kind of a signal.

"What now?" Dom asked, fidgeting in his seat.

"Don't rush me," Alex said grumpily. Now that they were here, he wasn't sure what to do. It being broad daylight, he was leery of just kicking the door in and shooting the place up. This called for some finesse, because above and beyond his desire to keep out of the clutches of the law, Alex wanted more than anything else to humiliate the killer, not simply put a bullet in him.

"You reckon he's home?" Dom asked in a soft voice.

"Maybe," Alex said. "A man with his kind of money can afford to sleep late and lay up with a woman until noon if he wants."

"Then let's go on in," Dom said. "Me from the back, you from the front. We'll catch him with his pants down and lick him in front of his woman. We'll show him who he can fuck with."

Yeah, Alex thought. He'll have a gun handy, woman or no, and if we make too much noise he'll kill one or both of us. As he thought this, he saw a little black boy, perhaps ten years old, round the corner a half-block down from them. He was about four feet tall and skinny as a rail, wearing a summer uniform of faded red shorts and nothing else.

Alex had an inspiration. He got a silver fifty-cent piece from his watch pocket, let his left arm hang out the open window, and began flipping the coin up in the air in a showy, ostentatious way. As he did so, he began to whistle "The Teddy Bears' Picnic," a happy, bouncy little tune he'd heard in a movie-show cartoon once. The gambit had the desired effect. The whistling attracted the little boy's attention and he began watching Alex's coin flipping display, instantly mesmerized by the height the coin reached before it fell back into Alex's waiting paw. After a moment or two, he approached the car slowly holding the stick of a lollipop with his right hand. As he got closer, Alex saw dust between his brown toes and bright, attentive eyes in a solemn face.

"Hiya, kid," Alex said in a friendly voice. "You doin' all right?"

The solemn little boy nodded twice, still sucking on his lollipop. His eyes followed the movement of the big silver coin as it flew up and down, up and down.

"How'd you like to make fifty cents?" Alex asked in the same friendly voice.

The little boy removed his lollipop and looked into Alex's face. "I'd like it, but my mama tol' me not to talk to strangers." He put the lollipop back into his mouth.

Alex nodded sagely. "A boy oughta listen to his ma. That's just common sense. I'm Alex. This is my brother, Dom," he said, jerking his chin at his brother. The coin continued to fly through the air, drawing the little boy's shining eyes to its path. "What's your name?"

"Matthew," the boy said. "Like the prophet in the Bible. My daddy's a preacher."

"That's real fine," Alex said. "Reckon bein' a preacher's

boy is hard work, bein' as everybody expects you to be good all the time. Am I right?"

The little boy nodded, still working on his sucker.

"Reckon you know a lot, too," Alex continued. "Bet you know just about everything that goes on in this neighborhood. Am I right?"

"Uh-huh," the little boy agreed.

"Like for instance, you prob'ly know the man lives in that house."

The little boy's eyes stopped tracking the half-dollar, and he threw a quick glance over his shoulder. Then he turned back to Alex.

"That's Archie's house. He's as bad as castor oil on strawberry ice cream. I keep hopin' that Jesus'll strike him down for all the bad things he done. He hurt my Uncle Bill in a fight six months ago—hurt him real bad. Uncle Bill was in the hospital for two weeks, and still limpin' around. Ever since then, I been hopin' somebody'd come over here and fix that mean bastard." The little boy's eyes got big for a minute when the bad word slipped out, and he blinked rapidly for a few seconds. "I didn't mean to say that word."

"I like a man what calls a spade a spade," Alex said. "You know if that gentleman's home, by any chance?"

"Naw," the boy replied. "He ain't. He got him a big black Dodge four-door sedan. Brand new. He ain't been here since yesterday afternoon. Reckon he's off with some woman. But I know a secret."

"What?" Alex asked, trying to keep from grinning.

"He usually leave his back door unlocked," the boy said. "A body could go in that way and lay for him if they wanted. 'S what I'd do if I had me a gun. I sneaked in there once hopin' to find one, but all's I found was a bunch of magazines with pictures of naked white women in 'em."

Alex grinned hugely, and flipped the half-dollar at the boy, who grabbed it out of the air like a frog snatching a fly.

"Thanks, mister," the boy said, his eyes big with

surprise. "But I didn't do nothin' to get this. My mamma and daddy wouldn't like me takin' it." He held it out to Mouton.

"You keep it, kid," Alex said. "Buy yourself some ice cream for yourself and don't tell nobody nothin'. Maybe if you're lucky, Archie won't be botherin' you nor your Uncle Bill no more."

The boy looked down at the big silver coin like it was the eighth wonder of the world, then back up at Mouton's grinning face. "Thank you, mister. Thank you a whole lot." He turned and walked away, a small skinny boy who already knew far too much about the doings of adults, and nothing about it to make him happy.

"What you wanna do now?" Dom asked. "Go inside and lay for him, maybe?"

Alex looked at the house and considered possibilities. Laying for Badeaux wasn't a half-bad idea, but they could be in there for a long time, and the cops would have a tag out for them after the mess at the Southport Club. There was nowhere good to stash the car, and in any case, they'd want it nearby in case they had to make a run for it. Annabelle had told him about the house on Melpomene, where Badeaux had one of his women. He might be there with her, now. He started the engine and put the old touring car in gear.

"Were we goin'?" Dom asked.

"To a place," Alex said. "Sit back and relax, so you'll be all rested when we get there."

Chapter 15

LUTHER PULLED up in front of Lincoln's house with his nerves jumping beneath his skin. Now that he was here, he felt nervous about what he was attempting. He'd never had any grandiose ideas about his savvy or his potential for greater things. The truth was, he'd been content to be Badeaux's flunky, even though Badeaux scared him and expressed a fair amount of contempt for him at times. But he'd worked for worse people than Archie Badeaux and he felt vaguely disloyal now that he'd embarked on this attempt to try to wrest control of Lincoln's patronage from him.

"Is this the place?" Carol asked. There was an edge in her voice that hadn't been there back in her bedroom. Or maybe it had been there and he'd been too besotted with sex to notice it.

"Archie brought me here a couple times," he replied. "I mostly hung around in the front while he had confabs with the big man."

"How many people has he got here?" Carol asked. She wasn't looking at Luther now. Her attention was focused at the front of the house and she was sitting near the edge of her seat, her body tense and rigid. It had lost all the softness he'd felt under his hands and legs earlier.

"Hard to say," he replied. "Although the times I been here, it's only seemed like the old man and this big black fella named Albert. He is one mean-lookin' sonofbitch, too."

She turned and looked at him. "You aren't scared of him, are you?"

He looked at her frankly, trying to understand in his mind why he'd let this woman talk him into this risky venture. It occurred to him that the smartest thing he could do would be to start the car up, turn it around, and drop her off, then get out of town while he had his whole skin. But unbidden, the sensation of feeling her moving underneath him leaped into the front of his mind, and he felt his body betraying him. He'd do it with her right here, right now, in broad daylight, if she'd say the word. But she wouldn't. She was all business now.

"I reckon a man who knows when to be scared is a better person to throw in with than somebody who claims he ain't never scared at all," Luther said stoutly. "I'm scared enough of that Albert not to let him get too close to me, nor come up from behind. He ain't nobody to fool with, but I don't reckon we're foolin' around, neither."

"No," she said. "We're not. Let's go in."

Every fiber of his reason told him not to, but instead he got out of the car, then came around to her side and opened the door. He held out his hand and she took it to help herself get out of the car. Even before he'd shut the car door, she was striding confidently up to the house. He walked after her, letting his right hand stray to the butt of his Remington automatic in his hip pocket. He didn't know why he had this premonition of danger—maybe he was just allowing himself to be spooked by the stories he'd heard about this crippled old man. But he reminded himself that *he* had use of both of his legs, and was a pretty smart *hombre*, besides. He'd managed to keep Archie happy for the past several years, and had been in his share of scrapes. You're doin' a piece of big talkin', he thought, for a man with sweat drippin' off'n his head.

He stepped up beside Carol and pushed the button to the doorbell, gently nudging Carol to the side so his would be the first face that Albert would see. It didn't take long for the door to open.

"Yeah? What do you want?" the big man said, his eyes looking unfriendly.

"It's Luther," he said. "You know, I work for Archie."

"I said what do you want?" Albert asked again, more distinctly.

"I want to introduce somebody to Mr. Lincoln," he said. "She's got some nifty ideas I think he'd like to hear." Luther put a winning smile on his face, and hooked his thumbs in the lapels of his jacket, like a small-town boomer about to show off some prize commodity he'd brought along.

"Mr. Lincoln don't see nobody," Albert said. "Get lost."

"Why—why, that ain't friendly, not at all," Luther sputtered. "Here we come all the way over here to talk some business and you treat us like street trash."

"Get away from here," Albert said menacingly.

"Back up," Carol said suddenly. "Back up or I'll splatter your black ass all over the hallway."

Luther and Albert looked over at her and found themselves looking down the bore of a .38 Colt Detective Special. She held it with the authority of a woman who knew which end of the barrel meant business. Albert backed slowly into the vestibule, his eyes large and dark with barely restrained murderous impulses.

"Honey, what're you doin'?" Luther asked in a voice pitched high with incredulity. "Mr. Lincoln ain't gonna—"

"Shut up," she said. She reached over, removed the automatic from his hip pocket, and pointed it at him. "Get inside, quick."

Luther did as he was told. He didn't recognize this two-gunned mama as the same delicate flower whose body he'd kissed every square inch of over the past couple days. That experience hadn't prepared him for the prospect of looking down the barrel of a gun. "Baby, you're bitin' off a mighty big chew. Sooner or later, Archie'll be along, and he'll kill you if Old Man Lincoln don't do it first."

She said nothing, but forced them quietly down the hall with black eyes like burning coal and the unwavering muzzles of her two pistols. They retreated until they'd reached the double doors to Lincoln's study. Carol thrust the .38 at Albert and indicated by sign language that he should open the doors. This Albert did, his eyes eating her.

As the doors opened, Carol herded her captives into the room, closing them behind her. Lincoln, sitting at his desk with a book looked up, saw the guns in Carol's hands, and froze. He left both of his hands on top of the desk, palms flat on the leather desk blotter. "You seem to have the advantage of me," he said mildly. "Might I inquire as to who you are, and what you want?"

"Does the name Lucinda Roker mean anything to you?" Carol asked.

The old man's lips compressed, and he squinted as he probed his memory. After a time, he shook his head. "No, not that I can recall." He surveyed her intently as he spoke, not at all worried by the guns she was waving around. Carol felt some amazement at his cool demeanor, but shoved those thoughts away. She couldn't falter now.

"Try harder," Carol said. "A young girl from a good family, that a sharp-talking gambler coaxed away and seduced, then turned into a whore and a morphine addict. You must remember." Carol tried to inject a note of sarcasm into her words, but she didn't hear sarcasm in the timbre of her voice. What she heard was the sound of hurt and despair; the sound of a much younger girl looking full into the face of an object of hatred and yet seeing the face of a father. She felt herself weakening, and wished more than anything that she'd stuck to her original plan, rather then impetuously grasping at Luther as a way of speeding up her revenge. She'd taken a risk that Farrell would find her in time to clean this up for her, but things were happening so fast now that they were getting out of her control.

Lincoln was silent for a long moment, his eyes flickering as he searched his memory again. "Lucinda Roker," the old man said finally, nodding slightly. "It was east Tennessee, wasn't it? Perhaps 1905 or '06?"

"Nineteen and seven," Carol said. "I was born ten months after that."

The old man nodded again. "I can recollect her face now that I see yours. But the eyes—the eyes aren't hers. I've seen those eyes when I've looked into the mirror of a morning and used the razor on my face. I don't get to look into the mirror much anymore—Albert, here, shaves me each morning. And what would your name be, my dear?"

"My name was Mattie when I was born," Carol said. "It's been other things since then. In Jackson I was Manda Hayes."

The old man's body stiffened, and his eyes became hooded. "Jackson," he said. "I never met you, but you ran the house off Madison Road."

"Yes," she said, nodding. "But I didn't do a very good job. I thought I was hiring good men. All they managed to do was get themselves killed. I had to put that bullet in your back myself. God damn me to hell for such a sloppy job." Her hands were quivering now with the weight of the guns and the responsibility she'd taken.

"So, it's you I have to thank for this," Lincoln said, gesturing with his hand at his crippled body. "You, to whom I gave a good job and paid solid money. Was it because of Lucinda that you wrecked everything I'd done and condemned me to this useless old man's body?" His face and eyes were as blank as stone, but for the first time since Carol had come into the room she heard a tremor in his voice. Whether it be fear, hate, or despair it was impossible to say, but she felt a small surge of triumph in getting that whisper of emotion from him.

"For her," Carol said, nodding. "And for myself, a little. You turned her into a whore. She died before her time. And you made a whore of me—and worse."

Lincoln smiled coldly. "Don't make your case out to be so special, my dear. I've had many women in my lifetime, and I lost count of the number of bastard children they threw. That was their lookout. Nobody made them come into my bed."

"Shut up," she said in a loud voice. "Shut your filthy mouth."

"Or what? You'll kill me?" he said. "You've already talked too much. If you're going to kill someone, my dear, shoot as soon as you see your target. Talk is fatal in these kinds of confrontations. It always allows enough time for someone else to turn the tables."

An explosion came from behind Carol, and her body shuddered. Her eyes rolled in her head as she tried to bring one of her guns level with Lincoln's head. She was going into shock, maybe dying, and she wanted to scream from the effort it took to squeeze the trigger. She heard another explosion as consciousness slipped from her grasp, and she wondered as she fell if it was her gun going off, or another's.

SAVANNA AND MARCEL returned to the Café Tristesse without having found Farrell, and Savanna was on edge. The trip to The Original Southport Club had yielded Carol Donovan's address, but they'd found the woman's home empty and the door half-open. They'd found Lincoln's name scrawled on the bathroom mirror, but it had meant little to either of them.

Marcel, showing considerable *sang-froid*, had gone to the telephone in Carol's living room and began calling people all over town, leaving word that Farrell was missing, and that he needed to get in touch with him urgently. From a few of Farrell's contacts, Marcel had learned enough about the mysterious Lincoln to give some idea of Farrell's possible predicament, but not enough to find the old man's lair.

Having run all of their options to zero, Marcel took

them back to the club, since he'd left word with everyone that they should contact him there. The youngster's face was flat and inscrutable, again reminding Savanna very much of Farrell.

Marcel parked his Ford behind the club and led Savanna up the steel stairs and through the rear entrance to the apartment.

An exhaust fan was pulling a cool breeze through the apartment, and Savanna took off her straw hat and shook her long brown hair loose. Marcel got a pitcher of sweet iced tea from the refrigerator and poured both of them a glass before calling down to Harry to see if he'd heard from Farrell. Savanna heard Marcel tell the bar manager to send someone up.

"Who is it?" she asked.

"A newspaperman named Whately," Marcel said. "I think he works for the *Weekly*." No sooner did Marcel speak than there was a knock at the door. Marcel went to it and opened it.

"Mr. Farrell in?" the old newshawk asked as he came in. He removed his hat and mopped his forehead with a wrinkled handkerchief. When he saw Savanna, he walked over and held out a hand.

"It's Miss Beaulieu, isn't it?" the reporter asked. "I used to spend some fine times in your place. Sure was sorry to hear you'd closed up and left town. You change your mind and decide to come home?"

She smiled. "Yes, I wasted enough time out in Los Angeles. I should be open again in about a week. You're welcome to come down and be my guest."

"That's mighty kind of you, ma'am." He looked around, then said. "Mr. Farrell about? I had some information I thought he could use."

"We've been trying to find him," Marcel said. "He's been out of pocket for a while, and I was beginning to worry about him."

The reporter raised his bushy eyebrows, and shifted his

eyes from Marcel to Savanna. "Well, I hope nothin's wrong."

"Probably not," Marcel said. "Mr. Farrell has a lot of things goin' on here in town, and he's just with somebody talkin' business, I reckon. Is what you had to tell him pretty important?"

"Well," Whately said, taking a cigar out of his pocket. "He was interested in that young woman who owns The Original Southport Club. I spent some time tryin' to nail down her story, and found out some surprising things. She ain't at all what she seems, which is probably what he was thinkin' all along."

Savanna could sense something behind the older man's words, and she leaned forward, her face attentive. "We'll probably see Mr. Farrell before you do, Mr. Whately," she said. "If you'll give us the gist of it, we'll try to get it to him."

The newshawk cocked an eyebrow at her, and saw a smile form on her face. When Savanna smiled, men always seemed to forget themselves, and that was perhaps why Whately decided to tell her what he'd found.

"Well, this gal ran a bawdy house in Memphis for quite a while and also ran a pornographic picture business on the side. She moved to Jackson very suddenly a few years ago, apparently because she discovered a man named Lincoln was there."

"Lincoln?" Marcel asked. "Why?"

"That I'm not sure of," Whately replied. "But go she did, and very precipitately. I talked to a friend in Jackson who said she ended up running a real high-class parlor house under the name of Manda Hayes. Nobody knows what their relationship might've been, or even if there was one, but we do know that Lincoln was lured to this house, possibly by this woman, where he was ambushed. Lincoln got four of them, but he took a bullet in the back and it was believed he was dead, although the cops up there never found his body. She disappeared right afterwards."

"So the cops think she was in on the hit?" Marcel asked.

"Well, the fact that she ran off doesn't look too good for her," Whately replied. "Apparently Lincoln didn't die, but was crippled. He showed up here about a year ago, and then this Carol Donovan, or Manda Hayes, or whatever her name is, also shows up down here."

"What's Mr. Farrell got to do with these people?" Savanna asked.

"Seems this Miss Donovan came to him for help with a gangster named Badeaux," Whately said. "Badeaux's Lincoln's leg-man in New Orleans. The connection's pretty easy to see once you got all the pieces."

"So Mr. Farrell thought that Lincoln was after her club," Savanna said.

"But that's not why she came to Wes—I mean Mr. Farrell," Marcel said. "It sounds to me like she wanted to finish the job she started in Jackson—"

"And wanted to use Farrell to help her do it," Savanna finished. "This doesn't sound good at all."

"And we don't have any idea where he might be," Marcel said. "He could be in a heap of trouble."

"Well," Whately said, consulting his notebook, "while I was doin' my research, I got one of my young men to run over to City Hall and check the City Assessor's tax roles. I got an address for a Jonathan Lincoln on the River end of Melpomene Street. If all else fails, we can go over there."

Savanna got up from her seat and went to the telephone. In a second she had the operator on the line and asked to be put through to the Negro Detective Squad at police headquarters.

"Negro Squad, Detective Gautier," a man said.

"This is Savanna Beaulieu talkin'," she said. "I need to speak to Sergeant Israel Daggett. It's a matter of life and death."

"Who did you say you were, ma'am?" Gautier asked.

"Savanna Beaulieu," she repeated. "I used to run the Club Moulin Rouge, and I'm a friend of the sergeant's. It's very important that I find him."

"Well, he's off on a manhunt, Miss Beaulieu," Gautier said. "I don't see how I can bother him right this minute."

"Listen," Savanna said. "I've got reason to believe that Wesley Farrell might be in serious trouble. You know who Wesley Farrell is, don't you, Detective."

"Yes, ma'am, I do, but—"

"Well, he's a friend of Sergeant Daggett's, too," Savanna said. "He's going to be led into a trap unless he's warned."

"Well, ma'am," Gautier said. "If you'll just let me get in a word, Mr. Farrell's *with* Sergeant Daggett. They're on their way to the Christ's Majesty Funeral Home right now. I just talked to them a couple minutes ago."

"Thank you," Savanna said quickly, then hung up the phone. She whirled on Marcel. "Quick, we got to get over to Christ's Majesty Funeral Home. You know where it is?"

"Sure," Marcel said. "Let's get goin'."

"Mind if I tag along?" Whately asked. "Smells like a story on the boil here."

"Come on then," Savanna said. "We ain't got time to argue with you."

IT TOOK BADEAUX and LeDoux about an hour to make it to the funeral home. It was getting into the late part of the morning, and a number of cars lined the street as mourners came to various visitations.

"I should of got me a fresh shirt," LeDoux said. "It's gonna look funny, me goin' into a visitation in my undershirt."

"We ain't goin' to no visitation," Badeaux said. "We're here to find out who Marcella Attaway's li'l friend is. When we find out, we're gonna take 'em outta here and squeeze 'em till they start to shit greenbacks."

LeDoux looked over at Badeaux, who was looking greasy-faced and red-eyed from the heat. "You ain't much for talk, are you, man?" he said.

Badeaux's baleful gaze fell on the ex-convict and he said, "We'll talk, all right, but if the sucker don't talk the right story, I'm gonna give him some incentive to come up with a better one." He fumbled out his snuff horn, stuck his thumb and finger into the white powder, then brought it to his nose and sniffed it loudly. He coughed and sneezed a bit before the cocaine hit his blood stream.

LeDoux just nodded. He'd lived among violent men all his life and he'd learned when to talk and when to stay shut. He opened the passenger door and got out, buttoning his double-breasted jacket and turning up the lapels to draw attention away from his disheveled state of dress. He put the derby on at a rakish angle, tipping it over so the bandage on his head was a bit less noticeable. Badeaux got out and buttoned his jacket, then looked up and down the street, checking for cops. Satisfied that the way was clear, he jerked his chin at LeDoux and they walked into the funeral home.

Inside the air was cool and the heavy maroon carpet under their feet was like walking on air. LeDoux noticed that they left deep footprints behind them as they walked. The heavy aroma of fresh flowers permeated every square inch of the place, and from somewhere LeDoux heard the strains of "Nearer My God to Thee" coming from an invisible organ.

There was a message board inside the lobby and the names of several funerals were listed on it. An arrow directed them to the Attaway funeral, up a flight of carpeted stairs. LeDoux took off his derby and, with his eyes, reminded Badeaux to do the same. Glaring, Badeaux removed the homburg he was wearing and tucked it under his left arm. He stalked up the stairs, with LeDoux a step behind.

At the top of the stairs they found doorways to several rooms, but LeDoux saw movement in the center room and beckoned for Badeaux to follow. The room was quiet. Only a handful of old women and men were there in small knots of threes and fives, talking quietly. None of them noticed the two roughnecks as they passed inside. LeDoux went to the casket and looked down on Marcella's remains. She looked small and broken in her elaborate brocade dress. Her makeup looked as though it had been applied with a paint brush.

"Poor old soak," he said to nobody in particular. "Money's supposed to make a body happy, but it didn't bring you nothin' but grief, did it?"

"You're talkin' to a corpse, man," Badeaux hissed. "Knock it off—you're givin' me the creeps."

They moved away from the coffin, and LeDoux spotted Avery standing to one side. The hammered-down little tavern keeper looked like a dark fireplug in his double-breasted blue pinstripe suit. LeDoux walked over to him, Badeaux right behind.

"Hey, man," LeDoux said quietly, shoving out his hand to his friend.

Avery took the hand and shook it. "Funny for things to end up like this, ain't it?" he asked. "You and me was just talkin' about poor Marcella the other night, and now here we all are."

"Funny," LeDoux said, "don't half describe it. The cops are lookin' for my ass right now 'cause they found out I was out there to see her, I reckon."

"What?"

"'S'gospel, brutha," the ex-convict said. "I been tryin' to find out who really killed her so I could get my ass outta the sling."

"Hell, nobody who knows you is gonna believe that," Avery said dismissively.

"Tell that to the cops," LeDoux said. "Look, Avery. Maybe you know the answer to this. I didn't think Marcella had no family left, but somebody musta been lookin' out for her. Who's takin' care of this funeral?"

"Well, it's the damnedest thing," Avery said. "I thought she was all alone in the world, but when I got here and started askin' around, some of the other folks said she had a third cousin, and it turned out to be Rogers Clifton, the president of the Homestead. How he could let that poor old woman live like he did is beyond me. I was to the house after the cops got out, and Jesus, it smelled like a bunch'a cats or dogs lived in that place. These rich guys, they ain't got no time for nobody but they own selves," he said, with a note of disgust in his voice.

Badeaux's eyes had lit with an unearthly light. His tongue came out and made a circuit of his lips like it was chocolate ice cream he was tasting. "Where'd this Mr. Clifton be about now, podnah?" he asked.

Avery looked over at Badeaux, seeming to notice him for the first time. It took him a brief moment to recognize who it was, and as he did, his features underwent a startling transformation. "Archie Badeaux," he said thickly. "What you doin' with him, Ernie?"

"We come here to talk to Mr. Clifton 'bout a few things, Avery," Ernie said, trying to make like everything was cool, and not quite succeeding. "You know where he's at?"

"Uh, I reckon he might be downstairs talkin' to Mr. DePriest. He runs the funeral home," Avery said. "Look, Ernie, you just got outta the pen. Don't be kickin' up no mess that'll get you sent back to 'Gola."

Badeaux turned his half-mad eyes on the little tavern keeper, his teeth showing like the fangs of a wolf. "Li'l man, you just stay outta the way, and you'll get to go home in one piece. I didn't come here to fuck nobody up so long as they behave, but I'll fill your ass so full of .44 slugs you'll make the floor cave in, you get me?"

Avery swallowed hard, his eyes bugging out. He nodded up and down frantically, unable to speak.

LeDoux cast an apologetic glance at his friend, then turned to hurry after Badeaux. He no longer cared about the money for himself, but he wanted to be there to stop Badeaux if he started to go over the edge. Now that he knew Ruby had been behind his betrayal, and with

Marcella Attaway murdered for it, the money had ceased to be anything but a burden to him and he no longer cared whether or not he found it. But Badeaux would not be deterred, and Ernie knew he could not let the hired killer do anyone else harm over it.

Badeaux reached the foot of the stairs and caught a funeral home employee by the arm, swinging him around. "Where's Mr. DePriest got his office?" he asked.

The young man, slender and bespectacled, looked at Badeaux strangely and pulled his arm gently away. "He's down that hallway, sir," he said. "But I think he's got somebody in there with him at the moment. If there's anything I—"

Badeaux brushed past him and stalked down the hall, shoving his homburg back on his head and tugging the brim down over his forehead. LeDoux caught up to him and placed a restraining hand on his shoulder. "Take it easy, man," he said softly. "We can't make no graves in here, or cops'll be all over us like cockroaches on a cake. Just take it light in there, and we'll get what we come after."

Badeaux half turned on LeDoux, his right hand shoved down inside his coat. His eyes were bright and hard and his lips had curved into that strangely pleasant smile of his. "Don't get in my way, punk. I don't need you for any of this."

They reached the office, and without bothering to knock, Badeaux worked the knob and pushed the door open. Two men were in the room, seated on opposite sides of a large mahogany desk. A brown man in his forties, dressed in a dark blue suit with a vest and *pince-nez* glasses perched on the bridge of his nose, looked up angrily from some papers he'd been signing. "What's the meaning of this?" he demanded. "It's customary to knock before entering a private office."

The second man was Rogers Clifton, and as he looked into Archie Badeaux's grinning face, he began to shrink back into his chair.

"Sorry, man," Badeaux said. "We just wanna have some words with Mr. Clifton, here."

"Then come back later," DePriest said. "This man has just lost a relative. He doesn't need to be upset with any unnecessary foolishness right now."

Badeaux reached inside his jacket and pulled out his .44 Smith & Wesson and held it down beside his leg. "Man, I'm sure sorry to be troublin' this brutha in his time of grief, but they's some money business we got to talk about, and it won't wait."

"Easy, man," LeDoux said, moving quietly and slowly to Badeaux's side. "I told you not to get all worked up in here. This is a funeral parlor. We can't be raisin' no ruckus in here." His hands were loose at his sides, and he watched Badeaux for an opportunity to grab the gun from him.

Badeaux turned to LeDoux, his eyes gone blank. "I told you not to get in my way no more." He shoved LeDoux away from him, bringing his big revolver to bear. LeDoux, half-prepared for such a move, was braced and shoved back, his left hand flying to the revolver as his right flew into a short arc to Badeaux's chin. Badeaux took the blow, but shook it off. His strength and resilience surprised LeDoux, who tried to clip him again over the bridge of the nose. Badeaux seemed ready for that move because he caught LeDoux's right arm at the wrist, and held it in mid-air in a vice-like grip. He countered LeDoux's grip on his gun arm by suddenly letting it go slack. The move threw LeDoux off balance, and in that instant Badeaux brought the revolver under LeDoux's guard and fired into his mid-section.

LeDoux's body shuddered and rocked back with the impact of the big slug. He continued to try to hold Badeaux in check, but the shock of the wound transmitted itself to every part of his body, and his strength drained away from him. His arms went limp, and as his grip relaxed, Badeaux whipped his gun against LeDoux's temple and he went down.

Rogers Clifton tried to slip past the two grappling men,

but Badeaux was faster. He shoved LeDoux's limp body away from him and brought his gun barrel down on Clifton's left shoulder. The blow shook the banker to his ankles, and he fell to his knees. Badeaux grabbed him by his necktie and dragged him upright, shoving the .44 against his neck.

"Now, you pissant mother-raper," Badeaux hissed. "You and me goin' for a li'l ride and you're gonna show me where the money is."

"W-what m-m-money?" Clifton groaned.

"The fuckin' Brinks payroll that the old woman found—LeDoux's loot. I know you got it, fuck-head, and you gonna give it all to me, right God-damn-now, or I'll blow your fuckin' head right into the corner."

"No, please—" Clifton pleaded, but Badeaux wasn't listening. He tightened his grip on the banker and dragged him out of the office.

"Don't get no stupid ideas, undertaker," Badeaux said to the mortician. "I'll kill anybody who comes after us." He punctuated his threat by firing at the telephone on DePriest's desk. The bakelite instrument exploded into a thousand fragments as the bespectacled mortuary owner ducked behind his desk.

Chapter 16

FARRELL AND the three detectives arrived at the funeral home as the clock struck eleven. The street was busy, as the mortuary was located in one of the more heavily traveled Negro business districts. There were several restaurants and cafés, and two Negro-owned movie theaters. It was like any normal morning but for the four armed men who got out of the police cruiser.

Daggett looked around the neighborhood, and suddenly pointed. "Look. Badeaux's here somewhere."

The other three looked across the street and saw the new '38 Dodge sedan with the New Orleans Motors emblem fixed to the rear bumper.

"What's the drill, boss?" Andrews asked.

"You and Maxwell take the back. If you can get in, sweep forward. Mr. Farrell and I'll go in the front. If you hear shootin', come in a hurry, but be careful. I don't want no civilians caught in a crossfire. Badeaux's crazy under most circumstances, but if he's been at the nose candy, he's liable to be flyin'. Better leave the shotguns here."

Andrews didn't like that part, but he nodded. "C'mon, Max. Let's get in there." The pair took off at a trot toward the rear of the establishment.

Daggett took off his Stetson and wiped perspiration from his forehead. His eyes were blinking rapidly from the prospect of violence. Farrell could feel his own blood pressure going into overdrive.

"Let's go," Daggett said. He unbuttoned his jacket and loosened the .41 Colt in his hip pocket holster. Farrell took out his .38 automatic, jacked a cartridge into the breech, then held the gun down beside his right leg, his finger just outside the trigger guard.

The two men made a strange sight, one dark brown, tall and long-limbed, wearing a dark blue suit, the other in wrinkled evening clothes with a pale gold complexion, eyes like diamond shards with pinpoints of fire in the center. They entered the mortuary and quickly consulted the schedule board for the Attaway funeral. They were about to move upstairs when the sound of a gunshot reverberated throughout the building. Daggett's long-barreled revolver appeared in his hand as though a magician had conjured it from the air. Before he could move in one direction or the other, a second shot sounded, followed by the crash of a door being kicked open.

Like a well-trained team, Daggett and Farrell separated, one moving right and the other left. There was almost no cover, but each found a place that would make him a less conspicuous target. Two men lurched toward them, one was Rogers Clifton, his arms flailing and his eyes bright with terror. Behind him they could make out Archie Badeaux holding his .44 raised to fire.

"Badeaux," Daggett shouted. "Let him go and drop the piece."

Badeaux, keeping the terrified banker between them, fired at Daggett's position, the shot blowing plaster dust past the detective's face.

Farrell lined up his gun, his teeth bared as he searched for a clean shot at the drug-crazed killer. But Badeaux's natural instincts as a predator were only keener for the cocaine in his head. He fired at Farrell, the slug tugging at the shoulder of his dinner jacket as the gambler pulled back behind his cover.

"You mother-rapers back off or I'll blow this goddamn banker's guts all over the wallpaper," Badeaux yelled in a high-pitched voice. "Do it now, or I'll kill him." He shoved his gun into Clifton's back, and the banker's body arched from the sudden pain. Clifton was whimpering like a scared pup.

"Do it, for God's sake," he screamed. "He's a lunatic—he'll do it, he'll do it."

Daggett's face was like a thundercloud and his mind recoiled at the thought of backing down, but he knew he had no choice. He signaled with his eyes and a jerk of his head for Farrell to back toward the mortuary entrance.

The two men retreated and made the porch, at which point they split into different directions and made for cover. Farrell ducked behind a tree and Daggett dove behind a parked car by the time Badeaux emerged with the struggling Clifton in his grasp. Seeming to divine the tactic that the other two men had devised, he continually shifted the banker from his left to this right, never giving his opponents more than a second or two for a clear shot. His physical strength, enhanced by the cocaine he'd snorted, seemed limitless.

Farrell thought for a brief second at just shooting into the tangle of their legs. No matter who he brought down, it would give them a chance at killing Badeaux. He shoved the long-barreled army automatic out in front of him, then began breathing in a shallow, controlled way. But Badeaux was on the alert for that. He snapped a quick shot at Farrell blowing tree splinters into his face.

By then they'd made the big Dodge and Badeaux shoved the banker in the driver's side door, clipping him over the ear with his gun as he did so. In a moment too rapid for Farrell and Daggett to track, Badeaux was behind the wheel, had the engine started, and was tearing away from Christ's Majesty. He threw out one last shot as they passed the police cruiser, and Daggett swore angrily as he saw the right front tire blow and flatten. He and Farrell ran out into the street with their guns raised, but, seeming once again to anticipate them, the Dodge rounded the corner on two wheels and was out of sight.

They were joined in the street by Andrews and Maxwell, both wild-eyed and breathing heavily from their sprint to the front.

"Well, that was sure smooth," Daggett said, but it was impossible to tell if he was expressing admiration for Badeaux's escape or sarcasm at their own inability to stop him.

"He left Ernie LeDoux inside with a bullet in him, boss," Andrews reported. "Mr. DePriest said he tried to stop Badeaux from kidnapping Clifton and Badeaux shot him. DePriest said he'd call for an ambulance."

"How's he look?" Daggett asked.

"Looks like it went through his left side," Andrews replied. "He might make it.'

"Better get back inside and call headquarters and get out an all points bulletin," Daggett ordered. "Get some other cars on him before he gets away from here."

"Badeaux's higher than a kite on heroin or cocaine," Farrell said. "But he's no fool. He'll know we'll have his joints and hideouts covered. But he might think we don't know where to find Lincoln."

"That's probably a good hunch," Daggett said, "but without some wheels, that won't help us much. Max, get to work on that tire. We got to get back out on the street."

At that moment, Marcel's brown Ford drew abreast of them. "We heard shots," the youngster said. "Anybody hurt?"

"None of us, anyway," Farrell said. "But Badeaux got away. He's probably half-way to Lincoln's place by now."

"Mr. Whatley," Marcel said, jerking a thumb over his shoulder, "got Lincoln's address. It's down on Melpomene."

"Sam," Daggett hollered as he stepped into the car, "you and Max do what you can here. As soon as you get your car back on the road, get over to Melpomene Street and call for some backup. If Badeaux decides to make a fight of it over there, it'll take some tear gas to get him out." He pulled the door shut.

Farrell jerked open the back door on Marcel's sedan and slid in beside Whately, and before he had closed the door, the brown Ford shot ahead like a spring- driven toy. He was thrown back by the acceleration, and his hat was knocked askew. As he found his seat and pushed his hat back, he noticed for the first time that Savanna was in the front seat.

"Savanna? You're in Los Angeles," he said stupidly.

"Was," she replied. "No longer. I decided to come home." As she looked into his eyes, she felt for the first time a rush of emotion that that nearly overwhelmed her. She blinked to dispelled the tears trying to collect there, and her throat felt clotted. There was so much she wanted to say, but as the car took the next corner, the tires shrieking in protest, it was apparent that talk of any kind would have to wait.

THE ANCIENT PIERCE ARROW bearing the Mouton brothers chugged slowly up Melpomene Street as they searched for the gray house. They were both feeling tense, and perhaps a bit afraid. They'd come too far to turn back now, but they knew enough about Archie Badeaux to fear him. They also didn't know what other dangers might lie at the end of their destination. Dom broke the old Smith & Wesson in his lap for the fourth time in the last half hour, still finding no more than six live rounds in the cylinder. He found himself wishing they'd thought to get a shotgun from somewhere. Archie Badeaux rated a shotgun.

"There it is," Alex said in a strangely calm voice. He eased the old car to the curb and shut down the motor. He shifted the .44-40 Smith & Wesson in his waistband and got out of the car. His brother, strangely silent, got out too, and walked to the front of the car to join him.

"What's the plan, brutha?" Dom asked.

"Let's hit the back," Alex said. "Chances are nobody's gonna be watchin' it. We can move toward the front and scoop up everybody we see. It'll give us an edge if Badeaux ain't there yet."

Wordlessly they walked across the street and entered the yard. Alex noted that the draperies were drawn, and he smiled at the realization that probably nobody was watching out. Lincoln probably thinks he's safe as a bear in his cave, he thought.

Walking lightly on their cork-soled shoes, the two men crept down the alley to the rear of the house. Finding the yard empty, they gained the porch and entered through an unlocked door. The kitchen was uninhabited, although the scent of pork slow roasting in the oven made their mouths run water as they drew their guns and passed into a dim hallway. Alex thought he heard voices up ahead, and he held a finger to his lips as he gestured with his gun at a closed door. In seconds they'd passed into a dining room furnished with a long table, chairs, and a big oak sideboard with a crystal water pitcher and footed glasses on top.

The sound of the voices was louder now, and Alex led the way toward a door beneath which a small puddle of light glowed. He crept toward it, gesturing with his gun barrel for Dom to follow. As he drew nearer, he opened the door a crack, peered through it and listened. Lincoln was speaking.

"Well, never let it be said that you can't be prompt," the old man said. "She'd about talked herself out. In another moment or two she might just have done what she came here for. And now, you miserable slug—start explaining how it is that you brought this murderous bitch into my home."

"Honest, Mr. Lincoln," Luther said, hanging from Albert's grip like a rabbit in the jaws of a hound. "She just wanted to make you a business proposition is all. I never—"

"Never thought she'd be dangerous," Lincoln replied dryly. "Spoken like a man being led around by his cock.

Tell me, were you that stupid before she took you to bed? Surely not—Archie would certainly have killed you before now. Perhaps he'll render me that small service when we can find him."

"She—she ain't dead, daddy," Ruby said shakily. She knelt beside Carol Donovan's body with her fingers at Carol's throat. She was dressed in a robe and held a .32 Colt automatic in her hand. Her eyes were wide with fright, and her face held the vague gray tinge that bespoke incipient nausea.

"Next time use a bigger gun," Lincoln said. "You shot her twice and managed not to kill her. Well, I suppose I should be glad you bothered to come down at all. Albert, take a look at her."

Albert, still holding Luther by one shoulder, clubbed his right fist and smashed it into Luther's temple. The man's body lost all its definition and collapsed on the rug like a sack filled with bones. Silently, Albert went to Carol's body, turned it over, and peeled back one of her eyelids. "She gonna die, Mr. Lincoln, but hard to say when. You want I should just twist her neck a li'l?"

"No," Lincoln said. "I might have a question or two for her if she wakes up. Collect her arsenal and bring it here."

Albert picked up the pistols from beside Carol's outstretched hands, then walked over to Lincoln's desk and dropped them on the blotter.

"If she found this place," Lincoln said. "I wonder who else knows about it? Badeaux brought a woman here once and I gave him hell about it. I should have killed that woman before he left with her, but it seemed unnecessary at the time. We'd better pack up and get out of here now," he said bitterly.

Alex shoved the door open and stepped through it. Simultaneously, Dom burst through the double hall doors. Each brought his big revolver level, Dom covering Ruby and Alex throwing down on Lincoln and Albert.

"That's right, cousin," Alex said to Albert. "Just make a

grab for one of them pistols and I'll kill you deader'n last week. Back up, goddamn you. You," he said to Lincoln. "Where's Archie Badeaux? We want him some kinda bad."

"Ha!" Lincoln exclaimed. "I'd like him, too, but I haven't any idea where he is. I'd like to know why he hasn't done what I pay him for, such as eliminating people like you and that young woman lying over there. Who the hell are you, if I'm not being too inquisitive?"

"Alex Mouton. That's my brother, Dom. Badeaux hired us to mess up that woman's nightclub, but we was set up. Wesley Farrell was there and kicked hell out of all my boys. I got to leave town and give up all I got because of that, and I want a piece of Badeaux's skin to keep me warm after I leave here."

Lincoln looked at Carol's prostrate form, then back up at Alex, shaking his head. "I suspect you've been had, my friend—not by me or Badeaux, but by that woman bleeding all over my carpet. I can't explain all of it to you, but I've heard of this Farrell. I suspect she used you to try and turn him against me. She's tried to destroy me before, and it's the only explanation I can offer. Unless I miss my guess, Farrell will arrive here soon, but we can't afford to be here—none of us—when he does."

Alex blinked his eyes uncertainly and his face registered his confusion. Lincoln's glib response had only served to perplex him more than he'd already been.

"Come, come, Mr. Mouton," Lincoln said. "Look around you. That woman has been very busy since she came to New Orleans. She's flummoxed you, she tricked that moron over there," he pointed at Luther, "into bringing her here, and she's undoubtedly tricked Farrell, too. The chances are good that Farrell, and perhaps others, will come here shortly and make an ever bigger mess than we have now. Put away your guns and leave, so we can leave ourselves. There's nothing else to do here." He wheeled his chair from behind the desk and out in the center of the room so he could look more directly at

Mouton. Before he could speak further, he heard the front door open explosively, then slam closed. The Mouton brothers, already tense and confused, stiffened and backed away from the half-open hall doors.

Rogers Clifton burst through the doors and fell headlong onto the carpet. Badeaux came in right behind, his face set like stone and his eyes like live coals. He was two steps into the room before it registered on him that something was wrong.

"What the fuck's goin' on here?" he yelled.

"As you can see, we're having a meeting," Lincoln said coldly. "Clifton what's the meaning of this?"

Clifton rose to his knees, his hand outstretched in supplication to Lincoln. "I was at the funeral home arranging for my cousin Marcella Attaway's funeral and this madman burst in, shot up the funeral director's office, then dragged me out at gun point."

"Shut up," Badeaux bellowed. "This slick-talkin' dick-head's holdin' out on you, boss. He's the one had the holdup money."

Lincoln fixed his lieutenant with a steely glare. "You're talking about the loot from the Brinks robbery a decade ago, I presume."

"Hell, yeah, that's what I been talkin' about," Badeaux yelled. "Is everybody here deaf or crazy?"

"You stupid fool," Lincoln said. "I pay you a king's ransom do to exactly what I say and nothing more, and instead you veritably set the city on fire looking for something that wasn't lost."

"Huh?" Badeaux said. For the first time since he'd entered the room, Badeaux's eyes lost some of their madness, and confusion took its place. "What you talkin' about?"

"I've known for almost three years where the money was," Lincoln said. "Do you think that I didn't know about my daughter's liaison with Ernie LeDoux? Did you believe that I wouldn't find out that she turned him in so the pair of you could take the money and run away with it?"

"I—I—" Badeaux stammered.

"If you'd left well enough alone ten years ago, we'd have gotten the money, but because you threw LeDoux to the police, we didn't get a chance to follow him to the hiding place and take it from him. I spent a small fortune trying to figure out where he'd hidden that money after you two fools lost it."

"Daddy—" Ruby began.

"Shut up," Lincoln thundered. "I suspected that LeDoux had cached the money with a friend, but since the friend he chose was pathologically honest, six years went by without any hint of the money turning up." Lincoln turned his obsidian eyes on Clifton, who still knelt on the floor. "But then it came to my attention that Marcella Attaway, the window of LeDoux's friend, Ben, was spending money on herself and her friends. I don't know how many poor Negroes benefited from her misbegotten largess before my people down here caught wind of it, but when she bought that large, rambling house on Leonidas Street, it all fell into place."

Lincoln wheeled the chair closer to Badeaux, whose face had collapsed in shock.

"It didn't take too much longer to discover that a distant relative, young Mr. Clifton here, had come down from St. Louis to join the Merchants and Farmers Homestead as head teller. He somehow found out about the money and began managing it for her. He'd buy her trinkets once in a while—a phonograph, a bracelet—and all the whiskey she could drink to keep her quiet." He leaned forward in the chair, his mouth smiling horribly as he looked down on Clifton. "But all the while, he was using the Homestead to launder the stolen money, then buying up property and small oil leases. Together with his cousin, he managed to spend about thirty-five thousand dollars by the time I got to him, but it had come back a hundred-fold thanks to his wisdom in investing in profitable ventures. When he suddenly became president of the Homestead, he was well on his way to becoming a man of consequence in this rather dreadful and miasmal city."

"And I would have, if you hadn't sunk your despicable claws into me, you vulture," Clifton said. His body was trembling, and his face was contorted with hatred.

Lincoln's eyes seemed to generate their own energy, and they flashed as though they were windows onto some hellish storm. "Vulture I may be, but at least I'm honest about my sins." He turned again to Badeaux, his face a study in contempt. "I owe the dying woman on the floor an apology if there were time to wait for her to regain consciousness. I thought she had undermined my organization here with her own petty hatreds, but I think, now, that some of the blame falls largely on your shoulders, Archie. I should have retired you with a bullet long ago, you stupid fool."

Badeaux had been mesmerized by Lincoln's monologue, but the insult was enough to jar him back to reality. He stepped back, jerked the .44 from under his arm, and brought it level with the crippled old man.

"Daddy," Ruby screamed, "No!" Her gun swung up and exploded, and as it did, the room was engulfed by a cascade of gunfire.

MARCEL HAD DRIVEN for all he was worth to beat Badeaux to the Lincoln house, but as they rounded the corner Farrell and Daggett could see Badeaux's Dodge in the driveway, the driver's door still open.

"Pull up there," Daggett said.

As Marcel brought the car to a stop, Farrell and Daggett jumped out of the car. Marcel flung open his own door, and Savanna did the same.

"Stay here, you two," Daggett said. "There's gonna be some hell raised in there in a minute, and I don't want you to get hurt."

"Farrell," Savanna cried.

He turned to her, looking into her eyes, seeing a million unsaid things and a million regrets there. He tried to say something, tried to think of some words that would heal the breach between them, but as Daggett rushed past him, he knew he didn't have the time.

She threw up a hand to stop him, but he was already gone.

"Damn," Whately said, getting out and standing behind the hood of Marcel's Ford. "This is gonna be one *hell* of a story." He got out his notebook and pencil, and began writing in a rapid scrawl.

"Marcel," Savanna said. "What'll we do?"

Marcel was looking at the house, his hands hanging loosely at his sides. He seemed to consider something, then made up his mind, his face flattening. His right hand swept the tail of his coat back and drew the old Iver Johnson .38 smoothly from his hip. "Everything I've got Wes gave to me. I've got to go in there." He started toward the house, and Savanna fell in beside him, reaching into her bag for the gun Farrell had given her. They were halfway to the house when the flat crack of gunfire shattered the late morning silence. Then both of them were running for the porch with long-legged strides, Savanna's straw hat flying from her head.

Farrell and Daggett, finding the front door slightly ajar, moved as a team into the house. As one scuttled ahead, the other covered him. Within seconds, they were in sight of the open hall doors. Then the sound of gunfire was so sudden and intense that it swept them backwards for a second before they drove themselves forward again.

Badeaux stood in the middle of the room emptying his .44 at Alex Mouton. Dom already lay on the floor, bleeding from several wounds. Lincoln, trapped in the midst of the room, gripped the wheels of his chair, maneuvering from side to side, looking for an opening to move out of the line of fire.

Daggett leveled his .41 Colt and shot Badeaux in the

middle of the back. Badeaux's body arched, and he half turned, his mouth stretched in a hideous grimace. As he tried to bring his gun to bear on the detective, Daggett shot him again, twice, in the body. He fell headlong into the floor, his eyes still focused on the detective.

Farrell fired at Alex Mouton. The shot took him high in the chest and spun him around. He smashed headlong into the wall and fell down. Then Farrell heard the high-pitched crack of a smaller gun and turned to see Ruby Richoux holding her gun out with both hands as she tried to shoot Daggett. Daggett was shooting at Albert, who had made the desk and grabbed up the two pistols lying there. He caught a round to the body and fell against the wall.

Farrell stepped to the side and raised his gun to fire at Ruby, but before he squeezed the trigger, he saw Marcel leap headlong through the hall door at the girl, knocking her to one side. As they fell, the Colt automatic spat once, then as Marcel closed his hand over her wrist, it fired again before he could wrest it from her.

In the sudden silence, Farrell could hear his own blood beating in his ears. He looked around the room and there, less than two yards from where Ruby lay, her arm still outstretched, Lincoln slumped, his arms limp alongside the wheels of his chair. His head was hanging over the back, his dark eyes fixed on the ceiling. He had a small, dark hole in his forehead with bright red blood oozing from it. Ruby's last shot had found a mark.

The girl saw Lincoln at the same moment Farrell did.

"Daddy! Daddy, oh God, no." Ruby's cries split the heavy stillness like a razor going through paper. She pulled herself away from Marcel and threw her body across his lap, screaming and sobbing. Farrell almost went to her, but then he saw Carol lying face up on the rug and he went to her side. As he touched her face, her eyelids fluttered, and opened.

"I should have waited for you," she said in a hushed whisper. "I got impatient...and tried to do it...myself. I wasn't as good as I...thought. I didn't do this very well...at all." She coughed, and flecks of bloody foam showed on her plum-colored lips.

Farrell nodded. "We got here as soon as we could. If you'd trusted me, things wouldn't have turned out like this. We could have gotten him another way."

She didn't seem to hear him. "Is he—dead?" She moved her eyes over to where Lincoln sat.

"As a mackerel," Farrell said. "That's all you came for, isn't it?"

She swallowed with difficulty, then, said, "I can't tell you...how long I looked for him before...before I tried the first time. When I heard he wasn't dead, I came looking for him again."

Farrell nodded. "Archie Badeaux never came to you at all, did he? That was a story you cooked up to hook me, then you pretended to be Badeaux when you hired the Mouton boys to wreck the club. That was how you set the hook. I would have found Badeaux and that would've led me to Lincoln. With five cents worth of luck, you'd have gotten the same result, and you'd be home drinking that expensive scotch."

"Luck," she said, smiling a little. "Used it all up...long ago."

"You can rest now," Farrell said, brushing the hair from her forehead, and cupping her face in his hand. "It's over."

She smiled and closed her eyes. It took Farrell a moment or so to realize she was gone. He got up and saw Clifton sitting on the floor beside the wheelchair, hugging his knees, the muscles of his face writhing like snakes under the skin.

Daggett walked over to Clifton and snapped handcuffs on his wrists.

"What-what are you doing?" He cried. "I'm Rogers Clifton, the president of Merchants and Farmers Homestead. These—these criminals kidnapped me. They were going to hold me for ransom, they were—"

"Save it," Daggett said. "You're under arrest for the murders of Malcolm Redding and Marcella Attaway. Better save all the talkin' you're gonna do to your lawyer."

Farrell walked across the room to where Alex Mouton sprawled against the wall. Blood was pouring through his fingers as he held them tightly against the bullet wound in his chest. Farrell knelt, shoved Mouton's gun aside, and then spoke to the man softly.

"I told you your brother was going to get you killed," Farrell said. "Why'd you come back after I let you go?"

Mouton's lips curved into a sickly smile. "You called it, man. Dom convinced me we needed to get even with Badeaux. We come here, and damn near pulled it off, too. Dom—is he...?"

Farrell nodded. "Yeah."

"Shit," Mouton said. He looked at Farrell and opened his mouth to say something, but instead he sighed, and then went limp against the wall.

Farrell stood up and half turned. As he looked up, he saw Albert Minshew on his knees, his face fixed in a baleful glare over the barrel of the Remington automatic. Farrell gritted his teeth, waiting for the bullet to come, and then four shots exploded so close together it was like they'd been fired by a machine gun.

Farrell grabbed his chest, certain he must be hit, but then Albert fell over on his face. Past his body, Farrell saw Savanna in the doorway, her little Colt held out in front of her the way he'd taught her. There were four holes in Albert's back, leaking a little bit of red. The first shot had probably killed him. It was a nice, neat pattern. An expert couldn't have done better.

Farrell walked toward Savanna as Daggett went to make sure Albert was dead. There was a nerve jumping in Savanna's face, and her expression was blurred. As he got to her, she collapsed against him. He took the gun from her fingers and dropped it into his pocket. The scent of her washed over him like a cooling wave on a hot day. Her hair smelled vaguely of coconut milk, and her brown skin of sandalwood. Her shape made his body tingle where it touched him, and he felt strangely like crying.

"I never knew it would feel like that," she said, strangling. "You never said it would be like that." A sob escaped her throat, and he patted her back like she was a small child awakening from a nightmare.

"It always is, honey," he said. "It always is." He was still whispering comforting sounds in her ear and patting her back when the ambulance and uniformed men arrived.

Epilogue

DAGGETT CAME into the interview room in the basement of police headquarters with two cups of coffee and a package of Pall Mall cigarettes. The uniformed officer at the door closed the door behind him, and he heard the bolt being thrown before he walked to the battered oak table and put first the coffee and then the cigarettes on the middle of the table.

Rogers Clifton sat there huddled in his chair, his coat and tie gone, his vest unbuttoned. His shirt collar was dirty and the sleeves rolled to his elbow were rumpled and smeared with dirty fingerprints. His eyes had that glazed look that a wounded deer's has when it can run no farther and it waits for the hunter to come up and deliver the *coup de grâce*.

Daggett took the cardboard tops off the cups of coffee, put one in front of Clifton, then put the other on his own side of the table. He tore open the cellophane on the cigarettes, tapped a few out, and offered them to Clifton. He came out of his daze long enough to take one, put it between his lips, then lean over to accept Daggett's light. He smoked in silence for a few minutes before speaking.

"What happens now?" he asked in a dull voice.

"Now you make things easy on yourself and tell me the whole story," Daggett said, taking a sip of his coffee. "The bank examiners are going over your books, and sooner or later they'll figure out how you laundered the thirty-five gee—that's why you had to kill Redding, isn't it?"

"I don't see why I should cooperate with you in the slightest," Clifton said. "I have nothing to gain by saying a thing."

"Maybe, maybe not," Daggett said, taking a cigarette for himself. Normally he didn't smoke, but there was something about being in the interrogation room—years of mingled sweat and fear and hatred that had permeated the walls and even the furniture—that he had to cover up, and cigarette smoke was the only remedy he knew. "But look at all we've got on you—your car parked outside the night of the murder, the glove left at the scene, the mate in your bureau, your name on the deed to Marcella's house. We finally traced the gun that killed Redding, and the pawn broker remembered your secretary coming in after it. There aren't that many young Negro women with that shade of dark blonde hair. You should have told her to wear a hat."

Clifton said nothing for a moment. Then he took a long drag from the Pall Mall, breathed it out again, and a look of defeat crept into his eyes. "It's funny, sergeant. The thing I most regret is deceiving Barbara that way. I was terribly attracted to her." He paused and dragged on the cigarette again. "We were supposed to have dinner later this week."

"She told me," Daggett said. "She's pretty shocked. I think she was a little in love with you, Mr. Clifton."

Clifton gave a short, bitter laugh. "If only I'd known that, we might've just run away from here together and kept all this mess from happening."

"How'd Redding figure out you were using the bank to launder the money?" Daggett asked.

"Bad luck," Clifton replied. "A man with whom I'd done some business knew Redding slightly. He apparently told him of a rather profitable oil lease deal I'd closed with him, and mentioned my name. Redding immediately realized that a head teller was in no position to be engaged in a business venture of that magnitude. He initially thought I was embezzling funds from the bank and investigated it. That's when he discovered the large sums of money I funneled into the bank."

"Being the head teller, I guess it was pretty easy for you to do that without anyone else tumbling to it," Daggett said.

"I should've stopped long ago and just been content with what I'd built up—moved on to somewhere else," Clifton said. "But I wanted to be president of my own bank. I had grand ambitions—to be able to help our people to realize their ambitions. Redding was too conservative. I saw more then one good investment walk out of the door because he didn't want to take a chance on them. I knew I could do better."

"If you laundered only about half the money before Lincoln caught you, where was the rest?" Daggett asked.

"When Marcella came to me about the money several years ago," Clifton began, "I immediately knew it had to be stolen. Ben lost all of his money keeping that tavern going. I didn't know until much later that it was the famous Brinks holdup money. I stashed it in one of our extra-large safe deposit boxes, which Redding also got into. He didn't know where the money came from, but he had his suspicions, and eventually figured out what I was doing," Clifton said wearily. "I'd found out that he was investigating me on the sly, and realized when he arranged to meet me away from the bank that he probably intended to force me to resign."

"But you couldn't then, could you?" Daggett said. "Lincoln had already found you and had you in his hip pocket."

Clifton nodded dolefully. "When Marcella found the money and began spending it and giving it away wholesale, somebody who knew that Ben Attaway had been Ernie LeDoux's friend got word to Lincoln. His people began nosing around, and eventually their investigations led them to me. He gave me no choice, really. It was throw in with him, or be killed."

"That blunt, huh?" Daggett said laconically. "But if he had you on such a tight leash, why not let Lincoln kill Redding and Marcella Attaway? He had a hell of a lot more practice at it than you did."

Clifton picked up his cardboard container of coffee for the first time, removed the lid, and drank a big gulp of it, seemingly oblivious to the heat rising from it. "With Redding it was fear," Clifton said as he picked up the package of cigarettes. He took another one, then lit it from the butt of his first.

"For all I knew," Clifton continued, "Lincoln would've had both of us eliminated. He had control of the payroll and most of the money I'd made from it. It occurred to me at the time that he didn't really need me anymore. He could kill the pair of us and take the money with impunity."

"I can see that," Daggett said, blowing out a long plume of smoke. "But why the old woman?"

Clifton's mouth was dry from talking, and he drank about a third of the remaining coffee in his cup, then licked his lips. "When she called me that night—after LeDoux's visit—she was nearly hysterical. She said if I didn't do something, she'd call the police, confess to taking the money, and ask for their protection. She was drunk, and in that state she might've been capable of anything." He paused to inhale a big drag from the Pall Mall, held it in his lungs, then let it feather out his nose and the corners of his mouth. "I held title to the house and had my own keys. I'd seen her like that before—drunk and unmanageable. I gave her enough time to pass out, then I drove over there in the small hours of the morning, let myself in, and killed her." He hit the cigarette again, then crushed it out in the tin ashtray on the table between them. The nicotine had calmed him, and he talked with a surprising dispassion.

"As long as we're talking so free," Daggett said, "what can you tell me about the deaths of Ezra Johnson, Ulysses Bautain, and Shirley Macomb?"

"Everything, I suppose," the defeated banker replied. "After Redding's death, I was the most senior bank officer, and because it was believed I had a good record, I was made acting president of the bank. There were others on the board of trustees who had agreed with my policy of more liberal loan policies."

"Uh, huh," Daggett said, to keep him talking.

"Lincoln apparently had agents of some kind in Washington, D. C. who learned of the Navy Department's survey of the area for the possible construction of an air training facility. The land they found most suitable was out on the eastern edge of town. Most of it was readily available and I managed to get it for a song. All but the two sizable parcels owned by the Johnson brothers and Ulysses Bautain."

"And in your new position as bank president, you could approach both men and make a pitch for their property," Daggett said.

"Yes," Clifton replied. "Neither of them knew for certain that the Navy actually wanted the land, but each had his own sources, and they'd received tips and rumors that the land might be worth more than a few thousand dollars if they bided their time. It was enough to make each of them dig in his heels and refuse to sell. When they balked, I had to tell Lincoln. You can guess the rest."

"What about the Macomb woman?" Daggett asked. "That was a stupid waste, and one of the things that tripped you up."

Clifton hung his head. "Of all of it, I regret that the most. I may have mentioned to Lincoln that I believed Bautain and his secretary were having an affair. He thought it might ease the pressure of an investigation if it was believed that the two of them had run away with each other. I was horrified when I learned the news." He drank the dregs of his coffee, and looked up at Daggett. "How did you find out about me? I was so careful to leave no trail."

"It's always the little things," Daggett said. "I had a feeling that I couldn't prove that the Redding murder was connected to the disappearances of Johnson and Bautain. Part of it was that Redding's was made to look like a suicide—he was left handed, but the wound was in his right temple. Then there was the puddle of vomit at the scene." The memory seemed to bother Daggett, because he shook out a fresh Pall Mall, put it in the corner of his mouth, and lit it. He inhaled deeply, then said, "I didn't have anything to put that together with until I found another puddle of vomit at the old woman's house. Professional killers don't puke after they kill—they don't care enough to get sick. That was the tip-off that they were both done by an amateur—somebody who still had a conscience. And you were the only link between the two of them. All I needed was the knowledge that you were Marcella Attaway's cousin."

Clifton nodded silently. He was quiet for several seconds, then he said, "What will they do with me, do you think?"

"Hard to say," Daggett said. "You might get the chair, but juries are funny. You've got the money to hire a good lawyer. You might get off with life, if you're lucky."

Clifton smiled. As he looked at him, Daggett saw for a moment what he might've looked like as a carefree young man.

"If I'm lucky," Clifton repeated. "You've a strange concept of luck, sergeant."

Daggett got up. "Come on. You'll want to call that lawyer of yours now."

Clifton stood up and walked to the door, waiting while Daggett knocked on it so they'd be let out into the hall.

A VERITABLE PROCESSION walked through the door of Nate Hopkins' office inside his building at the edge of the French Quarter. Along with Ralphie Daniels and his brother, Chester, there was Mrs. Naomi Brown, Marcel Aristide, and Fred Gonzalvo.

"Mornin', Mr. Hopkins," Marcel said. "I've got Ralph Daniels here to make good on his debt to you."

Hopkins looked up sourly. "About time. He was due here almost two days ago."

"That's all my fault," Marcel said blandly. "I'd arranged to bring him here, myself, but other business got in the way and it kept us from making the appointment. I came today to make good any interest on the debt you might think Ralph owes you.

Hopkins looked at the group, puzzled as to why they all were there, but he refrained from asking any questions. "All right, pay up and be done with it," he said in a harsh voice.

Ralph looked at Mrs. Brown, who smiled and nodded to him. He'd been able to get a partial refund on the railroad ticket, and she'd given him enough extra to make up for what he'd spent otherwise out of the seven hundred dollars. Thus encouraged, he stepped forward, removed the roll of bills from his trouser pocket, and laid it quickly on the desk in front of Hopkins.

The old man picked up the roll and counted it, wetting his thumb periodically to make thumbing the bills easier. When he was finished, he counted it a second time. Finally, he looked up at Ralphie. "All right, it's all here, but let me tell you somethin', boy." He leveled a menacing finger at Ralph. "Don't you never come into any of my places again, or let me hear of you goin' into anybody else's. Do it, and I'll have both your legs torn off and wrapped around your neck for a tie, you understand?"

The words shook Ralph, but he stood his ground, his face looking a little pinched. "No, sir, Mr. Hopkins, sir. Me and gamblin' have come to a partin' of the ways. I'm a new man as of today."

Hopkins looked at him balefully, then snorted. "Fine, now get out of my place and don't let me see you again."

Ralph turned shakily and walked out of the office, followed by the others. No one else had spoken a word, nor made any sound at all.

In the outer office, Chet put his hand on his brother's shoulder and said, "Let's be gettin' on down to the laundry, Ralph. We got a lot of work to do today."

"Mr. Daniels," Mrs. Brown said. "Might I ask you a question?"

"Why, uh, sure," Chet replied. He wasn't completely certain why Mrs. Brown was there, and her presence disconcerted him a bit.

"As I understand it, your brother owes you seven hundred dollars for taking care of his debt to Mr. Hopkins," Mrs. Brown stated.

"That's right," Chet said. "He'll be able to work it off in eight or nine years, I reckon."

"Have you any objection to gettin' your money back today?" Mrs. Brown asked.

Chet started. The question was so unexpected that it was like a thunderbolt. "Well, no, I don't reckon," he said slowly. "But where would it come from?"

"I've been doing some thinkin'," Mrs. Brown said. "I need a dependable handyman to help me take care of my property. Somebody young and energetic."

"Dependable?" Chet said. "Energetic?"

"Yes. How would it be if I paid you your seven hundred dollars today, and then Ralph could come to work for me immediately?"

Chet's mouth fell open. Marcel, standing off to the side, smiled, seeming to have known all along what was going to happen.

"Well, uh, I, uh, reckon it'd be all right, ma'am," Chet said finally. "Uh, you sure you know what you're, uh, doin' ma'am?"

"Perfectly," she said crisply. "Here, Ralph, turn around for me." She turned Ralphie around, then removed a checkbook and a fountain pen from her purse. Using

Ralph's back for a desk, she wrote in quick, bold strokes, blew on the check, then tore it off and handed it to Chet Daniels. He took it, looking stunned, unable to speak.

"Well, if that's all, gentlemen, I sure do appreciate y'all helpin' Ralph take care of his trouble with Mr. Hopkins. Y'all will have to come over for supper one evening soon. Come on, Ralph," she said, taking Ralphie's arm. "We got some planning to do." She quickly walked away with Ralphie, leaving the men behind.

Chet looked at the check, up at the retreating couple, then down at the check. "Damn," he said.

"Better get on down to the laundry, Chet," Marcel said. "You got a livin' to get. I'll be around to talk to you about some business expansion in the next week, okay?"

"Yes, sir, Mr. Aristide. Good day to both you gentlemen," Chet said, then he walked out of the office, looking down at the check like it was something from a fairy story.

"Let's go have us some breakfast, li'l brutha," Fred said. "I done worked up a powerful appetite watchin' all this high finance."

"Sure," Marcel said. "You're buying, right?"

Fred clapped him on the back. "Li'l brutha, you're all right. Can I ask you a question?"

"Sure," Marcel replied, opening the door to the street.

"Could you and Farrell use another man?"

"Fred," Marcel said, "timing is everything. It just so happens that Mr. Farrell gave me some extra responsibilities this morning, and I could use the help of a bright, capable fella like yourself. When can you start?"

IT WAS EXACTLY a week since Savanna Beaulieu returned to New Orleans, and the Club Moulin Rouge was open for business again. Louis Bras and his sextet, suddenly out of work after the tragic death of the owner of The Original Southport Club, were the opening act as the club opened its doors again. By nine o'clock, Anna-Lou Hamer dropped by and got up on the bandstand to sing with Bras and the boys. In honor of the occasion, she was dressed in a bright red gown and was crooning the lyrics to "I've Got My Love to Keep Me Warm," as Wesley Farrell came through the door.

Farrell, dressed in a silk jacket and trousers of desert tan, with a taupe colored shirt and a blood red tie, wore a red rose in his buttonhole. His beige Borsalino was tipped over his left eye, and he looked altogether like a man out on the town. Giving Billy Martin, the bar manager, a two-fingered salute off the brim of his hat, Farrell snaked his way through the tables and up the stairs to where Savanna's apartment and office were.

When he got to the head of the stairs the door was open a crack, so he knocked gently to announce his presence.

"It's open," Savanna called.

He walked through the door and took off his hat. He looked around, marveling at how the empty attic had been transformed back into a stylish apartment. Not finding her in her office, he walked across the hall and eventually found her putting a bundle of roses into a crystal vase. She stopped when she saw him, and walked out to meet him.

"How are you?" he asked after looking into her eyes for a moment.

"Okay, I guess," she replied. "For the first couple of days I wondered if I'd ever be able to live with it, but it got better after that—kind of like a bad dream that I don't remember so well anymore."

He nodded. "You did all right. It's not an easy thing to do, but you saw what was happening, and probably saved me and Iz both. It's not the kind of thing a man's apt to forget."

"No," she said. "I guess not." She looked down, and didn't seem to know what to do with her hands. "How—how are *you* doin'?"

He shrugged. "Pretty well. There was a lot of talk down at police headquarters, putting everything together for the cops. Frank didn't give me the hell I expected, but I got a couple of looks from him while I was telling my side of the story. I got them to give Ernie LeDoux a break. When he gets out of the hospital he's going to work as a bouncer for Avery's honky-tonk.

She nodded absently. "What about the girl?"

"In jail," he replied. "For a minimum of fifteen years, I reckon. That's if they have any pity on her, and sometimes they do, with a woman."

He ran out of talk, and found himself scuffing a toe around on the rug in front of him. He shoved his hands in his pockets, then took them out again, finally settling on folding them across his chest.

"I should've called you before now," Savanna said in a rush. "I—I guess I just got busy and lost track of the time."

"Getting a club back together, getting bar inventory up to snuff, and finding employees and a music act in a week qualifies as more than busy," he said with a small smile. "Sounds like somebody who wanted to come home—to stay—and get things back to normal." He looked around the room twirling his hat around in his fingers. "Place looks great," he said. He was running out of small talk, and was getting nervous. Any minute she might tell him she was busy and to get lost.

"Look," she said. "I got something on my mind and wanted to talk to you about it."

"You don't have to if you don't want," he said quickly.

"No, I gotta," she insisted. "What I did was wrong. I ran out on you without even a word, and I didn't say anything to you for months. You saved my life that time in Sleepy Moyer's house, and I just ran out on you. I—I felt like such a louse that after a while I just couldn't find the right words to call and say to you."

"It's all right," he said.

"No, it isn't," she said. "We been through a lot together. I owed you better than that."

He drew nearer to her, took her hand in his. "I owed you better than to try and slough off what had happened to you. What Sleepy did—I can't even imagine what it was like. I should've tried to understand you better. It wasn't until you were gone that I had the quiet to sit down and stop trying to push the thoughts away. I should've been there for you, and—well—I just didn't know how to do it."

She felt her head filling up with words and tears, and was scared to let go of all of them. She threw her arms around his neck and pulled his body into hers. He hugged her around the waist, and the strength of his arms was like a bulwark against the world at that moment.

"Don't ever leave me again," he said in her ear.

She felt a smile grow on her lips, but she didn't want him to see it—not just yet. "What'll you do if I do?" she asked.

"Come and find you. Make such a nuisance out of myself that you'll have to let me stay or come back here with me. I won't let you do it again, that's all I know."

She couldn't speak, but she nodded her head slowly, over and over. At first he thought she was just rubbing her face against his, and he was glad for it, but after a while, when the nodding went on, he knew what she was doing—answering him in the only way that she could at that moment, doing it over and over so he'd know she really meant it. He held her for quite a long time before she kissed him and made him take her downstairs to where the music and the people were.